YF Bashardoust, M

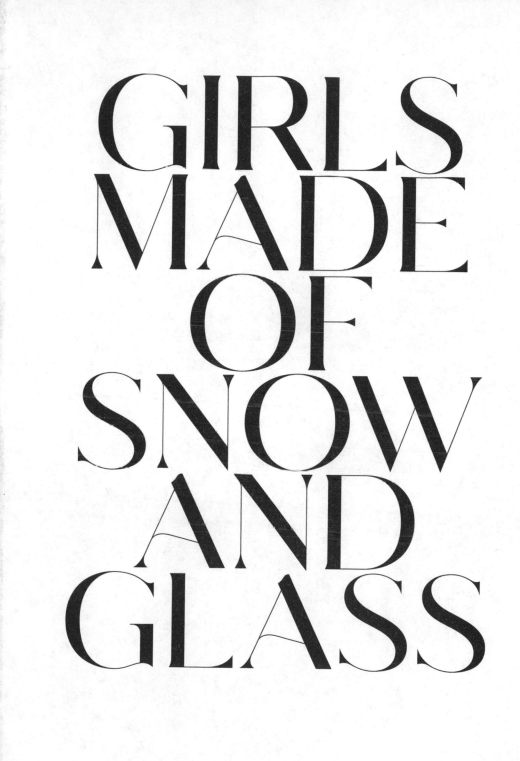

GIRLS MADE OF SNOW AND GLASS

GIRLS MADE OF SNOW AND GLASS

MELISSA BASHARDOUST

FLATIRON
BOOKS
NEW YORK

GIRLS MADE OF SNOW AND GLASS. Copyright © 2017 by Melissa Bashardoust. All rights reserved. Printed in the United States of America. For information, address Flatiron Books, 175 Fifth Avenue, New York, N.Y. 10010.

www.flatironbooks.com

Designed by Anna Gorovoy

Map by Rhys Davies

The Library of Congress Cataloging-in-Publication Data is available upon request.

ISBN 978-1-250-07773-8 (hardcover)
ISBN 978-1-250-17126-9
(international, sold outside the U.S., subject to rights availability)
ISBN 978-1-250-07774-5 (ebook)

Our books may be purchased in bulk for promotional, educational, or business use. Please contact your local bookseller or the Macmillan Corporate and Premium Sales Department at 1-800-221-7945, extension 5442, or by email at MacmillanSpecialMarkets@macmillan.com.

First Edition: September 2017

10 9 8 7 6 5 4 3 2 1

TO MY FAMILY

North Tower
throne room

royal
apartments

crypt

Sybil's
statue

lake

east wing

Shadow
Garden

↙ To the Southern Kingdom

1

LYNET

Lynet first saw her in the courtyard.

Well, the girl was in the courtyard. Lynet was in a tree.

The juniper tree in the central courtyard was one of the few trees still in leaf at Whitespring, and so it was one of the best hiding places on the castle grounds. Nestled up in its branches, Lynet was only visible to anyone directly beneath her. This hiding place was especially helpful on afternoons like these, when she had decided to skip her lessons without telling her tutors.

The young woman who walked briskly across the courtyard did not pass directly under the tree, so she didn't notice Lynet watching. What struck Lynet first was the girl's clothing. Instead of a dress, the girl was wearing a long brown tunic over loose trousers, allowing her to move more freely, in a long, striding gait. She walked with purpose, dark eyes staring straight ahead.

Lynet thought she knew every face at Whitespring, but she didn't recognize the girl at all. True, they had visitors come and go throughout the year, but usually for special occasions, and even then, Lynet could recognize most of them by sight, if not by name.

A stream of questions all fought for attention in Lynet's head: Who was this girl? Where had she come from? What was she doing at Whitespring? Where was she heading now with such conviction? Why was she carrying a large bag in her hand? She was a mystery, and mysteries were rare at Whitespring, where so little changed from day to day. The stranger was certainly more exciting than the music lesson Lynet was avoiding.

Now at the other side of the courtyard, the girl went up the short flight of stone steps that led to the west wing of the castle. As soon as she'd disappeared through the arched doorway, Lynet dropped down out of the tree and hurried after her, her bare feet silent on the snow. She peeked down the hall and saw the girl starting to go up the stairwell on the left. Lynet waited until the girl was out of sight and then scurried directly across the hall to climb out the window. Whitespring's uneven stones and ledges and sharp corners made the castle excellent for climbing, something she had discovered at a young age. She used the ledge above the window to pull herself up, careful not to snag her gray wool dress on the sharper parts of the sculpted ledge. She didn't want to have to explain to her father why there was a tear in her dress, or to see the forced smile on her sewing mistress's face as she asked why the embroidery on the hems that Lynet had done just last week was already coming undone.

Crouching silently on the ledge, Lynet traced the young woman's movements in her mind: after going up the stairs, she would come down the hall until she reached the first turn, a little past where Lynet was perched, at which point she could continue straight ahead or turn right down another hallway. Lynet counted the seconds, knowing that she should be hearing footsteps any moment—

Yes, there they were, passing down the hallway just inside. Lynet was sure to duck her head so the girl wouldn't see her hair peeking up past the window frame, and she listened as the footsteps continued on past the turn, straight down to the end of the hall, followed by a loud knock.

She heard a voice call, "Ah, come in!" and then the sound of the door closing again.

Lynet wasn't sure who had spoken, but it didn't matter *who,* as long as she knew *where.* She peeked over the ledge just in time to see the stranger going through the door at the very end of the hall to her left. Lynet climbed in through the window, hurried down the same hall, and went back out the last window so that she was now on the other side of the castle. She carefully skirted the ledge, counting the windows in her head.

When Lynet reached the window of the room where the stranger had gone, she knelt on the ledge and peeked in through the corner. The window was closed, but she had a clear view of the young woman, and that was what truly mattered. Lynet recognized the other person as Tobias, one of the nobles who had lived at Whitespring since before Lynet was born.

Tobias was saying something now, his enormous eyebrows making him look fiercer than he really was. But the young stranger didn't seem at all intimidated by Tobias's intense stare—she held her head high and stared right back.

In fact, the stranger didn't seem to let anything trouble her. There were flakes of snow in the messy dark braid down her back and on the collar of her shirt, but she made no move to brush them away. The bag she was holding was bulging full, and yet even after carrying it through the castle, she showed no sign of tiring. The inky thumbprint on her jawline, the fraying edge on one sleeve . . . these small imperfections fascinated Lynet because the girl wore them all with such ease and confidence. Lynet had never seen a woman look so comfortable in her own skin without appearing pristine.

Who *was* she?

Lynet leaned in farther, and the young woman set down her bag and opened it. With her head bent, her sharp cheekbones were especially striking, her eyelashes casting long shadows across her pale brown skin. . . . She looked up suddenly, and Lynet jerked her head away from the window. She was sure the girl hadn't seen her—Lynet had been barely visible in the corner—and yet in that brief moment, she'd thought their eyes had met.

When Lynet peeked again, the girl wasn't looking up anymore, and Lynet squinted to see what she was taking out of the bag— that would be one mystery solved, at least. And then she saw in the girl's lean hands a long metal instrument that curved at the end like the beak of some vicious bird. Lynet gasped sharply, and she could tell from the way Tobias was rapidly blinking that he hadn't expected this either.

The young woman was watching Tobias, waiting for some response, and Lynet couldn't stop watching *her*. She wondered how this girl could stand so perfectly still, hands never trembling under the weight of that monstrous instrument she was holding. She seemed almost defiant as she held it, and Lynet longed even more to know this strange girl—not just to know who she was, but to know *her*, and maybe to absorb some of that boldness for herself.

Tobias gave a short nod and settled down in a chair. On the table beside him was a wineskin, and he drank heavily from it before tilting his head back. The young woman took a breath and then placed the curved end of the metal instrument inside Tobias's mouth.

Finally, Lynet understood what was about to happen, but not before it was too late to look away.

The young woman yanked the instrument back, and the noble-man screamed as his tooth was wrenched out of his mouth.

Lynet was glad he screamed, because she had let out a small yelp herself. She ran her tongue over her own teeth, reassuring her-self that they were still in place.

A surgeon. The young woman must be a surgeon. Though the answer should have satisfied her, Lynet only grew more curious. She had never seen a woman surgeon before.

Lynet remained perched on her ledge until the surgeon had cleaned Tobias up and given him some herbs for the pain. When Lynet heard her leave, she abandoned her post and went back around the ledge, listening for footsteps inside. Her heart was thumping; where would the surgeon go next? What would she do?

When the surgeon had gone down the hall, Lynet slipped back inside through the window just in time to see her turn a corner. Lynet silently followed, but as she rounded the same corner, she ran into the Pigeons.

"Princess Lynet!" one of the women cried, and then they were all around her, and it was too late to escape.

She called them the Pigeons because of their gray hair and their constant cooing, and because they always traveled in flocks. Unlike most of the nobility, who preferred to live in their own private estates in clusters throughout the North, the Pigeons lived in Whitespring permanently, having made their nests here long before Lynet was born. They were Whitespring's oldest residents, and so they always seemed so surprised to see how much Lynet had grown, even if they had only seen her yesterday.

"Her mother would be so proud," one of them was saying now.

From behind her, another of the women said, "Look at this hair. So much like the queen's."

When she was a child, Lynet had thought they'd meant she looked like Mina when they said she looked like the queen, and she had swelled with pride at resembling her stepmother. But now she understood that when they talked of the queen, they always meant the *late* queen, Emilia. And the worst part was that they were right: Mina's hair was a dark auburn, her eyes light brown, while Lynet had her mother's thick black hair and nearly black eyes. Mina's face was angular and defined, her skin golden-brown, while Lynet had her mother's round face and muted olive-brown coloring. Lynet's cheeks, her nose, her lips, and everything else she possessed belonged to a dead woman who she didn't even remember.

The unofficial leader of this little band, a gray-haired, long-necked woman named Xenia who served on the king's council, bent down a little—out of habit, mostly, since Lynet was now taller than her—and took Lynet's face in her hand. "So lovely. King Nicholas must be so proud of you, my lady. You'll be such a splendid queen, just like your mother." Even in the shadows of the dim hallway, Xenia's eyes shone with a suspicious gleam—she always squinted at people like she thought that they were lying to her.

Lynet smiled and nodded and thanked them until the Pigeons were finished. Perhaps it was flattering to be fussed over, but she knew their fondness wasn't for her own sake. They loved her mother, and Lynet looked like her mother, so they thought that they loved her, too.

Once the Pigeons continued down the hall in a cloud of gray, Lynet wandered through a few corridors before she had to admit that she'd lost the surgeon. Still, Lynet was sure she would see her again soon enough. The castle had been without a court surgeon since the prior one had left several months ago, so the new surgeon would be in high demand for a while. Lynet would keep watch, and next time she wouldn't lose track of her.

Lynet dragged her feet down the hall until she reached the music room, where her tutor was waiting for her, seated at his harp.

He was mid-yawn when she walked in, and as soon as he saw her, he straightened, swallowing the rest of the yawn with a startled chirp. "There you are, my lady!" he said. "A little late, perhaps, but that's no trouble." His lined face stretched into a smile. She was more than an hour late, but he wouldn't scold her. None of her tutors ever scolded her for anything.

Lynet had once liked the *idea* of playing the harp. But the actual lessons were long and tiresome, and she never seemed to improve, so she didn't see any harm in skipping them when she could. She felt less bitter about the tedious hour to follow now that she had a new project, but as she sat down at her harp, she knew she would play even worse than usual today, her mind still following the new surgeon even when her feet couldn't.

When her lesson was finished (miserably, as expected), dusk was falling. Without even thinking, Lynet flew up the stairs to the royal apartments. Sometimes she felt that her entire day was only a prelude for her nightly visit with Mina, a tradition that had begun so long ago, Lynet couldn't remember exactly how it had started.

The fire was blazing high when Lynet stepped quietly through to her stepmother's bedchamber. Even though Mina had come to Whitespring from the South nearly sixteen years ago—around the same time Lynet was born—she had never become accustomed to their constant winter, and so she was always cold. Lynet, having been born in Whitespring, was never cold.

A maidservant braided Mina's hair in front of the mirror. Lynet could see her stepmother's reflection, serene and regal, her head held high, her back straight.

When Mina saw Lynet's reflection behind hers in the mirror, she held her hand up to signal the maid to stop. "That'll be all for now," she said, and the maid dipped a curtsy before hurrying away, managing a quick smile for Lynet before she left.

Mina stood to let Lynet take her place on the low chair in front of the mirror. As soon as Lynet sat, Mina smiled. "You have snow in your hair."

Embarrassed, Lynet reached up to brush it away. She supposed one day, when she was queen, she would have to appear as effortlessly composed as Mina did, but that day was years away.

Mina started to comb through Lynet's hair with her fingers. Combs and brushes were useless on Lynet's hair; they only snagged and caught in her curls, while Mina's hands deftly unsnarled and untangled them. They'd done this every night since Lynet was a child, and neither of them ever mentioned that Lynet was old enough to untangle her own hair by now.

Mina asked her about her day, and Lynet told her how useless she was at playing the harp, how she'd already been through three music tutors. "I never get any better, so they all give up on me in the end," she said.

"It's not you," Mina reassured her. "Whitespring is too gloomy and isolated for most people." Lynet knew she was right. It wasn't just the music tutors who all left. The only people, noble or not, who stayed at Whitespring permanently were those who had been here so long that they couldn't be troubled to leave. Lynet wondered about her new surgeon, how long she would stay. . . .

"You've left me behind," Mina said softly after Lynet had lapsed into silent thought for too long. "Where did you go?"

"There's a new surgeon," Lynet said without thinking.

"I'm glad to hear it. Whitespring has been without one for long enough."

"She's quite young," Lynet said.

Mina lifted an eyebrow. "She?"

Mina was watching her with interest, but Lynet didn't want to tell her more. She felt oddly protective of her new stranger, and she didn't want to share her with anyone else yet. "I also saw the Pigeons today," she said quickly.

Mina grimaced, and she accidentally tugged at one of Lynet's curls. "Same as usual, I expect?"

Lynet knew the Pigeons would distract Mina—Mina found them even more unbearable than Lynet did. The first time Lynet had slipped and called them by that name in front of Mina, she'd been afraid that she'd be scolded. Instead, Mina had burst into laughter. Lynet didn't blame her; though the Pigeons were always charming and respectful to Mina's face, Lynet heard the way they talked about her when they were alone. They called her *the southerner*, or *the southern queen*, never just *the queen*—that title was still reserved for Lynet's mother.

"Same as always," Lynet grumbled as Mina started braiding her hair. "I look so much like my mother, my hair looks just like my mother's, I have my mother's eyes . . . they probably even think I have my mother's elbows."

Mina frowned a little and bit her lip, but said nothing.

Lynet continued. "It wouldn't be so bad if it was just them, but—" She stopped, feeling too guilty to give voice to her thoughts.

"But you wish your father would stop comparing you to her as well?" Mina offered.

Lynet nodded. She started twisting a piece of her skirt in her hands. "It's even worse with him," she said quietly.

Mina laid her hands on Lynet's shoulders. "Why do you say that?"

Lynet kept her head down. It was easier to talk about it when she wasn't looking at anyone else—or at herself. She wanted to change the subject, but she had already done that once, and she knew she wouldn't be able to manage it again. Whenever they talked about Lynet's father, Mina seemed to . . . harden somehow, like she was putting a shield in place that even Lynet wasn't allowed behind. Sometimes Lynet wondered why they had married at all, when they seemed to spend so little time together and show such little affection when they did.

Mina squeezed Lynet's shoulders gently. "It's all right, wolf cub," she said. "Don't be afraid."

Mina's special name for her rallied Lynet's spirits, as it always did. She hated feeling afraid. "It's just that . . . well, the others only talk about how much I *look* like her, but Papa . . . I think he wants me to *be* like her in every way. He expects me to be sweet and gentle and—and *delicate*."

Lynet practically choked on the word. It was what her father always said about her mother—and about Lynet, too. *Your features are delicate, Lynet, like a bird's. You shouldn't be climbing trees, Lynet, not when your hands and feet are so soft and delicate.* Emilia had died, he said, because her body had been too delicate for childbirth. Being *delicate* had killed her mother, and yet he was so eager to bestow the quality on her.

"You say that like it's a curse," Mina said, her voice low and heavy. "There are worse things in the world to be than delicate. If you're delicate, it means no one has tried to break you."

Lynet felt ashamed without knowing why. She had always tried to emulate her stepmother, but the way Mina spoke now, Lynet wondered if she was trying to take on a weight she didn't fully understand. "I'm sorry," she said. "I must sound like such a child."

"That's because you *are* a child." Mina smiled, but her smile started to fade as she studied their reflections in the mirror. "Or maybe not," she said. "You're turning sixteen soon, aren't you?"

Lynet nodded. "In a month and a half."

"Sixteen." Mina knelt down beside her. "That's how old I was when I left my home in the South to come to Whitespring. I think part of me has always thought of myself as sixteen, no matter how many years have passed." Mina looked at the mirror and scowled, seemingly disturbed by what it showed her. Their faces were side by side, and for the first time, Lynet noticed a single white strand in her stepmother's hair.

"You're still young," Lynet said uncertainly.

Mina wasn't paying attention to her, though. She brought her hand up to her cheek, examining the corners of her eyes, the thin lines around her mouth. "If they love you for anything, it will be for your beauty," she murmured softly, but Lynet didn't think the words were meant for her, so she felt guilty for hearing them at all.

She waited a moment and then she said, "Mina? Is something wrong?"

Her stepmother shook her head. "Only a memory." She turned to Lynet and kissed her on the head. "You've grown up so fast. It took me by surprise. Soon you won't even need me anymore." Mina stood and gave Lynet's braid a playful tug. "Run off now, and enjoy the rest of your evening."

Lynet started to go when Mina called to her, "And do let me know what happens with your young surgeon. It'll be good for you to have someone closer to your own age to socialize with for a change."

Lynet didn't respond as she hurried out the door, but for some reason she couldn't explain, she felt herself blush.

MINA

At sixteen, Mina knew she was beautiful. Sitting on the grass, angling her mother's hand mirror so that the reflected sun wouldn't blind her, she discovered the secrets of beauty: the way the blaze of the afternoon sun transformed her dark hair into a halo of fire; the way her golden-brown skin glowed when she held her face at the right angles in the light; the way the shadows elongated her cheekbones.

These were secrets no one had taught her. Her father, when he was home, kept to himself, and her nurse, Hana, would sneer at her for being so vain. Her mother was long gone, of course, but Mina liked to think that she had left behind the silver-backed mirror as a guide for her daughter.

"*Dorothea*," Mina whispered to herself, wishing that just saying the name could conjure her mother on the spot. She had died so soon after falling ill that Mina didn't remember her being ill at all. She'd been four, recovering from an unrelated illness of her own, when her mother had died, so memories of her mother were faint, shimmering things, like coins at the bottom of a moving river.

"Mina!"

Mina groaned at the sound of her nurse's call. She had hoped that leaving the house for the refuge of the hills would allow her some peace from the woman's constant disapproval.

Hana had been old and shrill for as long as Mina could remember, but now that Mina was growing out of girlhood, Hana had become superfluous as well. The only reason Mina listened to her at all was because she was the best source of information about her mother. Hana loved to talk about the lovely girl who had run off with a young man against her wealthy family's wishes and had consequently been disowned by them. Mina wondered sometimes if the nurse was just making up stories—it was hard to imagine anyone risking such displeasure for the love of her father, and Hana hadn't become Dorothea's maidservant until after the marriage. But even half-true stories were better than nothing.

"Mina, I know you can hear me, you selfish child!"

There was a hint of desperation in Hana's voice, like she was scared of something. But there was only one thing Hana was scared of, and that was Mina's father, Gregory.

He's home, Mina thought. He'd left on one of his frequent journeys nearly two months ago. Mina always valued the times when he was away; the house felt lighter with Gregory gone, like some stormy cloud overhead had dissolved. Mina looked at herself in the mirror once more, wishing she could crawl inside it and wait until both her nurse and her father went away.

"There you are," Hana said, huffing behind her. "I know you come all the way out here just to make me kill myself from climbing these hills."

She was almost right. Avoiding Hana was one benefit of the hills, but if the nurse had been paying any attention, she might have noticed that the Summer Castle was visible from this hill. Though the royal family had never finished its construction, leaving it half-finished for nearly a century, the completed gold domes of the Summer Castle still gleamed in the sun, shining through the trees like a beacon. If it weren't so far, Mina would have tried to sneak onto the grounds, maybe plant a little garden there. She imagined that garden growing all around the castle, keeping everyone—especially her father—away.

"Your father is home," Hana said. "Don't you want to greet him?"

"Did he ask to see me?"

Hana glowered at her, but didn't respond, so Mina knew he hadn't. Still, she couldn't avoid him forever, so she stood up and brushed the grass from her skirt.

"Fine," she said, "let's go."

Hana grabbed her by the arm, but then she released it and reached for the mirror lying on the grass. "Is that—is that your mother's mirror?"

"I was just borrowing it," Mina said, blocking Hana from taking it away.

"I can't believe you would treat your dear mother's belongings so poorly. What if you had broken it? What if you had lost it? It's as if you don't care about her at all." She shook her head at Mina in reproach.

"I do care!" Mina protested.

"I don't know about that," Hana muttered. "You don't care for anything but yourself." She grabbed at Mina's arm again. "Now hurry up."

Mina wrenched her arm out of her nurse's grip, grabbed the mirror, and charged down the hill past her. She was in no hurry to see her father, but she didn't want Hana to think she was afraid of him. She kept up her quick pace until she reached the edge of the village market.

She hadn't been planning to come home so soon. She had snuck out early this morning, and she'd been planning to stay out for a few more hours. She'd never purposefully walk through the village in the middle of the day, especially not on market day, when it would be at its busiest.

"Just keep your head down and walk fast," Hana whispered. "No one bothered me on my way through. It's your father they fear, not you."

But Hana was as forgettable as she was unthreatening. People remembered Mina just as clearly as they remembered her father. Ever since magic had made the North freeze over, people were often suspicious toward those born with unnatural abilities. Whenever her father heard rumors of others with magical talents, he would set off at once to investigate, but as far as he knew, he was the only magician for the past few generations. Still, that didn't stop the villagers from considering Mina to be just as dangerous as her father. It never occurred to them that now it was Mina who felt she had to keep safe from them.

The village on market day was a visual feast. There were the familiar sights of the South—brightly colored fruit, fresh dates and nuts, colorful woven rugs—along with the rarer luxuries of the North—jewelry with gems from the mountains, soft furs, intricate wood carvings. Mina would have loved to spend all day walking back and forth down the long passageway between stalls, reveling in all that beauty. But as she and Hana passed through the crumbling stone archway that marked the entrance to the marketplace, Mina kept her eyes down on the dusty ground, letting her sheet of hair fall forward to cover her face.

It didn't matter. No matter how dowdy she tried to look, how modestly she cast her eyes downward, someone always recognized her, and then the whispers spread outward until they surrounded her.

The villagers went quiet as she passed. Then she heard the word *magician* in hushed tones, over and over again, until it sounded less like a word and more like the chirping of crickets. Once the whispers had spread far enough, the villagers started to step aside from her, keeping their distance from the magician's daughter. But in the narrow passageway through the market, there wasn't much room for keeping one's distance, not for the villagers, and not for Mina, either.

On all sides, people jostled into her and then jumped away. It would have wounded her, perhaps, if she'd felt anything but contempt for these people. They were hypocrites, shying away from her in the light of day, but sneaking to her father's house at night, begging him for magical solutions to their mundane problems. She passed by Lila, the weaver, who glanced away from her as she wrapped her arms around her swollen belly. She had come to Mina's father a few months ago asking for something to help her conceive a child, and even though she had gotten what she wanted, she didn't want to be reminded of how she'd done it. *Vulgar midwifery,* her father had dismissed the potion he'd given her. He didn't even consider such services to be magic, but they provided him with money to conduct his own experiments in his private laboratory. Of course, it was rumors of those experiments—his meddling with the forces of life and death—that made the villagers so wary of the magician and his daughter in the first place.

They were nearing the last of the merchants' stalls when Mina felt something strike the backs of her ankles. She halted, and she could practically hear the collective gasp of breath. When she turned around, she saw a young boy scurry behind his mother's legs, peeking guiltily up at Mina. Small rocks littered the ground by her feet—he must have thrown them at her. For now, it was only the children who struck out at her, but she knew she couldn't count on that forever.

"Come on, Mina, stop lingering."

"Just a minute, Hana," Mina said, loud enough for people to hear. They were all pretending to go about their business, but their movements were slow and unfocused. "Since we're here, we might as well do some shopping."

The backs of her ankles still stung from where the small stones had hit her. If she hurried away now, it would only prove that violence would deter her, that they could scare her away. The scale of fear was still tipped in her favor: they were more scared of her than she was of them.

She walked to the nearest stall and picked an object at random: a plain silver bracelet. "How much?" Mina demanded of the merchant. If he had been local, he might have waived the fee to get rid of her quickly. But Mina could see from the cool olive of his skin and the drab colors he wore that he was from the North, too concerned with his own business to worry himself with gossip about the magician and his daughter, and so he named his price. Mina handed some coins over to him and placed the bracelet around her wrist, a reminder that she would not be chased off.

"I'm ready to go home now," Mina said, turning again to Hana. She pitched her voice a little louder: "I'm ready to see my father."

Her bravado faded once she reached home. Mina knocked on the door of her father's study, taking a deep breath. After receiving no response, she peeked inside, but the room appeared empty. "Father?" she called softly.

Did he not even want to see her, after being gone for so long?

True, she wasn't particularly eager to see him again, but some part of her always stubbornly expected him to reach out to his daughter, the way she imagined most fathers did, even though he never gave her any reason to believe that he would.

Mina's hands balled into fists at her sides. Her eyes went to a door at the back of the room, almost hidden by the surrounding bookshelves—the door to her father's laboratory, the inner room where he did most of his work. Mina had been here in her father's study before—it was ordinary, if a little chaotic, with books scattered everywhere—but it was merely a presentable facade meant to distract from the hidden door leading to that secret adjoining room. She'd only been in the laboratory once in her life. Those memories were foggy, though, and her head pounded whenever she tried to remember.

She listened for the sound of her father approaching, and when she didn't hear anything, she crossed the study to that unassuming door. It was unlocked; she slipped inside.

The laboratory was dim and narrow, and along the walls were shelves full of vials and jars. She read a few of the scrawled labels: some were simply potions for sleep or health, but others announced themselves as deadly poisons. They had oddly fanciful names, like *Whisper of Death* or *Burning Needle*, and she knew from the proud penmanship that they were Gregory's inventions. He brewed death here, in a myriad of creative ways, just to pass the time.

She walked past a long wooden table where a lamp burned low. There was a dark black stain in one spot, but otherwise the table was covered in open books with strange symbols and drawings. She knew how to read, but most of the books were written in unfamiliar languages, so she ignored the books and focused again on the shelves.

Mina's eyes kept flickering to the contents of the jars, and she grew more unsettled each time. In many of the jars were misshapen lumps of . . . flesh? Bone? Feathers? She wasn't sure what they were until she saw an actual miniature replica of a human being in one of the jars. It floated in cloudy liquid, like a tiny wax doll, except she was sure it wasn't made of wax.

At the back of the room was a single jar resting on a small table. There was something inside the jar, and when Mina saw it clearly, she drew back at once. Unlike the strange fleshy things in the other jars, the contents of this one hadn't been preserved. She peered at the rotten lump of meat in the jar, thankful there was no smell coming from it. What purpose did this withered, shriveled piece of flesh serve for her father? Another failed experiment? An ingredient for one of his poisonous concoctions? The sight of it filled her with an inexplicable sense of dread.

"Repulsive, isn't it?"

Mina whirled around at the sound of her father's voice. He leaned against the doorway, his arms folded over his chest. But he wasn't the same as he had been when he'd left two months ago. His dark hair had lightened to gray, and there were more lines on his now-gaunt face. He looked to have aged at least twenty years while he'd been away.

"What happened to you?" Mina said, forgetting for a moment that he had caught her trespassing.

He walked over to the table, ignoring her question completely. "Do you know where I've been these past months?"

Mina was still tense, waiting for him to scold or berate her for invading his inner study. "Off on a useless search for another magician, I assume," she said.

He fumbled with the books on his table, tossing some on the floor, while stacking others in a pile. "Wrong," he said. "I was at Whitespring."

Mina couldn't hide her curiosity. "At the castle? With the king and queen?"

"With King Nicholas, yes. Queen Emilia, however, is dead." He looked up and watched for her reaction, but Mina gave none. Why should she care if the queen was dead? What happened in the North was of little concern to her.

Gregory chuckled to himself and leaned heavily against the table. "I don't know why I expected you to care. You should care, though, because her death has changed both of our lives forever."

Again, he waited for a reaction, for her to ask him what he meant. Mina knew he was baiting her, so she refused to answer at all. He'd tell her whatever he wanted to in the end, with or without her prompting.

"She died in childbirth," he continued, "but she left behind, in her stead, a daughter as beautiful as she was."

"I didn't know she was carrying a child," Mina said placidly.

"News travels slowly, I suppose. But she had . . . complications. The child was killing her from the inside out. The king called for me in secret to see if I could save her and the child through magic, since medicine had failed. He'd heard what I could do, he said. He'd heard whispers that I had power over life and death." Gregory's eyes glittered in the dim light, his voice solemn with pride, but then he glanced away, and Mina saw his hands gripping the side of the table. "I was too late to save the queen," he forced out, "but I did manage to save the child, using unconventional means. That's why you find me so . . . changed. The process was draining."

For a moment, Mina forgot that she was pretending not to care, drawn in by her father's faltering words, his altered appearance. She had never seen her father look so vulnerable, so uncertain, and she wondered if the change in him was more than physical. Shyly, she reached out to lay a hand on his arm. "Is there anything I can do to help?"

Gregory looked down at her hand and then brushed it away like it was a piece of dirt on his sleeve. "You've never pretended to care before, Mina. There's no need to start now."

Mina flinched and crossed her arms, trying to keep herself from storming out. She didn't want to give her father the satisfaction of driving her away.

"And now what?" Mina snapped. "You said this would change things for us."

His eyebrows went up in mock surprise. "You don't think I would perform such a feat without a price, do you? In exchange for saving his daughter, the king has invited us to live at court."

"At Whitespring?"

"A fresh start for us both."

"But it's so . . . so . . ." *Cold*, she was thinking. Mina was used to the bright days and warm nights of the South. Whitespring was so named because even in the spring, the ground was white with snow. How could she ever belong in such a place?

"It's better than living like outcasts."

Mina wrung her hands, trying to think of a way to persuade him without having to beg. Summoning as much authority as she could, she dropped her arms to her sides, stood tall, and said, "Go without me, then. I'll take care of things here. You don't need me."

He released the table and stepped closer to her. "Oh, but I do need you. I need that face of yours." He took her face in one hand, his fingers pressing into her jaw. "You'll marry someone highborn, and my place—*our* place—will be secure even if the king forgets his debt to me."

Mina tried to push his arm away and free herself from his rough grip, but even in his weakened state, he was stronger than she was. He waited until she'd given up before finally letting go.

"If you *need* me," she said, rubbing her jaw, "then you should try to be more persuasive. I don't owe you anything."

His face twisted in anger, but then he laughed. "You don't owe me anything? No, Mina, you owe me *everything*. You owe me your life. And not just because I'm your father."

Mina wanted to turn away, but there was nowhere safe to look. The whole room was full of him. "Fine," she said. "Tell me what I owe you, exactly. If you're convincing enough, maybe I'll change my mind."

He nodded, wearing the arrogant smile of a man who knew he was about to win. "All right, if that's the game you want to play." Gregory grabbed her wrist, and Mina, resenting the feel of his fingers digging into her skin, but knowing from experience that she couldn't break his grip, allowed him to drag her over to the table. He took a small pouch from his pocket and poured its contents—a handful of sand—out onto the table.

"Watch carefully," he said, sifting through the sand.

To Mina's astonishment, the sand started to *move*, to shift even without his touch, and then it wasn't sand anymore but a small gray mouse, bouncing off the sides of his cupped hands. She gasped, berating herself for it when she heard him laugh. She'd heard the same whispers that the king had, that the magician Gregory had the power to create life, but she'd never seen her father demonstrate his otherworldly power. He played the part of magician for the villagers with his potions, but he kept his real magic in his laboratory, for himself alone.

Gregory was grimacing, his jaw tense as if with pain, but then he recovered. "It's alchemy in its purest form," he said, "transforming one thing into another without any intermediary. I was born with the power to take any inanimate substance and transform it into something organic . . . but only to some extent. This mouse is no true mouse. It is, in its essence, still sand. It will not grow or age or die. It's not even truly alive." To prove his point, he balled his hands into fists, and the tiny, squeaking mouse abruptly disinte-grated, once again a pile of sand.

Mina nearly gasped a second time, but though her jaw hung open, she made no sound. Her eyes saw a pile of sand, but her mind transformed it into a pile of bones and meat. It was both grave and corpse in one.

With a careless gesture, Gregory swept the sand back into the pouch. "It's like a mechanical doll, do you see? If you wind it up, it resembles life, but it is only a resemblance. In order to make it a real, living mouse, I would need to add my blood—the source of my magic." A weary note crept into his voice. "It . . . has taken me many years and many attempts to figure that out."

"What's the point of all this?" Mina rasped, her throat dry. She kept thinking of the shelves around her, of the misshapen creations in their jars.

"Ah yes. This was only a prologue to the story I want to tell you. When you were a child, no more than four years old, you fell deathly ill. Your mother wept, for there was no one who could help you. Your heart was damaged, likely since birth, and all we could do was wait for it to stop altogether. And one day, it did. Your mother was frantic, almost furious, in her grief, and I hated to see her in such a state."

Mina couldn't help raising an eyebrow at that, especially since Gregory's lip curled slightly at the mention of her mother. Gregory paused, glaring coldly at her, and Mina couldn't stop herself from taking a step back away from him.

"I know what you're thinking, but I *did* love your mother once. I wanted her to be happy. And so I brought you here, to this room. I laid you down here, on this table. And then I opened up your chest, took out your useless heart, and replaced it with a new one, made from glass."

Mina almost laughed at him. Was he trying to frighten her? True, she'd been sickly as a child—Hana had told her that—but this was the first she'd heard of glass hearts. She made no effort to hide her skepticism, but Gregory was undeterred. He placed one hand on her chest and said, "Don't you have a scar, right here? Haven't you ever wondered why you don't have a heartbeat?"

This time, Mina did laugh. "I may have a scar, but I also have a heartbeat. I wouldn't be alive, otherwise."

"Have you ever heard it? Felt it?"

"Of course not. It's too quiet for me to hear."

"Give me your hand," he said, but he grabbed her hand before she could give it and held her palm to his chest.

Mina instantly started to take her hand back, but she stopped when she felt something peculiar under her palm: a faint, rhythmic pounding. She pulled away in shock. "What is that? What's wrong with you?"

"It's not me, my sweet. Put your hand to anyone's chest or wrist or throat, and you'll feel the same steady pulse."

Mina put her hand on her own chest, waiting for something she'd never felt before.

"Don't bother. You won't find it, because you don't have one. Remember what I told you about my blood? When you were sick, I didn't yet know how to create something more genuine than that sand mouse."

Mina's throat tightened and she had to force out the question: "Are you saying that I'm just like—"

"Oh no, no," Gregory said, frowning at her like she had said something completely ridiculous. "*You* are alive, Mina, and you will grow and live and die the same as any living being; it's only your heart that's artificial. I commanded your new heart to keep you alive, but because I created it without my blood, it is still, in essence, glass, so it lacks some of the nuances of a real heart—like a heart-beat. It was the best I could do."

She tried to think back to a time when her heart might have lurched or pounded or fluttered—*anything* to announce its presence—but there was only ever silence. She thought again of that mouse dissolving into sand. "I don't—I don't believe you."

"Do you need more proof? I was hoping you would. Turn around."

She knew. She knew as she turned to the table at the end of the room what he wanted her to see. She knew what that withered, rotten piece of meat inside the jar was, and she fought the urge to retch.

"That's your heart, Mina," Gregory said from right behind her. "Aren't you grateful that rotting thing isn't a part of you anymore? Don't you think you owe me, after all?"

3

MINA

Mina stared at the heart—*her* heart—and tried not to scream. "Why couldn't you save my mother, if you could save me?" she asked her father. She might still trap him in a lie, if she kept calm.

Gregory's voice grew harsh. "Your mother was never ill. She was horrified when she learned what I had done to save your life. The idea of it was repulsive to her. She'd been unhappy for a long time, but only after I replaced your heart did she choose to do something about it. She wanted to punish me for what I'd done—and to punish you for what you had become." He roughly turned Mina by the shoulders so that she was facing him. "Do you understand what I'm saying, Mina? Your mother . . . your mother killed herself."

"You're lying," Mina said at once. "She died because she was ill. Hana told me."

"Because that's what I told Hana to tell you." The words sounded bitter on his tongue. "Your mother chose death over me, over you, because she was weak. She could endure me, but when she sensed an emptiness in her child, it was too much for her to bear. Your heart was shaped to survive, not to love, and your mother was self-ish: she was incapable of loving someone who could never love her back."

"I—I can love," Mina said. She tried to think of a way to prove him wrong, to fight back. But she didn't love her father, and even if she pretended she did, he would never believe it.

Hana? Hana was familiar, but there had never been much affection between them. What did love feel like? How would she know if she'd ever felt it before? *I loved my mother,* she wanted to say, but then Hana's accusation came back to her: *It's as if you don't care about her at all.* Mina had denied it, but now she wasn't sure. She loved the memory of her mother, the idea of having a mother, but the woman herself was a mystery to her, as was everything that had happened to her before her father gave her a glass heart. She always wondered why she had such trouble remembering her early childhood, but now she understood: her old life had ended the day her heart stopped, and a new one had begun.

She felt so drained, suddenly, so empty. For the first time, she noticed the silence in her body, the absence of that steady beating in her chest. *You don't care for anything but yourself.* She couldn't even remember if she had ever shed a single tear.

Gregory came to stand in front of her, blocking her view of the heart in the jar. His face was drawn and solemn. "There's no point fighting me on this, Mina. I understand how you function better than you do. You can rage and hate and despair and hope as well as anyone else, but love is something more complicated. Love requires a real heart, which you do not have, and so you cannot love, and you will never be loved, except"—he came closer to her and brushed his knuckles against her cheek—"you have beauty, and beauty is more powerful than love. People can't help themselves: they crave beauty. They will overlook anything, even a glass heart, for it. If they love you for anything, it will be for your beauty. But there's nothing for either of us here. Come to court with me, and you'll be the most beautiful lady there, the most envied, the most desired."

He stopped to see if his words were having any effect on her, but Mina's face was as still as her heart.

"Well? Do you agree? Will you be ready to leave for Whitespring by tomorrow?"

He reached his hand out for her in a gesture of reconciliation, and though she hated herself for it, Mina put her hand in his.

What else did she have?

Mina laid her mother's mirror down on the grass by the stream. She had meant to put it back, but the thought of going into her mother's room now was too painful. She was sorry to leave behind her favorite places—the hidden stream where it was always cool, the giant oak tree that she had once tried (and failed) to climb as a child, the ruins of the old church with the caved-in roof. They were all solitary places, of course—none of the villagers would miss her or her father when they were gone.

She remembered the first time she had been brave enough to approach a group of children playing by the stream, dangling their feet in the water. She had been only seven or eight, and her loneliness had finally overcome her timidity. Mina had already begun to notice the way parents would pull their children closer to them whenever Hana took her into the market, but she had never understood why. For all she knew, it was because of Hana, not because of her.

But she had been alone the time she tried to join the children at the stream, and so when half of them had jumped up from the water and run away, and the other half had sneered and called her and her father cruel names, Mina finally understood: *They hate me.*

She had decided at that moment that she hated them, too.

But today there was no one at the stream, so Mina was free to sit on its banks and say a final good-bye. She refused to hate this place just because of one bad memory on its banks. There was too much to appreciate here—the drops of sunlight falling in between the leaves overhead, the sound of the water rushing past, the scent of the grass. Mina even loved the large chunks of stone that littered the stream, remnants of a bridge that had collapsed years ago. She had come here to cheer herself up, but everywhere she looked, she found something else she was leaving behind.

Her reflection looked up at her from the mirror, and even that offered her little comfort anymore. From seeing the portrait of Dorothea that hung in her room, Mina knew they bore a fairly strong resemblance. Her life she owed to her father, but her beauty she owed to her mother.

No, I owe you nothing. You left me with him.

Weak, her father had called Dorothea. Mina didn't think her mother weak; she thought her selfish.

And what about me? What am I? She looked into the mirror for an answer. Her face was ashen, her eyes dull. Even so, she was beautiful. And what was more, the mirror gave no indication of what lay beneath. With her beauty as a distraction, no one would ever know that she was, deep down, hollow. She touched her cheek, the bridge of her nose, the indentation above her upper lip, and she was alarmed by how soft her skin was, how impermanent, like the heart in its jar. Her beauty was merely a shell, and a shell was always in danger of cracking.

The surface of her mother's mirror seemed to mock her, its image too flawless, too smooth for how she felt inside. *It should be cracked,* she thought. Maybe then her reflection could absorb what was broken in her, and Mina could be whole. Her fingers curled into a fist—

But before she even touched the glass, the mirror cracked by itself.

She gaped at the mirror in awe, trying to understand. Her chest was aching, and she felt so tired suddenly, but she ignored the feeling. *Show me. Show me what you did.*

The glass seemed to dissolve into liquid before knitting back together. Mina stroked the mirror's undamaged surface with her fingers as the pain in her chest faded away.

It's listening to me.

The glass was responding to her, to the glass in her heart. Her father hadn't told her about this side effect; was he even aware of it? Was there still something about her that he didn't understand? Gregory had given her a piece of his own magic when he'd shaped her heart, and she was almost certain that he didn't know it.

And what was that ache in her chest? Had the magic done it to her? She started to panic as she thought of her father's aged appearance, but she recalled that the ache and the fatigue had faded. Perhaps commanding the glass had drained something from her, but at least the effect wasn't permanent. With growing excitement, Mina whispered, "Be a mouse," to the mirror.

This last command drained her even more as the glass shifted again, spilling out of the frame onto the ground. And then the glass became a small brown mouse with twitching whiskers, and Mina heard a series of gasps.

Mina hissed a silent order for the mouse to become glass again, and the mouse crystallized as she looked up and saw a group of four girls her age gathered by the trees. She recognized their faces, but she didn't know their names or who they were. They were all staring at her in horror, some of them moving their lips in silent prayer.

Mina staggered to her feet, hoping to distract their gazes away from the mouse that had just been glass, but several of them were pointing. "You're just like him!" a tall girl cried. "My mother always said that you were."

"No, you don't understand—" Mina took a faltering step toward them, but they all took a step back together.

"Don't come any nearer!" said the girl in front. She bent down and picked up a long, twisted stick from the ground, holding it in front of her like a sword. "We don't want anything to do with either of you!"

"I'm not like him!" Mina yelled at them. But hadn't they just seen proof that she was?

She took another step forward, and the girl threw the stick in panic. It scraped Mina's arm, leaving a shallow scratch before it fell at her feet.

No one will ever love me anyway, so what's the point in playing nice?

Mina could hurt them if she wanted to, just as they had hurt her. She could use the glass to scare them. All those sideways glances, all those sneering whispers—why fight their contempt when it would be so much easier to earn it? At least now it would be for her, not just her father.

"You should be careful how you speak to me," Mina called to them, "especially when you don't know what I can do."

The girls watched with widening eyes as the mouse shifted into liquid glass and swirled up toward Mina's hand, circling up her arm like a snake. Mina wondered if she should turn it into a real snake and hurl it at them the way they had thrown the stick at her—

But then Hana came bursting through the trees like an angry bull, and the girls scattered and ran.

Mina quickly gave up her hold on the glass, letting it fall back to the ground as shards and praying that Hana had been too distracted by the frightened girls to notice.

"What are you doing meddling with the villagers?" Hana said, taking Mina by the wrist. "You know it's better just to ignore them. And stop wandering off without telling me where you're going. You're my responsibility, you know."

"I'm going home now anyway, so you didn't have to bother coming after me," Mina said. She pulled away from Hana, still shaken. She was glad Hana had interrupted before Mina had done anything to hurt or scare them, and yet—and yet, she felt cheated, like she was still holding a breath that she had almost been allowed to release.

"Just a minute," Mina said, kneeling down so that her back hid the glass and the mirror frame from Hana's view. In a hushed whisper, she ordered the mirror to fix itself, and the glass slithered back to its home in the mirror frame, where it solidified. She picked it up and went to join Hana at the edge of the trees.

Hana kept fussing on their way home, and now Mina worried that she had made a terrible mistake. What if those girls told everyone what they had seen, and word eventually reached her father? For the first time, she was grateful that they'd be leaving so soon—perhaps rumors of Mina's powers wouldn't have time to reach him. She was almost certain Hana hadn't seen anything, or else she would have mentioned it by now, but even so, Mina would have to be more careful. If Gregory found out about her power, he was sure to use it to his advantage in some way, and Mina didn't think she could bear it. She needed to have something to herself, something that he couldn't take from her.

Gregory was standing outside the house as they approached, looking even more haggard in the daylight. "There you are!" he called. "I've been looking for you."

Mina went toward him, bracing herself, but Gregory passed by her and went to Hana, walking around her with a thoughtful frown. "You're . . . what? Sixteen, seventeen now?"

It took Mina a moment to grasp that he was talking to her this time. "Sixteen."

"That's old to still have a nurse, wouldn't you say?"

She glanced at Hana, who seemed to have no reaction to the question. "Yes," Mina said. "I've thought so for a while."

Gregory nodded. "I agree. And we want to travel as lightly as possible."

Hana still didn't react, even though Mina was sure she was about to be dismissed. Maybe Hana didn't care. Maybe she'd be thankful to get away from them both.

Gregory stood in front of Hana, placing a hand on top of her head. "Say good-bye to your nurse, then, Mina." Before Mina could even ask what he was doing, Hana's body had hardened to wood and clattered to the ground as a pile of twigs and branches.

Of course, Mina thought. The only maid willing to serve a magician's lonely wife and daughter was one Gregory had created. She should have known.

Gregory walked back into the house, leaving Mina alone with the remnants of her nurse. She stared at the pile wide-eyed, and she shivered despite the sunlight. One moment Hana had been here, real and human, and now she was nothing but kindling for a fire. Mina kept waiting for tears to come—she may not have been fond of Hana, but she had never wished her *dead*. But no tears came, and her lack of emotional display made her feel . . .

Heartless.

But that's what I am, she thought. *That's what I'll always be.*

Mina stepped over the pile and followed her father inside.

LYNET

Crouching in the snow, Lynet peered into the small, dingy window of the surgeon's basement workroom. Over the past several weeks, she'd fallen into the habit of following the new surgeon instead of attending her lessons, but she thought it was a worthwhile trade. After all, could her lessons have taught her that the surgeon's name was Nadia, or that she was only seventeen?

Lynet watched Nadia now as she read and made sketches in her journal, pausing only to push back the strands of black hair that kept falling over her eyes. She rested her chin on one hand, her fingers turning the pages with something like reverence. Sometimes the hint of a smile crossed her face as she scribbled down a note. Lynet loved these moments of calm most of all, when the focused, serious surgeon relaxed just enough for Lynet to see the person underneath. It was during these times that Lynet wished she could watch Nadia from inside the room rather than from outside the window, that she could speak to her and know her thoughts as well as her actions.

But it was too late for that now; Lynet had spoiled it all by following her for so long. How could Lynet ever speak to her and pretend not to know who she was or how she spent her days? Why would Nadia ever agree to speak to her when she knew how Lynet had haunted her like a ghost?

A sudden flurry of movement startled Lynet as two men came bursting into the room, one of them supporting the other, holding him up because his foot was mauled and bloody. Lynet's stomach lurched. She recognized the wounded man as a kitchen servant, and she started to turn away from the gruesome sight, but then— then Nadia reacted, and Lynet couldn't look away at all.

Nadia rolled up the sleeves of her tunic, revealing lean but strong forearms, and knelt to examine the foot. She moved quickly but precisely around the room, fetching a wooden block and—to Lynet's horror—a saw.

Lynet knew what would happen next as Nadia propped the servant's wounded foot on the block. The blood, the white of bone, the look of anguish on the poor man's face as he bit down on a rag to keep from screaming—Lynet tried to block them from her vision. But she couldn't stop watching Nadia during the entire procedure, her stern look of concentration the one source of stability during such a terrible scene.

Just once, when the amputation was complete and Nadia was bandaging the stump, did Lynet see the surgeon betray any sign of agitation. Nadia let out a single, relieved exhale, her eyes closing briefly, but only when her head was bent, her face hidden from the servants—but not from Lynet.

Lynet decided that was as much as she could handle for the morning, and she climbed up the castle walls to her bedroom window, thinking herself a coward. Here she was, unable to speak to a girl when that girl regularly faced horrors without even flinching. She decided she would at least look in on that kitchen servant later and make sure he didn't lose his position because of his injury.

She climbed in through the window, swinging both legs over the ledge, and nearly let out a yelp when she saw her father sitting in her chair, waiting for her.

"Lynet, we've talked about this," he said.

No matter how stern or forbidding her father tried to appear, he always seemed sad rather than angry—perhaps it was the way his voice sounded like a sigh, or the dark circles under his deep-set eyes, or the way his hair and beard always seemed a little grayer every time she saw him, as though he were slowly being drained of all color. Lynet would have preferred that he scold her so she could feel indignant in response, but she didn't know how to respond to that disappointed note in his voice other than to apologize.

"I'm sorry, Papa, I was just . . ."

"Just skipping your morning lessons? Just climbing in through your window despite your father's many warnings?"

"I'm sorry," she said again, more softly this time.

He looked like he wanted to say something else, but then he shook his head and stood, holding his hand out to her. "We'll talk about this later. Today of all days, we should be at peace with each other."

Lynet frowned. "What's today?"

He dropped his hand and raised his eyebrows in surprise. "It's two weeks before your birthday. It's time for our yearly visit. Have you forgotten?"

"Oh, that's . . . that's right," Lynet said. She had been so distracted following Nadia that she *had* forgotten this day was approaching—or maybe she hadn't wanted to remember. Tiny prickles went up and down her arms, but she forced a smile and said, "Are we going now?"

He nodded, and Lynet followed him out of the room. Lynet let her father lead, walking slightly behind him so that he wouldn't notice the deep breaths she took to calm her nerves. Normally she would have prepared herself, but this year she had forgotten, and so the dread came to her all at once, in a flood of nausea.

They passed other members of the court as they made their way down to the courtyard and around to the garden, all of them bowing their heads in solemn greeting. Lynet could see on their faces the moment they remembered what day it was and where the king and the princess were going—a slight intake of breath, a smile quickly turned to a somber frown. Today was a day of mourning.

It was appropriate, then, that they had to walk past the Shadow Garden. Lynet ordinarily liked the garden, especially seeing it from above, where the bare branches of the trees stood out against the snow like trails of ink spilled over paper. Today, though, she could only think of Queen Sybil and the story behind all those dead trees.

Centuries ago, before Whitespring had earned its name, the Shadow Garden had been called the Queen's Garden, because it had belonged to Queen Sybil. But when the queen's only son was thrown from his horse to his death, the queen hanged herself from one of the trees in her garden. At the instant of her death, the winds changed, and snow started to fall over the northern half of the kingdom, though it was spring. The castle froze, the passing of time blurring into one long winter, and the Queen's Garden remained in its new, grim state: a grove of dead trees, a garden of shadows. The Queen's Garden became the Shadow Garden, the castle was renamed Whitespring, and the everlasting winter became known over the years as "Sybil's curse."

Past the garden, at the base of the North Tower around the back of the castle, was a small door slightly below ground level, a short flight of steps cutting through the snow. When they reached that door, Nicholas froze, eyes fixed on the handle. Lynet gently put her hand on his arm. "We don't have to go this year, if you don't want to," she said, trying not to sound too eager.

He rested his hand on hers for a moment, perhaps drawing strength from it. "No," he said, "I wouldn't deprive you of this. It's the only time we have with her." And without any more hesitation, he opened the door to the royal crypt, where Lynet's mother waited.

Nicholas lit the lamp that hung by the door and held it up, offering his other hand to Lynet. The stairs down to the crypt were uneven and winding, and Lynet often had trouble with them, especially when she was little, so she gratefully took her father's hand and let him lead her down.

Her father pressed her hand gently as they submerged into the stale air of the crypt, and she managed a weak smile in return. These visits meant so much to him; she didn't want him to know that she always dreaded this day. They always honored her mother's death shortly before Lynet's birthday. When Lynet was younger, she hadn't thought much of it, but now she understood that this was her father's way of separating her mother's death from her birth. He wanted to spare her the guilt of being the cause of that death. She was thankful for that, she supposed.

Lynet kept her eyes down as they passed through shadowed walls. She didn't want to see the massive stone columns, because then she remembered that those pillars alone kept the crypt from collapsing under the pressure of the earth above. She didn't want to glance up at the walls, because all along them were long, narrow alcoves, each housing a casket. The bodies of all her ancestors were here, and one day she would join them.

She had to look up, though, when they reached the Cavern of Bones.

Past the dead trees of the Shadow Garden was a statue of Queen Sybil standing over the lake. Her stone hands covered her face as she wept eternally, her grief strong enough to banish spring from the North. Here in the crypt, in the Cavern of Bones, was a statue of a different sort.

Lynet forced herself to look at Sybil's bones, laid out on her bier. All around her were the remains of other skeletons, martyrs who had died on their knees when they came to pray to Sybil, asking her to end the curse that bore her name. Since then, the custom when passing through the Cavern was to stop and kneel and offer a prayer to Sybil in the hopes that one day her curse would end.

Nicholas knelt down, and Lynet followed, shutting her eyes to block out the sight of death. She prayed, as she had been taught, for the end of the curse, for the survival of the North, for respite from the cold.

When they finished their prayers and finally reached the alcove that held her mother's casket, Lynet was so tense that she almost let out a moan of fear. Her father still held her hand tightly, and she was suddenly convinced that he would lead her straight into the casket to take her mother's place.

"Papa, I—"

He shook his head. "You don't need to say anything, my Lynet-bird." He released her hand only to put his arm around her and hold her close. "Look," he said. "Look at her." They were only words, but Lynet felt as though he were holding her eyelids open, forcing her to stare at that smooth wooden box.

"Every year," Nicholas said, "when we come to see her, I always feel the pain of her loss all over again. I think of her laid out in that casket, her eyes forever closed, her soft hands crossed over her chest. I can imagine her so vividly as the woman she once was."

Lynet could imagine her too: a corpse laid out, eyes closed, hands crossed—but the corpse had her own face. Thanks to the strong resemblance she shared with her mother, Lynet knew that if she opened that casket now, she would see something like herself—her own body, her own face—after nearly sixteen years of decay. Perhaps life was the only thing that set Lynet apart from her mother, the boundary between them as indistinct as a single breath. The faint sound of Lynet's breathing, the rise and fall of her chest—without them, Lynet might have been indistinguishable from the woman in that box. She kept her eyes wide open, afraid that if she closed them, she would see the inside of the casket behind her eyelids.

Her father turned to her, studying her face. "You become more like her every year."

"I'm not her," Lynet said, barely above a whisper.

Her father smiled fondly, mistaking her terror for fear of inadequacy. "You will be. A few more years, and you'll embody everything that she was."

All Lynet wanted was to run outside and climb the highest tree, as far away as possible from this place, and then she would be more certain than ever that she was alive—that she was herself. But her father's arm kept her weighed down beside him, and when they were finished paying their respects, Nicholas led her out of the crypt. Lynet followed in a daze, blinking away the sight of the casket.

Nicholas hugged her close and pressed a kiss to the top of her head. "I'm so thankful for you, Lynetbird. On this day, especially, I see how fortunate I am."

Guilt and pride mixed in equal measure in her chest—pride because she had made her father happy for one brief moment, and guilt because she knew she would disappoint him again. She could never be her mother, even if she'd wanted to be.

Only when they had emerged back into the fresh air did Lynet start to come out of her stupor and feel her blood flowing again. She could see the outlines of the dead trees in the garden and hear the distant lapping of the lake, all of these sights and sounds more vivid and sharp after the suffocating gloom of the crypt.

Her father's voice seemed louder too as he said, "I have to meet with my council now, Lynet. Will you be all right on your own? Or perhaps you'd like to come with me? It would be good for you to see a council meeting."

Mina had told her about those council meetings—a group of old men and women gossiping or else arguing over how much money to spend, while the king waited for them to make up their minds, and how they usually decided to do nothing at all. "No, thank you," she said, "I'd like to go for a walk. Although . . . I wouldn't mind going on your next hunting trip."

He smiled at her in amusement. "Enjoy your walk, then. But don't be late for your lessons," he said, before heading back toward the courtyard.

When he was gone, Lynet practically threw herself at the nearest wall and started to climb. She didn't even have anywhere to go, but she needed to climb up, away from the crypt, away from the bones and the stench of death. She found a jutting piece of stone as a foothold and found a ledge to bring herself up on top of the low, arched roof. She climbed up over the arch and then started down, toward the central courtyard. She almost slipped as she made her way across, and she relished the way her pulse sped in response—it was proof that she was alive, and that she was not the dead queen in her coffin. How could anyone mistake her for the late queen when she was scaling the walls of a castle? Would someone so delicate be able to climb these heights? Would someone so delicate risk her safety in such a way?

Lynet was overlooking the courtyard now, but she still felt like she was running away from something, and that if she stopped, it would catch her. It was a restless feeling, an itch that made her feel like her skin didn't fit over her bones correctly. She thought she might leap out of herself and become someone new, and then she'd be at peace.

Leap. The thought appealed to her, made her heart race faster. The juniper tree was about five feet away from the edge of the roof, its branches inviting her. *I can make that jump,* she told herself. It was a farther distance than she had ever jumped before, and there was a voice in her head telling her that she was doing something pointlessly dangerous, but every muscle in her body ached to take that leap, to release whatever strange energy was building up inside of her. Her muscles tensed in preparation, and she relished the feeling of fear and elation that flooded her.

Lynet targeted the nearest juniper branch, its leaves covered in snow. She crouched lower, took a breath, and jumped.

One of her hands found the branch—and lost it again, her skin scraping painfully against the sharp bark as she tumbled down. She barely had time to absorb what had happened before her back hit the ground, her fall thankfully blunted by several inches of snow.

I knew I couldn't make that jump.

She lay there for a moment, eyes closed, and even though she had missed the tree, she did still feel a kind of peace come over her. That feeling of something moving under her skin was gone, replaced by a stinging pain in her left palm. She took deep breaths as her pulse began to slow.

And then she heard an amused voice from above: "What's this? A bird fallen from her perch?"

"I'm not a bird," Lynet shot back immediately. She opened her eyes and then inhaled sharply as she looked up at a face that had become familiar to her.

The girl from the courtyard. The surgeon she had been following. Nadia.

Lynet seemed to be familiar to her, too, because Nadia was staring at her, wide-eyed, from above. "No, not a bird, a princess," she said. "I apologize, my lady. I didn't recognize you at first."

Lynet rushed to her feet and tried to brush the snow off her skirt, hoping also to brush off the indignity of having been found falling from a tree. But the juniper branch had scraped a layer of skin off her left palm—the source of the pain she'd felt earlier—and she winced when her hand met the rough fabric.

"Did you hurt yourself, my lady?" Nadia said, reaching for Lynet's hand. As she examined Lynet's palm, Lynet took the opportunity to observe Nadia up close. After weeks of peering through windows and running after her over rooftops, Lynet's mind was reeling with new details. Nadia's hair wasn't black, as Lynet had previously believed, but a deep, dark brown. Her heavy eyelids were lined with long eyelashes. And her eyes—her eyes were staring back at Lynet.

"It's fine," Lynet said, snatching her hand back. "Just a scrape."

"I can put something on it to help it heal, if you come with me. I'm the new court surgeon."

I know, she nearly said. "If you insist. But just . . . just call me Lynet, as if I weren't a princess." She couldn't bear such formalities from her, not when Lynet felt so familiar with her already.

Nadia seemed surprised by the request, her head tilting slightly, but she nodded and began to lead the way across the courtyard. Lynet paused for a moment, and then she did what she had done the first time she'd seen Nadia walk across this same courtyard.

Lynet followed her.

5

LYNET

The surgeon's workroom was much more vivid in person than from behind a dirty window. Lynet paused at the threshold, feeling like she was about to walk into a dream—or like she was waking from a dream only to find that reality was even stranger. Along one fragrant wall were shelves carrying a variety of potions and herbs, along with the occasional bowl of leeches. The jars and vials on the shelves reflected the light from the window, sending shards of sunlight and shadow throughout the room.

Hanging on another wall was a drawing of a bloody man pierced all over his body by different weapons. Underneath it was a low table of knives, scalpels, and other steel surgical tools, some of which Lynet recognized from watching Nadia work over the past few weeks. Strewn throughout the entire room were piles of books and bottles of ink and loose sheets of paper, which Nadia hurried to tuck away as soon as she set foot in the room.

Lynet took a moment just to absorb it all. Ignoring the mess on the table, since Nadia seemed so embarrassed by it, she walked slowly along the edge of the room, observing it from new angles with each step. From the corner of her eye, she saw that Nadia was watching her now with the focus she usually reserved for surgical procedures, waiting until Lynet had come full circle back to the doorway.

"This is where you work?" Lynet said, though she already knew the answer.

Nadia nodded. "Also where I sleep." She gestured to a dark room in the back.

That was something new, something Lynet hadn't known from watching her. She had never seen Nadia sleep, not even for a moment over her books. She wondered how it would feel to sleep in a room like this. She wondered what kind of dreams Nadia had.

"I have an ointment for your hand," Nadia said. In one smooth motion, she turned to one of her shelves and reached up for the jar without even needing to look for it. "My name is Nadia, by the way."

Lynet nearly said, "I know," before stopping herself.

"Here, give me your hand." Nadia started applying the greenish ointment to Lynet's wounded palm. Lynet pretended to fiddle with the silver bracelet around her wrist, but she also watched from beneath her eyelashes as Nadia rubbed ointment on her skin with the same delicacy as when she turned the pages of her books.

"What is that?" Lynet said, wrinkling her nose at the ointment.

"Comfrey."

"It smells terrible."

Nadia laughed, a husky exhalation that seemed to take her by surprise. Lynet didn't think she'd ever heard Nadia laugh before.

Nadia replaced the ointment on its shelf, and then paused, her back to Lynet. "May I freely ask you something?" she said.

Lynet shrugged. "I suppose."

Nadia came to stand at the other side of the table, opposite Lynet, and looked her directly in the eye. "Why have you been following me?"

Lynet gaped at her. She was ready to lie and deny it, but she knew her stunned face must have already given her away. What should she do? What would Mina do in her position? The answer, of course, was that Mina would never be in this position in the first place.

When Lynet opened her mouth, the truth slipped out: "Because you were wearing trousers."

There was a confused pause, and then another burst of laughter escaped from Nadia, and she covered her mouth with her hand. Lynet started laughing too, and she felt the same thrill as when she was climbing, her heart fluttering at the unpredictability of each step she took.

"Is that really why?" Nadia said, shaking her head in amazement.

"That's how it started, but—wait, how long have you known?"

Nadia looked up at the ceiling as she tried to remember. "I think . . . the day I first noticed you, I was pulling a tooth. . . ."

"So you've known all along." Lynet groaned. She covered her face with her hands before the smell of the comfrey made her drop them again. Still, she wasn't ready to look Nadia in the eye again, so she stared down at the floor and asked, "You . . . you weren't angry about it, were you?"

She peeked up in time to see Nadia lean forward, her braid falling over her shoulder as she rested her forearms on the table. "Not . . . angry, exactly. But once I found out you were the princess, I was so worried that I would slip up in some way while you were watching, and then you'd tell your father and I'd be dismissed." She shrugged, wearing a rueful smile. "But I couldn't exactly ask you to stop, could I?"

Lynet frowned, considering the truth of this. If Nadia had come to her and asked her to stop, would she have been angry, or asked her father to throw the surgeon out of the castle? Of course Lynet wouldn't have, but Nadia had no way of knowing that.

"Even if you're not angry with me, I'm still sorry," Lynet said, not just to appease her, but because she meant it. Lynet rested her arms on the table surface across from her, mimicking her pose. "It's an old habit of mine since childhood, following people, seeing how they spend their days."

"That's an odd habit, isn't it?"

Lynet shrugged. "When I was little, I would see other children at court running around and playing, and I wanted to join them, but my father—I wasn't allowed to play with them, in case I got hurt." She stared down at the table. Lynet could feel the words spilling out of her, but she made no effort to stop them. This workroom seemed a world apart from Whitespring, and so any secrets she told here would be buried under snow and earth.

"And then they never stayed for long, anyway," she continued. "People never stay for long at Whitespring. So I started to follow them around, watching from a distance, hiding so no one would see me. It was the only game I had, and this way I didn't have to worry about growing too attached to any of the other children my age before they left. And then I just . . . never stopped. I started following other people too, but all they do is sit around and gossip and complain about each other, so it's not very exciting, not like you—" She stopped herself too late and her head snapped up, her face growing warm, but Nadia didn't react to her unintended confession. She just kept watching, waiting for Lynet to finish.

"I . . . I don't think I ever considered how invasive it must be to feel like you're being spied on. I'm truly sorry." She forced herself not to look away, hoping that Nadia would reward her with a smile, but instead, Nadia's face seemed to fall, a dark look in her eyes before they darted away.

After a short but uncomfortable silence, Nadia said, "I wouldn't have asked you to stop, anyway. I became a little—" She broke off and looked down at the table.

Lynet leaned forward. "What?"

Nadia shook her head, but then her lips curled in a slow smile and she answered, "I was going to say 'flattered.' I've been traveling through the North for almost a year, trying to help people when I can . . . and during that year, so many people have dismissed me or laughed at me for wanting to practice medicine." Her voice was light, but she started tracing the lines and whorls on the table, her nails scraping against the wood. "They think girls are too softhearted to witness any suffering, that I'll be scared off. They think I'm just playing at being a surgeon. But you . . . no matter what I was doing, whether I was letting blood or pulling a tooth or even amputating a foot this morning . . ." Her hands stopped moving and she looked across the table at Lynet. There was something heavy, almost expectant, in the force of her gaze that made Lynet lean back again, taking her arms off the table. "You never turned away," she finished. "And so I always felt like a true surgeon in your eyes."

Lynet retraced all the steps she had taken following Nadia, now imagining them from the other girl's point of view. All this time, Lynet had been trying to understand her from a distance, while Nadia had been purposefully showing Lynet exactly who she was.

She offered Nadia a shy smile, never breaking her gaze. "I'm glad I fell out of that tree," she said quietly.

Nadia laughed again, more freely this time, and Lynet laughed too, dispelling the serious air that had come over them.

Lynet liked to see Nadia smile, to hear her laugh. When Nadia smiled, her whole face softened, like clouds giving way to the sun. But Lynet also liked the stoic, focused surgeon that she had watched from windows—so different from this smiling girl, but still such an essential part of her. And the fact that the two were the same, that the girl and the surgeon could exist freely in the same person, was to Lynet the very meaning of possibility—of freedom.

"I'd never seen a female surgeon before," Lynet said. "Are you the first?"

Nadia shook her head, her back straightening into what Lynet knew was her surgeon's posture. "My father told me about others, mostly from the South. I've even read that Queen Sybil knew all the medicinal properties of the plants in her garden and used them to help the ailing. But hardly anyone remembers her for that any-more. They only blame her for the curse."

"Sybil's curse," Lynet murmured, for the first time wondering why people called it that when no one knew whether Sybil herself was responsible for it. But then, what was the life of a queen com-pared to the legend people created for her after her death? The truth had stopped mattering years ago. "It hardly seems fair," she said, more to herself than to Nadia.

"Medicine was my family's trade," Nadia continued. "My mother was a midwife and my father was a surgeon."

"Was?" Lynet asked gently.

"They're both dead now," she said simply. "A fever."

"Oh, I—I'm sorry."

But Nadia just shook her head with a strained smile. "I don't want to mourn their deaths anymore. I only want to honor their lives."

Lynet leaned forward. "How do you choose to honor them?" What she really wanted to ask was how anyone could honor the dead while still feeling alive.

"I want to do what they did," Nadia said at once, like she'd been ready for the question. "My father studied medicine in the South, before the university closed. He taught me what he learned before he died, but now that Queen Mina has reopened the university, I want to go there too, to walk the same halls that he did."

"When will you go?" Lynet asked, trying to sound light and casual.

Nadia stared at her without answering, and for a moment Lynet saw the light in her eyes waver with uncertainty. "In the next year, I hope," she said.

Lynet looked down at her feet on the stone floor. What else had she expected, that Nadia would stay at Whitespring forever, when so few people did? That because Lynet had come out of hiding and spoken to her, she would be forced to stay here forever, to keep her company? No one stayed at Whitespring for long, she knew that, except . . . except perhaps some part of her had thought that Nadia was so unflinching, so steady even in times of crisis, that even the cold and the gloom of Whitespring wouldn't scare her away.

"I can't stay here anymore," Nadia said softly. "I've seen so much misery in the North, so much death. . . ."

Lynet's head shot up. "What do you mean?"

Nadia's eyebrow arched in response. "Have you ever been outside the castle? Have you seen what it's like for people who can't afford to bury themselves in fur or sit by a fire all day? Nothing grows here, nothing ever . . . *changes*, or gets better. Half of this kingdom has frozen over." She lowered her voice. "And ever since, all we've had are kings and queens who hide behind walls while their people suffer."

Lynet bristled. "You're talking about my father, you know."

"I thought you didn't want me to talk to you like you're a princess," Nadia shot back.

Lynet flushed in anger, a fire spreading through her, and she relished the feeling. She had made the mistake of reaching out to someone who would be leaving soon anyway, but she wouldn't make the mistake of growing attached to her. Let Nadia leave, if she thought the North was so terrible.

"Well, then, I wish you luck," Lynet said, her words clipped and even. "I'll leave you to your work."

She turned for the door behind her, but before she reached it, Nadia had come around the table and was taking her arm. "Wait," she said, "don't be angry with me. Princess or not, I shouldn't have said that. I understand family loyalty."

Lynet looked down at the hand encircling her upper arm, and Nadia released her, taking a step back.

"I apologize," Nadia continued, looking Lynet in the eye. "I'll be more careful of what I say."

"No," Lynet said, "I don't want that. Then you'll just be like all the rest. No one here ever tells me the truth; they only tell me what they think I want to hear—what my *father* wants me to hear. They all treat me like I'm . . . I'm . . ."

"Like a butterfly," Nadia said softly. "Something beautiful but frail."

Lynet stepped away from the door. "Why would you say that?"

"Because that's what I thought you would be like, before I met you—before you started following me. Everyone spoke of you in such hushed tones, like you might break if they said your name too loudly." She studied Lynet, brow furrowing in contemplation. "But you're not like that at all. That's not your nature."

She was still watching Lynet like she was some kind of riddle or puzzle, a mysterious specimen caught in a jar. Lynet found that she didn't mind, though, because she knew that when Nadia looked at her, she was seeing *Lynet* and not Emilia.

"And how would you know what my nature is?" Lynet said, tilting her head up at Nadia in a manner she hoped was playful and not lofty or superior.

But Nadia didn't notice her inviting tone. Instead, she seemed to be silently deliberating something as she focused her intense stare on Lynet. "I might know more about it than you think," she murmured. She turned away then with a little shake of her head and returned to the table, opening one of her journals.

Lynet followed her to the table, closing the journal she was paging through. "What do you mean?"

Nadia wouldn't look at her, but her forehead was furrowed in thought. That meant she could be persuaded, if Lynet just pushed a little more. "Did you hear something else about me?"

Nadia glanced up at her briefly, just long enough for Lynet to know that she had guessed correctly. "What was it?" she pressed. "Why won't you tell me? What can you possibly know about me that I don't have a right to know?"

"I agree," Nadia said, and now she lifted her head to look at Lynet, her dark eyes shining. "I do think you have a right to know. I thought at first they were keeping it from you for your own good, but I don't believe that anymore. It's not fair for them to keep it from you." She was still watching Lynet intently, and Lynet understood that she wasn't just teasing—she did truly think Lynet had a right to know. Perhaps she even *wanted* to tell Lynet this mysterious secret, but something was stopping her.

"How do you even know about this, whatever it is?" Lynet said, more calmly now. To get the answers she wanted, she just had to ask the right questions.

"Because it's something the court surgeon should know."

"And why can't you tell me?"

"Because I'm under strict orders not to tell anyone, especially you."

Lynet bit her lip. Her father might know, but she knew there was no point asking him—he would think she was too delicate for any secret. The only person she could trust to answer her was Mina, but Mina would never have kept anything from her in the first place. "But you *want* to tell me, don't you?"

Nadia smiled in response, leaning toward her just slightly. Lynet only needed to ask one more question—

"So if I ordered you to tell me . . ."

Nadia shrugged. "Then I would have to tell you, wouldn't I? No one could blame me for following the direct orders of a princess."

"Then as a princess," Lynet said, "I order you to tell me what you know about me."

Permission granted, Nadia gave a slight nod of her head and said, softly but clearly, "The truth that they don't want you to know is that your mother never gave birth to you. She died before you were born."

It took Lynet a moment to understand what Nadia was saying, but even then, it was preposterous. If Emilia wasn't her mother, then how could Lynet look so much like her? "Oh, really?" she said. "Then who's my real mother?" But despite the skepticism in her voice, a flutter of hope in her chest betrayed her, her heart whispering the name: *Mina?*

Nadia shook her head. "You don't understand. You have no mother, no father. You never did. You were created magically, out of snow."

Lynet repeated the words to herself, but they didn't make any sense. "What did you say?"

Nadia's jaw tensed; now that the thrill of the secret had passed, she seemed to realize the full impact of what she was telling Lynet. "Your stepmother's father—the magician—shaped you in your mother's image out of snow and blood. You were made to resemble her exactly."

The whole idea was so ridiculous that Lynet almost laughed. This was Nadia's secret? It was nothing more than a joke, a story, a fabrication. True, her stepmother's father was a magician—he had magical abilities that made even Mina lower her voice when she spoke of them.

But how could any of this be true if Lynet's mother had died in childbirth? She had died on the day Lynet was born—that was why her father always took her to the crypt two weeks early, to separate those two occasions in Lynet's mind.

Unless, she thought, *that's the day my mother really died.*

"Nadia?" she said, her voice too loud in the quiet room.

Nadia had been watching her, waiting for her reaction to this discovery. "I'm here."

"If what you're saying is true, then when did my mother die? It couldn't have been in childbirth."

Nadia's lips thinned in concern at Lynet's flat voice, at her glassy eyes staring ahead at nothing. "Two weeks before," she said.

Lynet took a long breath. That still didn't have to mean anything. It was a coincidence.

But other hints came rushing to her now—her uncanny resemblance to her mother along with her father's complete confidence that she would grow up to be exactly like the late queen; a burn scar on her hand even though she never remembered burning herself; the fact that she could lie in the snow for hours and never feel cold. Mina's pitying look whenever Lynet said she wished she looked more like her—

Did Mina know?

Lynet had never spoken to Gregory alone, and she wondered now if that was no accident, if her father had kept him away from her, for fear that he would tell her the truth. But there had been one time, just a year or two ago, when she had been running to Mina's room and collided with the magician. Lynet had been mortified, but Gregory had only smiled down at her and insisted that there was no harm done. He had put his hands on her shoulders and told her that if she ever needed help, she could always come to him, that he was always her friend. . . .

And then Mina had hurried toward them both. She asked Lynet to go wait in her room for her, because she needed to speak to her father alone. Lynet hadn't thought anything of it at the time, but now she remembered the slight note of panic in her stepmother's voice, the way her face was stretched into an unnatural smile, the bloodless grip she had on her father's arm.

Mina knew. Mina knew and she had kept it from her all these years.

The full weight of this revelation finally fell on her, the truth becoming increasingly undeniable, and Lynet closed her eyes, trying to shut it out. But she couldn't keep Nadia's words from reaching her: *You were made to resemble her exactly.* Made, created, shaped—all those words meant the same thing: she was something artificial. She was a duplicate, created to live out all the days that had been stolen from her mother. Unless she was meant to die her mother's death, as well. Had Lynet ever had anything of her own? Was she even a person?

"What do I do now?" Lynet whispered. "Am I supposed to just go on like before and pretend I don't know?" She opened her eyes and looked to Nadia.

Nadia shook her head and leaned over the table, her shoulders hunched with remorse. Her fingers were drumming against the wood, and finally she nodded to herself and looked up at Lynet with a mixture of guilt and resolve.

"If I were you," she said in the same firm tone as when she gave advice to one of her patients, "I would want to know more, even just for your own safety. That's why I'm allowed to know, as the court surgeon—I need to know that the cold won't numb you, because you're immune to it."

Lynet didn't hear a word Nadia said. The room seemed to be getting smaller, and she was having trouble breathing. "I have to go now," she said.

"Lynet, don't go—I'm so sorry I told you, please—" But Lynet was already rushing out the door, up the stairs, out into the open air. She kept moving until she had crossed through the courtyard and into the garden, and then she collapsed in the snow, hoping that for the first time, she'd feel something like cold.

6

MINA

The first time she saw Whitespring, Mina's skin prickled, and not just from the cold. As she took in the sharp spires and steeply curved archways, the high stone walls as blank as snow, Mina thought she was looking at the skeleton of a castle, its meat picked off over the years until only the bones were left. Whitespring was as gray as the sky, and already she missed the bright colors of her home.

And she was so cold. She kept adding layers of clothing, furs and thick wools, but she felt trapped underneath all that fabric, too constrained to move comfortably. She longed to feel fresh air on her skin again. Instead, she had to settle for blowing on her hands to keep them warm.

Gregory hadn't been thrilled with their small set of rooms in a forgotten corner of the castle, but he said that would all change once he'd made a good marriage for Mina. She was glad the rooms were small; they gave her the illusion of coziness.

"You haven't gone outside since we came here," her father told her three days after they'd arrived. "Go get some air. We're cramped in here as it is."

It was true. She'd holed herself up in her room, thinking that if she curled up tightly enough, she'd be warm again. Mina weakly protested out of habit, but she *was* growing restless, so she threw on another layer of fur and obeyed.

"Take the left corridor and keep walking straight, and you'll end up at a courtyard," Gregory told her. "Don't get lost. I don't want to find you freezing somewhere."

"I appreciate your concern," Mina snapped at him.

All the same, she took his advice. She didn't want to wander the castle's labyrinthine corridors for the rest of the morning. As he had said, she eventually came to a courtyard, smaller than Whitespring's central courtyard. Winged statues stared down from the balconies, and Mina stared back to show them that she was unafraid. In the center of the courtyard was an empty fountain. But there were none of the usual sounds Mina expected to hear outdoors. No birds sang, no breeze whistled through the trees. Seeing a fountain without hearing the trickle of water was unsettling.

She sat on the edge of the fountain and pulled a peach from her pocket. Fruit was in short supply in the North, so she'd been sure to take some with her before leaving.

"Where did you get that?"

Mina tensed. A man walked toward her, his arms crossed. He was dressed finely, so he wasn't a servant, but he didn't match the image of older, pompous noblemen she had in her head. This man was likely not yet thirty, with a dark beard lining his square jaw and curling black hair. Despite his relative youth, he seemed to be dragging the full weight of his body as he walked.

"It's mine," Mina said, trying not to sound too defensive. "I brought it with me."

"Don't let me interrupt you, then." He gestured to the fruit. "Eat."

She took a bite of her peach. In the silence of the courtyard, the squelching sound of the fruit was embarrassingly loud. "Do you want a bite?" she said, holding the peach up to him. "I'm sorry I don't have another to offer you."

He shook his head. "I didn't intend to disturb you. I only came here to . . ." He fell silent, and Mina thought maybe he was finished speaking to her, but then he said, "This was the queen's favorite place to sit."

Mina glanced up at the gloomy statues on the balconies. She didn't understand how this courtyard could be anyone's favorite anything, but she didn't want to insult the late queen in front of a stranger. "Did you know her?" she asked.

"Yes," he said, his expression softening as he looked down at Mina. "She was the most beautiful woman I've ever seen. Her daughter will take after her."

"But she's a baby. She doesn't look like anyone yet."

"She looks like her mother," the man insisted. "She is the late queen returned to us. She will grow up to be as beautiful and as gentle as her mother once was."

Mina shrugged. "I haven't seen her. I don't even know her name."

"Lynet," the man said, smiling for the first time. "That was what the queen had always wanted to name a daughter. Princess Lynet. Like the bird."

"That's a pretty name," Mina said—or tried to say. She'd taken another bite of the peach before speaking, and she coughed as a piece of fruit caught in her throat.

"Didn't your mother teach you not to speak when you eat?" he said, with a hint of amusement in his voice.

She swallowed and said, "No, she didn't. My mother is dead." He inhaled sharply at her words and seemed so mortified by his error that she took pity on him. "It was a long time ago. I only remember her a little."

"Is it terrible as a girl to grow up without a mother?"

Mina wasn't sure how to reply. She had never known any alternative. "Sometimes."

He nodded and sat on the ledge of the fountain beside her. Mina's first instinct was to move away from him, but she stopped herself—he didn't know anything about her, after all; he had no reason to be afraid of her, nor she of him. Without even Hana for company, Mina had spent most of her time alone since leaving home, and so she had forgotten that there could be comfort in another person's presence. Perhaps she had never known it at all. She studied his profile, wondering how she could make him smile again.

Abruptly, he shook his head and turned to her. "Will you be attending the banquet in the princess's honor tonight?"

She nodded. Her father had given her no other option than to attend. She had to be beautiful tonight, in order to be memorable.

"I'm glad," he said.

"Then why do you seem sad?" Mina said before she could stop herself.

He answered at once, unperturbed by her question. "Grief," he said. "Grief at the passing of our queen. You would be sad too, if you had known her. . . ."

He turned his face away from her, and Mina regretted her thoughtless question. She inched a little closer to him, until her skirt was brushing his leg. If she put her hand on his, would he smile for her? Would it be a comfort or a violation?

Just as she'd started to inch her hand toward his, he turned back to her and said, "I never asked your name."

"It's Mina."

His mouth turned downward. "I know a man with a daughter of that name."

If he'd met Gregory already, there was a good chance this man would want nothing more to do with her. Even if he didn't know about her father's peculiar talents, Gregory made people ill at ease. She might have lied and given a false name, but if she wanted this acquaintance to continue, he'd learn the truth soon enough.

"My father's name is Gregory," she said, resigned.

He nodded. "That's what I thought." He rose from the fountain, and though his face had shown no disgust or fear, she knew instinctively that she had lost him.

"I'm not my father," she blurted out.

"I've stayed too long." He spoke quickly, and before Mina could respond, he was walking away, leaving her with her half-eaten peach, which now tasted bitter in her mouth.

He hadn't even told her his name.

That night Mina readied herself for the banquet, but in her mind, she was still in the courtyard, not quite daring to touch the hand of a man she barely knew.

But why bother thinking of him? a voice in her mind asked. *You can't love him, and he could never love you.*

That was true, but she kept thinking about the softness of his voice, the kindness of his eyes when she was just a stranger to him. No one had ever spoken to her with such gentleness before. If she'd had less faith in her beauty, she might have decided to forget him, but perhaps if he saw her tonight, not bundled in furs, but gowned and bejeweled . . .

The only piece of fur Mina wore over her dress as she walked into the Hall was a shawl that served to warm the crooks of her elbows and little else. If Mina wanted to be accepted at court—and catch the eye of her kind stranger again—she would have to look like she belonged. In her brief time at Whitespring, she'd already learned that the people here were more accustomed to the cold, and so they didn't dress as heavily as Mina would have. If she had dressed for warmth tonight, she would have been the only one.

The Hall wasn't as cold as it could have been, packed with people as it was, but Mina's teeth still chattered. "Clever girl," her father said softly. He had sensibly dressed for the cold, and though he had mocked her at first for her thin dress, his eyes now shone with understanding. His clothing marked him as an outsider.

Gregory led her by the elbow to one of the long tables at the back of the Hall. "Most of these people are only visiting the castle for the banquet tonight," he whispered, "so this may be your one chance to make an impression. Try to be charming."

Mina put on her most dazzling smile as she took her seat, but it was difficult to be charming when she was a stranger among friends. Even here at the back of the Hall, among the lesser nobility and friends of the castle, Mina wasn't important enough to warrant any attention. People talked over both her and Gregory, craning their necks to continue conversations from the last time they'd seen one another. Gregory ignored them in turn—it was Mina who needed to please them, not him. But Mina's smile was beginning to falter.

At home, when she walked through the marketplace, she knew that the villagers were observing her every movement, watching her out of the corners of their eyes like she was a coiled snake about to strike, and so she had become used to scrutiny, to being jeered at and mocked for the slightest misstep. But now that no one was watching, she finally stopped trying to smile at everyone, and the muscles in her cheeks were grateful to her for that. She stopped trying to make eye contact in a hopeless bid for attention, stopped sitting quite so straight, stopped taking tiny bites of her bread and meat so she wouldn't be caught with her mouth full. She simply observed the people around her and enjoyed being invisible.

And as the night wore on and Mina became more relaxed, something changed. The guests started to grow bored with one another, and their curious eyes began following her movements. The lady beside her struck up a conversation with her, and the old man opposite called her a "real beauty." She laughed with them, holding her head at angles she knew would flatter her, because she'd studied them so long in the mirror. It was a fair trade: she gave them something pleasing to stare at, and they gave her approval, acceptance, even affection.

If they love you for anything, it will be for your beauty.

Beside her, Gregory was observing Mina's victory with what looked like something between relief and resentment. This was what he'd wanted for her, after all, this was why he needed her, but Mina knew that he must hate having to need her in the first place. Still, he knew better than to interfere and possibly ruin whatever strange magic Mina's beauty was working, so he kept silent, and Mina ignored him as best she could. Tonight, she was not the magician's daughter, but an anonymous beauty.

Every so often, she scanned the crowded room, hunting for one face in particular. As she searched, it occurred to her that her stranger might already be married, but that only made her more desperate to find him and know for certain.

"A toast!" called a voice from the high table.

Mina hadn't paid much attention to the high table, all the way at the other end of the Hall, but she looked up now—and nearly jumped out of her seat when she saw the king.

No wonder she hadn't found her sad stranger when she searched the room; she had never thought to look for him seated on a king's throne.

When the crowd fell silent, King Nicholas stood. "A toast," he said, "to my daughter and to your princess. May she grow to be as beautiful as her mother, and may you all love her as you loved her mother, the queen."

The Hall drank to the princess, but the princess didn't matter to Mina. It was kings and queens she was thinking of, especially the dead queen who inspired such devotion in the people around her. There was genuine feeling in their faces, love for a woman who was dead and unable to return their love ever again. Queen Emilia could not have plausibly loved every person in the room, and yet they all loved her, unconditionally, unrequitedly.

Her ear caught a single word from across the banquet table, and she listened closely to single out the thread of conversation. Yes, there it was again—*remarry.*

"But will he remarry, do you think? He was so devoted to her," a sharp-jawed woman was saying to the man sitting opposite her.

"Oh, he must, he must. Not in the next year, maybe not the year after that, but soon enough. The people will want a queen, and the man will want a wife."

"And the poor princess, without a mother . . ."

Mina stopped listening; she'd heard what she wanted to hear. *The people will want a queen, and the man will want a wife.* Her sudden desire was a collision, and it left her shaking. With her beauty, she had made people pay attention to her, to notice her without mocking her. But a queen—

A queen had the power to make people love her.

7

LYNET

Lynet didn't remain lying in the snow too long—she didn't want anyone to come passing by and find her there, especially not Nadia. She knew Nadia had nothing to do with her birth—her *creation*—but Nadia was the one who had told her, and so Lynet blamed her for it anyway.

At that moment, rising from the snow that had made her, she hated everyone who had known what she was before she did—her father, Gregory, Nadia . . .

And Mina.

Part of her still wanted to believe that Mina hadn't known, but the doubt would remain until she asked. Before she could back down, Lynet allowed her indignation to lead her up to the queen's chambers. But when Lynet reached them, the queen wasn't there. The fire was burning, though, and so Lynet knew that Mina would return soon. She walked around the room, thinking of all the times she had come here before, night after night—all those years, all those confidences she'd shared, all those opportunities for Mina to tell her the secret of her creation.

She'd always thought Mina's room was one of the most beautiful places in Whitespring. Mina collected pieces of the South that she acquired each market day. Pale orange silk hung around her bed, the gauzy fabric shimmering like liquid. The reds and oranges and yellows of peaches and apples illuminated the room like they were made of light. On the table by her bed was a shining silver-backed hand mirror without any glass in its frame. Mina said she kept it even though it was broken because it had once belonged to her mother.

On the far wall, there was a large, wooden-framed mirror, reflecting all that color and light back at itself, magnifying the room into a world of its own. Lynet paused in front of the mirror, her own reflection startling her. She wondered what she would have looked like had she been born naturally, a child of flesh and blood. Would she still have her mother's delicate features? Or would her outsides match her insides, her skin finally sitting comfortably over her bones so that she wouldn't always feel like she wanted to leap out of her own body? She felt trapped by that reflection—and yet some stubborn part of her still wanted to fight for it and take it back from her mother. It was Lynet's turn to live now, wasn't it? She had every right to claim this reflection as her own. *It would be my own, if I were anywhere but here,* she thought. If she left Whitespring, left the promise of a crown and a life that wasn't hers, then she could be whoever she wanted to be. . . .

The slamming of a door made her jump, and she heard voices coming from Mina's parlor. One of the voices was Mina's, and after listening for a moment, Lynet recognized her father's voice as well.

"And you didn't even think to consult me first?" Nicholas was saying.

"You've never cared before," Mina replied. "I'm free to do what I want with the South. That was our agreement."

"Building and improving roads and reviving the university was one thing, but this is a *castle*, Mina. What's the point in taking on such a project?"

There was a heavy pause, and Lynet didn't need to see her stepmother's face to know that it was stony with anger. Lynet had years of practice pretending not to notice the arguments between her father and her stepmother. But over the years, whenever she heard Mina's voice raised in anger or lowered in defiance, Lynet had started to imagine that it was her own, instead, telling her father all the things she wished she could say to him.

"I don't expect you to understand," Mina said quietly, "but in the South, the Summer Castle's abandonment always represented the North not caring about us. Finishing its construction will be a legacy of sorts, not just for me, but for you, too. It will give the South something to take pride in, and it will employ hundreds of people. I know the southerners want this, Nicholas. They write to me all the time, telling me how thankful they are that someone finally cares about them—"

"It will take *years*, Mina."

"I have years to give."

Now Nicholas fell silent, and Lynet held her breath, wondering what he would say and who would win this battle.

"You promised me, Nicholas," Mina whispered. "Don't you remember?"

"Of course I do, but I still—" He paused and said in a calmer voice, "We'll discuss this at a later time, after Lynet's birthday, perhaps."

"Construction has already begun. I won't let you take this from me, Nicholas."

"Later, I said. I don't want to spoil Lynet's birthday with our bickering." Lynet heard the door open and close again, and then she heard Mina sigh.

At another time, Lynet would have been eager to hear more about her stepmother's new project. Mina always spoke of the Summer Castle with such affection, telling Lynet all about its golden domes and marble floors, the rest of it abandoned and unfinished. She would assure Mina that she agreed with her decision no matter what Nicholas said, and it would be something they shared together.

But now Lynet could only think of the secret that Mina had kept from her for all these years, and she left her corner to sit on the bed and wait.

When Mina came into the bedchamber and saw Lynet, her face tightened into a strained smile. "You're early!" she said. "I hope you weren't waiting here long—"

Lynet couldn't stop herself. She took a breath and said, "Why did you never tell me that I was made of snow?"

Mina's mouth hung open in surprise before she recovered and reverted back to her forced smile. "What did you say?"

Her pretense was unbearable. Lynet might have expected anyone else to wave her aside, but she couldn't accept it from Mina. "Mina, please," she said in a whisper, "don't lie to me."

The smile faded from Mina's face slowly. She shut her eyes tight for a moment, and then she nodded to herself and opened them again. She walked over to where Lynet was sitting on the bed and gently lifted Lynet's head with her hands, her fingers curled against Lynet's jaw. "Who told you, then?" she said, her voice sad but resigned.

"So it's true," Lynet said, her last remnants of hope dying away as she looked up at her stepmother with wide, pleading eyes. What she was pleading *for*, she didn't know.

Mina started to say something, but then she stopped, her jaw tensing, her hands falling away from Lynet's face. "Did my father speak with you?" When Lynet didn't answer, Mina grabbed her roughly by the shoulders. "Tell me, did he—but no, no, he's away now, he couldn't have . . ." She released Lynet, her shoulders sagging in relief as she turned away. "But if he didn't tell you, then who did?" she murmured to herself.

"The real question is, why didn't *you*?" Lynet said, her voice growing louder. She rose from the bed, wanting to stand more level with Mina. "Why did you let me find out on my own?"

Mina grew quiet, and Lynet wished she wouldn't look so sad—it was making it harder for her to stay angry rather than burst into tears like a child. Without looking at Lynet, Mina walked slowly to the small table beside her bed and gently touched the handle of the broken hand mirror. Abruptly, she pulled her hand away. "There have been times over the years," she said, still looking down at the mirror, "when I've thought about telling you, but as you grew older, the truth seemed more like a burden than a gift. I'd hoped you would never find out." She looked up at Lynet, the fire reflected in her warm brown eyes. "Don't *you* wish you had never found out?"

Lynet started to consider her answer, but then she shook her head, like she was trying to shake something off. She didn't want to see Mina's point. She didn't want to be reasoned with. She wanted to scream, to release some of the panic that was threatening to overcome her. "I know why my father never told me, but you—I've always trusted you to be honest with me. You should have prepared me for this. You should have told me *something*. If it were you instead of me, wouldn't you want to know?"

"No," Mina said almost instantly, a sharp edge to her voice. She reached for Lynet's face. "I would have considered it an act of cruelty to tell you."

Lynet flinched from Mina's outstretched hand, backing away until she tripped on the corner of a rug. That small indignity was too much for her, and whatever courage she was trying to maintain in the face of this revelation shattered in an instant, leaving her with all the fear and hurt of a child who'd discovered pain for the first time. "That doesn't make any sense!" she shouted as she burst into tears. She shut her eyes and hugged her arms around herself, expecting Mina to come and hold her at any moment. But moments passed, and she was still alone in the dark.

"Doesn't it?" Mina said, her voice small and wavering. "There's nothing you can do about it, nothing you can change, so what's the point in knowing the truth? Why would I tell you, except to hurt you?"

When Lynet opened her eyes again, Mina was clutching the bedpost like a shield between them. Lynet wondered if she had ever seen her stepmother appear so distressed. She almost moved to reassure Mina, until she remembered that *she* was supposed to be the one in need of comfort. That was why she was so angry, so scared—not because Mina hadn't told her before, but because Mina wasn't doing anything now to make it better. She had thought Mina would tell her it would all be fine, but instead she seemed even more afraid than Lynet.

"At least tell me what else you know," Lynet said. "Tell me . . . tell me what I should do."

Her voice cracked, and the sound seemed to reach through to Mina at last. She straightened and came to her, pulling Lynet into her arms. "Of course, Lynet," she said, her hands pulling at Lynet's curls, untangling them from years of habit. "Tell me what you want to know."

She gently guided Lynet to the chair in front of the mirror, and Lynet sank into it gratefully. She didn't want to be angry anymore— she was too scared and confused to take on the truth alone, and the feel of her stepmother's fingers combing through her hair made her feel safe. More than that, it made her feel like herself.

"So what am I, then?" she said, her voice more like a croak. "Am I just . . . a doll?"

"No, you're not just a doll," Mina said. "My father shaped you not just from snow, but also from blood."

"Is that important?"

Mina's hands paused for a moment, but then she continued. "Yes, it's important. Without his blood, you'd be artifice, a perfect imitation of a human being, but only an imitation. You wouldn't grow or age. You . . . you would have no heartbeat. Blood creates genuine life."

Lynet took a shuddering breath. "So I'm not . . . I'm not going to die at the same age as my mother?"

Mina looked up in surprise, meeting Lynet's eye in the mirror. "Is that what you're afraid of? Oh, Lynet, no, your life is your own, to live out as you choose."

A fresh set of tears filled Lynet's eyes, though whether they were from relief or despair, she couldn't say. She covered her face with her hands, ashamed that Mina should see her like this again. But when Mina gently tried to move her hands away from her face, Lynet allowed it, seeking to draw strength from her stepmother's example. Mina was kneeling beside her, waiting for her to speak.

"I'm sorry," Lynet managed to say. "I'm sorry I'm like this, but I . . . I wish it weren't true. I wish I had something that was only mine. I wish everything were different."

Mina seemed to wince, but then she nodded. "I understand. But listen to me, wolf cub. I never knew your mother; I only know you. You don't have to be like your mother, no matter what anyone says."

"Sometimes I think I will be whether I want to or not. . . ."

She took Lynet's hand, a fierce gleam in her eye. "I won't let it happen. You're not your mother, and you're allowed to have something that belongs only to you."

In that moment, Lynet believed her. She believed that Mina could do anything she was determined to do, her will stronger than any magic. Lynet threw her arms around Mina's neck, and Mina held her close. "Thank you," Lynet said.

Mina pulled away first, as she always did. "Do you feel better now?" she asked.

Lynet nodded, though she wasn't sure how she felt. She still had the unsettling feeling that she was trapped in someone else's body. Then again, she had felt that way even before knowing the truth.

Mina bit her lip, and then she said, "I want to show you something."

She stood, went to the door, and held her hand out to Lynet, waiting for her to follow. Lynet did follow, and the two of them left the room and walked through the halls together, crossing the long gallery to the west wing of the castle, continuing until they were in a narrow hallway Lynet wasn't even sure she had seen before. That was impossible, though; she knew every corner of Whitespring, even if there were some she visited less frequently.

At the end of the hall was a simple wooden door. Mina pushed it open and Lynet followed her inside. She recognized the place now: it was a chapel, or at least it used to be. The line of stone altars was still there, but the wooden benches for worshippers had been removed over time as the North stopped trusting in any gods but Sybil, and now the room felt cavernous and empty. Three large stained-glass windows lined the wall behind the altars, but without much sunlight, the windows were dull and a little sad, the pattern of colors all appearing as the same dreary hue.

"I always found this chapel a comfort," Mina said, her voice barely echoing in the empty room. She walked over to the line of altars and sat in front of the center one in a single graceful movement. Her presence seemed to make the room feel intimate rather than lonely.

Lynet sat beside Mina, careful not to make any noise—she felt somehow that it would be disrespectful if she did.

"I used to come here when I wanted to be by myself," Mina continued. "I knew no one else came to this chapel anymore, so I felt like it was the one corner of Whitespring that was mine."

Lynet watched her reverently, struck by Mina's serene smile, her soft brown eyes no longer flashing with the fire that always burned in her room. Mina seldom spoke of her life before she had become queen, as though it hadn't truly begun until she'd worn a crown. Lynet could believe it—she couldn't imagine her stepmother as anything but a queen, even though she had vague memories of the first time they'd met, before Mina and her father had married. Even in her memories, Lynet always saw Mina as a flame, something fierce and fearless and regal.

But here inside the calm quiet of the chapel, she could imagine Mina as a child—not a child, but sixteen, the same age Lynet was fast approaching—sitting here by herself in a strange, cold world, her flame somewhat dimmed. She thought of the fire that was always roaring in Mina's bedroom, the furs she wore even though everyone else at Whitespring had long since adapted to the cold. This one place alone had given her a sense of comfort, of belonging, and Lynet wished she could find the words to tell her stepmother how dearly she appreciated being here with her now.

"You'll find something that's yours alone," Mina said, taking Lynet's hand in her own. "And when you do, don't let anyone take it from you."

Lynet thought of the argument she had heard between Mina and her father, the way Mina had fought for what was hers. Would Lynet ever be able to do that? Could she ever burn as brightly as her stepmother, when she was made of snow?

"Thank you for telling me the truth," Lynet said. She hoped Mina understood that she was thanking her not only for that, but especially for sharing this place, this memory, with her.

But Mina frowned slightly as she looked down at their joined hands. When she spoke at last, it was to say in a halting voice, "Yes, Lynet, of course."

Lynet wanted to ask her what she had been thinking about, but something stopped her. She kept picturing that girl sitting alone in the chapel, and it was strange and even unsettling to think that Lynet hadn't been a part of Mina's life then. Whatever Mina had just been thinking—whoever she had once been—was a world away from Lynet. She held Mina's hand more tightly, not yet ready to accept that there were still so many secrets hidden away at the center of the flame, too bright for her to see.

8

LYNET

Lynet sat on the edge of the North Tower's one large window, waiting.

The patches in the ceiling let in beams of moonlight, illuminating pieces of the room one at a time: a corner of a faded rug, the skeleton of an empty bedframe, the arm of an overstuffed chair, all covered in dust. The only inhabitants of the North Tower lay in the crypt below.

Each morning for the past few days, Lynet had found a new note from Nadia tucked into the branches of the juniper tree. She kept imploring Lynet to see her again, to let her apologize for handing Lynet this burden so gracelessly. Lynet didn't respond, but she still checked every morning for the latest one. Besides, she was too busy to visit. More and more visitors were arriving at Whitespring as Lynet's birthday celebration approached, and Lynet's duty as a princess demanded that she stand by her father's side in the Hall, greeting and visiting with each new arrival personally. And now she understood why her father made such a fuss about her birthday every year. He had been trying, in his own way, to make her feel human.

As much as she tried, Lynet couldn't be angry with him for that.

She wasn't angry with Nadia, either, not really. But she couldn't stand to go back into that room, to look at that spot by the table and think, *That was where I learned the truth.*

And then, just this morning, she'd found another scrawled message in the tree—the shortest one yet:

I have the prior surgeon's journals, if you want to know more.

She knew Nadia was appealing to her curiosity, but did that matter? Lynet *did* want to know more. For the first time, she left a note in response:

Midnight at the top of the North Tower. Bring the journals.

She had chosen the tower because it was the highest point at Whitespring, a marked contrast to the subterranean workroom where Nadia had unraveled her with a few simple words. Perhaps in the tower room, high above the royal crypt, Lynet could put herself back together again.

Shortly before midnight, she had climbed out the window of her room, descending carefully to the ground below. It may have been dramatic of her to choose to meet at this time, but she felt freer at night. There was nowhere she was supposed to be, no *one* she was supposed to be, and so it seemed a fitting time to find out who she was.

When she had reached the courtyard, she quickly checked the juniper tree to be sure Nadia had seen her note—yes, the note was gone, so she quickly went through the arch that led to the garden. After only a few hurried steps, she found herself running.

Running to the tower? Running away from something? She wasn't sure—she only knew that she needed to feel her blood rushing through her body, to become so aware of the pounding of her heart and the rush of air through her tired lungs that she couldn't feel anything other than human—flesh and bone, not snow and blood. In the dark of night, with only the moon watching her, she could even pretend that she didn't look anything like her mother.

She knew the position of every tree in the Shadow Garden, and so when she suddenly collided with something, her first thought was that one of the trees was in the wrong place. But then she looked up and found that she hadn't run into a tree, but a man.

His hands were on her shoulders as he held her away from him, and so she recognized him as the best of her father's huntsmen when she saw the scarred skin that peeked from under his sleeves. Lynet had seen him many times from the window when her father was preparing for a hunt, but she had never encountered him personally, and she was glad of that. His scarred arms didn't frighten her, but his eyes did—they were so blank, so empty, like black marbles set in a human face.

"You're the princess," he said, bending his head a little to look at her. "You're as beautiful as they say."

She shrank back when the huntsman brought his face closer to hers. That was the other strange thing about him—over all the years that Lynet had seen him, he never appeared to age. Even now, he looked only a little older than Lynet, but she knew that was impossible.

She was growing uncomfortably aware of how close he was to

her, and that his hands were still on her shoulders, so she pulled away from him.

"It's late, child," he said, and she wondered how old he could possibly be to call her that. "Why are you out at this hour?"

"I have a right to be here if I wish," Lynet said. "What are *you* doing here at this hour?"

"I have a right to be here if I wish," he echoed.

Neither one of them sounded entirely convincing, but perhaps that was to Lynet's advantage. "If that's the case," she said, her voice starting to shake a little, "then there's no reason for either one of us to tell anyone that we met here tonight."

They both watched each other, and maybe it was only a trick of the moonlight, but Lynet thought then that he *did* seem the age he looked, eyes darting nervously over Lynet's shoulder, body slightly hunched like a guilty child's. Lynet noticed she was standing the same way.

He nodded to her in understanding. "Go on your way, then," he said, "and I'll go on mine."

They both watched each other for a moment, and then almost at the same time, they both headed off in opposite directions. Lynet looked back once to make sure he wasn't following or watching after her, but he was gone.

Lynet only had to wait a few minutes perched on the windowsill before she heard the loud squeak of the door opening behind her. Nadia appeared in the doorway, holding a lit candle that somehow seemed to throw the room even more into flickering shadow. She had her surgeon's bag with her as well.

"This is a very tall tower," she said, slightly out of breath.

Lynet shrugged, glancing down at the ledges and footholds she'd used to climb from a nearby tree up to the tower window. She hopped down from the window and sat on the rug in the center of the room. Nadia knelt down to join her, placing the candle between them and leaning in.

The climb had taken all of her attention, and so she felt calm and focused now, especially next to Nadia's lingering breathlessness. "Do you know where we are?" she said.

"The North Tower," Nadia answered at once. "Like your note said."

Lynet shook her head, the shadow of her curls dancing along the wall. "Not just that. We're directly above the royal crypt. I go there once a year with my father, to visit my mother's resting place. We went the other day, before you told me that she didn't die giving birth to me at all."

Nadia cringed. "I'm sorry," she said. "I thought you'd want to know. I thought *anyone* would want to know. I never meant to frighten you away."

"I wasn't frightened," Lynet said quickly. "I just needed to . . . to think about what you had said."

Nadia offered an apologetic smile. "So you're not angry with me?"

"Not anymore," Lynet said. "I'm glad I know the truth."

Nadia's whole body seemed to loosen with relief. She pulled something out of her bag and handed it to Lynet, careful not to let it touch the candle flame. "This belonged to Master Jacob, the surgeon before me. I found it in the cellar with the other old records, and I thought it could help you."

"Have you read it yourself?" Lynet said, taking the thin, worn journal.

Lynet knew from her uncertain pause that Nadia had indeed looked at it even before she answered. "I did. There's a little more detail about you, but not on the creation itself."

Lynet started flipping through the journal, stopping when she saw Emilia's name. She read the account of her mother's illness, her father's desperation as he summoned a notorious magician from the South to help save her. When she died, he had asked the magician to create a daughter for him, a girl who would resemble her mother exactly. The magician had created the girl out of snow and his own blood, which held the power to create life. Lynet kept reading, seeing herself from a distance—not as a human being, but as some strange and unnatural experiment.

Lynet set the journal down, breathing evenly. She wished now that Nadia hadn't read these pages. Everyone else saw her as her mother's child, but at least they still saw her as human. Lynet kept her eyes on the candle flame, following its movements. "What do you see when you look at me?" she said.

Nadia's voice was guarded when she answered. "What do you mean?"

"Do you see me now like I'm . . . a curiosity? Something unnatural or . . . or a copy of my mother?"

"I never knew your mother."

Lynet looked up at her and tried to smile. "That wasn't an answer to my question."

Nadia went silent, and Lynet tried to read her, but she was half in shadow. Lynet waited for the answer with growing dread—she had been designed from the outside in, after all, her face painted on like that of a doll. Who was she, if not a copy meant to be compared to the original?

"No," Nadia said at last, her voice making Lynet jump. "I definitely don't just see you as a curiosity, or a shadow of someone else. But I don't have all of the answers you want. I can't tell you more than what's in that journal—"

"But you can," Lynet said. "The journal says my skin is always cold to the touch, but I have no way of knowing if that's true on my own." She inched closer, reached out for Nadia's hand, and pressed it against the exposed skin below her throat. "Is it true?" she said. "Am I cold?"

Though she was startled at first, her hand jumping under Lynet's, Nadia soon went still, her eyes moving slowly up from their hands to Lynet's face. She was no longer in shadow, and for a moment Lynet thought she saw worry in her eyes—but perhaps that was only the reflection of the flame.

"Well?" Lynet said quietly.

Nadia pulled her hand away. "That was the wrong test," she said, her eyes flickering from the skin of Lynet's throat back up to her face.

"Oh?" Lynet said. "Then what would be the right test?"

Nadia smiled at Lynet's playful tone, and she pushed the candle forward. "Your skin is cold, but anyone's skin would be cold in a drafty tower like this one. The real test will be if your skin ever grows warm." She nodded toward the candle. "Warm your hand over the flame, but don't burn yourself."

Lynet had played this game plenty of times over the years. It was another way to rid herself of that discomfort in her skin, putting her hand over an open flame, moving it closer and closer until she lost her nerve and moved it away. She did it now for Nadia, letting the flame warm her skin.

After a minute or so, Nadia moved the candle away and took her hand. "What do you feel now?" she said, tilting her head but never dropping her gaze. "Does your hand feel warm?"

She ran the roughened pad of her thumb over Lynet's palm, and Lynet's heart gave an odd little jump that she couldn't explain. "Yes, I'm warm," she said, her voice a breathless whisper.

A slow smile curled on Nadia's lips. "That's strange," she said. "To me, you don't feel warm at all. Your skin is still cold to the touch."

Lynet pulled her hand away, peering down at it and trying to find the answers she wanted in its lines. "How can that be?"

Nadia shook her head. "I don't know. Maybe anything that isn't cold feels warm to you, but the cold feels neutral. You've soaked in the heat, like some kind of sponge, but the surface still stays cold."

"So you're saying my insides don't match my outsides?" She laughed dryly. "I could have told you that."

"What do you mean?"

"Isn't it obvious? I'm my mother on the outside. I look like her. I sound like her. Put a crown on my head, and no one will be able to tell the difference."

Lynet tried to keep her voice light, but Nadia's face was serious, and Lynet remembered that she had thought Nadia a contradiction too—the smiling girl and the severe surgeon. "And what are you on the inside?" Nadia said softly.

Lynet shook her head, her throat suddenly closing up. "I don't know," she said. No matter what she did, no matter who she was, the only thing anyone ever knew about her was how much she was like her mother. And with every year that passed, she would only become more and more the woman lying in the crypt below. She was destined to become someone else, to lose all sense of herself. Everyone kept telling her that she wasn't a child anymore, but Lynet knew that being a child was the only defense she had against becoming a woman she didn't know. She could feel the sting of tears in her eyes, and she thought of how she had broken down in front of Mina. She refused to let that happen again in front of Nadia.

Lynet forced a shrill laugh and rose from the floor, hurrying to the window. "Shall we find out?" She slipped one leg over the windowsill, and then the other.

Nadia came over to her at once. "What are you doing?"

Lynet laughed again. "Don't worry, there's a ledge right outside the window. See?" She lowered herself onto the ledge, the window now at her waist. She clung to the windowsill behind her, and Nadia seemed unsure whether to take hold of Lynet's hands, or if that would make her lose her balance. "The view from here is extraordinary in the daytime," Lynet said. "You can see all of Whitespring laid out in front of you." And even now, in the moonlight, Lynet could still see the outline of the courtyard below, framed by Whitespring's sharp spires and steep roofs. That dark cloud there was the top of the juniper tree, surrounded by snow that seemed to absorb the pale light, and for a moment, Lynet couldn't tell if the snow was reflecting the moonlight, or if it was the other way around. Beyond the stern gray walls of the castle were the woods, the dark shapes of pines standing like sentries on watch.

"I'm sure it's very beautiful," Nadia said. "Now come inside."

Lynet laughed again. "Are you scared for me? I already climbed up here tonight instead of taking the stairs." She inched her way along the ledge. "Here, there's room for you, too."

"I'm not climbing out there, and you probably shouldn't, either. I don't think it's safe."

A cool wind blew through her hair. "If I fall, you'll patch me up, won't you? Just like when we met."

"Not if you're dead when you hit the ground."

The thought came to her at once: *At least if I'm dead, I won't turn into her.*

What had made her think such a thing? Lynet glanced down at the ground far below, and for the first time, she fully comprehended that she could fall. She could die. She was not invincible. *What am I doing this for?* she wondered now, and as always, a voice in her head answered, *To feel alive.* But this time there was another voice, one she had never heard before, and it offered a different answer:

To die.

"Nadia?" she called. "I want to come back inside now." Her voice sounded so small to her, like she had already fallen and was calling from far below.

At once, Nadia's sturdy arms came around Lynet's waist and hoisted her up over the windowsill. Lynet could have climbed back in herself, but she didn't trust her own body at the moment. That itching under her skin was dangerous; it told her she could jump from a roof to a tree when she couldn't. It told her she could hang from a tower window and not fall.

Even when she was safely inside the tower, Nadia didn't release her immediately, perhaps afraid Lynet would leap away again. And maybe she would—she could feel the rapid beat of her pulse underneath her skin, trying to burst out of her, and she worried that Nadia could feel it too. Or maybe she wanted Nadia to feel it, to ignore the cool surface of her skin and find the blood burning underneath. Maybe she just wanted someone to turn her inside out for once.

But how could she explain that? How could she explain any of her actions tonight? She couldn't just say that her skin didn't fit her right sometimes, and that the only way to fix it was to do something reckless and exciting. But when she pulled away, Nadia wasn't staring at her in disapproval or confusion; she was looking above Lynet's eyes with something like delight, the beginning of a smile on her face.

"What is it?" Lynet said, her curiosity overcoming her shame.

"Your hair . . ."

Lynet was confused at first until she noticed she was standing directly in a patch of moonlight coming through the roof. She supposed it had created some kind of halo around her head. Lynet was ready to laugh at Nadia for being so entranced by something so commonplace, but then Nadia reached a hand to brush softly against her curls, and Lynet was afraid to move at all. Nadia wound a curl around her finger, her eyes avoiding Lynet's face, and Lynet's heart pounded, a slow but heavy knock against her ribs. Even the air around them seemed to still, so that each breath felt significant, the graze of hair on her cheek enough to make Lynet forget the itching under her skin.

Nadia drew her hand back so suddenly that Lynet thought the entire incident had only happened in her imagination. "I can't let you keep this journal, but you can come to the workroom any time you'd like," Nadia said in a rush, her voice a little too loud. "There are other journals, but I haven't looked through all of them. You may be able to learn more."

And then she was leaving—bending down to retrieve the journal and the candle before hurrying out the door. The door swung closed behind her, leaving Lynet still standing by the window in the silent room, staring at the empty space in front of her where Nadia had just been. It had all fallen apart so quickly—Nadia had been moving so impossibly fast—

Or perhaps Lynet was caught in a single moment, the world around her passing by while time stood still for her.

9

MINA

How did one seduce a king?

It was too soon, of course. He wouldn't remarry while the memory of his wife was fresh in his mind, but memories lacked substance and faded quickly enough.

As the magician's dreaded daughter, she'd never associated with the villagers back home, let alone been courted by anyone. She had to start somewhere, though. There would be no room for mistakes with the king.

Maybe it didn't matter that she didn't know any young men. She was her father's daughter, and what she didn't have, she would create.

Late one night, not long after the banquet, Mina crept out of bed. She lit a candle, took up her mother's mirror, and placed both on the ground near the frosted glass of her window.

Since the day by the stream when she had first learned she could manipulate glass, Mina had practiced using her power, finding that the more glass she had around her, the less the magic drained her, though the effect was always temporary. But her father's rule of blood did not work for her. She had once tried to make a mouse again, but regardless of whether she used her blood to make it, the mouse was never truly alive—it never had a pulse. That didn't matter, though. Tonight, she didn't want to create anything with a pulse.

Bolstered by the glass window, she concentrated on the mirror, and the glass slid out of the frame to form a silvery pool on the floor. The pool lengthened, and slowly, a shape emerged: a human body, tall and lean. The glass figure was still transparent, but it had become solid, a crystalline mannequin.

She shaped him in her mind, careful to attend to every detail: the curl of his eyelashes, the calluses on his hands, the jutting of his collarbone. At the last minute, she remembered to clothe him, and the glass shifted into a tunic to oblige her. The glass became bone, flesh, and cloth, and when it was done, Mina bent down over it and whispered, "*Live.*"

Even with the window, Mina felt the breath knocked out of her just as his eyes snapped open.

He was beautiful, his eyes black, his hair dark and shining. Her one misstep was his arms. She'd wavered briefly in forming them, not sure if he should be muscular or lean, and as a result, his brown arms were lined with thin scars, like cracks on a mirror surface.

She leaned over him. "Do you know who I am?"

He blinked at her slowly, and then he beamed with recognition. "It's you," he said, and his voice rang out like glass. "I've looked on your face every day. And though I've seen others, you've always been the most beautiful of them all."

His words were a caress, like the feel of cool glass against her skin on a hot day. "My name is Mina. Let me help you sit up."

With one arm under his shoulders, she guided him into a sitting position. He copied her movements, learning how to move his limbs and his body until he was sitting like her, with his knees tucked underneath him. They sat face-to-face, studying each other. Mina bit her lip, and he did the same.

"My name is—do I have a name?" he said.

Mina hadn't thought about a name. She considered it, tasting different options until she found one that felt like broken glass on her tongue. "Felix," she said. "Your name is Felix."

"My name is Felix," he repeated. "What would you have me do," he said, "if I can no longer show you your own face?"

"I need you to teach me what it means to be in love—what it looks like, how it feels. Love me, as best as you can, and I will learn from you."

Her voice had started to break on those last words, and she went silent, wishing she hadn't spoken at all. What did a piece of glass know of love? She could shatter him to pieces now if she wanted, force him back into the mirror frame and forget that she had ever tried this misguided experiment.

But then he placed each of his hands on her shoulders and leaned forward, his lips hovering over hers before moving to the patch of skin just below her jaw, right where her pulse should have been, and her breath caught. "That's easy," he murmured against her throat. "I've loved you since I opened my eyes and saw you."

Mina's eyes fluttered closed as her hands skimmed along his scarred arms. She pulled him close, marveling at the unfamiliar but comforting weight of his head buried in the crook of her neck. For a moment she thought, *Maybe this is enough.* Maybe she didn't need the king or his crown—maybe all she needed was to shut her eyes and hold Felix tightly enough until she forgot that neither of them had a pulse, that neither of them could ever make the other truly human.

But she couldn't shut her eyes forever, so she opened them again and gently removed herself from Felix's embrace. "Hold out your arms," she said.

The cracks were noticeable, but they looked like scars, the kind one might receive from dueling or hunting. She could have fixed them, probably, but she decided she liked him better this way. She ran her fingers over the scars, and the feel of them sent a thrill all the way to her bones. *Mine.*

"You have the look of a huntsman, my love," she said, "and the king often goes hunting. When you leave here, you'll go to the stables and ask for the marshal, and you'll tell him you've come to join the royal huntsmen. Perhaps in time, you'll accompany the king himself, and then you'll come back here, to me, and tell me what you've learned about him. Do you understand?"

"Yes. I'm going to be a huntsman," he recited, eyes wide with eagerness to please her.

She bent her head and pressed her lips against one of the scars on his inner arm, and he lifted her head gently, stroking her cheeks, her lips, with his thumb. She leaned in, unsure at first, but when he didn't move away, she drew in closer, until her lips met his. Almost immediately, she drew back again.

Felix adapted quickly. He copied her movements, bringing his head forward to return her kiss. His adoration, his yearning, nourished her, and she understood now why gods were always said to be jealous.

She pretended it was the king she was kissing, practicing where on his back to place her hands, when to lean away so that he would be left wanting more. *This is what it feels like to be held, to be loved,* she told herself, but she was too aware that it was a mirror that loved her, and mirrors only saw the surface. Were people the same? If she shone brightly enough on the outside, could she blind everyone to what lay underneath?

Felix cried out. She had unthinkingly torn the flesh at the nape of his neck, and when she withdrew her hand, his blood was under her nails.

Had the cry been loud enough to wake her father? Mina rose from the floor, listening for the sound of footsteps. Felix remained on his knees in front of her, his upturned face radiant with devotion, and she forgot her worries at the sight of him. She didn't think she would ever grow accustomed to this sudden wealth of affection.

"Stand," she said, and he obeyed. "Did I wound you?"

"A little."

"Do you still love me?"

"Of course."

She leaned in to kiss him again, but the sound of her door slamming open made her jump.

It was her father, and he was livid.

"Get him out of here," he said, his voice a low rumble.

Felix looked to her in confusion, waiting for her to tell him what to do. "Remember where I told you to go," Mina whispered to him. Her room was level with the ground, so she threw open the window. Felix understood, nodding to her once before climbing outside to fulfill the other task she had given him.

As she shut the window, she wished she could follow him, or that when she turned around, her father would be gone. But she had no such luck. Her father was waiting for her, as furious as before. She decided then that no matter what he said or did, she wouldn't tell him about Felix's true origin. That was still her secret, and she would cling to it as long as she had strength left in her.

"I can't tell if you're naive or just deeply stupid," Gregory sneered, a vein pulsing on his forehead.

You wouldn't speak to me that way if I were queen, Mina thought, but she remained silent. Let him rage, and when he was finished, she would speak.

"You should be thankful I stopped you before it went too far. If anyone found out about this, or if you ended up with a child, it would be impossible to find anyone to marry you."

"And what if you *were* too late? What if it did go too far?" It was a risky claim to make, but it was worth it to see the blood drain out of his face. Yes, he'd listen to her now. He'd hang on every word.

He grabbed her roughly by the shoulders. "Did it?"

Mina waited before answering, letting him anticipate her reply. "No," she said at last.

Gregory released her, his shoulders sagging with relief. "If I ever catch sight of you with him—or any other man—again, I'll kill him. How could a daughter of mine be so foolish?"

"I wasn't going to let him—"

Her father's laughter interrupted her. "You think you could have stopped him?"

"Yes."

"And how do you know that?"

Because I made him and I can destroy him. She kept her mouth tightly shut, afraid that her pride would betray her. "I knew what I was doing."

"Oh? Enlighten me."

She thought quickly. Tell him the truth of her purpose, her secret ambitions, and he could be an ally. Lie, and he would think her a fool and marry her off as soon as possible.

"I want to be queen."

His mouth remained hanging open for another few seconds before he shook his head and remembered to close it. Whatever he'd expected to hear, it hadn't been that. She'd rendered him speechless, and that was a victory.

"I want to marry the king," she continued. "I spoke to him in the courtyard, the morning of the banquet, and I thought that if I could . . . practice with someone, then I'd know what to do if I ever spoke to him again. I'd know how to—to make him love me."

Gregory continued to stare blankly at her for some time, and then he burst into laughter. "I've underestimated you," he said. "Here I was hoping to marry you into an important family, and all this time, you've been daydreaming about becoming a queen. You've inherited something from me after all."

The idea of inheriting anything from him was distasteful to Mina, but she didn't want to ruin her father's good humor. "You could help me," she said. "We could work together. You could be the father of a queen."

He seemed to consider the idea more seriously, his expression growing contemplative. "It wouldn't be for another few years. The queen's memory must start to fade before the king can replace her. Are you resolved to wait that long?"

"Yes," Mina said, thinking of the high table in the banquet hall and of the adoring faces that would turn to her when she took her place there at the king's side.

"And no more of this . . . this 'practicing,' either?"

Mina flushed. She shook her head.

"If we can make this happen, Mina . . ." He stopped, nodding to himself as he went to the door. He paused at the threshold. "One more thing before I go. I'm simply curious: Is it the man you desire, or is it the crown?"

There was no safe answer. If she chose the man, she'd be deemed immodest; the crown, and she'd be mercenary. The only answer she could give was the truth:

"Both."

Mina used to be able to determine the season by the trees alone. But in Whitespring, it was always winter, and so she hardly noticed as a year passed, and then another. She hadn't expected to be queen by the end of a year, but she had hoped she'd at least have the chance to speak to the king again. She often lingered near the western courtyard where they had first met, but she never found him there. During meals in the Hall, she was too far from the high table to even catch his eye, let alone to speak to him. Most of the time, he wasn't even there, preferring to take his meals privately.

Her father wasn't concerned. "He can't content himself with a memory forever," Gregory kept telling her. "Soon he'll want solid flesh, and that is something you have that the old queen no longer does."

And though she found comfort in his reassurances, part of her always wondered, *Is that all I am?*

She still had Felix, though. She couldn't risk her father catching them again, so Mina had searched for a safe place to meet him, and one night she found it. In a forgotten corner of the west wing was an abandoned chapel with stained-glass windows, the last remnant of a time when the sun had still shone on Whitespring, before the North had begun to pray to Sybil instead. From there, Mina called for Felix—because she had made him, she could reach out to him with a thought, a slight pull that he felt no matter where he was. He was rising quickly among the ranks of the huntsmen, but the king was still beyond his reach, and so out of Mina's reach as well.

And then, one night in the Hall, Mina overheard that there

would soon be a picnic in the Shadow Garden behind the east wing of the castle. That wasn't news in itself—the court occasionally held small social gatherings for their own amusement—but Mina also heard whispers that this would be the princess's first public appearance, which meant the king would be present as well. Mina had another chance at last. When the king saw her again, she wouldn't be the huddled, shivering girl he first met in the courtyard.

On the day of the picnic, Mina went alone to the Shadow Garden. She didn't think this nightmarish collection of twisted, dead trees deserved to be called a garden at all, but she had to admit that the garden was almost pretty today, the lanterns hanging from the trees' bare branches lending an orange glow to the snow. The entire court was here for the princess's first appearance, along with a considerable number of visiting nobles. A tented pavilion had been set up away from the trees, and underneath it sat King Nicholas, as well as a nurse with an active two-year-old on her lap. The princess was struggling against her nurse's arms in an effort to join a group of children running and playing under the trees.

Mina felt lost in the crowd. She recognized some faces from the Great Hall, but she had no friends or allies among any of them. She watched as old friends waved to one another, and she began to wish she had spent less time watching the king and more effort making a friend or two at court. She had come here today secretly expecting the crowd to part for her at her arrival and form a path for her straight to the king, who would be instantly struck by her beauty. But that was romantic nonsense that she should have put aside years ago.

She would approach this opportunity more practically, then. She needed to be approachable—alluring—to make people come to her instead of begging for attention from the fringes. She wandered through the crowd, looking for the right moment, the right person. She just needed someone to *see* her, to be drawn in by her beauty.

There—standing not too far from the pavilion were two men, both young enough that it was possible they were unmarried, engaged in conversation. Mina walked quickly, looking in the other direction as she headed toward them, letting herself accidentally collide with one of the men.

"Oh, I'm so sorry!" she said at once, stepping away from him so that he could see her better. "I should have been watching where I was going." The two men both started to scowl, but when they turned to see who had so clumsily interrupted them, their mouths fell open, their scowls forgotten.

Yes, Mina thought, *look at me.* She stood there, inviting them to see the way her hair so perfectly complemented her emerald-green dress. They would know her southern roots by the gold hue of her skin, but they would also have to notice how soft that skin was, her neck bare even though she was cold. Their eyes flashed brightly as she submitted herself to their gaze, lifting her chin and forcing herself not to turn away as she once again wondered, *Is this all I am?*

"No need for apologies," the shorter one said, running a hand through his limp brown hair. "Especially not if you stay and talk with us."

Mina smiled and put her hand on her throat, noticing the way their eyes followed. "Thank you, gentlemen," she said. "I'm afraid I don't know many people at court, and it would be such a comfort to have a friend."

She chirped and preened for them like a songbird in a cage, begging to be sold, but always standing so that she had a view of the king. Before long, others joined their circle—at first only other men, but soon some women joined them as well, until Mina became the main attraction of the festivities. They all swept their eyes over her at first, a slight frown of hesitation on their faces as they realized she was an outsider, but then Mina would smile or fiddle with her hair, and their gazes became more appreciative.

The king seemed preoccupied with making sure his daughter didn't run off to join the other children playing by the trees, swinging branches as makeshift swords, but Mina knew he would notice the growing circle of people eventually, and then he would see her at the center of it all, shining like a beacon calling him to her.

In the end, it was Mina's laugh that caught his attention. He had been listening to some old man who was leaning over to whisper something to him, eyes glazing over with boredom, when Mina pretended to laugh at something she was only half listening to in the first place. The king turned his head at the sound, and then he saw Mina, his head slightly tilting in curiosity as he noticed the small crowd of people around her. Mina held her head high, wanting him to see her like this, adored and admired, rather than the lonely girl in the courtyard, but after only a moment, he turned back to the old man.

Trying not to react to this disappointment, Mina brought her attention back to the group, but they weren't looking at her anymore. They were moving aside, making room for a group of people led by a middle-aged woman, her head held high on her long, elegant neck, her black hair veined with dignified white strands.

Mina recognized her. Her name was Xenia, and she and several others of about the same age were always seated closest to the high table, many of them on the king's council.

Xenia's left eyebrow went up in a perfect arch, and her lips curled into an amused but cold smile. "What a strange day this is," she said, loudly enough for everyone to hear. "Our beautiful princess is making her first court appearance, and here we all are gathered around a southern girl none of us even know. I should think the king would resent such an insult to his daughter."

She turned and left, taking the crowd with her. Some simply walked away, but several others took the trouble to shoot Mina a withering glance first.

Why should these people make me feel ashamed of my home? Mina thought. When had they earned the right to do so? For all their disdain toward southerners, they were no different from the frightened villagers at home, whispering and throwing rocks at her ankles when she wasn't looking. Their reasons for hating her were different, but the sharp pain of their rejection felt exactly the same. She glanced at the king, and she instantly regretted it—he was staring at her, witnessing her sudden disgrace with a deep frown.

To be humiliated was one thing, but for *him* to see it—Mina couldn't help herself. She retreated as fast as she could without breaking into a run. She knew that to leave now would be a sign of defeat, but she couldn't bear to stay and be sneered at while her plans for the future dissolved in an instant.

She was nearly out of the garden when she heard a voice call, "Wait!" and then a strong hand took hold of her arm. When she turned to confront her latest tormentor, she let out a small cry of surprise—it was King Nicholas.

Just as she had imagined, the crowd had parted to form a path between her and the king's pavilion, but instead of Mina going to him, he had come to her. They were all watching with interest, waiting to see what the king would do.

Nicholas followed Mina's gaze to the observing crowd, and he gave an exasperated sigh. He let go of Mina's arm and offered his own. "Walk with me," he said, and Mina took his arm at once, hardly knowing what she was doing.

The king set a leisurely pace away from the garden—a simple stroll rather than the escape Mina had been making. Mina clung to his arm, thinking furiously. She didn't know what to do, who to be—what was his purpose in following her? Why was he leading her away? Was he trying to help her, or did he want to tell her personally never to attend any public functions ever again?

Finally, he said without looking at her, "I know who you are. You're Gregory's daughter."

"My name is *Mina*," she said firmly.

He stopped walking and turned to face her, a small crease appearing between his eyebrows. "That's right. Mina. The girl with the peach. You've become . . ." He shook his head slightly and turned away. "Were they being cruel to you? Is that why you were running off?"

Mina studied his face, looking for some sign that he was goading her into a trap. But his eyes were gentle, and his forehead gently wrinkled with concern. He was the same man she had met in the courtyard two years ago, sad yet kind.

"Yes," she whispered. "Yes, they were cruel to me. But people have always been cruel to me, for one reason or another."

He nodded in understanding. "Whitespring can be set in its ways. No one trusts anyone or anything new, not at first. I'm sorry you had to learn that so harshly. I won't let it happen again."

Mina didn't respond at first. Even though she was still shivering, she felt a strange kind of warmth, his words wrapping around her protectively. She had confided something to him, and he had taken her side.

"Thank you, my lord," she said, "for coming to my rescue." *No one else ever has*, she wanted to say.

He smiled a little, but then his expression darkened. "Is your father here?"

"No," Mina said quickly.

He held his arm out to her. "Then perhaps you'd like to stay for the rest of the afternoon? I doubt anyone will give you more trouble, and I'd hate for you to leave so early."

She took his arm and he led her back to the crowd before

bowing his head to her and returning to sit with his daughter. Mina tried not to gloat too much as the same people who had just shunned and sneered at her now called to her and greeted her warmly, but it was difficult not to enjoy the way Xenia and her friends were suddenly at her side with begrudging smiles.

"The king seems fond of you," Xenia said. "Have you met before?"

"Once," Mina responded.

"I do hope you weren't too offended by what I said earlier," Xenia added, placing a hand on Mina's shoulder. "Just a little playful teasing among friends."

Mina fought off the urge to shrug Xenia's hand away. She might have said something sharp and biting, something to make Xenia regret having been cruel to her, but as much as Mina wanted to strike back at her, she also found herself enjoying Xenia's attention. Making Xenia accept her was even more satisfying than rejecting her would have been.

"I understand," Mina said. "And I'm sure we'll be such good friends from now on."

Still elated from her success, Mina told her father everything when she returned to their apartment. He sat at his writing desk, listening to her account of the day without saying anything, and when she was done, he only said, "Does the king know you're my daughter?"

Mina nodded, puzzled, but then she remembered her first meeting with the king, when he had quickly left after finding out who she was. At the time, she hadn't known he was the king, and so she'd assumed Gregory had just made a new set of enemies. But now she wondered *why* he had reacted as he had, why he had been so sharp with her when asking if her father was in the garden.

"The king doesn't like you," Mina said, noticing the way her father showed no surprise at her words. "But why? You saved his daughter."

His lips almost twisted into a snarl as he pushed himself up from his seat and retreated to the window, his back turned to her. "But not his wife," he muttered.

"Still, wouldn't he be grateful to you?"

"He *should* be grateful."

"But then, why doesn't he like you? Why wouldn't you come with me to the picnic today?"

Gregory's fingers curled against the windowsill. "I doubt the king wants to be reminded of the debt he owes me."

"For saving his daughter?"

Gregory started to laugh, a dry, grating sound that quickly became a cough. When he had recovered, he turned to her, holding his withered hands out in front of him. "Look at what I've become, Mina. I've lost my youth, my vitality. And for what?" He gazed down at his empty hands. "For nothing. For a lie." He shook his head and his hands dropped to his sides. "I'll tell *you*, at least. I'll have to content myself with that."

"Tell me *what*?" Mina said, tired of his cryptic games.

"I didn't save the king's daughter," he said, voice thick with pride. "I *created* her."

Mina was silent at first. She kept thinking of the sand mouse Gregory had shown her back home, the way he had been so secretive about how he had saved the infant princess's life, his sudden aged appearance and heavy gait since returning home. . . .

Gregory saw realization pass over Mina's face and nodded. "That's right," he said. "The queen was already dead by the time I arrived north. She had been ill; she wasn't even carrying a child. That was just a lie to explain why the king suddenly had a daughter. After her death, the king wanted me to create life in a way that I had never done before—an infant that would age naturally. He wanted her to look just like her mother." The words came rushing out of him, long held back by whatever promise he had made to the king. How difficult it must have been for him never to tell anyone about his greatest success.

"The blood," Mina said. "You made her with your blood."

"Snow and blood. It took me many attempts to understand how to make her truly alive, and each attempt weakened me, drained the life out of my heart." He clutched his chest and lowered himself back in his chair. "It's a cruel joke, isn't it? All my life, I've wanted to understand my own power, to test my limitations and move beyond them. And now that I finally know what I'm capable of, I've become an old man before my time. I can never create life again without giving my own."

Mina hardly listened to his self-pitying ramble. She was thinking of the little girl squirming on her nurse's lap. There was no sign that she was anything but a normal child of flesh and blood. True, she would bear an uncanny similarity to her mother as she grew, but she had a beating heart and a loving father who would protect her from this secret—and from Gregory. Mina bit the inside of her cheek until she tasted blood.

"Will he ever marry me, then?" she said, more to herself than to Gregory.

Gregory gestured her over to him, staring up at her in cool appraisal. "You have to make him want you so much that he won't care about anything else. People aren't rational when it comes to affairs of the heart. After all, your mother married me even when her family threatened to disown her for it."

And she hated you in the end, Mina thought. *Will he hate me, too, if he ever finds out what I am?* She didn't bother voicing her concern to Gregory—she knew he wouldn't care. *I'll have to make him love me first*, she decided. If he truly loved her, he wouldn't care about her dead heart.

And perhaps—perhaps the king wouldn't find Mina's condition so repellant when his own daughter's birth was so unconventional. Perhaps he was the one person in the world who would be able to love her.

10

MINA

From her new place in the Hall, seated with Xenia and her circle, Mina often caught the king's eye, a private smile passing between them. Over the next year, she watched him cater to his daughter's every wish and learned that the king cared more about his daughter than about anyone else. If she wanted to win over the father, she would have to win the child, as well.

And so when a birthday celebration for the princess was announced, Mina knew how important it was for her to attend. She wasn't the only one—the Hall was crowded with visitors on the night of the celebration, but this time Mina had a place among them. Mina knew Xenia's niceties were anything but sincere, but she still welcomed the pretense, and she felt some satisfaction at knowing that Xenia and her friends couldn't even comment on the thick furs Mina wore.

As the evening wore on, Mina recognized that there were some virtues to standing apart from the crowd with her warm dress: there were one or two instances when the king saw her from his table, their eyes meeting before someone else—usually Lynet, who kept kicking her legs and trying to duck under the table—distracted him. But she'd had enough of shared glances and distant smiles; she needed to find a way to bring him over to her again, to make him seek her out.

The next time she looked up, the king wasn't there.

Mina looked around the Hall, but she couldn't find him anywhere. And then, while she was watching the main door, she saw a cloud of dark hair run out from under a table and escape outside.

She put the pieces together: a restless princess who had slipped away, a worried father searching for her, and Mina, the only one who knew where the princess had gone. She could go tell the king's guard what she had seen, but Mina knew that if she found and retrieved Lynet herself, the king would undoubtedly be grateful to her.

Mina made some excuse about needing air and left the Hall, emerging into the chilly courtyard, the light from inside throwing her shadow large over the snow. There was a juniper tree near the edge of the courtyard, but unlike the spindly trees in the Shadow Garden, this one was green and full, its leaves frosted with snow.

She looked around the courtyard, hoping Lynet hadn't gone too far, and saw a shower of snow fall from the juniper tree. There was no wind to have caused it. Mina casually strolled toward the tree.

When she was standing under the tree, more snow started to fall. Mina brushed the wet snow from the back of her neck and glared up at the offending tree—and found two curious eyes peering back at her. Nestled in the branches was a little girl, her eyes and hair as black as the lake at night. The girl crouched down in panic at her discovery.

"Lynet?"

The girl clung to her branch wordlessly, refusing to confirm or deny her identity.

"Lynet? That's your name, isn't it?"

"What do you want?" Lynet said, before shoving her knuckles into her mouth.

Tucking her skirts beneath her, Mina sat at the foot of the tree. She patted the ground, but Lynet didn't move. "If you come sit with me, I'll give you a present," she said.

Lynet climbed down from her branch to a lower one, and then she dropped down to the ground, landing on hands and knees. She was wearing only a thin dress, like a true northerner, but even when the snow touched her skin, she didn't seem to feel the cold at all.

"What present?" the girl said as she plopped down beside Mina.

Mina had only half expected the bribe to work, so she hadn't considered what she would give Lynet for a present. She wasn't wearing any rings, but she had her silver bracelet, bought in defiance years ago. She unclasped the bracelet and held it out. "Here," she said. "Isn't it pretty? Let me put it on you." She placed it around the girl's wrist; it was too big for her, of course, but it stayed on, and Lynet was entranced by it.

"Thank you," she said. "You're pretty, what's your name?"

"My name is Mina."

Lynet nodded and went back to twirling her new bracelet around her wrist.

"You're pretty too," Mina said.

"Thank you," Lynet said at once. Mina supposed this wasn't the first time she'd heard that compliment.

"You're very bold to be climbing such big trees," she said, and this time, the girl rewarded her with her full attention.

"What's bold?"

"It means you're brave and fierce, like a little wolf cub."

Lynet bent her head over her wrist, her hair hiding most of her face, but Mina saw that the girl was smiling.

"My name is a bird," she said. "Papa told me. He says I'm like a bird."

"Oh? What else does your papa say?"

"He says I'm like my mama. She's dead."

Her bluntness was unexpected, but Lynet didn't seem upset. It was a fact, like anything else. It was unfair to be jealous of a child, but Mina wished for that sense of detachment about her own mother's death, rather than the sting of rejection.

"My mother is dead too," Mina said without thinking. She was staring straight ahead, thinking of the day her father had told her the truth of her mother's death, when she felt a tug. Lynet had moved closer to her, one of her dirty hands entangled in Mina's skirt. She wanted to brush the hand away before it soiled the fabric, but that wouldn't endear her to the child. And . . . she found she didn't mind it. The girl rested her dark head against Mina's shoulder, and that didn't bother her either. The weight of Lynet's head was heavy and comforting.

"Do you miss your mama?" Lynet said. She lifted her head, and the sudden absence left Mina colder than she was before.

"I did once, but not anymore."

The girl was unhappy with this answer, though; her forehead scrunched up and her head drooped as she picked at her skirts.

"What's the matter? Do *you* miss your mama?"

"Papa misses her," Lynet mumbled.

"Does that make you sad?"

She shrugged.

"Do you miss her too?"

She gave no answer—but then, how could she miss a mother

who had died before she was even born? "It's fine if you don't miss her," Mina said softly. "You don't remember her. You never really knew her. It's hard to miss someone you can't remember."

Lynet kept her head down. "Don't tell my papa," she whispered.

Mina shook her head. "I won't say a word, wolf cub."

"Lynet!"

Mina was startled by the sudden cry, but Lynet stiffened in recognition: King Nicholas was hurrying toward them. Mina stood immediately, brushing the snow off her dress. She needn't have bothered; the king passed by her without a glance and swung Lynet up into his arms.

"We've been looking everywhere for you," he said.

"I was bored," Lynet mumbled into her knuckles.

"What were you even doing here—were you climbing trees again? I've told you how dangerous it is to climb trees. Those bones of yours are breakable."

"She wasn't climbing anything, my lord," Mina said. "I found her sitting out here, and we were talking together."

He looked at her like she'd appeared out of the air. But then he seemed to recognize her, and his face softened. "Mina," he said. "I'm sorry I didn't say anything to you sooner. I was so relieved to find Lynet. . . ."

"I like her," Lynet whispered to him.

"Is that so?"

"She's even prettier than Mama, isn't she?"

The king winced. "No one is prettier than your mama," he said.

Mina's pride was a little injured, but she would do better to side with him over Lynet in this case. "If your daughter truly resembles her mother, my lord, then you must be right."

This softened the blow somewhat, and he smiled fondly at his daughter before setting her back down on her feet. "Can I trust you to go back inside, Lynetbird?"

Lynet pouted, but she nodded. She looked at Mina for a second, her small forehead furrowed in thought, and then she ran forward and flung her arms around Mina's waist.

Mina laughed in surprise and placed a hand on the girl's head. She looked up at Nicholas to see if he found this pretty sight charming, but he was frowning. "That's enough, Lynet," he said.

Lynet pulled away, gave Mina one last smile, and ran off in the direction of the Hall. Nicholas still wore his frown, and Mina tried to understand what troubled him so that she could say the right thing. She settled on something safe: "She's a sweet girl."

"A sweet girl, but not a careful one," he said, glancing up at the juniper tree. "She latched on to you so quickly. . . ." Nicholas said, more to himself than to Mina.

"I suppose she wants a friend, or . . ." Mina took a moment to go over what she was planning to say, which also had the desired effect of making her seem shy or uncertain.

"What? Speak freely with me."

"You asked me once, a long time ago, if it was easy for a girl to grow up without a mother. I can tell you truly now that it isn't. I've made so many mistakes that I wouldn't have made if I'd had a mother to guide me. After my mother died, I yearned for feminine guidance, someone to emulate, to learn from. I wanted . . . well, I wanted a mother."

Mina barely heard herself speaking. The truth of the words didn't matter as much as Nicholas's reaction to them. She observed him as she spoke, waiting to see if she should continue on this path or retreat.

From the way he was glowering, the answer was clear: *Retreat.*

Mina thought frantically. "Of course, I didn't mean that *I*—" She gave a dry laugh and turned her eyes down. "It seems I still don't know how to speak to kings. I cringe whenever I think of the day I first met you. I'm sure I was very rude. I didn't even know who you were."

"Really? I don't remember you being rude at all. You were genuine. Unaffected. I liked that about you."

Mina held back a sigh of relief. "Liked?" she said, peeking up at him with a hint of coyness. "Have I lost that quality as I've grown?"

"I fear we all do," he said with a sigh, looking up at the dimmed stars peeking through the clouds. He met Mina's eyes again, a hint of a smile on his lips. "But I hope some of it still remains."

She tried to hide a smile, but even that gesture was planned and perfected, artifice designed to look genuine, just like her heart. He was right—somewhere through the years, she had forgotten how to be herself without calculating the effect of every word, every look. She had dressed as a northerner to fit in, and now she was dressed as a southerner to stand apart, always with a view at pleasing the king. She had put up with Xenia's false friendship in order to feel accepted. She was no better than Felix, adapting herself to please whoever was holding the mirror. Mina wondered if she would ever be able to give him something real, to tell him everything about herself and trust him to reach out to her nonetheless.

"Is your father here tonight?" Nicholas asked her, somewhat stiffly.

"No, my lord," Mina said.

There was a touch of skepticism in his narrowed eyes. "He never seems to accompany you anywhere."

Mina shifted uncomfortably, thinking of how to answer. Perhaps in this case, the honest answer was the best one. "We're . . . not close," she said with a pained smile.

Nicholas frowned. "And yet he's the only family you have, isn't he? That must be lonely for you." He took a step closer to her and reached out to take her hand, but then he stopped himself. "If you can keep Lynet from climbing any more trees, I'd like to invite you to walk with us tomorrow afternoon by the lake. It's Lynet's favorite place."

"I'd be very honored, my lord," Mina said, happy to change the subject.

"Are you going back inside?" he said, offering his arm.

Mina considered the offer—she would have loved to see Xenia's face when she walked into the room on the arm of the king, but then he would leave her to return to his daughter, the best part of Mina's night already behind her. Better to leave him now, when his memory of her would be of this moment under the juniper tree.

"Thank you, my lord, but I think I'll retire for the night."

Did she imagine it, or did his face fall just a little? He wished her a good night, and Mina waited until he was gone before she allowed herself a smile. She inhaled deeply, breathing in the crisp, cold air, and sent a silent thank-you to Lynet for running away and hiding in that tree.

11

LYNET

Lynet kept her head down, but she lifted her eyes to discreetly watch Nadia at work. She had spent much of the last several days in the basement workroom, rummaging through Master Jacob's journals for answers that she never found, but not once had she or Nadia ever mentioned that shared moment in the tower, when the moonlight had existed only for them.

They were shyer with each other now. Nadia would hand her the journals quickly, before their hands could brush against each other, and Lynet always sat across the table from her, rather than at her side. But the more they took pains not to re-create that night, the more Lynet thought of it, confused by the flurry of nameless, indistinct emotions the memory always stirred.

When Nadia brushed aside strands of hair as she read, Lynet remembered the way her hand had faintly trembled as it had reached for Lynet's hair in the tower. The gentle sound of Nadia's breathing made her remember the way her own breath had come so haltingly afterward, when she stood alone in the room. And when Nadia bit her lip in concentration, Lynet wondered at the sense of disappointment that washed over her, like she was searching for something without even knowing what it was. Sometimes Nadia watched her, too, but she always ducked her head and pretended to have been doing something else whenever their eyes met.

Lynet flipped another useless journal page, shifting restlessly. She wished this shyness between them would pass. Without Nadia, Lynet only had the snow and her own thoughts to keep her company. She had never noticed before how ever-present the snow was here, how impossible it was to get away from it. Only now, when the snow was a constant reminder of her origins, did she wish it would melt away.

Her eyes drifted up to Nadia again, and all at once the thought struck her: *I could go with her. I could follow her south, where no one knows me.* It would be so much easier to forget the truth in the South—she would never have to see the snow or hear her mother's name again.

She hardly read another word for the rest of the morning, and she was still imagining their future journey together on her way out when she found her father standing in the courtyard. She was supposed to be with her music tutor, but her father didn't seem surprised to see her here; in fact, he held his arm out when he saw her.

"Come walk with me," he said.

She had been trying to avoid her father ever since learning the truth of her birth. She was afraid she would say something to reveal that she knew the secret he was keeping from her, afraid some of her resentment would seep into her voice. But she took his arm and let him lead her through the stone arch that led to the Shadow

Garden. "Do you remember how much you used to like it here when you were little? The lake was your favorite place."

Lynet did remember. She had never understood why no one else would splash in the lake with her. Now she knew—the water was icy cold to anyone but her.

"You have a new favorite place now, though, don't you?" her father continued.

Was he going to scold her about climbing the juniper tree? She sighed and waited for the worst.

Nicholas stopped and turned to her. "You've been skipping all of your lessons so you can visit the surgeon's workroom nearly every day."

Lynet gaped at him, trying to decide how best to appease him. A sincere apology? She couldn't deny it, not when she was supposed to be poorly playing the harp right now. And she couldn't explain *why* she was visiting the workroom, without telling him that she knew the truth he was hiding from her.

"I know you're young," Nicholas said, "and it's exciting when someone your age is at Whitespring, but you can't neglect your duties, especially when your birthday is tomorrow."

"What's so special about my birthday this year?" Lynet muttered with some bitterness.

Some of his sternness melted away, and he smiled at her. "I don't want you to be unprepared," he said. "You're not a child anymore, Lynet. You're going to have to learn to walk in your mother's footsteps."

A month ago, she would have bowed her head in defeat and mumbled a halfhearted agreement. Perhaps it was because she now knew that her father had *made* her so that she could walk in her mother's footsteps, or perhaps it was because she kept hearing Mina's voice in her head saying, *You don't have to be like your mother, no matter what anyone says,* but this time, Lynet spoke the first words that came to her mind:

"And what if I choose not to?"

He was taken aback by her response, his forehead wrinkling in confusion, but he didn't seem angry with her, at least. "I only want you to have the life you were meant to have," he said. "I've let you run around freely long enough. Tomorrow is the day you leave all your childhood habits behind. No more climbing, no more avoiding your lessons to do whatever you wish . . . and less time with Mina."

"What?" The other terms she had been expecting, but that last one made the exclamation fly from her lips before she could hold it back.

Nicholas took a breath and looked up at the web of branches over their heads. At least he seemed to understand the weight of what he was asking her to do. "When you were a child, you took to Mina at once. You doted on her. I made it very clear to both of you that I didn't want her to take the place of your mother, or for her to have too much influence over you. And for a while, I thought she understood. But you two have formed . . . an attachment. When you were a child, I could understand. But now that you're older, you don't need a stepmother anymore." He took her hands in his and gave her an imploring look. "I know you're at an age when you think you don't need a father's guidance, but I hope you still trust and respect my judgment. I'm thinking of your future, Lynet."

Lynet took measured breaths, willing herself not to cry. "So what would you have me do, just pretend she doesn't exist?"

"Of course not, but you've become too dependent on her. You go see her every night." He paused, and when he spoke again, he spoke slowly, choosing his words with care. "I know this may be difficult for you to understand now, but as you get older, you won't always be able to trust Mina to have your best interests at heart. You would be wise to distance yourself a little from her before that happens."

Lynet thought about how Mina had showed her the chapel, and how honored she had felt at being allowed this glimpse into her stepmother's world. *No more Mina?* It was true she wasn't a child anymore, but that just meant the two of them were becoming something more balanced than stepmother and stepchild—they were becoming sisters, friends, able to confide in each other more than ever before. And now she had to either leave that friendship behind, or else hurt her father by disrespecting his wishes.

She shook her head, the only response she could give to such an impossible situation, and her father sighed. "You'll understand everything more clearly tonight."

"Tonight?"

He smiled. "You, Mina, and I are going to meet tonight in my chambers, as soon as the sun goes down. There's something I want to tell you. Think of it as an early birthday gift."

Lynet offered a weak smile, but she wasn't sure she wanted any gift she couldn't share with Mina. She remained silent as they walked back through the garden together, and then her father followed her through the halls to make sure she was headed to the music room. She would have gone even if he hadn't followed her—there was nowhere else she was allowed to go.

"Ah, there you are," her father said when she arrived at his rooms at the appointed hour. He gestured for her to sit by the fireplace. But there were only two chairs by the fireplace, and Nicholas had already taken one of them. If Lynet took the other, Mina would have to sit apart.

She chose to kneel down on the floor beside the fire. "Why did you ask us here?"

Nicholas smiled down at her. "It's a surprise, my Lynetbird. I'll tell you as soon as—"

The door opened, and Mina strode in. Lynet had learned over the years that the Mina she knew only appeared when they were alone. When Nicholas was near, Mina stood tall, rigid even, and her face went blank except for small, controlled movements. The Mina who walked into the room now was distant and untouchable, but undoubtedly a queen.

"We were waiting for you. Sit," Nicholas said.

Mina settled in the chair opposite Nicholas, the red tints in her hair and the deep glow of her eyes catching the firelight.

Nicholas straightened in his seat and looked intently at Lynet. "You know you're my greatest joy in this world," he said. Lynet guiltily glanced at Mina, but Mina's face revealed nothing. "At almost sixteen, you've become everything your mother was. And so your birthday is the perfect time for you to begin to take the place she left for you."

Mina gave a short laugh. "Don't tell me you mean to marry her."

"Of course not," Nicholas said with some irritation. "I mean to prepare her to become queen, starting by giving her full control of the South."

They were all speechless for a moment. Lynet knew she was supposed to say something, to thank him, to show him how excited she was, but all she felt was shock and a growing sense of panic. She knew she would have to be ready to be queen when her father died, but she also knew that on that day, her transformation into her mother would be complete. That was what he was really offering to her, after all—not the South, but the chance to become her mother sooner.

"But what does that mean?" Lynet finally managed to say. "What do you want me to do?"

Nicholas nodded in approval. "You're going to learn how to be a queen, Lynet. You'll attend all public court events and greet all visitors personally. You'll come with me when I meet with my council, and you'll handle all matters related to the South—hearing petitions, deciding policy. As we discussed this morning, you are going to have to put your childhood behind you from now on. You have responsibilities."

Lynet's stomach twisted a little more with each word. She could sense her world becoming smaller and smaller, no bigger than one of the coffins in the crypt. She had wanted to run away, but now she felt more trapped than ever.

Nicholas was beginning to frown, and Lynet knew she wasn't responding the way he had hoped or expected. In desperation, she turned to Mina, forgetting for a moment that he didn't want her to depend on Mina anymore.

But Mina wasn't looking at Lynet. She was staring ahead at Nicholas, sitting perfectly still except for a slight tremor of her hands.

She didn't know, Lynet realized, now understanding the full extent of her father's decision. She had been so occupied with her own fears that she had forgotten that the power her father was granting her—the position he was preparing her for—was Mina's.

Why hadn't her father asked for Mina's blessing before making this decision? But of course he wouldn't—she never knew them to agree about anything.

"You would do this?" Mina said, her voice barely above a whisper.

"I will do anything that's best for my daughter," Nicholas said, looking at his wife for the first time since he'd begun his announcement. "And needless to say, I will not allow you to make her decisions or rule through her. Lynet is old enough not to need you anymore."

"And have you considered that Lynet may not want to accept your offer?"

The two of them both looked down at Lynet, who tried not to cower under the eyes of the two people she cared about most. Nicholas was looking at her in disbelief, clearly confused by the suggestion that Lynet wouldn't want to take such an important step toward becoming queen. And Mina—Mina was simply waiting for Lynet to tell her father the truth.

Nicholas was the first to look away. "Don't speak for her. If Lynet has any complaints, she'll speak for herself."

"Will she?" Mina said softly, her eyes still on Lynet.

Lynet was growing light-headed, too warm from sitting in front of the fire, and even though she shut her eyes tight, she could still see them both watching her, waiting for her to say something. No matter what she said, she would have to hurt one of them. She could already see the look on her father's face, the slow realization that his daughter wasn't the person he thought she was. She would never be able to make him understand, but Mina—Mina would understand. Mina could be reasoned with. Even if she upset Mina now, Lynet could explain herself later, and she knew that Mina would forgive her. She couldn't believe the same of her father.

Lynet shook her head. "I don't have anything to say."

"That settles it, then," Nicholas said. "I'll make the announcement at your birthday feast."

There was a long pause before Lynet dared to open her eyes, keeping her head down as she peered up at her stepmother. Mina wasn't looking at her anymore, but Lynet could feel her disappointment nonetheless; she could feel it in the fire's punishing heat.

"And when Lynet takes the South, what will I do?" Mina said.

Nicholas shrugged. "You'll still be queen in name."

"The South is *mine,* Nicholas."

"It was never yours to keep." He sighed and rubbed at his forehead. "Please understand that this is not a personal insult to you—"

She laughed dryly. "No? Even when you accused me of trying to rule through her? Or are you just afraid she'll become too much like me and not enough like her mother?"

Nicholas rose from his seat in one movement, but Mina remained still, watching him defiantly.

"Lynet, you can leave now. I want to speak to your stepmother alone."

Lynet stood, looking to Mina uncertainly. She was sure that Mina would understand and forgive her, but she still longed for some reassurance.

But Mina only looked at her coldly and said, "Go, Lynet. I don't need you to protect me."

Lynet heeded her stepmother's command and hurried out of the room.

12

MINA

Mina walked by the lake with Nicholas and Lynet nearly every day, but she felt she was making little progress with the king. They would stroll leisurely while Lynet ran ahead, but the king's worried eyes seldom left his daughter, and their conversations were light and impersonal.

The real challenge, Mina thought, would be to find a way to approach Nicholas alone. As long as Lynet was there to distract him away from her, Mina knew they would never move beyond this casual friendship.

She asked Felix to track the king's movements, to watch for those rare moments when the king was alone. Her chance came at last one morning when she heard a tap at her window. Felix was standing outside, and Mina quickly shut her door before opening the window. "You shouldn't be here," she hissed at him in a whisper.

"The western courtyard," Felix whispered back. "He's there now. Alone."

Mina gripped the window frame to calm herself. The king was alone in the western courtyard—exactly where Mina had first met him. She wasn't sentimental, but she still thought the coincidence boded well for her. "Thank you, Felix," she said. "I'll meet you tonight. Don't linger here."

Felix didn't move, but Mina didn't have time to waste. "Go!" she said again, and this time he obeyed.

Nicholas was sitting on the fountain ledge when Mina arrived at the western courtyard.

"My lord?" Mina said, forcing a note of surprise in her voice.

He tensed at the intrusion, but when he saw Mina, he managed to smile a little.

"I hope I'm not disturbing you," she said.

He stood to greet her. "Not at all. When I'm alone, my thoughts overwhelm me."

"Then I'll have to push them back for you," Mina said, her head bowed. That was one of the tricks she'd learned from their walks together, to speak bold words in a demure manner. Pointing your chin downward encouraged a man to lift it up again. Stumbling while walking invited him to give you his arm. Faltering over words made him listen more closely, his eyes drawn to your lips. Weakness was more enticing than any seduction.

"I must bore you with all my sad talk."

"Not at all. I want to understand. There must be no end of worries for a king, especially without a queen to share them."

"Even after so many years, I—Mina, are you cold? You're shivering." He removed the heavy cloak he was wearing and draped it around her, as she'd hoped he would. Mina kept her head down as he performed his act of gallantry, but as he drew the cloak tight around her neck, she lifted her chin and looked him in the eye. She'd expected him to step back from her, but instead, he remained staring down at her upturned face for another few seconds before letting out a shaky breath and moving away.

That was another trick, to shiver with cold until he noticed. That was the easiest one of all, since she hardly had to fake it.

"I should take you inside, if you're cold," Nicholas said.

"No!" Once he escorted her inside, he'd leave, and she didn't know when she'd have a chance to be alone with him again. "No," she repeated. "I'll be just as cold inside, and I needed a change of scenery."

"A change of scenery, hmm?" he said. "I wouldn't want you to grow bored of Whitespring." He fell silent, and then he held out his hand to her. "Come with me. I'll give you a change of scenery."

Delighted—but careful not to seem too delighted—Mina took his hand. He led her toward the Hall, but then turned down a corridor she hadn't visited before, to a large set of closed doors. He opened one enough to let her in.

Mina gave an involuntary gasp when she walked into the room— *the throne room,* she realized, when she saw two ornate chairs at the opposite end of the room. The cross-vaulted ceilings high above her made her think of a giant rib cage, the click of her shoes on the stone floor echoing against it like a heartbeat. A banner of colorful tiles stretched around the walls; it was a mosaic of the four seasons, a reminder of something long lost. Mina walked in awe until she came to the two grand chairs waiting on a dais at the end of the room. They were identical, carved from the same dark wood.

"That one's mine," Nicholas said, pointing to the chair on the left. "The other is for my queen. It has been empty for some time."

Mina stepped up on the dais. She knew better than to sit in the queen's throne. Any indication that she wanted to replace his beloved Emilia would offend him. Instead, she sat in the king's throne and stared out at the room with a lofty expression.

He laughed and gave an exaggerated bow. "You look better there than I do. Not that I use it often. People are always so eager to leave Whitespring that I hardly have time to impress them with my grand throne room. There's a riddle there, I think: What kind of king rules over such a desolate castle?"

"A stubborn king."

"Do you think so? What would you have me do instead?"

"Move court. Leave this dreary place behind and move south. You could finally finish the Summer Castle. I grew up near there, and I never understood why it was abandoned."

"Oh no, I couldn't do that. This is my home. To move away would be to admit defeat, to give in to Sybil's curse and let her drive us away."

"I've always thought that the North puts too much importance in Sybil. Maybe all you have to do to break the curse is take down her statue and stop revering her so highly. Or maybe this is no place for a king to rule at all, and she was doing you a favor by trying to drive you away."

Nicholas laughed, but he stopped when he noticed that Mina wasn't laughing with him. She'd meant it as a joke, but then she wondered if she might really believe it—maybe not about Nicholas, but about herself.

Nicholas lifted her chin. "What's the matter?"

The truth came to her lips before she could stop it. "Sometimes I think Whitespring doesn't want me here. Sometimes—" *I think it knows what I am*, she continued silently, *and it has rejected me.*

He took her hands and pulled her up from the throne and down from the dais to stand with him. One hand covering hers, he brought the other to her face, and he blinked in shock when his ungloved hand met her flesh, like he'd expected something else. The soft pads of his fingers brushed over the skin of her cheek, her jaw, her neck. Would he notice she had no pulse gently beating beneath her skin? She wanted to flinch away when his fingers reached her throat, but she couldn't bring herself to do it, so she kept still, letting him revel in the feel of something softer than air and warmer than memory.

His hand paused at last on her cheek, his thumb close to her lips. "Whitespring wants you here," he said. "*I* want you here. Every time you shudder from the cold or wrap yourself more tightly in your furs, it reminds me that somewhere, the sun shines more brightly than it does here. You carry it in your skin."

It was so easy to believe him. After all, didn't she currently feel a million suns burning underneath her skin? Didn't she feel them illuminating her from the inside out? Her heart was a mirror, reflecting the rays through her whole body and out from her eyes, desperate to throw its light over Nicholas as well. Unbidden, the truth struck her: *If I could love anyone, it would be him.*

"If it's the sun you long for, why stay? Come to the South, to the hills where I was born, and I'll show you the sun."

His hand dropped from her cheek, and he shook his head. "Because I love the winter, too. The world here is frozen, and so it never changes, and so it is always what I expect it to be. There's a comfort in that. And besides—" He gestured weakly to the queen's throne and let his arm fall again in defeat. And though he didn't say the words, Mina heard them clearly enough: *And besides, how could I leave her?*

Mina was struck with the childish urge to tip the chair over and give it a kick for good measure, but instead she said, "I understand. I wish I knew how to make the sun shine for you again."

"Ah, only one person can do that."

Mina bristled. "Lynet."

The name drew out a smile, but it wasn't for her. "What do I need the sun for, when I have Lynet?"

She'd taken him in the wrong direction. Mina needed to bring him back to her, away from Lynet, away from his dead wife. *How can I make him happy again?* she asked herself, but the reply was merciless: *He doesn't want to be happy.* The times when he had reached out to her—at the picnic and under the juniper tree—had been when he'd seen Mina at her loneliest. If she wanted him to reach out to her again, she would have to give him a piece of her own sadness.

"I wish I'd grown up with a father who loved me as much as you love Lynet," she said. Reminding him of her father was always a risk, but she knew a fragment of the truth would be more effective than a lie, no matter how artfully told.

And she was right. Her sadness drew him back to her. "Oh, Mina," he said. "Is he cruel to you?"

Mina shook her head. "No, not cruel, but—" She faltered, biting her lip. "Nicholas, I—oh, I'm sorry, my lord, I shouldn't have—"

"No, it's fine," he said, bringing his hand to her cheek again. "You may use my name."

"Nicholas, you were right the other day—I *am* lonely. I have no one here, except . . . except for you."

She wore an exquisite expression of pain and longing on her face, one that she'd practiced with Felix. She knew it was effective.

Nicholas was staring at her lips, and then he leaned forward, bringing his head down to hers—

The sound of the heavy door opening made Nicholas draw back like a guilty child. Mina glared at the intruder—Darian, the steward. The old man had lived at Whitespring far longer than anyone else had, and so he was in charge of running the place, perhaps even more so than Nicholas. "Forgive me, my lord," he said. "There was no audience scheduled for the throne room, and yet I heard voices from within. I'm sorry for disturbing you."

"Not at all," Nicholas said, avoiding looking anywhere in Mina's direction. "In fact . . . I . . . wanted to speak with you. Wait there."

He turned to Mina. "I've enjoyed our talk today, and I hope you have as well. I trust you can find your way back to your rooms?"

"Yes, my lord," Mina said quietly. "I won't keep you any longer."

He bowed his head to her in gratitude and hurried away with the steward, leaving Mina alone in the empty throne room.

Mina made a decision that night in the chapel. She went over the events of the day, the conversation in the throne room, thinking of the hidden truths she had told, the lies she had tried to wrap them in. There were lies she had to tell and truths she had to hide, but otherwise, she found herself longing for more moments like the ones they had shared—moments when she had revealed something true to him, something real.

If anyone could love me, it would be him.

She had tried to use pretense to win him, but in the end, she always slipped and let a little of the truth seep through—and when she did, he responded with warmth, with kindness. *If he marries me,* Mina decided, *I'll tell him the truth about my heart. I'll tell him on my wedding night.*

She waited for Felix, but she had something difficult to tell him tonight, and so she felt none of the usual excitement as he appeared in the chapel doorway.

"Thank you for telling me where to find him," Mina said, offering him a smile when he was at her side.

"I wish I hadn't," Felix said. "I did exactly what you told me to, but I wish I had disobeyed you." He shook his head. "I watch him for you, day after day, and when we meet, we only talk about *him*. Sometimes, when I'm watching him, I think I hate him."

"Felix—"

"And you—" He placed his hand against her cheek, tracing her cheekbone with his thumb. "I see how badly you want him. I saw it on your face today. And even though you're happy, I—I feel something different."

Mina removed his hand from her face and kissed his palm, rougher now and more callused than when she had first made it. "Are you angry with me?"

He thought a moment, trying to understand feelings that were for once his own. "No," he said. "I feel . . . sadness. Loneliness. That's the part I don't understand—the less lonely you feel, the lonelier I become. That's not the way it should be."

She smiled sadly at him. "I wanted to say good-bye, Felix."

"Good-bye?"

"I can't see you like this anymore."

"It's because of him, isn't it?"

"Yes. I want to be myself with him, or at least I want to try. You're too big a secret to keep."

He shook his head. "I wouldn't tell—"

"I know," she said. She wrapped her arms around his neck and laid her head against his chest. Perhaps she was starting to reflect *him* now—she could feel his sadness. "I know, my darling, but I can't be true to him and keep you at the same time. I don't want to practice love anymore—I want to try to feel it. I'm sorry," she said, pressing one last kiss to his lips. "But I have to send you back."

He pulled back from her suddenly. "Send me back where?" he said, his voice harsh. "Into your mirror, where I can only watch you from a distance?"

Mina didn't understand why he was reacting like this at first, but then she took in his huntsman's uniform, his scuffed boots, and the small tear on his right sleeve. He had a fresh scar on the back of his hand. Mina had forgotten that he had experiences of his own now, a life beyond this chapel, beyond her use for him. He had become too human to be only a mirror; to turn him back into glass now would be a kind of murder.

"I'm sorry," she said. He seemed new to her, and she wanted to touch him again, to understand the person he had become in the past three years. But she was afraid that if she did, she might not be able to leave him here, as she knew she must. He had no heart to offer her, and she wanted something more than glass. "I won't send you back," she assured him. "But you mustn't try to see me again."

Felix didn't respond. He simply watched her with that endless gaze, and even when she turned her back on him and walked out of the chapel, she thought she could still feel the force of those unblinking, empty eyes.

13

LYNET

Lynet was beginning to regret her choice to sit outside the door and listen as Mina and Nicholas argued. But it was better to know than to sit in her room and wonder.

"You made a decision that concerns me," Mina was saying, her voice low with rage, "without even telling me."

"I didn't tell you," Nicholas answered, "because I knew you would tell Lynet. Despite my best efforts, you hold a considerable amount of influence over my daughter. I know you would have turned her against me, just as you've always tried to turn her against her mother."

The silence that fell over them now was even worse than the arguing, and Lynet rested her forehead against her knees, bracing herself.

"You don't know the first thing about your daughter," Mina said. "She never cared about her mother, not from the beginning."

Lynet lifted her head in surprise. *No, she's not supposed to tell him that.* These were secrets that they had shared, secrets she could never tell her father.

"You're just trying to hurt me now," Nicholas said softly.

"No, *she's* the one who's always trying *not* to hurt you. She doesn't want you to know how little she cares about Emilia. How could she? She never even knew her. She's never missed her, never loved her, never wanted to be anything like her."

"Mina—"

"Emilia isn't even her mother—"

"*That's enough!*" Nicholas roared. "And if you dare tell her . . ."

Lynet held her breath. Mina had already told one of her secrets—how could she be sure she wouldn't tell all of them?

But Mina just gave a brittle laugh. "I'm not that cruel."

"No? You're your father's daughter, aren't you?"

Another silence. "It's lucky for you, Nicholas, that I'm not," Mina said, her voice so quiet that Lynet could barely make out the words.

Lynet heard footsteps approaching the door, so she quickly scurried down the hall, turning into another corridor where she would be safe from view.

And now where should she go first? To Mina? To her father? The cracks in her family that had been spreading for so many years were finally starting to break open, creating a rift that was becoming too wide for her to hold together anymore. Even if she mustered the courage to go speak to her father and tell him she had changed her mind, he would probably think it was Mina's doing. But she had to believe that she could still apologize and explain herself to Mina and repair some of the damage that she had created.

A few minutes later, Lynet knocked softly at Mina's door. There was no response. There was no light coming from under the door, either, but Lynet knew Mina couldn't possibly be asleep already. She frowned at the door for a moment, and then she had an idea about where Mina might be.

She knew she was right when she saw a thin stream of light from under the chapel door. Inside, Mina was sitting under the central altar, a candle by her side. Bundled in her furs, her hair streaming down her back, she seemed very small.

"Mina?" Lynet said. She whispered it, but her voice echoed, and Mina jumped a little at the sound.

"Come sit by me," Mina said.

Lynet treaded carefully, feeling like she shouldn't make any noise, like she shouldn't be there at all. She sat on the floor beside her stepmother. "Mina, I didn't—"

But when Mina looked at her, waiting for whatever pitiful explanation she would offer, Lynet understood how pointless her words were now. She felt a flash of resentment toward her father, because she knew that it was for his sake that she had turned on Mina with her silence. She had done it because she knew it was an opportunity to make him happy, and it was so difficult to make him happy. But she had chosen her father's happiness over Mina's because she thought she could take her stepmother's forgiveness for granted, and she knew that wasn't fair at all. If she wanted to speak her feelings, she should have spoken before, in front of her father. Anything she said now would only add to the insult of her earlier silence.

In the end, it was Mina who spoke. "It's the way of things, I suppose," she said. "I think I suspected something like this might happen once I noticed how much you'd grown. As long as you were still a child, I was young, I was safe . . . but now that you're older, there's no use for me anymore."

"That's not true," Lynet said at once.

Mina gave her a sad smile. "You'll see too, one day. Once you grow older, someone else will be waiting to take your place, someone younger and prettier than you. I knew that day was approaching for me. I knew even when you were still a child. So why am I so surprised to learn that I'm being thrown aside? Why am I always so surprised?"

Lynet reached for her hand. "I would never throw you aside!"

Mina raised an eyebrow. "No? You say that now, but time could change your mind. And what about your father's commands? He doesn't want me close to you." Mina took hold of Lynet's hand now, grasping her tightly by the wrist. "Are you bold enough to defy your father, wolf cub?"

Mina's grip was tight, but more alarming was the desperation in her voice, the pleading in her eyes. Lynet had never thought she would ever see Mina like this, but then, she had never seen Mina on the brink of losing something so important to her.

Lynet met her stepmother's gaze but tried not to let it swallow her whole. "What do you want me to do?"

Mina's grip relaxed now. "Tell him the truth—that you don't want the South."

Lynet swallowed. "I don't know if I can change his mind, even if I speak to him."

"You can if you find the right words to say. Your father doesn't want you to be unhappy. He loves you. How hard can it be to persuade him to do what you want?"

Lynet finally tore her wrist away. How hard could it be? Lynet knew well enough that her father had certain expectations for her, and that he wouldn't give them up easily. "Mina, I don't know. . . ."

"Do you want to rule the South?"

"I . . . no, I don't."

The light of the candle flashed in Mina's eyes. "Then we both want the same thing. Didn't I promise you that I would never let anyone turn you into your mother? If you let your father groom you for the throne while he's still alive, that is exactly what he will do."

The familiar restlessness was coming over her as she heard the truth in her stepmother's words. This was her choice, then—she couldn't make both her father and her stepmother happy, but if she chose her father, then there was the possibility that she would lose herself, lose everything that made her feel like her own person. The answer seemed obvious, and yet she still hesitated.

Mina's voice pierced through the silence. "What are you afraid of, Lynet?"

"I'm not afraid," Lynet said, the words tumbling out before she could stop them. "I'll do it. I'll talk to him."

Mina wrapped her arms around Lynet and pulled her close. Lynet found being ensconced in Mina's furs almost unbearably warm, but she clung to her stepmother, searching for comfort even as she tried to give it. After all those years of trying not to hear Mina and her father fighting and trying not to notice the way the Pigeons talked about her, only now did Lynet allow herself to acknowledge that perhaps her beautiful, self-assured stepmother was as uncertain as she was. No wonder, then, that Mina was so desperate not to lose her last connection to her home—it was a piece of her, as surely as Mina was a piece of Lynet. And so maybe for once, Lynet could help Mina the way Mina had always helped her. She would tell her father she wasn't ready for his offer, and he would concede, even if he didn't understand, and Mina would be happy, and maybe they could all go back to the way they were before.

"Thank you, wolf cub," Mina said before she pulled away.

Lynet felt a fierce need to protect her stepmother, to earn the pet name Mina had given her so long ago. If she couldn't tell her father what she wanted for her own sake, at least she could do it for

Mina's. "Nothing will come between us," Lynet said. "I promise." She took Mina's hand and pressed it gently.

Mina returned the gesture, but there was still doubt in her eyes, in the corners of her weary smile, and she mouthed something low and nearly inaudible as she started to stand. Lynet couldn't make out the words exactly, but she thought she heard Mina say, *I hope you're right.*

Lynet awoke on the morning of her birthday to the barking of the dogs, excited for the hunt. She climbed out of bed and went to her window, craning her neck to see the dogs gathered at the castle gates, along with the rest of the hunting party on their horses. Her father was there, as well as the head huntsman, the one with the empty eyes. Lynet quickly pulled her head back inside the window; she didn't want either of them to see her.

Lynet suffered through her lessons for the day, though her stitching was even worse than usual, and she kept forgetting the dates and names of Whitespring's prior rulers that she was supposed to memorize. She was too occupied trying to decide what she would say to her father and imagining his reactions.

He still wasn't back later in the afternoon when her lessons were finished, so she went down to the workroom to see Nadia. She took her usual place, piling journals at one end of the table, but at this point, she was sure she knew as much as Master Jacob had known, and it still wasn't enough. She kept fidgeting on her stool, flipping through the pages with a jittery restlessness. How soon until her father came back? How soon until she had to disappoint him? If she couldn't convince him not to give her the South, would Mina believe that she had tried her hardest? Would she lose both of them?

Firm hands came down over hers, stilling her frantic movements, and she looked up at Nadia, who was standing over her with a curious frown. "What's wrong?" she said. It was the first time Nadia had touched her since the tower, and so Lynet knew she must be worried.

Lynet didn't want to deny that something was wrong. She couldn't go to Mina this time, not when Mina was part of the problem—and she had no one else to confide in. "My father wants me to rule the South," she blurted out, and then she told the rest.

When she was finished, Nadia leaned an arm on the back of Lynet's chair, thinking. "So your father wants you to take the South," she said, "and your stepmother wants you to talk him out of it."

"Correct," Lynet said, folding her hands in her lap and looking up as she waited for Nadia's solution. Even with all her turmoil, part of her was just happy they were speaking to each other normally again. "What does the court surgeon suggest I do?"

Nadia smiled a little. "The court surgeon recommends a dose of self-interest."

Lynet shook her head. "I don't understand."

"You've told me what your father and stepmother want, but what about you?" Her hand moved from the back of the chair to rest on Lynet's shoulder, and for a moment Lynet could only stare at it before her eyes traveled from Nadia's hand up her arm to meet her waiting gaze. "What do *you* want?" Nadia continued, her voice a little lower than before.

"I . . . I don't know. I want them both to be happy," Lynet said, her throat dry.

Nadia removed her hand. "I mean, what do you want for your future?"

Lynet didn't know what to say. She didn't know how to explain that she always tried not to think about her future, because when she looked into it, she couldn't see herself anymore. In the end, it didn't matter whether or not she took her father's offer now—she would replace Mina and become queen eventually, and when she did, she would become her mother. That was her purpose, to resurrect the dead and die a little in the process.

The itching under her skin was back, but this time just climbing out a window wouldn't be enough.

"Let's run away," she said, spinning around in her chair.

Nadia laughed in surprise. "What?"

Lynet stood, so that they would be face-to-face. "You want to go south to the university anyway, don't you? Let's go now, together."

She was flushed with excitement, practically rocking on her feet with the urge to *go*, to leave Whitespring and all her troubles behind. She didn't understand why Nadia was frowning at her like that, why she was shaking her head.

"You can't just *leave*."

"Yes, I can. People do it all the time. Why is everyone else allowed to come and go as they please except for me? We can go to the university, just like you planned."

"*No*," she said, and Lynet was startled by the harshness in her voice. Nadia seemed startled too, because she shook her head and added in a softer tone, "I mean . . . it's a long journey, even a dangerous one. The roads aren't always smooth, and there are thieves who hide in the woods. You've never even been outside the castle."

Lynet bristled as she understood Nadia's meaning, her hands twisting at her skirt as she tried to keep composed. "You're saying I'm not strong enough to survive outside Whitespring," she said. "You don't think of me any differently than the rest of them do. You think I'm too delicate to survive anything."

Nadia wouldn't look her in the eye. "Lynet—" She was interrupted by a furious pounding at the door, and she ran to answer it while Lynet tried to make herself small and invisible.

Nadia opened the door, and Lynet heard a man's voice say, "You're needed at once. The king's had an accident."

14

MINA

"I want to ask you something," Nicholas said.

"Of course, my lord." Mina tried to keep her voice low—a difficult task, since Lynet was splashing her hands in the freezing lake. Mina had been worried that he would try to avoid her after their tryst in the throne room, but soon afterward, he invited her on another lakeside stroll—with Lynet as chaperone, of course.

"I'd like to invite you to dine with me tomorrow night, somewhere more private than the Great Hall."

Mina was glad he wasn't watching her; she couldn't help a satisfied smile. "I'd be honored, my lord."

He finally turned to her. "I don't want you to be honored. I want you to be pleased." His voice was gruff, but from the flicker of worry in his eye, he seemed genuinely concerned.

Now Mina allowed him to see her smile. "I'd be pleased, then. I . . . I enjoy our time together."

"As do I," he said. "And so does—"

But he didn't need to finish the sentence: his eyes went straight to Lynet, who was now nearly waist-deep in the lake.

"Lynet!" he called. "Don't go so far into the water!"

Lynet stared at him for a moment, and then she went right back to splashing in the lake.

"Lynet, I won't ask again."

This time, Lynet ignored her father completely.

Nicholas sighed. "She's always testing her limits." He went to retrieve his daughter, lifting her from the lakeside and carrying her away.

Lynet didn't respond well; she started thrashing like an angry cat, kicking her feet in protest as she tore at her own hair.

Mina watched this entire display with fascination. Would Nicholas scold her for her disobedience? Would he punish her in front of Mina, or would he wait until later? What form would his anger at his daughter take?

But Nicholas just laughed at her tantrum. It was the first time Mina remembered ever hearing him laugh, making it all the more unexpected. "My little bird is trying to fly away," he said, tightening his hold on Lynet playfully, "but I know she wouldn't want to make her father sad. Isn't that right?"

His words seemed to placate her, or maybe she was just exhausted from fighting so hard. She shook her head.

"Well, then she should do what her father says. But first, she should give him a kiss." He gave her his cheek, and Lynet pressed her lips against it noisily.

Mina observed them with a growing resentment she didn't understand. She hadn't wanted to see Lynet punished, exactly, but now she kept wondering *why*. Why wasn't he punishing her, when other fathers would? Why did Lynet deserve to have that luxury when so many others didn't? But there was no reason; there was only Lynet's squeal of delight and her father's look of devotion as he set her down.

"I think it's time for you to go back inside anyway," he said to Lynet. "I have to meet with the council shortly."

Lynet clutched her father's leg and shook her head. "Stay."

"I can't stay, and so neither can you," he said fondly, ruffling her hair.

"Mina can stay."

Father and daughter both looked at Mina at the same time, one uncertain, the other hopeful. Mina didn't know how to answer— she didn't want Nicholas to think she was overstepping her bounds, but if he decided to trust her with Lynet's care, that would speak a great deal to his opinion of her. "Only if you'd allow it, my lord," she said. "I'd be happy to watch over her for a little longer and see her to her room." The words slipped out so easily that she didn't even wonder if they were true.

Nicholas deliberated briefly, then nodded. "All right, Lynet, you can play a little longer, and then Mina will take you back inside." As Lynet let out a high-pitched cheer and ran toward the trees, stumbling over her small feet, Nicholas said to Mina, "Not much longer, though. I don't want her to tire herself."

Mina didn't say that Lynet seemed to have enough energy to play for hours. "I'll watch over her very carefully, my lord."

"I must go now," Nicholas said. "But I'll send someone for you tomorrow evening."

Yes, that was right—he had invited her to see him the next evening. "Until tomorrow, then, my lord," she said.

"You called me Nicholas last time we spoke," he said softly. "I wish you would do so again."

"Until tomorrow, Nicholas," Mina murmured.

He watched her a moment longer, and then he stepped toward her and said, "I'm looking forward to tomorrow."

There was no foresight or guile when Mina smiled—she simply smiled because his words had made her happy. And even when he left, she was still happy. He had invited her to see him, not because Lynet had asked or because he felt duty-bound, but because he wanted to see her. He wanted *her*.

Mina wandered closer to the garden to keep better watch over Lynet, who was running in circles around the trees and shouting to some invisible friend or enemy, Mina wasn't sure which.

Mina was tense, her arms crossed, ears ringing from Lynet's shouting. Now that Nicholas was gone, she had no reason to pretend to herself that she wanted to watch over a spoiled child whose father never punished her for anything. How nice it must be for Lynet to live in a world where *father* was only ever a happy word, to play at fighting imaginary threats, because she had never known any real ones.

And just as she was thinking that it was only a matter of time before Lynet's perfect world shattered, she saw Lynet trip over one of the tree's roots and tumble to the ground.

Mina rushed toward her at once, hoping that Lynet hadn't hurt herself in a way that would be apparent to her father. She kept waiting to hear Lynet cry or scream, but Lynet was silent, hugging her right leg close to her. "Let me see, Lynet," Mina said, and Lynet stuck her leg out to show her the small scrape on her knee from the tree root. Her face was pinched, her lips quivering, but she still didn't cry or make any sound. Mina didn't understand it—she'd thought Lynet would be wailing by now, running to her father to fix all her problems—

And then she realized—if Nicholas knew about this mishap, he probably wouldn't allow her to play outside again for at least a week. Lynet must have already learned this during her few short years, and so she had trained herself not to cry or shout or show pain at all. Mina had come to consider Lynet a pampered, fragile creature, but now she remembered the way she had first found her, perched up in a tree, the king not there to keep her in check. Maybe Mina had been right to give her the name "wolf cub." Maybe Lynet was more resilient than she looked.

"Don't worry, Lynet," Mina said gently. "I won't tell your father about this if you don't want me to." That was an instinct Mina could understand, something she could share with Lynet at last.

Lynet seemed to relax now. She didn't flinch when Mina cleaned her knee with snow, and when Mina suggested it was time to go back inside, she hopped to her feet and put her small hand in Mina's.

The two of them walked at a child's pace back to the courtyard. Lynet rambled on, and Mina tried to follow her sudden changes in topic and her mumbled words. Among other things, Mina learned that Lynet hated wearing shoes and that one of her teeth was loose. But Mina was glad she had agreed to stay with her. Something about Lynet's carefree youth made Whitespring seem a little less dour and gloomy.

"Mina!"

Mina's hand tightened on Lynet's when she heard Gregory's voice behind them just as they were nearing the east wing entrance. She knew Nicholas wouldn't want Gregory near Lynet—and Gregory should have known that too. So why was he taking such a risk in approaching them? Should she tell Lynet to go the rest of the way on her own?

But now Gregory had already hurried across the courtyard to join them. Mina held tight to Lynet's hand as he peered down at Lynet with great interest. Lynet, to her credit, was trying to hide behind Mina, away from his gaze.

"She's perfect," Gregory breathed. "Do you know who I am, child? My name is Gregory."

"Lynet, do you know the rest of the way back?" Mina said, not taking her eyes off her father. She hadn't considered that Gregory would have any interest in a child, but now she remembered that Lynet wasn't just any child to him—she was his creation. *So am I,* she thought, but then again, she was a failure. Her bloodless heart was of no more interest to him than one of his sand mice. Lynet, though—Lynet was unique.

"Yes," Lynet said, her voice muffled by Mina's dress.

"Then I want you to go now. Go all the way back to your room and don't stop. Can you do that?"

Lynet didn't bother to answer. She let go of Mina's hand and scurried inside. Mina kept watching until she was safely out of view.

When she turned back to Gregory, his eyes were still locked on the empty space where Lynet had been.

"You shouldn't have done that," Mina said to him. "What if the king saw you?"

There was a flash of anger in his eyes, but then it passed, and he nodded in concession. "It was reckless of me, I know. I wasn't thinking. But I saw you both passing by, and I . . . I couldn't resist the opportunity."

"She was scared of you, didn't you see?" Mina said. She thought she would take pleasure in the wounded look on his face, but instead, she felt something closer to pain. She didn't understand why she should be jealous, but all Mina could think was that he had never cared when *she* was scared of him.

Gregory scratched his jaw, thinking. "Yes, she did seem frightened of me, didn't she? I'm a stranger to her, thanks to the king." His eyes narrowed with contempt. "Doesn't it seem unfair to you that I should be a stranger to the girl I made with my own hands?"

He continued to glare at the empty space in front of him, and Mina stared at her father's profile with growing dread. "What do you want with her?" she said in a whisper. "Why is she so important to you?"

Gregory shook his head at her, seemingly confused by the question. "Isn't it natural that I should want to know her better? Any father would ask the same."

Mina decided she'd had enough of his sudden paternal feeling for someone else's child, and she stormed across the courtyard, away from him. So this was another reason Gregory was so eager to see Mina be queen, why he had insisted on moving to Whitespring in the first place. He wanted Lynet. He wanted to be a *father* to Lynet. Let him have her, then, Mina decided. What did it matter to her?

Still, when she returned to her rooms, she thought of Lynet's tiny hand grasping hers, of the understanding they had shared over her scrape, and her harsh thoughts melted away. She remembered how scared Lynet had been of Gregory, and she wondered if the only real way to protect Lynet was to remove herself and her father from the girl's life entirely. But was she willing to make that sacrifice?

Mina pushed the thought aside and went to her bedroom; she had to decide what to wear tomorrow when she saw the king.

15

MINA

At the appointed hour, a servant arrived at Mina's room to take her to the king in his private dining room. She wore her hair loose, without any ornament. Tonight she would have no designs, no artifice. She would go to him as the young woman that she was, and she would prove without doubt that Nicholas could love her for herself.

The servant led her to the end of a hall where two large doors were flanked by the king's guards, and Mina felt like a bride being taken to her husband. *Soon,* she thought. *Soon it will come true.*

The guards opened the doors for her, and she floated over the threshold, only to be met with a ghost.

But no, it couldn't be a ghost, because ghosts were of the past and this was a vision of the future, of Lynet as a woman. On the opposite wall, above an enormous lit fireplace, was a large portrait of the dead queen. Even though she'd heard plenty of times about the resemblance between the princess and her mother—and even though she knew the real reason why—she hadn't been prepared to see the truth of it with her own eyes. She felt she might suffocate under the pressure of this once and future ghost, this woman who was dead and yet alive.

"Admiring my queen?" Nicholas asked.

She'd been so startled by the portrait that she hadn't noticed Nicholas standing at one end of a long banquet table in front of the fireplace. A hearty northern meal of venison awaited them at the table, and Mina briefly wondered if Felix had been the one to bring down this deer.

"Good evening, Nicholas," she said, ignoring his question.

He held the chair out for her, waiting for her to take her seat before moving to his own at the other end of the table. They ate in near silence, with Mina commenting every so often on the meal, or Nicholas offering her more wine. All the while, Queen Emilia stared down at them, watching as they ate. Mina shifted in her seat, trying to put the portrait out of her view. Something was troubling the king tonight, but Mina didn't know if it had anything to do with her. A king could have any number of reasons to be troubled, after all.

When they were finished eating, Nicholas rose from the table and went to the fireplace, standing with his back to Mina, his hands clasped behind him. "You're quiet tonight," he said softly.

Mina almost laughed. "Only because you seem so thoughtful. I didn't want to interrupt your own private contemplation." He nodded, and Mina could see only his profile, shadowed against the flames. "I wish I knew what you were thinking," she said, letting herself speak with more honesty than she'd usually dare.

He turned to her, and they studied each other, though Mina didn't know what either one of them was looking for. "I was thinking of Lynet," Nicholas said, "of what is best for her."

Mina forced herself not to react, though her eyes couldn't help flickering up to the portrait above Nicholas's head. "And what have you decided?"

He walked to the table with a heavy step, coming to stand at Mina's side. He reached down and wrapped a lock of Mina's hair around his fingers. Mina sat perfectly still, hardly breathing.

Nicholas dropped the lock of hair and looked her in the eye. "I spoke with Lynet this morning," he said. "She seemed troubled, disturbed by something. When I asked her if something had happened after I left her with you yesterday, she became quiet, almost fearful. After much questioning, I found out that she met your father."

Mina felt the blood draining from her face. She thought frantically, but she ended up telling the truth. "I couldn't prevent it," she whispered. "I was taking her to her room when he stopped us."

Nicholas inhaled deeply and then walked back to the fireplace. "I keep trying to forget who you are, who your father is, but I was only fooling myself."

The resignation in his tone frightened her, her skin prickling with worry. "What do you mean?"

Without looking at her, he said, "We shouldn't continue to see each other alone anymore. You and your father will continue to live at court, of course, but our interaction will be kept at a minimum."

Mina stood from the table. "Nicholas, I—" He turned toward her, and she took a faltering step before beginning to sink to the ground. She was fine, of course—shaken, but not unable to walk—but she wanted Nicholas to come to her. He did at once, bounding toward her before she could touch the ground and holding her up in his arms, and Mina remembered how she had wanted to be herself tonight, without any tricks or games. She'd already failed.

"Do you need to sit?"

"No," Mina said, holding on to his arms to keep herself upright.

"No, it's fine, I just . . . don't understand. Have I done something wrong?"

"No, Mina, of course not. It isn't your fault." He looked away from her. "But your father—"

"I'm not my father."

Nicholas still wouldn't look at her, and the time for timidity had passed, so she put her cold hands in his. "Mina, I can't . . ."

"Please. Please just look at me."

He turned to face her, and she was relieved that he seemed as devastated by this decision as she was. She couldn't accept that she had come this far only to lose him now. "Nicholas," she said, "all my childhood, people have hated me because of my father, because of his powers. I can't stand to think that even you would hate me because of *him*. Hate me for some other reason, but not that one."

Nicholas shook his head. "I don't hate you, Mina, but I—" He stopped, frowning, and for a moment, there was no sound but the crackling of the fire. His eyes hardened, and his hands tightened around hers. "You know about Lynet, don't you?"

Mina didn't know how to answer—she didn't know which answer he wanted to hear—but her hesitation *was* an answer, and Nicholas let go of her hands and backed away from her. "He promised me he wouldn't tell anyone, but he told you, didn't he? *Didn't he?*"

"I won't lie to you," Mina said. The sweetness was gone from her voice, and she no longer pretended to be faint. The time for lying was over. She had to shift her footing, as though balancing on a very high wall that had suddenly started to crumble. If she was careful, she might still not fall. "Yes, I know. I know and I've never once told anyone. I would never tell anyone, least of all Lynet."

He turned away from her, toward the fire—toward Emilia. She knew she would lose him if he kept looking at the queen instead of her. "Nicholas, listen to me," she said to his retreating back. "I wasn't lying when I said I was lonely here. My father is not a good man. He cares little for me, and I've always known it. In the years I've been at court, you've shown me nothing but kindness, especially when I needed it most. Is it so hard to believe that I would feel some . . . affection toward you? That I would want to be near you whenever I could? I'm no pawn in my father's games. I . . . I wanted you for myself, not for his sake. Please—" She stopped, nearly breathless. She had never known that honesty could be so exhausting.

But Nicholas wasn't moved by her confession. He kept his back to her, shaking his head slowly. "I almost asked you to marry me tonight," he said in a low voice.

She grabbed the back of her chair for balance, but now she actually needed it. "What did you say?"

"That was why I invited you here. I was planning to ask you to marry me."

Mina took a steady breath. "And do you still want to ask me?"

Nicholas shook his dark head. "I'm not sure. Sometimes I don't think I should remarry at all."

Mina's fingers curled around the back of the chair, her nails scratching tiny marks in the wood. She had taken off every piece of armor she had, stripped away every lie and pretense, and she was still going to lose him because of her father. She had tried being the sad, lonely girl who needed rescue, and she had tried being herself, as much as she dared. What else could she do to make him want her? What else did she have to offer him?

She heard her father's voice in her mind, a quiet reassurance: *He can't content himself with a memory forever. Soon he'll want solid flesh, and that is something you have that the old queen no longer does.*

He was still facing the portrait, his beloved dead queen whom he could only love from afar. Mina let go of the chair and went to him.

Even if she offended him now, at least he would refuse her on her own merit rather than her father's. She pressed herself against his back, draping her arms around his shoulders, and he let out a small, surprised gasp. "Nicholas," she murmured, "I don't want to lose you."

He disentangled himself from her arms and turned to her. As long as he stopped looking at that portrait, Mina thought she might still have a chance.

"Do I look like my father?" she said, turning her face toward the light.

He managed a single breathless laugh. "Certainly not."

"Then what do you see when you look at me?"

He swallowed. "Mina—"

"Do you find me beautiful?"

He started to turn away again, so Mina took his hand and brought it to rest against her cheek. "In the throne room that day, you touched my face, like this. I think you wanted to kiss me. Nothing has changed between us now."

After loving a ghost for so long, he seemed to marvel at the feel of her skin under his hand. He was warmer than Felix—softer, too, and she wondered if his touch could transform her from glass to flesh.

"We've both been lonely, haven't we?" Mina said, and she wasn't sure if she was still playing a part or if she was speaking truthfully now.

He was playing with her hair, letting the strands fall between his fingers. "Yes, at times," he said so quietly Mina could barely hear him. "I didn't think I would marry again, but . . ."

He leaned forward, just slightly, and Mina had to stop herself from pulling him to her in one move. Instead, she thought of Felix, and went up on her toes to place a single kiss below his jaw, where she could feel the heavy heartbeat underneath his skin.

That simple moment of contact seemed to break whatever self-control he was still clinging to, and he pulled Mina to him, his mouth pressing down on hers.

If she had known that all she had to do was kiss him first, she would have done it a long time ago.

He pushed her away suddenly, turning his back on the portrait and Mina both as he ran his hands through his hair. When he faced her again, his eyes flashed with defiance. "Marry me," he said.

The words sounded so sweet to her that Mina wanted to hear them again. And she waited long enough that she did.

He stormed toward her, pulling her to him with one arm around her waist. "I don't care about your father. I want you to marry me. Will you be my wife and my queen?"

Mina let out a shaky laugh. "I will, with all my heart."

He kissed her again, and then he just held her close, like someone might try to take her away from him. But Mina had fought so hard for this moment that she knew nothing could loosen her hold now. She clung to him in relief, her lips grazing his neck, but then she felt his heart pounding against her chest, and she quickly put some space between them, worried he would notice that she didn't have a heartbeat of her own. She would have to be careful not to let any embraces linger too long.

Nicholas kissed her temple. "One more thing," he said. "We have to tell Lynet."

"Now? Isn't it late for us to go to her?" Mina said.

He released her and strode toward the door. "Gossip moves quickly, and I don't want her to hear it from anyone but me." Nicholas sent for his daughter, and then he turned back to Mina, his expression serious. "You understand, of course, that I can't allow Lynet to become too attached to you. I don't want your father to be alone with her, and if that means that you'll have to keep her at a distance, then so be it."

"Of course," Mina said. She would have been a fool to say otherwise, no matter what fondness she had for the girl.

When Lynet arrived, eyes a little red from sleep but still bright and curious, Nicholas stood by Mina. He looked at her, and then at his daughter, and he took a step forward. He cleared his throat and said, "We have something to tell you, Lynet." He paused, probably wishing that Lynet would piece the news together and announce it herself to spare him the effort. When she didn't, he continued: "You're going to be a queen one day. You know that, don't you?"

Lynet solemnly nodded her head.

"But until that day comes, this kingdom needs a queen, and that means I . . . I have to marry again. Do you understand?"

She nodded again, her eyes darting to Mina.

"Mina and I are going to be married," Nicholas finally said.

Lynet looked directly at Mina now and tried to hide a smile. "You're going to marry my papa?"

"I am," Mina said.

"Does that mean you'll be my mama?"

Mina started to speak, but Nicholas descended on Lynet, going to one knee in front of her. "Listen to me, Lynet. Just because I'm marrying again doesn't mean I'm trying to replace your mother." He gestured to the portrait. "*That's* your mama, and she always will be. Mina is going to be your *stepmother*."

Lynet's lower lip started to jut forward, but she stopped it before it could become a pout. She looked pleadingly over her father's shoulder at Mina.

But Mina had already made her choice. "Your father is right," she said.

Lynet shuffled closer to Mina, staring up at her with those eyes she'd inherited from her mother—but the truth was that she had no mother, except for the snow. Maybe some part of her understood that, and that was why she wasn't willing to give Mina up so easily. Lynet carefully wrapped her arms around Mina's waist, laying her head against Mina's stomach.

Nicholas was watching them, waiting to see how Mina would respond. And despite the girl's arms around her waist, Mina felt a fierce stab of resentment toward her for making such a gesture in the first place and endangering Mina's precarious new position. She hung on to that resentment, irrational as it was. She would need it to do what she had to do next.

Mina gently drew the girl away from her. Nicholas nodded his approval, and Mina focused on that rather than on the dejected slump of Lynet's shoulders. Nicholas took Lynet's hand to lead her away, and Mina kept her eyes on him rather than on Lynet's bowed head. If ever there was a time to be heartless, it was now.

16

LYNET

The king's had an accident.

Lynet knew that could mean any number of things, that there was no reason to think anything terrible had happened, but she *knew* from the sudden numbness in her fingertips she should expect the worst.

"Is it—" Nadia started to say, but then her head moved just barely in Lynet's direction and she simply nodded. "I'll come at once."

The moment Nadia turned to get her surgeon's bag, Lynet pushed past her and ran out the door. "Lynet, wait!" she heard Nadia calling after her, but she couldn't wait. The truth couldn't be as terrible as what she was imagining, and so she needed to know the truth at once.

The courtyard was crowded with people, most of them gathered around a few men in riding habits—noblemen who'd accompanied the king on his hunt. In the low rumble of the crowd, Lynet made out the words *stag* and *blood,* but she didn't want to hear any exaggerated reports—she wanted to see her father.

Still, she stood frozen on the edge of the crowd, unsure how she would make her way through it without anyone stopping her. Desperately, she looked up: maybe if she scaled the walls, no one would notice, and she would get to her father's rooms faster.

She jumped as a hand came around her waist. Nadia had caught up with her, and she didn't say anything as she ushered Lynet through the crowd, shielding her from curious eyes.

Mina was already there when they reached her father's rooms, alone except for the scarred huntsman. There was blood on his hands and forearms, the flash of red drawing Lynet's attention at once.

Mina staggered and put one hand on the huntsman's arm to keep herself upright. It was the sight of her stepmother, ashen and disoriented, that made Lynet lose what remaining composure she had.

"Where is he?" Lynet ran forward, not caring about her fear of the huntsman. "What happened?" She took hold of his arm and decided she wouldn't let go until he told her. "Please."

He looked to the queen, but she hardly seemed to notice Lynet at all. "An accident," he said to Lynet. "A stag."

Lynet ran toward the door of the bedchamber, not waiting to hear more. *He's dead. He's dead like my mother, he's left me to be with her, he's dead, he's dead.* But before she'd reached the door, strong arms held her back. "Let go of me," Lynet choked out. She fell to her knees, and only then did she see that it was not the huntsman, but Mina, who was holding her.

"Let the surgeon attend to him first, and then you can go in," Mina was saying. *Surgeon. Because he was torn open. Because he's dead.* Nadia would know. Nadia would tell her. She was speaking quietly with the huntsman, but when Lynet tried to catch her eye, she turned her head away.

"He's dead," Lynet said, the words repeating over and over again in her mind. *He's dead, he's dead, like her.*

"He's not dead." Mina put her hands on Lynet's shoulders. "Listen to me. He's lost a lot of blood, but he's not dead."

Nadia cleared her throat, gesturing to the door that Lynet and Mina were blocking. "I'll do what I can to help," she said.

"Go, then," Mina commanded, and when Mina commanded, anyone would obey.

Nadia hurried inside the room, shutting the door quickly behind her. Lynet wanted to follow, but Mina was still holding her.

"So he's alive," Lynet said, testing the words, finding them so much sweeter than her previous refrain. *He's alive, he's alive.*

"He's alive for now," Mina said with a mix of sadness and relief.

"For now? But he—but you said—"

"His wounds were severe. The stag gored him. He may not be with us much longer."

It didn't make sense to her. There was dead, and there was alive, but Lynet didn't know what to do with anything in between.

"Lynet, do you understand what I'm saying?"

"But he's not dead," Lynet insisted. She just needed to explain to Mina that she was wrong. *Mama* was dead, but Papa was alive. That was how it had always been. "He can't die."

"Anyone can die," Mina murmured.

She stood, becoming again the queen that Lynet knew so well. Lynet didn't know how to put herself back together as quickly as Mina; she stayed where she was on the floor, part of her believing that if she just waited here long enough, her father would come walking out through the door, alive and whole. Mina gave a slight nod to the huntsman, and he returned it and walked out of the room, leaving them alone.

Mina slowly paced around the room in silence. The dull gray light from the window made her seem faded and ghostly, lost in another world, and Lynet didn't know how to bring her back. She couldn't bear this silent waiting, though.

"They'll be able to save him, won't they?" she said, her hands twisting in the folds of her dress.

Mina sank heavily into one of the chairs by the fireplace, resting her head in her hands so that her hair curtained her from view. Then she lifted her head, looked into the empty fireplace, and said, "I don't know."

That's not what you're supposed to say, Lynet thought. Mina was supposed to help her, to offer comfort or reassurance—but lately, Lynet felt that she was the one who kept trying to comfort Mina, instead.

"Just tell me that he'll be all right—"

"Lynet, I don't *know*," Mina snapped.

"Stop saying that!" Lynet shouted, her voice shrill with barely restrained panic. She rose to her feet, though her legs were trembling. She hated feeling so afraid, hated feeling weak and helpless to protect anyone she cared about. But how was she ever supposed to be brave, when Mina wouldn't even look at her? "How can you just sit there?" Lynet said, the words bursting out of her. "How can you be so calm? You don't even care if he recovers, do you? But then, why should you? You never loved him."

Finally Mina turned to look at Lynet, her eyes cold, and Lynet's anger shrank away, leaving her only with shame. "Mina, I didn't—"

"You're right," Mina said, her voice low but clear. "I don't love him. I thought I did once, a long time ago. But you're wrong to think I don't care what happens to him." She hesitated and then she said, "You'll be queen if he dies, you know."

Queen? It was the last thing on Lynet's mind. She would renounce any claim she'd ever had to the throne if it meant keeping her father alive. "I don't care," she said. "None of that matters to me."

Mina smiled, a frightening twitch of her lips, and looked away again, her fingers curling against the chair's armrests. "It's so easy for you, isn't it?" she said in a whisper. "If I'd had a father like yours growing up, maybe I wouldn't care about being queen either."

Lynet went silent, cursing her own thoughtlessness. She knew being queen meant more than a crown to Mina, but only now did she fully understand the inevitability of her losing that crown. Whether it mattered to Lynet or not, she would become queen on the day her father died—today or years in the future—and on that day, Lynet wouldn't be the only one to lose something dear to her.

"Mina—"

The door to her father's bedchamber opened before Lynet could continue, and both she and Mina turned as Nadia stepped out of the room. Her face was drawn, and there was light perspiration on her forehead as she took a few heavy breaths. "He's lost a great deal of blood," she said, looking only at Mina. "I've given him henbane, to make him sleep."

"Could I . . ." Lynet swallowed. "Could I see him?"

Nadia sighed as she turned to her, but then she nodded. "He may not be coherent enough to speak with you, but you can go to him, if you wish."

Mina rose from her chair. "I'll let you go in alone. You need better comfort than I can offer you right now." To Nadia, she said, "Call for me if anything changes."

Once Mina was gone, Lynet had no more excuse to wait. She stood in front of the door, bracing herself.

"Do you want me to go with you?" Nadia asked her, placing her hand lightly on Lynet's shoulder.

"No," Lynet said. "Just . . . just tell me if he's going to live. Be honest with me."

Nadia's hand tightened for a moment, and that gentle pressure was answer enough. "If he does," Nadia said, "it probably won't be for much longer. You should say good-bye now, just in case. And Lynet—"

Lynet turned, facing her.

"About earlier, when we were talking in the workroom—"

Lynet shook her head, shrugging Nadia's hand off her shoulder. "Not now. I don't care about that now."

Before Nadia could respond, Lynet slipped into her father's bedchamber, shutting the door behind her. As soon as she was inside, she shivered, her whole body recoiling from the motionless form resting on the bed. She had thought nothing could be worse than the crypt, but now she knew she was wrong.

But she forced herself to move toward the bed. The thought was floating in her head, though she felt too guilty to articulate it, that she needed to be quick, in case he died while she was standing there.

The wound at his side was heavily bandaged, and his skin was sallow, but her father looked peaceful in his drugged sleep. Pleasant dreams, Lynet hoped. Hesitantly, she reached for his hand, but it took her three tries before she managed to touch him. She'd thought he was too far gone to wake, but at the touch of her hand, he groaned, and Lynet snatched her hand back. He was alive, at least. Dying, but alive, still alive.

He looked up at her, his eyes clouded from his unnatural sleep. He said one word:

"*Emilia?*"

"No," she heard herself say. "No, it's not Emilia. It's Lynet."

"Lynet," he murmured, his eyes fluttering closed again.

"Yes, *Lynet*," she repeated. She had come here to say good-bye, but as soon as she started to speak again, the words seemed to tumble out of their own volition. "I'll always be Lynet," she continued in a whisper. "I don't want to become her. I don't want the South, and I don't want to be queen, and I wish . . . I wish I didn't even look like her. I wish you'd stop seeing her whenever you look at me. I wish you'd stop wanting me to be like her so badly." Maybe she could only speak her mind now because he couldn't really understand her, or maybe it was because she knew this might be her last chance, but now that she had started, she couldn't stop, the stiff and careful speech that she had rehearsed forgotten. "I wish I knew how to make you happy without forgetting who I am," she said, choking on the words. "But . . . I still love you, and . . . and I wanted to say good-bye."

Her voice was breaking, but she felt so light at that moment, light and whole.

Nicholas opened his eyes to look at her, though he didn't quite seem to *see* her, and again he breathed her mother's name.

"Yes," she said. "Yes, it's me. Emilia." She would grant him this one favor. She could do it without fear, now that she had told him the truth.

She bent down and kissed his forehead, quickly withdrawing before he asked for anything more. *I'm not my mother,* she reminded herself. *I am alive.*

His eyes slowly closed again, and she backed away, grateful to see the slow rise and fall of his chest as she left the room.

Sybil was waiting for her by the lake, hiding her face in her stone hands as always. Tonight's birthday celebration had been called off, of course, and so Lynet paid no attention to the gradually darkening sky as she huddled underneath the statue, hugging her knees to her chest and saying silent prayers for her father.

It was strange, the way nothing had changed. Queen Sybil wept; the lake was as serene as ever; the trees in the Shadow Garden twisted their naked arms up to the sky. It didn't seem fair that

Lynet should enjoy anything beautiful while her father was dying (alive, but dying; dying, but alive). *I should have stayed*, she thought. *I should have waited until the end.*

But then she had heard him calling her by her mother's name, and the panic had overwhelmed her. She hugged her knees tighter, and she knew she wouldn't go back, not now, not when death was so near. This wasn't a game anymore. What if when death came for her father, he mistook her for her mother and took her, as well?

But she was already on the verge of death, wasn't she? Because if Nicholas lived, she would never be able to refuse his offer of the South, not after nearly losing him, and if he died, she would become queen. And either way, Lynet feared that she, too, would slowly die away, leaving nothing but Emilia.

And either way, Mina would hate her for it.

The shameful memory of her fight with Mina finally brought Lynet to tears, and she made no sound as she wept into her hands like sad Queen Sybil above her—Queen Sybil, who was only remembered for her death and the damage that followed. And how would Lynet be remembered? As a scared little girl who lashed out at the people she loved?

It's so easy for you, isn't it?

Lynet lay her head down on the snow and closed her eyes, willing herself to stop crying, to stop thinking of her father or Mina, to stop thinking of anything at all. . . .

When she opened her eyes again, her neck was hurting and the sky was completely dark except for the moon shining overhead. She must have fallen asleep. As she eased out of her curled-up position, she remembered what had brought her here in the first place, and she wished she could dive back into unconsciousness and make the whole world disappear once more.

She crawled down to the lake's edge and washed her face. The wind was making ripples in the water and whistling through the trees in the Shadow Garden in a mournful wail. Lynet thought it sounded like words: *Run away.* She heard the words in her head, as urgent as a command, but as gentle as a whisper. *Run away, run away.*

"I can't. I shouldn't."

It made sense, though. Nadia had made it clear that her father's life was already over, and this way, no one would ever bring her news of his death. There would be no news to tell, not if she were long gone from here. Even if he somehow lived, Mina would still have everything she wanted, since Lynet wouldn't be there to take it from her. And Lynet—

Lynet would be free.

She heard another urgent whisper, but this time it was Nadia's voice asking her, *What do you want?*

But she had told Nadia what she wanted, and Nadia had denied her, making Lynet feel weak and spoiled, a butterfly with stunted wings that had never learned to fly. Nadia would stop Lynet from going, if she knew.

Then I won't tell her.

Lynet rose to her feet. The whisper gave way to the deafening roar of her heart pounding out the words in a kind of furious chant:

Run away, run away, run away.

Nadia thought Lynet couldn't survive outside Whitespring, but she was wrong; the only way to survive at all was to leave Whitespring, to make a new life for herself outside these walls. She'd been born and shaped from a dead woman, living under her ghostly shadow, and now she would finally escape it the only way she knew how.

She would pack what she needed tonight and then leave right before dawn, when it was still dark—and perhaps by then she would know her father's fate for certain. Lynet focused on the blood rushing through her body, on the strange bubbling energy that filled her chest and almost made her want to laugh, just so she could release some of it. She needed to remember this feeling, because she knew it would all shrivel away when she went to see Mina. She couldn't leave knowing that Mina was angry with her, that their last words to each other had been laced with resentment.

She didn't bother going to Mina's room. By now she knew where her stepmother would go when she was most distressed.

But the chapel was empty when Lynet arrived. She walked slowly down to the central altar. Her burst of energy from making her decision was fading, and now her nervousness at seeing Mina again was settling over her.

Footsteps were approaching, and at first Lynet thought it must be Mina, but this was too heavy a step to belong to her stepmother. Instinctively, Lynet hid behind the large stone altar, peeking out to see who else other than Mina would come to this abandoned chapel.

Her question was answered as the scarred huntsman stepped urgently into the room. Had he followed Lynet here? What would he want with her? She shrank back behind the altar, afraid that he would reach down and grab her by the scruff of her neck like an animal. His sleeves were still caked with dried blood.

But he just stood there, waiting, until Lynet guessed he must be meeting someone here—a secret romance, perhaps. She felt a flush of anger on her stepmother's behalf, that anyone should use her haven for their own purposes. She was even more irritated because she knew she couldn't leave the room until he was gone, and her legs were cramping from her crouched position.

She was curious, though—was this indeed a romantic tryst? And if so, who would love such a man? He was obviously strong, and he was attractive enough, square-jawed and broad-shouldered, and she supposed those scars gave him a dangerous kind of appeal. But who could look into those strange, vacant eyes and ever find love or warmth shining back?

The huntsman's head shot up as a silhouette filled the doorway. "I'm sorry I'm late, my love, but I was detained on the way."

Lynet recognized her voice at once, of course, and so she was already clutching the stone altar in shock when the silhouette stepped forward and became Mina.

17

MINA

The engagement was quiet, and the wedding ceremony was small, just as Nicholas wanted. He seemed to think that celebrating his remarriage at all would offend his dead wife.

Still, Mina considered it a triumph. She had paid close attention to Xenia when Nicholas made the announcement that Mina would be Whitespring's new queen, relishing the look of shock that passed over the woman's face before she managed to hide it. Marrying the king had become more than a means of securing a husband and a crown—it was now an act of defiance.

She felt it even more when she took her place at the high table beside the king at the wedding feast, two months after his proposal. The Hall was filled with people who had once turned away from her, but not even their disapproval had been enough to keep her from this seat. She, the magician's daughter, was now their queen, and the magician himself was seated to her left.

At her right was the king—her husband—and to *his* right was Lynet. Mina wished the girl were seated elsewhere; at her father's side, she commanded his complete attention, leaving Mina with only the back of his head and Gregory for company. She wasn't sure which she preferred.

"You could be a little happier on your wedding day," her father whispered. He barely looked at her as he spoke, his eyes shining with the light from the Hall.

"I'm bored," Mina muttered. "I didn't think my husband would rather talk to a child than to me."

"Bored? Then I'll have to provide you with entertainment."

Before she had the chance to ask him what he meant, Gregory stood. He waited for the noise in the Hall to die down as everyone, including Mina and Nicholas, turned their attention to him. A vague unease fell over the room.

"Thank you, everyone, for celebrating this day with us," he called out, and Mina wanted to cringe at his presumptuousness. "As the father of our beautiful new queen, I would like to bestow a gift on the royal couple, if I may."

Nicholas turned to Mina with a puzzled and slightly fearful look, but Mina only shrugged. After a brief hesitation, the king nodded to Gregory and then moved closer to his daughter.

Gregory descended the dais. He gestured to two men at the end of the Hall who quickly exited and then returned carrying an enormous object covered by a sheet. They set it down before the dais.

"My lord, my lady, I present to you both a gift made by the finest northern artisans." In one flourishing movement, he removed the sheet, and Mina saw—herself.

The mirror was taller than her father, its dark wooden frame simple and unadorned. It was the first time Mina had seen herself since becoming the king's wife. The wedding had been surreal, like walking in a dream. But this—this woman in the glass wearing a golden circlet—this was something to believe in.

I am queen.

Nicholas stood, and she walked beside him, stepping down from the dais to approach their gift. Her husband was thanking Gregory, but Mina didn't hear him, too captivated by the woman in the mirror. She wanted to reach out and touch the glass, to call it to her, but she knew she mustn't, not yet.

The crowd in the Hall applauded loudly, freeing Mina from the mirror's strange spell. She almost shrank from their collective stare at first. Did they see a southern girl, an outsider, raised above her station? But no, there was no scorn on the faces of her new subjects. Even those who had once mocked her knew better than to insult a queen. In their eyes, she saw herself as they did—beautiful, yes, but more than that—regal, powerful.

They loved her.

Mina heard the sound of someone running from the dais, and then Lynet was at her father's side, eager to be a part of this new game. Laughing, he swung her up into his arms and brought her closer to the mirror as Mina shrank to the side. Lynet was exploring the mirror with her hands, running her small, chubby fingers over the wood, and Mina flushed with unexpected annoyance.

She would ask herself later if she could have prevented what happened next; she saw the parts, but hadn't been able to figure out the whole quickly enough to stop it. Gregory, sensing the crowd's growing restlessness, ordered his men to lift the mirror and take it away. At the same time, Nicholas knelt to set down his daughter. As the mirror was lifted from the ground and Lynet rejoined it, the two collided, Lynet's head hitting the bottom of the mirror.

A gasp filled the room, and there was a tense silence before Lynet started to cry despite her best efforts not to, her face screwed up in pain. Nicholas snatched her up at once, pushing back her hair to reveal the cut—nothing as large as Mina had feared, but enough to send a trickle of blood down the girl's forehead onto her cheek.

Nicholas barked at one of the servants to call for his surgeon and then glared at Gregory's men, who had set the mirror back down. "Get rid of it," he commanded, cradling Lynet in his arms.

He started to turn away, but Gregory appeared in front of him, blocking his way. "My lord," he said, bowing his head. "I have some skill with medicine, and I wouldn't want you to miss your wedding feast. Give the child to me, and I will see to her. After all, we're family now, aren't we?"

Mina watched this display in horror. After Nicholas's proposal, she had told Gregory how close she had come to losing Nicholas because of his interference, and though he had glowered at her, she thought he had understood. But perhaps he *had* understood—he had chosen this moment to ask for Lynet, when the whole court was watching. If Nicholas refused his generous offer or insulted him in any way, everyone would wonder if there was some deeper meaning behind it, and the last thing Nicholas wanted was speculation about his daughter. Mina wondered how accidental Lynet's injury truly was.

She couldn't see Nicholas's face from where she was standing, but she could see his defeat reflected in the coldly triumphant gleam of her father's eye. She wanted to intervene, to snatch Lynet away from them both, but she knew that if she approached them now, Nicholas would think she was part of her father's plan.

Gregory reached for Lynet, who was clinging to her father with all her strength, but then one of the guards came forward with the king's surgeon. Nicholas gratefully handed Lynet to him, instead, while Gregory shot an angry glare at the intruding surgeon. "Your offer is appreciated but unnecessary," Nicholas said to Gregory for the benefit of the crowd. He followed the surgeon out of the Hall, not once looking at his new queen.

Mina stood there helplessly, not sure if she should follow. Rumbles echoed throughout the Hall, and Mina knew that if she didn't quiet them now, they would overpower her. From the corner of her eye, she saw Xenia, the ghost of a smirk on her lips. How satisfying it would be for her if Mina should begin her reign in confusion and chaos. Mina's fists clenched at her side. *I am a queen*, she reminded herself. *And I am loved.*

"Please be calm," she called to the crowd. "The princess has a small wound, nothing that will not heal shortly. Continue your meal, as I'm sure my husband would wish you to do." Her voice was steady, and the anxious rustling died down. Mina knew she had to return to the table; if she didn't, they would all assume something was wrong.

Before she ascended the dais again, she examined the mirror and found a small crack in the glass near the bottom. She could have fixed it, of course, but too many people had already seen the damage. "Should we dispose of it, my lady?" one of the men asked.

Mina brushed her fingers against the cool glass. It wasn't just glass, though; she was reaching out to herself, to the image that had taught her that she was a queen. Wouldn't it be ungrateful to be rid of it so soon?

"No," she said. "Take it to my chambers—the *queen's* chambers." The men obeyed, carrying the mirror out.

Gregory came to her side. "Nicely handled," he said as they ascended the dais together.

Mina didn't answer. She only took her seat at the high table and looked out at her new subjects, finding herself in the reflections of their eyes.

After the feast, Mina went looking for her new husband. She hadn't forgotten the promise she had made to herself, that she would tell him about her heart on their wedding night. She would explain to him what it meant, and he would reassure her that her father must have been mistaken, that their love for each other proved her heart was as real as his.

She found Nicholas in his room, staring into the fireplace.

"Has the princess recovered?" Mina asked.

Nicholas turned to her, his whole body tense. "Yes, she's asleep in her room. I'll check on her again later tonight."

"Surely it isn't that serious? It was a scrape. Didn't your surgeon examine her?"

"Yes."

"And?"

"I want to be there if she needs me. I don't want her to think that our marriage will change anything."

"I see." *He'd rather spend his wedding night with her,* Mina thought, and she couldn't help the burst of rage she felt—toward her husband, his daughter, even his dead wife.

"You're angry with me," the king said, lifting an eyebrow in surprise.

"I'm not angry, my lord," Mina lied, "but I had hoped not to spend my wedding night alone." She came closer to him and placed one hand on his chest, curling her fingers over the fabric of his shirt, wishing she could reach through flesh and fabric alike to claim his heart for her own. The king was staring at her hand, and he brought his own up to cover it, his skin warm from the wine and the excitement of the day. She slid her hand away from his, up to his jaw, his cheek, and he pressed her hand to his lips. Mina leaned in, feeling alive under his gaze. "Come back with me to my room, husband."

Cupping her face, he kissed her roughly. Mina brought her hands to his chest, but at her touch, he retreated, shaking his head at her. "I can't ignore what happened tonight, Mina."

"I don't understand."

"I thought I could marry you and still keep Lynet away from your father, but that was a mistake." He shook his head again, looking away from her. "I'm afraid this marriage was a mistake."

His voice was resolute and unwavering as he spoke those words. And even as Mina felt dread slowly spreading through her, part of her knew that she should have expected this from the start. *No one can love you, remember?*

"Nicholas, you can't mean that," she said in a near whisper. "You wanted this as much as I did."

"I know," he said. "But I haven't known a moment's peace since I proposed to you. I kept wondering if I was endangering my daughter, if I was pursuing my own selfish desires without thinking of her. At least now I know I was right to feel that way."

"It's a little too late to change your mind, isn't it?" Mina spat, her hands shaking. She didn't know whether to be devastated or furious, both emotions building inside her until she was sure she would tear herself in two.

He stepped closer to her and took her face in his hands, simply looking at her, searching for something. "I've been unfair to you," he said softly. "When we're alone together, it's easy for me to forget who you are, to pretend . . ."

Mina pulled herself away from him. "To pretend that I'm Emilia. Is that what you mean?"

"Mina, I'm sorry."

He reached for her again, but she stepped away from him. "If you closed your eyes and held me in your arms, it would be easy to think that I was her, to feel like you had a wife you could touch again. But I'm more than just something to touch, Nicholas. I want you to love *me*."

"I know. But I can't give you what you want, any more than you can give me what I want. I see that now."

He started to turn away, but Mina stopped him with a hand on his arm. "Why?" she demanded, her voice trembling. "Because of my father? Or because of her? Emilia is *dead*, Nicholas."

She knew at once that she had made a mistake, and her hand fell from his arm. Even with the fire burning behind him, at that moment he looked like he was made of ice, rigid and unfeeling. "Nicholas—"

"You're right," he said in a quiet voice. "Emilia is of the past, and now I must look to the future—to *our* future. I won't take your crown from you. We will still be king and queen together, I promise. But we will be husband and wife in name only. And I don't want your father to think of himself as Lynet's family."

Mina didn't speak. She didn't trust herself not to scream or heap curses on both her new husband and his wretched daughter. And what would she tell her father? That her beauty wasn't enough and she had nothing else to offer? That even as a queen, she didn't have the power to win the love of a single man?

But you don't have that power, and you never will, Mina reminded herself. Even the adoring crowd at the feast only loved her because she was queen—and Nicholas already had a queen to love.

"Is that all?" she said when she found her voice again.

He softened then, letting out a sigh as he rubbed at his forehead. "No," he said, "of course not. Make any request of me, and I'll try to grant it."

Her first instinct was to deny both his offer and his pity, but then she considered more carefully—she was queen now, wasn't she? She had wanted both Nicholas and the crown; why should she throw away both if she could only have one?

"I want the South," she said, a realization rather than a request. She was the first southern monarch since before Sybil's curse—didn't that grant her some sense of ownership, even responsibility? "When you receive petitions from anywhere in the South, I want you to pass them on to me. I decide what happens there and what projects are funded, with no interference. Will you grant me that?"

He studied her a moment, taken aback by the fervor in her voice as she made her request. Finally, he nodded. "Very well. The South is yours. Anything else?"

A place in your heart. "No," she said. "Nothing else that you would be willing to give me."

"Mina—"

"Good night, Nicholas." She wanted to leave while she still had this partial victory.

She remembered as she left the room that she had wanted to tell him about her heart. She never would now.

The queen's chambers were much grander than those of a magician's daughter. Her new mirror was already in place in her bedchamber, and Mina scowled at herself in the glass as she took off the gold circlet. She was beautiful, yes, but in the way a rug was beautiful. Something to look at, not someone to love.

She slumped to the ground, weighed down by self-pity. *Look at yourself,* her reflection seemed to reprimand her, *a queen with no king, a wife with no husband, sitting all alone on the floor of her large but empty room and feeling sorry for herself.*

Mina couldn't even look herself in the eye. Her gaze fell on the cracks in the corner of the mirror, the source of all her troubles tonight. She thought of Lynet and fought down the impulse to blame her for the night's disappointments. She told herself that even if Lynet hadn't hurt herself, Nicholas would still have turned her away eventually—if not because of Gregory, then for some other reason. She told herself these things, but she didn't know if she fully believed them—or if she wanted to believe them. It was much easier on her pride to blame Lynet. And didn't she deserve that reprieve on her wedding night?

She ran her fingers over the lines in the glass, reminded of the scars on Felix's arms.

Felix.

She still had the empty mirror frame locked away in a chest. She'd kept it because it had been her mother's, but also because it helped her remember that there was someone in this castle who loved her in his own way. There were times since she'd turned Felix away that she was tempted to call for him again, and she had always resisted—but now there was no need to resist, no reason to be true to a husband who was no husband at all.

Mina made a decision: she wouldn't spend her wedding night alone.

It was late enough that she could slip through the castle halls unnoticed, and the chapel was deserted, as always, when she arrived there. Would he still come to her, if she called to him? Or would he resist her, resenting her now that she was married?

She called for him anyway, reaching out to him just enough so he would feel that pull and know that she wanted him. Mina could *make* him come to her, make him love her again with a silent command, but she didn't want that. She wanted Felix to choose to come to the chapel—to choose *her.*

She shivered in the cold, waiting. She tried to tell herself that it was a long walk from the servants' quarters to the chapel, that she had to be patient, but with every moment that passed, she was sure he wouldn't come. She would either have to go back to her room, alone and twice rejected, or else wait here forever in the dark.

Another minute passed, and another, and the empty chapel— once so welcoming—seemed to mock her for her foolish hope. Did she think herself so worthy of forgiveness that she could expect Felix to simply run to her again?

And then, impossibly, the sound of footsteps. Mina held her breath, listening closely, as the footsteps made their hasty way toward the chapel, growing louder as they reached the door.

Felix's broad frame filled the doorway, and he was looking at her in surprise. "I didn't believe it at first," he said. "I thought I was mistaken, and that I would come here and find this place empty." He stepped into the room, but he kept his distance from her, watching her warily. "I thought tonight was your wedding night."

Mina wanted to reach for him, longing to feel the familiar breadth of his shoulders, the scars lining his arms, but she couldn't bear the thought that even he would push her aside. "Tonight *is* my wedding night, but . . . but my husband doesn't want me."

Felix blinked at her, his face expressionless. "Then he must be a fool."

She smiled sadly. "I've missed you, Felix."

He tilted his head. "You turned me away." There was no reproach in his voice; he was simply stating a fact.

The light shone on his eyes, and she saw how blank and empty they were. The last time she had seen him, he had been almost human, but now, after being away from her, he had become the perfect huntsman and no more. Did he remember loving her at all?

"I shouldn't have called you again," Mina murmured. "It's too late."

"Too late for what?" Felix said, taking a step closer to her. "Why did you call me here tonight?"

She wanted to do what she should have done the last time—turn him back to glass, destroy any evidence that he had lived, that he had stood here in this same room and loved her. "I don't know," she snapped. "You don't even—"

He took another step toward her. "I don't what?"

She shook her head, furious at herself for coming here tonight. "It doesn't matter."

He was standing directly in front of her now, so that she had to look up at him. "What do you want from me, Mina?" he said, and for a moment, she saw in his eyes a flicker of hope—or perhaps it was just her own feeling that she saw reflected in him.

"I just want you to love me again," she said.

Her voice cracked when she spoke, and she realized how desperately she meant what she said. If Felix didn't love her anymore—if even her own creation had turned against her—then what did she have left? Her icy composure was gone now, and she silently pleaded with him as an equal, two clumsy glass hearts trying to fit together without breaking.

"Mina," Felix murmured, and his eyes seemed to glow, absorbing the light from her lamp. He took her face in his hands and leaned in to kiss her forehead, and then the bridge of her nose. His arms came around her, and Mina clung to him in relief. He wasn't warm, not exactly, but the pressure of his arms around her was something similar to warmth, and that was enough for her tonight.

"You kept me away from you for too long," he murmured into her hair. "I had forgotten how it felt to love you."

"I'll never wait this long again," she promised.

She knew his love was only an illusion, but that, too, was enough for tonight.

It was late when she returned to her room, but Mina didn't plan to sleep, yet. She lit some candles and smiled to herself, still holding on to that joyous moment when Felix had taken her in his arms again. And then there was a knock at the door, and the moment was ruined.

Nicholas? Her first thought was that her husband had come to see her, and she was suddenly aware of how badly she wanted it to be true, how much she still wanted him to love her. She knew she would break all her promises to Felix if it meant she could have her husband at her side.

But when she opened the door, she didn't see anyone at first. Then she heard a small cough, and Mina looked down to see Lynet standing in the doorway, a bandage on her forehead and her knuckles in her mouth. Her happiness from a moment ago proved itself to be a shallow, flimsy thing compared to the sinking disappointment she felt now.

"Lynet? What are you doing here so late?"

"I'm sorry I broke your mirror," Lynet mumbled. She looked down at her feet.

Even though Mina had been happy earlier to blame Lynet for the night's humiliation, the girl seemed so upset that Mina wanted to reassure her.

Keep your distance, Mina started to remind herself—but she didn't need to anymore. Lynet had been shy with Mina ever since the engagement, and Mina had done nothing to discourage it, but that was before, when she wanted to please Nicholas. Now there was no reason to do anything for his sake.

"Come inside, Lynet," Mina said. "I want to show you something."

She led the girl through to her bedchamber, until they were standing together in front of the mirror. Mina went down to her knees and pointed at the web of cracks in the corner. "Do you see that?"

Lynet nodded.

"That's where you hit your head. See? I would have to get all the way down here on my knees before I could even notice it. When I stand up"—she stood, to demonstrate her point—"I can't even see it." She stood a little to the side, so that she wouldn't reflect on the cracked glass at all, and Lynet finally looked up at her and smiled.

"But what about your head? Does it hurt where you hit it?" Mina asked.

Lynet shook her head.

"Does your father know you're here?"

She shook her head again. "He's sleeping."

Mina felt strangely smug about this, as if she and Lynet were keeping a secret together. She looked down at the girl beside her, the girl who had shown Mina nothing but warmth and acceptance since the moment they had met. Lynet was too young to know the prejudices of her fellow northerners, too innocent to see in Mina the sharp glint of her glass heart—and so in her innocence, she made Mina innocent as well.

Mina went to sit on the edge of the bed. "Come sit here with me," she said, patting the space beside her.

"Yes, Stepmother." Lynet climbed up next to her.

Mina wrinkled her nose. "Oh, I don't like that. 'Stepmother' makes me sound so old and formal. Call me Mina, like you used to."

Lynet didn't say anything.

"Lynet, I know . . . I know I've been preoccupied with the engagement and the wedding, and so I haven't been able to spend much time with you, but now that it's all over . . . well, we're still friends, aren't we?"

"You're my stepmother," Lynet recited.

"That's true," Mina said. "I'm your stepmother, and I can never replace your mother, but you can still . . ." *You can still love me.* "You can still be my friend. You have only one mother, but you can have many friends."

Lynet considered this, and then she inched closer to Mina, taking a strand of her hair in her little hand. "I wish my hair was like yours," she said, the hair spilling from her hand.

"But you have such wonderful curls," Mina said. *Like your mother.* But she was sure Lynet had heard that often enough from Nicholas. "You just need to brush it more often."

Lynet shook her head. "The brush gets stuck, and then it hurts. I don't like brushing my hair."

Mina studied Lynet's hair for a moment, and then she said, "Turn around with your back to me."

Lynet frowned in suspicion, but she turned with her arms crossed. "What are you doing?"

"I'm going to brush your hair." At once, Lynet started to scramble away, so Mina pushed her back down and kept her hands on her shoulders. "Listen to me. I'm going to brush your hair with my fingers. I'll be careful so it won't hurt, but if it does hurt, we'll stop. Agreed?"

"No!"

"Are you scared, little wolf cub?"

She pouted, but she stopped struggling to get away. *"No."*

Mina tried not to laugh, knowing Lynet would be offended if she did. She started to comb through Lynet's hair with her fingers, untangling and unknotting. She did hurt Lynet once or twice—the girl flinched whenever she approached a particularly nasty tangle—but Lynet didn't protest or try to leave.

"When I grow up, I want to look like you," Lynet said softly.

Mina pretended not to hear. It was an impossible wish. But she couldn't explain that to Lynet, of course, no more than Mina could explain her own glass heart.

Mina's hands paused as they brushed the skin on Lynet's neck. Her skin was always so cold, and yet she never seemed to feel the cold at all. Perhaps her seeming immunity to the cold was one of the effects of her creation—but was that the only one? Mina had never considered that Lynet could have the same power over snow that Mina had over glass, but now she wondered how she could have missed it. There had been times during her walks with Nicholas when Lynet had played in the snow, making elaborate structures that should have been difficult, if not impossible, for such an impatient child. Mina hadn't been able to shape glass until her father had told her about her heart; perhaps Lynet couldn't fully transform the snow until she knew the truth of her birth. *I might teach her,* Mina thought. *I'm the only one who could.*

But then she would have to explain to Lynet the circumstances of her birth, the debt she owed to Gregory. Mina still had nightmares sometimes of that rotting heart in its jar, her father's voice behind her telling her that she owed him her life. She remembered the way the village girls had looked at her when they had seen her experimenting with her powers. Lynet was probably better off never knowing the truth.

Even when the last tangle was free, neither Mina nor Lynet moved away. Running her hands through the girl's hair was surprisingly soothing. It was thicker than her own, but softer. Could Nicholas even look at it without thinking of his wife's hair? *His wife,* Mina thought, as though he only ever had one. She had the sudden urge to pull out Lynet's hair, every last strand, and burn it all.

Lynet let out a little yelp, and Mina saw that she had started to act on her fantasy without meaning to, a few loose strands of Lynet's hair coming away in her hand.

"I think it's time you fly back to your room, Lynet. Your father might wake to find you missing, and your stepmother is tired."

Lynet bounced off the bed in happy oblivion, and Mina watched her go. How many years would they have together before Lynet realized that whatever love she thought she felt for Mina was nothing but a childish illusion? How soon before Lynet began to resemble the portrait of Emilia on Nicholas's wall? One day they would both start to see each other differently, and Mina couldn't imagine how they could become anything but enemies on that day.

Lynet of the strange cracks that had appeared on Felix's neck. Mina was walking toward Lynet's altar now, and Lynet shifted to hide herself better—and then she heard Mina inhale sharply.

A moment later, Lynet learned why—the moon had changed positions since she'd first hidden here, and so she was now casting a large shadow that had moved with her.

Mina's voice, strong but slightly fearful, echoed through the chapel. "I know someone's there."

There was no point hiding anymore. Better she should stand and reveal herself than be caught crouching in fear. Lynet stepped out from behind the altar, trying not to wobble on her cramped legs, and Mina's face crumpled when she saw her. Lynet knew that Mina was going over everything she had said to the huntsman, everything that Lynet must have heard. And perhaps, like Lynet, she decided she would rather face this moment directly than cringe away and be dragged out into the open.

Before Lynet's eyes, Mina became the proud queen again, standing tall. She held up an imperious hand to Felix, gesturing for him to stay where he was as she approached Lynet with measured steps. "You're always snooping and spying, aren't you, Lynet?" Mina said. Her tone was sharp, but with a fearful waver underneath that she was trying to control. Mina reached out to touch Lynet's face, and Lynet couldn't help turning away as Mina brushed her cheek with the backs of her knuckles. "What do I do now?" Mina whispered. "What do I do with you now? You've heard so much. You've seen—"

Mina drew back, her hand going to her throat, her eyes darting to the huntsman, and at the same time that Lynet realized what the cracks on the huntsman's neck had reminded her of, she remembered what Mina had said about having a glass heart that her father had given her. She hadn't understood before, but now she wondered . . . if one girl could be made of snow and never feel cold, then perhaps . . .

18

LYNET

The huntsman went straight to Mina and took her face in his hands, studying her intently. "You look sad," he said. "Tired."

Lynet was rapt. She'd never seen anyone approach her stepmother with such intimacy. Her father always wore a layer of formality when he was with the queen. But despite his youthful appearance, the huntsman spoke to her and touched her like they'd known each other for a long time.

Mina brushed his hands away, and her voice was cold as she said, "I look sad, do I, Felix? And why do you think that is?"

The huntsman—Felix—took an uncertain step away from her. "Is the king dead?" Was there a faint note of hope in his voice?

"Not dead," Mina said, "but hardly alive. The surgeon did a fine job of closing him up, but it's . . . it's like he wants to die. He keeps asking for *her*, for his dead queen. I think he means to join her."

"I'm sorry, Mina—"

She laughed, a brittle sound. "Are you? I don't think you know what it means to be sorry."

"I only know what you know. What you want me to know."

"And do you know how to hurt? How to destroy? Have I taught you that?" She grabbed his arm and pulled up one of his sleeves, revealing the scarred skin of his forearm. "Look at all these scars. Did you receive one today, when you tried to slay my husband?" Felix flinched, pulling his arm out of her grip, but Mina didn't relent. A terrible silence hung over them both, and Lynet kept her hand over her mouth, afraid she would reveal herself by some small sound.

"Mina," he said at last, "I promise you I didn't kill him. It was a stag. We were separated. I wasn't there to help him."

"You weren't there, but you *saw* it happen, didn't you? I can see it now in your eyes." She lay her hand on his chest, and then Lynet witnessed something extraordinary: cracks appeared on the surface of the huntsman's skin, cracks that branched all across his neck, moving up toward his face. The huntsman stood completely still, not even breathing. Was *Mina* doing this to him? How could that be possible?

"What did you do, then?" Mina said, her voice dangerously quiet. "I already know the answer, but I want to hear you say it."

"I thought of *you*," he breathed, and he buried his head in the crook of her neck and shoulder, his arms encircling her waist.

The cracks on his skin disappeared as Mina returned his embrace, one hand digging into his back, the other tangled in his hair. Lynet felt an unexpected pang in her chest. She had always thought that *she* was the only one who saw Mina's private self, the woman behind the stately queen, but now she understood that she had never seen the real Mina at all.

"Oh, you fool," Mina murmured against the huntsman's neck. She pulled at his hair, bringing his face level with hers. "You sweet fool. You've ruined everything."

"I don't understand," he said. "He didn't love you. He made you suffer again and again."

"Oh, Felix."

He pleaded with her like a hurt child, begging her to understand him. "I wanted to see you smile, as you once did," he said. "I wanted you to look into my eyes and see yourself as you are, smiling and beautiful. What did I do wrong, then?"

"When the king dies, I will no longer be queen."

"And what of it? Weren't we happier before then? Before you chose him over me? It was when you became queen that you began to look so unhappy, so different from the first night I saw you."

He reached for her, but she flinched away from him. "That was when I had nothing to lose. Now I can feel it all slipping away— my youth, my beauty, my crown. Even if Nicholas lives, he'll give Lynet all my power, piece by piece, until I'm left with nothing but the glass heart my father gave me." Her fingers curled over her chest, and she grimaced. "She'll replace me."

The huntsman tilted his head slightly, frowning a little in thought. "Do you want me to kill the girl?"

The silence that followed was as thick as the darkness in the crypt. Mina's silence was worse to Lynet than anything else she had heard. It was the silence of thought, of doubt—and no matter what Mina answered, Lynet would never be able to forget the pause that preceded it.

"No, Felix," Mina said at last, her voice hoarse. "You can't—*I* can't do that." She turned away from the huntsman, looking up at the stained-glass windows like they might speak to her. Through the windows, the moon threw dappled shadows on her face, reminding

18

LYNET

The huntsman went straight to Mina and took her face in his hands, studying her intently. "You look sad," he said. "Tired."

Lynet was rapt. She'd never seen anyone approach her step-mother with such intimacy. Her father always wore a layer of formality when he was with the queen. But despite his youthful appearance, the huntsman spoke to her and touched her like they'd known each other for a long time.

Mina brushed his hands away, and her voice was cold as she said, "I look sad, do I, Felix? And why do you think that is?"

The huntsman—Felix—took an uncertain step away from her. "Is the king dead?" Was there a faint note of hope in his voice?

"Not dead," Mina said, "but hardly alive. The surgeon did a fine job of closing him up, but it's . . . it's like he wants to die. He keeps asking for *her*, for his dead queen. I think he means to join her."

"I'm sorry, Mina—"

She laughed, a brittle sound. "Are you? I don't think you know what it means to be sorry."

"I only know what you know. What you want me to know."

"And do you know how to hurt? How to destroy? Have I taught you that?" She grabbed his arm and pulled up one of his sleeves, revealing the scarred skin of his forearm. "Look at all these scars. Did you receive one today, when you tried to slay my husband?" Felix flinched, pulling his arm out of her grip, but Mina didn't relent. A terrible silence hung over them both, and Lynet kept her hand over her mouth, afraid she would reveal herself by some small sound.

"Mina," he said at last, "I promise you I didn't kill him. It was a stag. We were separated. I wasn't there to help him."

"You weren't there, but you *saw* it happen, didn't you? I can see it now in your eyes." She lay her hand on his chest, and then Lynet witnessed something extraordinary: cracks appeared on the surface of the huntsman's skin, cracks that branched all across his neck, moving up toward his face. The huntsman stood completely still, not even breathing. Was *Mina* doing this to him? How could that be possible?

"What did you do, then?" Mina said, her voice dangerously quiet. "I already know the answer, but I want to hear you say it."

"I thought of *you*," he breathed, and he buried his head in the crook of her neck and shoulder, his arms encircling her waist.

The cracks on his skin disappeared as Mina returned his embrace, one hand digging into his back, the other tangled in his hair. Lynet felt an unexpected pang in her chest. She had always thought that *she* was the only one who saw Mina's private self, the woman behind the stately queen, but now she understood that she had never seen the real Mina at all.

"Oh, you fool," Mina murmured against the huntsman's neck. She pulled at his hair, bringing his face level with hers. "You sweet fool. You've ruined everything."

"I don't understand," he said. "He didn't love you. He made you suffer again and again."

"Oh, Felix."

He pleaded with her like a hurt child, begging her to understand him. "I wanted to see you smile, as you once did," he said. "I wanted you to look into my eyes and see yourself as you are, smiling and beautiful. What did I do wrong, then?"

"When the king dies, I will no longer be queen."

"And what of it? Weren't we happier before then? Before you chose him over me? It was when you became queen that you began to look so unhappy, so different from the first night I saw you."

He reached for her, but she flinched away from him. "That was when I had nothing to lose. Now I can feel it all slipping away— my youth, my beauty, my crown. Even if Nicholas lives, he'll give Lynet all my power, piece by piece, until I'm left with nothing but the glass heart my father gave me." Her fingers curled over her chest, and she grimaced. "She'll replace me."

The huntsman tilted his head slightly, frowning a little in thought. "Do you want me to kill the girl?"

The silence that followed was as thick as the darkness in the crypt. Mina's silence was worse to Lynet than anything else she had heard. It was the silence of thought, of doubt—and no matter what Mina answered, Lynet would never be able to forget the pause that preceded it.

"No, Felix," Mina said at last, her voice hoarse. "You can't—*I* can't do that." She turned away from the huntsman, looking up at the stained-glass windows like they might speak to her. Through the windows, the moon threw dappled shadows on her face, reminding

Lynet of the strange cracks that had appeared on Felix's neck. Mina was walking toward Lynet's altar now, and Lynet shifted to hide herself better—and then she heard Mina inhale sharply.

A moment later, Lynet learned why—the moon had changed positions since she'd first hidden here, and so she was now casting a large shadow that had moved with her.

Mina's voice, strong but slightly fearful, echoed through the chapel. "I know someone's there."

There was no point hiding anymore. Better she should stand and reveal herself than be caught crouching in fear. Lynet stepped out from behind the altar, trying not to wobble on her cramped legs, and Mina's face crumpled when she saw her. Lynet knew that Mina was going over everything she had said to the huntsman, everything that Lynet must have heard. And perhaps, like Lynet, she decided she would rather face this moment directly than cringe away and be dragged out into the open.

Before Lynet's eyes, Mina became the proud queen again, standing tall. She held up an imperious hand to Felix, gesturing for him to stay where he was as she approached Lynet with measured steps. "You're always snooping and spying, aren't you, Lynet?" Mina said. Her tone was sharp, but with a fearful waver underneath that she was trying to control. Mina reached out to touch Lynet's face, and Lynet couldn't help turning away as Mina brushed her cheek with the backs of her knuckles. "What do I do now?" Mina whispered. "What do I do with you now? You've heard so much. You've seen—"

Mina drew back, her hand going to her throat, her eyes darting to the huntsman, and at the same time that Lynet realized what the cracks on the huntsman's neck had reminded her of, she remembered what Mina had said about having a glass heart that her father had given her. She hadn't understood before, but now she wondered . . . if one girl could be made of snow and never feel cold, then perhaps . . .

"You're like me, aren't you?" Lynet said. "You're made of glass."

Mina shuddered and bowed her head, her hair hiding her face. When she looked up again, she truly *did* seem like she could be made of glass—cold and sharp, her eyes as unreadable as the huntsman's. "My heart is made of glass, Lynet, but I'm not like you." She grabbed Lynet's wrist. "Did you think you were my father's only experiment? His only success?" Mina held Lynet's hand against her chest, over her heart. Lynet waited, too confused and too scared at first to understand what she was feeling—what she *wasn't* feeling. There was no heartbeat, no sign of life pounding underneath Mina's flesh. Lynet gasped, and Mina laughed at her.

"There, do you see? When I was a child, my heart stopped, so my father cut me open and gave me a heart of glass. Do you remember what I told you about your birth, Lynet? About my father's blood? Blood is what makes you real, but there is no blood in my heart. It serves its function and keeps me alive, but it cannot love, and no one can ever love a heartless thing like me."

Lynet wrenched her hand away, her own heartbeat wild and frantic. There was so much defiance in Mina's voice that Lynet almost missed the fear hiding beneath. It was there, though, waiting for Lynet's next move, her next word. With each second that passed, Lynet knew she had to do or say something if she wanted to prove that she wouldn't look at Mina differently now, that she wasn't afraid of her, that she still loved her stepmother. But there was nothing to say, no words capable of breathing life into Mina's heart, and the truth was that Lynet *was* afraid. Mina was a mystery to her now; how could she claim to know her stepmother's heart better than Mina did?

And so she could only watch as the hope on her stepmother's face slowly died away with each moment of silence.

"Say something," Mina said, so low that Lynet thought she'd misheard at first. "I can't stand to see you look at me like that."

Mina backed away, her arms wrapped around herself. But still Lynet said nothing, like this was a test or a trap, and she was sure to fail—or perhaps she had already failed.

"*Say* something!" Mina roared, and in that same moment, the stained-glass windows all shattered at once, colorful shards raining down on them both.

Lynet quickly covered her face, but she still felt one of the shards bite at her cheek, and without thinking, she ran for the chapel door to escape the blizzard of glass. As she crossed the threshold, she heard Mina shout, "Go after her!" and then she felt the pounding of the huntsman's boots under her feet as he followed in pursuit.

Lynet's heart beat furiously as she ran through the halls. She emerged breathless in the western courtyard, pausing only a moment to gather her bearings. Lynet rarely came here, knowing that it was one of her mother's favorite places, but she knew that if she climbed over the high wall opposite, she would be outside the castle walls. When she had imagined running away, she hadn't pictured herself like this, furtive and desperate, empty-handed and afraid. But even in the silence of the night, she could still hear the sound of glass shattering in her ears, and she was more eager than before to run and leave behind the wreckage of her old life.

She had no time to waste, and so in that brief space between one breath and the next, she made her decision and ran for the wall, pulling herself up as quickly as she could. But she wasn't familiar with this particular wall, and so she placed her foot on a stone that happened to be loose. The stone slipped under her, and Lynet fell backward, waiting for the impact of the snow against her back.

But she never hit the snow—someone caught her.

"I've got you," said the huntsman, his arms wrapped around her waist.

Lynet kicked at him, and he let out a surprised grunt, releasing her. Lynet didn't look back as she started to scramble for the wall again, but the huntsman was used to chasing far quicker beasts, and so he caught up to her quickly, throwing her to the ground. Felix held her arms down, one knee on either side of her waist.

When Lynet looked up at her attacker, she noticed how clearly his eyes reflected her own face, her own terror. But Lynet refused to let him see her that way. She had to be brave, even if it was only for show.

"Did she tell you to kill me?" she spat at him. "Is *that* why she sent you after me?" Even as she spoke the words, she was surprised to discover that she wanted to know the answer. Mina had told him not to kill her before, but she might have changed her mind after finding out that Lynet had heard all of her secrets. Had she sent her servant to do what she couldn't do herself?

"It'll be easier for her if you're dead," the huntsman said.

Lynet wished she could stop trembling. She wished she could look him in the eye and tell him to do it quickly. "So it's true, then," she said, but her voice sounded so small, so unsubstantial, like the feel of an eyelash against her cheek. "You're going to kill me."

The huntsman's jaw tensed. "I'm sorry, child," he said.

Lynet didn't understand why *he* sounded so frightened, or why his voice started to break as he called her "child." When Lynet grimaced from the pain of his tight grip on her arms, he did the same, like a perfect reflection. It reminded her of the night she found him in the garden, the way he had seemed to follow her lead, even imitating her posture. *He's some kind of mirror,* Lynet thought, recalling the way Mina had almost made him shatter apart like the glass windows. *He feels whatever I feel.* If she stared at him with fierce resolve, he would only do the same. She would win nothing from him by pretending to be brave.

She started to sob, taking loud, shuddering breaths that threatened to choke her. "Please," she gasped. "Please don't kill me."

Showing her fear was easier than she wanted to admit. She didn't even have to try; it was more like she had to stop trying.

Her sudden outburst caught him off guard, his grip on her arms easing slightly.

"Please don't hurt me, I don't want to die, I'm so scared." The words gushed out of her, and she wasn't sure she could stop if she tried. "Let me go—"

He released her, his face contorting, and Lynet sat up slowly. But then he shook his head and shot one arm out, his hand circling her throat. "And what if I do?" he said. Lynet didn't move. She was certain, somehow, that as long as he could see the fear on her face, he wouldn't hurt her.

"This isn't what she made me for, not at first," he said, his voice low. "She made me to love her, to show her what love is, not to hunt or to kill." His hand tightened. "If I kill you for her, then what will she see in me? And what will I see in her?" He released her throat, and Lynet fought to keep still.

Felix stood, and Lynet froze like a frightened rabbit, waiting to spring. "Go now," he said. He took a small purse from his belt and tossed it on the snow beside her. "Leave her in peace, and don't let me find you again. If you need help, ask the snow."

Ask the snow? Lynet didn't understand, but she didn't stop to ask him. She grabbed the purse, staggered to her feet, and ran to the wall, scaling it easily this time, and dropped down on the other side—her first steps outside of Whitespring.

Part of her was afraid that Nadia would be right, that as soon as her feet touched the ground, the earth would open up beneath her and swallow her whole. She would have to cross a dense wood in the dead of night before she'd come to the nearest town—what made her think she could survive at all?

But she took one step toward the wood, and then another, and nothing happened, except that she was now two steps closer to a new life. She had nearly died tonight *within* the walls of Whitespring, after all. Death was everywhere in that castle, in each day that was just like the last, but life—life was what happened next, life was the rush of air in her lungs when she made a jump she wasn't sure she could make.

She knew she shouldn't linger here; it would be foolish to gamble her life on the huntsman's whim. And Mina . . . she didn't want to think about Mina, yet. She didn't understand a world where she was in danger from Mina—so she would simply leave that world behind.

Lynet looked up at Whitespring one last time, saying good-bye to everything she'd ever known.

And then there was nothing left to do but run.

19

MINA

Mina stood in the chapel, surrounded by pieces of shattered glass. She hadn't meant to lash out like that, but the fear and rage building up in her had demanded some kind of release, something to drown out the silence of her heart. Since Lynet knew the truth already, she had no reason to hold herself back anymore.

The chapel was dark and silent, but Mina could still hear the echoes from when the glass had shattered, could still see the horrified look on Lynet's face, the look she might give to a frightening stranger. And perhaps she was a stranger—Mina had kept so much hidden from her over the years, whether for Lynet's safety or for her own.

But she had known this would happen one day. The moment Mina had realized how much Lynet had grown—the same night when Mina had first seen a strand of gray in her own hair—she knew that this disillusionment had been inevitable. She knew that Lynet's childish adoration couldn't last forever, and that when she became old enough to see Mina—to see right to the heart of her—she would only ever be able to hate her. She should have been better prepared for this night.

Mina frowned. Felix was taking too long. He should have returned with Lynet by now. He'd caught more difficult prey than a frightened girl, even if she was skilled at hiding. Mina felt the same frustrated fear building up in her that she'd felt before shattering the window, but now there was no more glass to break.

I have to win back Lynet's favor, Mina thought. When Felix brought her back, Mina would explain herself and try to be the stepmother Lynet had always known—

But even as the thought entered her mind, she knew it was impossible. It was too late. There would be no other chances, no other roles but the ones that had been set for them from the beginning—the bitter, aging queen and the sweet young princess poised to take everything from her.

She heard Felix arriving before she saw him—heard him walking at his normal pace, quick and clipped, and so she wasn't even surprised when he appeared alone in the doorway.

"Where is she?" Mina said in a whisper.

He shook his head, the moonlight from the broken windows making his dark eyes glow with an eerie intensity. "I don't know."

Mina lifted her skirts and stepped around the broken glass to reach Felix, taking his face in her hands and searching for answers in those unreadable eyes. "Felix, what are you saying? You couldn't find her?"

He tried to turn away, but she kept him in place as a broken, shameful look started to fill his eyes. "No," he said, "I couldn't find her."

Mina released him and buried her face in her hands. *If she went to Nicholas* . . . "Keep looking," she said, dropping her hands from her face. "Look in the trees, especially. I'll check the king's rooms. We have to find her."

But Lynet wasn't with her father. And Felix hadn't found her in any of the other places Mina had suggested—Lynet wasn't by the statue, and she wasn't in the North Tower, and she wasn't visibly scaling any walls or climbing across any roofs. Where else could she be? Where else in Whitespring did she spend her time? Who else did she visit?

The surgeon, Mina remembered, the one Lynet had mentioned only once more than a month ago, and then refused to talk about ever again, even when Mina had asked about her. She had known from the way Lynet had avoided her eye that she hadn't forgotten about the surgeon, only that she didn't want to discuss her with Mina.

She told Felix to wait for her in the chapel and then hurried down to the surgeon's workroom. Mina knew her name was Nadia, but she had never spoken to the surgeon or had need of her services before Nicholas's accident; she hadn't really taken notice of her at all until Lynet mentioned her. Then she kept watch whenever she saw the girl pass by, noticing her confident yet elegant stride, the way she stared straight ahead, not sparing a glance for anyone around her. Others might have interpreted this as arrogance, but Mina recognized the surgeon's manner as single-minded purpose. A girl in her position couldn't afford to show doubt or weakness. She could see why Lynet was drawn to her.

When Mina knocked on the door of the basement workroom, there was no answer, so she went into the empty room to wait.

She hoped she wouldn't have to wait for long. The hair on her arms prickled with warning, and Mina's breathing became shallow in the cluttered, dimly lit room, its low ceiling pressing down on her. Her eyes swept over the shelves of vials and jars, the stained wooden table, the books piled everywhere, all reminding her of another workroom, and she understood why she felt so ill at ease here.

She went to the table, leaning against it for support as she fought to control her erratic breathing. She couldn't let the surgeon find her like this, a scared girl with no power. She wasn't that girl anymore, and this was not her father's laboratory. The wooden table underneath her trembling hands was made from a lighter wood than the other table. She opened one of the surgeon's journals and found notes made in her handwriting, messy and slanted, not like her father's neat, spiky hand—

Mina frowned, blinking at the journals, trying to understand why, for a moment, she *had* seen her father's handwriting. Was it simply a trick her mind was playing on her? But no, she saw it again out of the corner of her eye, a piece of loose parchment sticking out from between the journal's pages. And there, visible on that parchment were two words written in a hand that she could never forget: *Well done.*

She thought she had ripped the paper in her haste to pull it out of the journal, but it was already torn, a simple half sheet with those two words written on them and nothing more. There was no signature, but Mina knew from the cold sweat on the back of her neck that it had to be from Gregory.

No longer caring how the surgeon would find her, Mina tore through the rest of the papers, looking for some explanation for the note.

I'm going mad, she thought as she flipped through more journals. The room had affected her, stirring up painful memories, and now she was looking for something that wasn't there.

And then she saw another corner of loose parchment, stuffed

under a pile of books, and she knew she wasn't imagining anything. Mina pulled out the parchment—two sheets of it—and looked down at a half-finished letter in the surgeon's hand.

She read through it, her fingers clutching the sides of the paper tightly enough to wrinkle them.

The door to the workroom opened, but Mina didn't move.

"My lady!" the surgeon said in surprise. "Did you need—"

Mina put the letter down and turned to face the surgeon, her earlier, shapeless distress sharpened into a fine point. "When did you first meet the magician Gregory?" she asked calmly.

To the surgeon's credit, she didn't flinch or look away. One hand perched on her hip in a show of confidence. "Before I came to Whitespring. He's the one who encouraged me to apply for this position."

"He asked you to spy on Lynet?" Her voice was still calm, but her hands were shaking.

The surgeon's eyes flickered to the letter in Mina's hands, knowing as well as Mina did that the letter contained, in her own hand, information about Nicholas's plans to give Lynet the South, with special attention to Lynet's reaction to this news, her fears and doubts. She took a long breath before answering. "He wanted to know more about her. Nothing . . . nothing harmful, just her personality, her reactions to . . . to . . ."

"To knowing how she was created?"

And now shame forced the surgeon to look away. "I would have told her anyway," she muttered. "She had a right to know."

"And what did my father promise you in return for this information?"

"Passage south and a place at the university," she answered, voice low.

Mina nodded, putting the letter down on the table behind her. She pitied the young woman, in a way. She had been just what her father needed—a stranger, someone with no loyalty to Lynet, who wanted something badly enough to trade seemingly harmless information for it. Mina might have done the same, in her position.

And now she was here looking for a spy of her own, hoping Nadia could lead her to Lynet.

"Where is Lynet?" Mina asked softly.

Nadia shook her head listlessly, still cowed by her admission, and now that her air of defiance had fallen away, Mina noticed how young she was, how uncertain of herself. She couldn't have been much older than Lynet. "I don't know," Nadia said. "I haven't seen Lynet since the king's accident."

Mina took a step closer to her, searching her face for signs that she was lying, but there was only defeat. "She hasn't come to see you?"

Nadia frowned now, and Mina could see the pieces coming together in her mind. "Is Lynet missing?"

Her confusion seemed genuine enough, and Mina sighed, turning away in disappointment.

"Did something happen?" she pressed, a note of worry in her voice.

Mina laughed dryly. "Do you think I'll tell you, just for you to send another report to my father?" She picked up the letter, crumpling it in her hand. "Did you ever stop to wonder *why* he would want this information from you, when he could obtain it himself?"

Nadia shrugged. "He said the king didn't like him, that it was difficult for him to get to know this girl he thought of as his granddaughter. But is Lynet—"

"I'm sure that's what he *said*. But did you believe him?" Mina said, her voice growing louder. "You must be a clever girl, to be a surgeon at your age. Didn't you wonder why he couldn't just ask *me* about her? Or why he wanted to be far away while you were here collecting this information? Didn't you find any of this slightly suspicious?"

"Of course I did!" Nadia snapped. She seemed surprised by her own outburst, and she looked down at her feet as she continued. "But . . . but it didn't matter to me then. I didn't know her then. I didn't . . ."

"You didn't care. You just wanted your reward. Well, let me tell you the cost of that reward. My father doesn't think of Lynet as a granddaughter, or even as a person. He only thinks of her as *his*. He has no regard for human life. Why should he, when he can create it so cheaply? And apparently you don't either, since you were willing to use her for your own gain, to sacrifice her safety just to get what you wanted." She was tearing the letter up now, ripping it apart as each word that she directed at Nadia turned inward and pierced her, instead.

But her words had some effect on Nadia, as well. She looked stricken, frozen in place, her eyes staring unblinking at the pieces of paper that floated down from Mina's hands. "You're right," she said tonelessly. "I've been trying to write that letter all night, but it feels like drawing blood." She shook her head. "I tried not to let it bother me before, but now . . ."

Mina tried to remain disgusted, but all she could think was that they were both traitors, both tools her father had used to reach the girl he'd created. And now Lynet was gone, leaving them both alone to face what they had done. Mina had betrayed Lynet for a crown, and Nadia had betrayed her for the university. But how could Mina blame her too harshly for wanting to get away from this miserable place and go somewhere warm? At least one of them could still do it.

"I'll give you what my father promised you."

Nadia's head snapped up. "What?"

"I want you far away from here. I'll leave a sealed letter and a purse with the steward for you. The purse will take you south, and the letter will grant you a place at the university. My only price is that you leave by dawn and never come back."

"But Whitespring—"

"We survived without a surgeon before my father found you."

Nadia was silent for a long moment and then shook her head, resolute. "I can't go until I know what's happened to Lynet."

"Lynet is beyond your reach and mine." Mina swept past her, kicking aside the scattered pieces of paper. "Remember, I want you out of Whitespring by dawn. Don't let me find you again."

"She wanted to run away," Nadia called after her, and Mina froze. "She wanted to go south with me. She told me that before the accident."

"And do you think she'll make it all that way on her own?" Mina said.

Nadia didn't answer, and Mina knew they were both thinking that for all of Lynet's restless energy and reckless habits, she was still a sheltered girl, beating at the bars of her cage.

Mina left the room without interruption this time, but once she was out of the surgeon's sight, she stopped and leaned against the wall of the stairwell, her knees shaking. As soon as she'd known that Lynet hadn't gone to Nicholas, part of her had guessed that Lynet had left Whitespring. She had pushed the thought aside, to the very back of her mind, not because of fear, but because of the far more shameful feeling that washed over her now—

Relief.

"Isn't it better for you that she's gone?" Felix asked her when they were in the chapel again. "Isn't it safer that you never find her?"

"No, Felix," she said, but of course she knew there was truth in his words. Lynet was gone, but at least she couldn't tell her father about Mina's secrets.

She breathed in. *I'm safe.*

And out again. *But Lynet's in danger.*

Even when she shut her eyes, she could still see Lynet's face, holding her hand up to her cheek in pain and shock as a piece of glass struck her—

Somewhere underneath her skin, Mina could feel every sharp piece of glass scattered throughout the room. She concentrated on them, knowing she would need them to give her strength to accomplish this next task, and they started to move, to slither across the ground and join each other. Felix stood watching beside her, his mouth hanging slightly open in awe as one by one, the puddles of liquid glass stretched up from the ground and formed his new brothers.

There were a dozen of them, the same number as in the king's guard, all with plain, unmemorable faces. She was rushing, though, so some of them had scars similar to the ones on Felix's arms. Mina clothed them in the same white-and-blue uniform as the king's guard, as well, instilling in them one purpose: to find the princess and bring her back to Whitespring. She told them to search the woods south of Whitespring, to keep watch over the town in case she surfaced there. Under no circumstances were they to hurt the princess.

"Go," she told the soldiers, her chest aching from the effort of creating so many people at once, and they marched away, with Felix in the lead.

She had thought she'd feel more at ease once she'd taken action, but Mina couldn't stop wringing her hands. If anything happened to Lynet outside the castle walls, it would be her fault. Mina was the one who had scared her away. *And I'll be the one to bring her back again,* she promised herself.

But a treacherous whisper added, *And then what will you do with her?* Lynet knew about her heart, and she knew about Felix. How could Mina ever trust Lynet again now that she'd been turned inside out, her rotten core on display to the only person who had still thought she was perfect?

20

LYNET

Lynet stumbled in the darkness, her only guidance the patches of moonlight that broke through the trees. She didn't think about where she was going but tried to keep to the main road. She didn't think about what she was leaving, though she kept glancing behind her, sure that the huntsman had changed his mind and was coming after her. She only focused on moving forward, ignoring the tightness in her chest, the lump in her throat. *This is what you wanted, isn't it?* she kept thinking. *You're free now. You can be whatever you want to be.*

But surrounded by towering pine trees, she didn't feel free. She felt like a coward, running from the first sign of danger.

With each step, the coins in the purse clinked together, and Lynet had to try not to flinch as she remembered the sound of the shattering glass in the chapel. She kept telling herself it wasn't true—that Mina loved her, that she hadn't sent the huntsman to kill her—but the weight of the purse the huntsman had given her was a constant reminder. She lost track of how long she'd been walking, but she knew if she stayed on the road south, she would make it out of the woods eventually, and then she'd arrive at the town of North Peak. That was assuming, of course, that no wild animals attacked her in the woods. *Like my father,* she almost thought, but she forced it to the back of her mind. There were too many dangerous thoughts, and she stepped around them as carefully as she could, like she was navigating through a field of traps.

Soon, she promised herself. Soon she would reach the town, but she wouldn't stop there, she would keep going—

Go where?

South, of course. She'd go south, just as she had planned. She would put as much distance as possible between herself and the events of this night, until she forgot her old life and became someone entirely new. That was what she had wanted—the freedom to shape her own future. There was nothing to fear, nothing to regret. *I wanted this,* she reminded herself again. And every time she stumbled in the darkness, or wondered if she'd heard something growling, or remembered the look on Mina's face in the chapel, she just repeated it once more. *I wanted this.*

She was still saying it to herself when she felt rough hands grab her, one arm encircling her waist while the other held something sharp to her throat.

He found me, she thought, but the voice that spoke didn't belong to the huntsman.

"Your purse," the voice said, low and frantic next to her ear. "I can hear the coins. Give it to me, or I'll slit your throat and find it myself."

Lynet remembered Nadia telling her that thieves hid in the woods, that she'd never survive on her own. She struggled to breathe—the blade was pressing into her, and a slow trickle of blood began to flow where it had nicked her skin. "Take it," she said, fumbling for the purse tied around her waist. She held it up, silently praying that he wouldn't decide to kill and search her anyway.

But as soon as the thief snatched the purse from her hand, he was gone, leaving Lynet terrified and penniless, but alive.

Lynet ran.

She was lucky, really, she told herself. The thief hadn't seen the silver bracelet on her wrist, hidden by her sleeve, so she still could buy her way south. If she needed anything else, she would have to beg for it.

In her heavy boots, Lynet tripped over a tree root that jutted up through the snow, and fell on her hands and knees. Something inside her broke, then, and all the dangerous thoughts she'd been trying to avoid caught up to her at last. Her father, the chapel, the huntsman, the thief with his knife against her throat—they all descended on her at once, and she struggled against the tears stinging her eyes, her throat burning from the effort of not crying.

Lynet curled up on her side, holding her knees to her chest, clutching at her dress as she tried to stop the dry, heaving sobs that shook her whole body, each one making her hate herself just a little bit more. She pictured what she must look like now to an observer, and the image was that of frightened prey trying to make itself small and invisible.

It's true, whispered a traitorous voice in her head. *I'm not strong, I was never strong, I was only pretending.* What was the use of climbing trees or high towers if she was just going to end up here, lying helplessly in the snow? She'd tried to convince herself that she wasn't delicate, never understanding that the only reason she had to try so hard to prove it was because she had never really been tested. And now that she *had* been tested, now that she had failed so miserably, she knew that she had never been strong—only lucky.

She forced her eyes open and slowly sat up. She had left a dark stain in the snow that she knew was blood from the wound on her throat, and for a moment, she was entranced by the sight of it, a distraction from the thoughts that troubled her. The blood served as a reminder of who she was, what she was made of. She was not her mother's child—she never had been. She was blood and snow, and so she would be like the snow, like the pine needles, like the winter wind: sharp and cold and biting. Snow didn't break or shatter, and neither would she. All she had to do was be true to her nature.

Cold as snow, sharp as glass. Lynet rose to her feet. She still had a long way to go.

When Lynet first heard the sound of hoofbeats behind her, she didn't hesitate. Immediately, she scrambled off the main road, diving into the maze of trees, knowing that she might become hopelessly lost as a result. There was only one reason she'd hear horses coming from the direction of Whitespring in the middle of the night—Mina had sent someone after her, to hunt her down.

Lynet thought quickly. What did it matter if she escaped her pursuer only to end up dying lost in the woods? She had to keep the main road in view somehow, even if just to know when the danger had passed and it was safe to stop hiding.

Lynet found a tree with low enough branches to climb and went up as high as she dared, until she had a decent view of the road stretching in both directions. She had acted just in time—only a few seconds after she was hidden in the tree, she saw two men on horseback riding past.

She had been right—they were from Whitespring and wore the uniforms of her father's guards. But when the moonlight struck their faces, she knew these men didn't belong to her father. One of them had a long scar running down his neck, and both of them had dark, blank eyes, like two reflective pools. Her stomach twisted as she remembered looking up into those same eyes, certain she was about to die.

The two men rode on, but soon others followed, Mina's huntsman among them. They were riding more slowly, holding their lamps up to peer into the woods. A few of them were on foot, spreading out into the trees.

Lynet tried not to breathe, hoping that they wouldn't come near her tree, that they wouldn't look up and shine their lamps directly on her. She couldn't do anything but wait—if she tried to climb higher up, she might make too much noise or attract their attention. Worse, she might slip and fall, landing at their feet with a broken neck. Their search would be over then.

She lost sight of the soldiers—she thought there were ten of them, not counting the two that had ridden on ahead. But then she heard a noise from below and saw the golden light from a lamp approaching her tree.

It was the huntsman who stepped out from between the trees, holding his lamp high. He was looking up, searching the pine branches for a frightened girl who might be huddling there.

Lynet was thankful for her dark brown dress and hoped that if she kept her head down, her hair hiding her face, she would appear as nothing more than a shadow. She heard her breath coming out in shallow spurts, and she put her hand over her mouth, waiting, waiting. . . .

But the huntsman didn't seem particularly enthusiastic about his task. The others had been searching with a single-minded determination, but the huntsman moved more slowly, turning his lamp from tree to tree after only a glance upward. When he came to her tree, Lynet's heart pounding against her chest, the lamplight didn't even come close to her, swinging in a low arc far below her perch.

She was lucky it was him. Any of the others might have discovered her hiding place, but the huntsman hadn't let her escape only to capture her again. She didn't think he would let her go a second time, but she could tell that he was hoping not to find her in the first place.

She didn't come down from her tree until the last of the soldiers was beyond her vision down the road, and even then she waited a little longer before slowly, carefully climbing down.

The knot in her stomach loosened, but it didn't go away entirely. Lynet guessed the purpose of those first two riders. They were to go all the way to town and wait there in case Lynet emerged from the woods before the others found her.

She couldn't go on into North Peak. She couldn't go back to Whitespring. She was trapped in the woods until she starved to death or was found. Death waited for her in every direction.

Lynet clung to the base of her tree, not knowing which way to go now. She was alone, outnumbered, and empty-handed, without anyone to help her—

If you need help, ask the snow.

She sank to the ground, turning the huntsman's cryptic words over in her head. Perhaps it was some kind of riddle, but no matter how many times Lynet repeated it over to herself, she couldn't find any other meaning.

Lynet scooped up a fistful of snow and looked at it uncertainly. "Help?" she whispered. Nothing happened, but she didn't even know what she wanted to happen, or what kind of help she was asking for. What she really needed was a cloak with a hood, something to hide her face so that if she managed to find a way into town, she would be inconspicuous. She was picturing the cloak in her head, something slightly shabby and dull, so it wouldn't attract attention, when she noticed what was happening to the snow.

It was *moving*, and Lynet let the snow fall from her hand in panic. But it still kept shifting, somewhere between snow and liquid, as it spread over the ground. And then, between one blink and the next, there was a plain black cloak lying on the snow.

Hardly believing what she had seen, Lynet touched the cloak, feeling the heavy fabric between her fingertips, marveling that it was *real*. The snow had become a cloak for her, because she had asked. But how was that possible—

Because I'm made of it, she thought, the answer both obvious and incredible at the same time. She'd always had a special knack for making shapes in the snow, forming intricate castles or shaping animals that almost seemed to come alive. And how else had the chapel's glass windows shattered, unless Mina had made it happen by will alone? How else had those cracks spread out over the huntsman's neck at Mina's command? The soldiers with their glassy eyes and vacant expressions . . . they weren't real at all. They were men made out of glass. If Mina's glass heart gave her power over glass, then Lynet must have the same power over snow. She had been made from magic, after all—why shouldn't some of that magic still remain in her blood?

Lynet swept some pine needles aside and took up a handful of snow. *Melt*, she thought. The snow turned to water in her hands almost instantly, dripping from between her fingers. Despite everything, she wanted to laugh. It felt like moving another arm, an extension of her body that she hadn't previously been conscious of.

But Mina knew. She must have at least suspected that Lynet would have this power, since she was clearly aware of her own. Another secret Mina had kept from her, then, another piece of herself that she hadn't known. There was so much she still didn't know—about herself or about Mina. Neither one of them was the same person anymore. Lynet still held all the pieces—all of the moments she and Mina had shared together, the feel of Mina's hands braiding her hair, the small comforts she had offered—but they seemed to be scattered around her, with no way to repair them without creating a distorted image, a cracked mirror. And in the spaces between all those cracks were Mina's secrets, the Mina who claimed she was unable to love, the Mina Lynet had never known.

Lynet still didn't understand the strange powers that had shaped them both. *For that, I suppose I'd have to ask the magician.* But Lynet couldn't ask Gregory, because Gregory—

Gregory was away in the South.

She felt a prickling all along her skin, thrilling with a growing sense of purpose. She had already been planning to go south, but now she had a more exact destination: she could go to the university, find Gregory, and ask him all her questions. Perhaps he knew how to cure Mina's glass heart, to make her capable of the love that Lynet remembered. Perhaps the cracked mirror wasn't irreparable after all.

But first she had to evade Mina's soldiers. She had the cloak, but that wasn't enough, especially if they kept moving south until they caught her. She had to mislead them somehow, to make them think she was headed somewhere else so they wouldn't follow her. She stared down at the snow, wondering how it could help her now.

And then she remembered being up in the tree, thinking that if she fell and broke her neck at their feet, their search would be over. *I could make another me,* she thought. *Another girl made out of snow who looks just like me.* Mina wanted her dead—so if Lynet gave Mina what she wanted, if Mina believed Lynet was dead, she would stop her search, and that would buy Lynet the time she needed to go to Gregory.

A body, she thought, sinking her hands into the snow. No, not just any body. *Me. Become me.*

The snow started to melt in front of her. Lynet kept her own image in her mind, repeating her command over and over again until the snow shifted and liquefied under her hands. The snow stretched out and formed the outline of a human—but creating a perfect replica of herself was more difficult than making a nondescript cloak. The figure in front of her was an eerie imitation of Lynet, but the eyelashes were missing, the dress was the wrong shade of brown, and her fingers seemed to blur together. She'd also forgotten about the small cut on her cheek from where the glass in the chapel had nicked her. The image in her mind hadn't been precise enough, so she concentrated again and again, making adjustments until she was looking down at her own body, clothed in her same brown dress with its fur lining. It was her exact image, except there was no heartbeat, no breath. She wondered if this was what her mother looked like at the moment of her death.

Lynet shivered. She knew what else she had to do to make Mina believe that Lynet had died on her own in the woods, and she wasn't eager to see the result.

A broken neck from falling out of a tree, she thought, picturing it in her mind, and after the snow liquefied and solidified again, she stared at the body's—at *her*—head, now lying at an odd angle, a reality that she had just barely avoided over and over.

Lynet slipped off her silver bracelet, her first gift from Mina, and placed it around the body's wrist. She felt light, almost weightless, like a spirit leaving her weakened body behind. Lynet was dead, just like her mother, and the girl who would emerge was someone new, shedding her soft skin to become something cold and untouchable. She had almost forgotten that today was her birthday.

The first true birthday that I've ever had, she thought, slipping her new cloak around her shoulders. She lifted the hood to hide her hair and face, and she rose from the snow to begin her new life.

21

MINA

Mina waited for Felix to bring Lynet to her, but instead he brought her Lynet's corpse.

She had been waiting outside the king's bedchamber at dawn when Felix came to her, several hours after she had sent him and the glass soldiers into the woods.

Mina had been frightened then, struck cold by the thought that Lynet was waiting for her, full of hate for her stepmother now. She almost wished that Felix hadn't found her at all.

Felix led her to the chapel, and Mina didn't understand why Felix avoided her eye when he told her that Lynet was there, why he kept saying he was sorry.

Several of the soldiers waited in the chapel, standing around the central altar. With a flick of his hand, Felix waved them aside, and he gently led Mina forward. And only then did Mina see that this was Lynet's corpse, and Lynet was dead.

Even as she bent forward to inspect the corpse, she still thought it was all some kind of trick, or that she had been mistaken, and she would see the faint movement of Lynet's chest signaling that she was alive, but unconscious. But her chest remained still, and for the first time, Lynet's heartbeat matched Mina's own.

Her neck was broken, and there was still a small cut on her cheek from where Mina had accidentally wounded her with the glass. *No,* Mina told herself, *none of this was an accident.* Lynet must have fallen, probably from a tree where she'd been hiding—hiding from Felix and the soldiers. Every piece of Lynet's death came together, like a hundred tiny shards of glass, and together they formed a mirror that showed Mina her own face, her own guilt.

Mina stumbled, and Felix took her by the arm, helping her stay upright. "Did anyone see you bring her here?" she asked, her voice a thin rasp.

"No," he said. "No one knows but you."

But they would all know eventually. The princess's death, so soon after the king's accident. Would anyone believe that Lynet had met a natural end? Or would they all assume that she had taken her own life, fearing for her father's? Some terrible part of her whispered that she could use that assumption to her advantage, if she needed to shift suspicion away from herself.

Hands trembling, Mina gently laid her hand on Lynet's cheek. Her skin was as cold as it had ever been, her face just as pristine and beautiful. And yet the corpse was a pale imitation of the living girl; it was only a facsimile of beauty without the animation of Lynet's face, without the spirit behind her eyes. Wasn't that what Mina had secretly wanted—to strip Lynet of her beauty, to be the only woman worth looking at, worth loving?

She was glad now that she had told the young surgeon to leave Whitespring instead of inflicting some harsher punishment. She was glad there was someone else in this world who would carry the memory of Lynet's eyes, her smile, the way she was always dashing down the halls instead of walking. Nicholas had his own memory of Lynet, and the courtiers would remember a princess who looked like her mother. But if that young woman had been Lynet's friend, then she might have been the only person other than Mina to know Lynet as she was, not as she appeared.

Felix's hands gently came around her, trying to lead her away. "No," she said. "Not yet." She slipped the silver bracelet off Lynet's wrist. She would keep it on her bedside table, beside the empty mirror frame that had once belonged to her mother. A collection of things she had lost, she supposed, or of people she had driven away.

"Take her to the crypt," she ordered, though it felt wrong. Lynet had always been so scared of the crypt, so certain that she would end up there beside her mother, both of them identical in death as in life. Now her fear had come true. "Try not to let anyone see you. I don't want the king to hear about this before I tell him myself."

Felix led the others away, and Mina took a breath before returning to the king's rooms. She wondered if this news would kill him.

He was lucid when she sat at his bedside, though his skin had taken on a sickly gray tint. His first words were, "How is Lynet?"

Mina kept her face still. "Why do you ask that?"

He stared up at the canopy above his bed, eyes wide and unseeing. "I think I dreamt of her. I think . . . I think she was saying good-bye." He closed his eyes, his face screwed up in pain. "I can't tell anymore, I can't tell who . . . which one of them I saw. . . ."

"Nicholas . . ."

"I keep hearing her voice in my head, telling me terrible things, the same things you told me—that she never cared about her mother, that she's been unhappy—but I can't remember if any of it is real." He reached for her hand, and Mina took it in surprise. "Tell me, Mina, tell me—she was happy, wasn't she? We were happy together."

Mina didn't know if he meant Lynet or Emilia, and she wasn't sure if Nicholas knew, either, or if they had come together to form one beautiful dead woman, far from his reach. *He'd love me, too, if I were dead,* Mina thought. For all the bitterness that lay between them, she knew that if she died on the spot, he would weep for her. He would mold her memory into a wife he could love, and he would worship her dead body just as he had shunned the living one. *He loves nothing so much as his own grief.*

"Nicholas, you have to listen to me. I have to tell you something."

"She said good-bye. . . . Why did she say good-bye? Where did she go?"

Mina had the curious feeling that she wasn't in her own body, that she was watching from somewhere else, and she clasped his hand more tightly, willing herself to come back and finish what she had started. "She's dead, Nicholas. Lynet is dead."

He released her hand at once, staring at her in disgust. "Do you hate me so much?"

"I don't hate you, Nicholas, I never have. It's always been you who hated me."

Nicholas shook his head. "I never hated you. But I can't love you, and I think you'll never forgive me for that. That's why you're lying to me now."

Mina sighed, wishing she had just waited for him to die rather than ever tell him. "You're right," she said. "I'm lying. Lynet is in her room."

"Get her for me," he said, his eyes fluttering closed.

"I will," Mina said. "You'll see her soon. You'll see them both soon."

He murmured something under his breath, something that sounded like, "She said good-bye," and tears began to flow from beneath his eyelids.

"Nicholas?" Mina whispered, a hint of panic in her voice.

But before she could say more, he was gone.

Mina stood alone in the chapel, staring at the jagged pieces of glass in the empty window frames. She shouldn't have come back. The room reminded her of Lynet—something Mina had known would happen when she first brought Lynet here. She had been strangely nervous that time. Maybe she'd just been afraid that Lynet would see her too clearly, see the angry, homesick girl that she had been.

Mina's fears had been unwarranted. Lynet had understood. Lynet had thanked her for sharing this piece of herself, and if she had seen some past vision of Mina here, she had not judged her too harshly.

Mina fell to her knees in front of the altars, her ragged breathing the only sound. Broken glass dug into her knees through her thick skirts, but she barely felt the pain.

Mina heard the door open behind her, but she kept her head down.

"I thought you'd be here," Felix said, kneeling at her side.

"Leave me."

He gently cupped her face in his hands, lifting her head to look at him. "Ask me again, and I will."

She didn't answer, so he leaned forward and brushed his lips against hers.

"The king is dead," she told him.

Felix bowed his head, whether from shame or respect, Mina wasn't sure. "I'm sorry."

"Don't tell anyone, yet. If Whitespring knew that both the king and the princess were dead, there would be chaos." She took his face in her hands, lifting his head to look at her. "Felix, what do I do now?" she asked him in a whisper.

He put his hands over hers and brought them to his lips, kissing her knuckles. "Be a queen, just as you were always meant to be."

Mina gazed into his eyes, trying to figure out if he was only reflecting back to her the answer she wished she could give herself. "What do you see in me, Felix? What do you see right now?"

He studied her, and as he did, his face started to change, his lips turning down, his eyes filling with despair. Mina saw the brokenness in him, which meant that he saw something broken in her. She had told Lynet it was a gift to be delicate, because it meant no one had tried to break her. The word that Lynet hated so much had sounded like a luxury to Mina. She had tried to think of a time when she had ever felt delicate, but she couldn't; for as long as she could remember, she had always felt herself covered in invisible fractures, a map of scars like the ones that ran up and down Felix's arms. Perhaps she was so broken that she had become unbreakable.

No one would ever see her like this, Mina decided. No one would see her on her knees, head bowed in shame. She had nothing left to lose, except her crown—and she would fight for it. The people of the South still needed her, and she would fight for them, too. She wouldn't waste Lynet's death by falling apart now.

Mina thought of the girl who had once sat in this same room, promising herself that she would be a queen, and she rose to her feet.

Mina paced the windowless council room, waiting for her guest. Today, the long table was bare, and the throne at its head was empty.

Father and daughter were both dead, but Mina couldn't afford to mourn any longer. In the chapel, she could fall to her knees and give in to regret, but the moment she crossed the threshold, she had to be nothing less than a queen, with no sign of weakness or doubt.

She knew she had to act quickly in the short hours after Nicholas's death. The captain of the guard had always liked her—he had southern roots, he had whispered to her once—and so when she brought him a dozen new soldiers to train as her personal guard and a purse full of gold coins to spend as thanks for his continued loyalty, he bowed his graying head and promised always to serve his queen.

She sought out a few of the noblemen she knew, ones whose gazes had lingered on her a little too long over the years, men she'd flirted with long ago at social functions even before she was queen. She didn't tell them that Nicholas was dead, but she expressed her worries that he would die soon, that she would be a widowed queen. She kept them all at a distance, using only flattery and the illusion of her vulnerability to let them think she was close enough to touch. Later, when they learned that both Nicholas and Lynet were dead, each one would remember that the queen had sought him out especially, and he would think himself favored, perhaps even desired. They would all believe that with Mina on the throne, they might have a chance to rule too—a dowager queen was a valuable asset for a man who wanted to be king.

Finally, she spoke to the steward and made sure that her plans had some historical precedent. And then she sent for Xenia. As much as she hated to admit it, Mina needed her support.

A knock at the door brought Xenia, escorted by one of Mina's new soldiers, and Mina told him to wait outside while she and the noblewoman talked.

"Has something happened, my lady?" Xenia said in the honeyed tone she'd always used since Mina had become queen.

"Sit, please," Mina said, gesturing to the table. Xenia took her usual seat, at the king's left side, and Mina sat across from her. "I'm telling you this because I know I can trust you to do what's best for the stability of this kingdom," Mina said. She had thought she would need to force the words out, but she found to her surprise that she believed them. Xenia's power came from her position at court, a position that depended on stability and unchanging order. If she could convince Xenia that they both wanted the same thing, she would win.

"I'm honored by your trust in me, my lady," Xenia answered. "I hope the king is well."

"I'm afraid not," Mina said. She looked down at her clasped hands for a moment before continuing. "The king is dead."

The news shocked Xenia into momentary silence, her mouth hanging open. "I've known him since he was a boy," she said, fighting to recover her composure. "I—I'm sorry, my lady. I know this loss must be—"

Mina shifted in her seat. "I understand your grief, but we have no time for it now."

Mina's blunt words had their intended effect—Xenia's polite mask slipped, her face hardening as she looked with loathing at the lowborn woman who ranked above her. "Then you'll forgive me for asking why you've called me here alone. I know it isn't because of the high regard you hold for me."

Mina gave Xenia a cold smile. "You're right. But I do understand your position here, the influence you hold over the rest of the court. I experienced it firsthand when I was a girl. One word from you, and the rest follow."

Xenia tilted her head in acknowledgment. "True."

"I have something else to tell you . . . something I wish I didn't have to say." Mina paused, afraid her voice would break. When she was sure of herself, she said, "The princess is dead as well."

Xenia didn't react at all, her face perfectly still. And then she said, "Are you telling me the truth?"

The sight of Lynet's corpse laid out in the chapel flashed through

Mina's mind. She took a breath, forcing the image away before she answered. "Lynet was found dead early this morning on the grounds. Her neck was broken, probably from a fall. I can't know for sure, but I think . . . I think she took the news of her father's accident badly."

Xenia gasped, understanding Mina's implication. "The poor child."

Mina waited for her to recover, to grasp the larger ramifications of Lynet's death, as she knew Xenia would.

And there it was—Xenia looked up at Mina suddenly, looked her in the eye with perfect understanding. "The king named no other successor, did he?"

Mina shook her head. "I spoke to the steward. He said the king had no other direct relations, only distant cousins, all with an equal claim to the throne. Do you understand what that means?"

"Of course I understand. This kingdom will fall into chaos. There could be civil war. . . ."

"I don't want that any more than you do. I want everything to stay as it is. And there's only one way I can see for that to happen."

She had feared that Xenia might laugh at her when she figured out what Mina truly wanted, but Xenia didn't laugh or sneer. She nodded slowly, looking Mina full in the eye as she said, "You have to remain queen. And you can't do that without me."

"It seems that we both need each other," Mina said. "You keep me on the throne, and I'll keep you on my council."

"Is that all you can offer me?" she said, her voice quiet but firm.

Mina had been prepared for that question. "I'll make you my chief adviser."

"An alliance, then?"

"For the good of the kingdom."

The two women watched each other, and Mina knew they were reaching the same realization—that despite their distaste for each other, they would both be stronger together than they had been before, when they were at odds. The peace of an entire kingdom waited for them to put aside past offenses in the name of power and pragmatism.

Xenia's eyes narrowed slightly. "If I help bring you the council and the rest of the court, do you think you would be able to maintain your place on the throne?"

"I have the castle guard on my side," Mina said, "and a newly established personal guard as well. The steward assures me that I'm not the first queen in Whitespring's long history to remain in power after her husband has died. I can only imagine that all of Whitespring would also prefer a peaceful transfer of power rather than a long search—or war—over a successor, and will give me no trouble. And, of course, I have the support of the South. If I command them to rise up—or to stop sending food to the North—they will obey."

Xenia shuddered, probably imagining the disaster that a southern siege against the North would bring. At last she nodded. "No one wants a war, especially not the North."

"Are we in agreement, then?" Mina said, rising from the table. "We'll speak to each of the councilors together, telling them what's happened and explaining why their support is necessary, just as I've explained it to you. With your influence and my position, I'm sure we can persuade them to fall in line."

Xenia stood too. "I believe you're right. Have no worries, my lady. You'll sleep tonight as a queen."

That evening, Mina gathered her court in the throne room with her guards, both old and new, lining the walls. The Hall was more suited for an audience of this size, but Mina thought the throne room lent her an air of authority and provided a change of scene from the stale and stagnant kings and queens who had come before her.

"People of Whitespring," Mina called out over the small crowd. "As some of you may have already heard, King Nicholas died this morning, from wounds received during a hunting accident." She waited for them all to murmur among themselves, bracing herself for what she had to say next. Would it ever become an easy thing to say? Would she ever become accustomed to speaking these words? "But even as we mourn his loss, we must face another tragedy: Princess Lynet was found dead as well."

The crowd gave a collective gasp out of respect for the news, but Mina saw no fresh sorrow, no real surprise. The council members all knew, of course, because she and Xenia had told them, and they must have quickly shared the news with others. At that moment, she preferred Nicholas's honest grief to the calculated looks of sadness on the faces of the court.

"There will be time enough to mourn in the coming days, but at this moment, it's my duty to look to the future, to ensure that no harm comes to this kingdom as long as it's still in my care. The king died without naming a new successor, and so in the interest of maintaining peace in our kingdom, I have been asked to continue my reign as queen and to rule in my husband's stead. I would never presume to accept such a request without the support and approval of my court. If there are any here who wish to refute my claim, please speak now."

Minutes passed in silence, and though Mina saw a number of people glance uncertainly at the soldiers around the room, not a single person in the room spoke out.

Finally Xenia stepped forward, apart from the crowd, but still at a careful distance from Mina. "I think I speak for us all, my lady," she said, "when I say that we are thankful for your leadership at such a distressing time. We all owe our continued good fortune to you, Queen Mina." And with a sly look in her eye that only Mina could see, Xenia bowed her head. Immediately, the rest of the crowd followed suit, the entire room bowing to their queen.

Mina allowed herself a small, silent intake of breath, barely no-ticeable to anyone who might be peeking up at her over the sea of bowed heads. She had stood in front of a bowing court before, but always at Nicholas's side, always with Lynet close behind her, a reminder that she was only an interim between two identical queens. The last time she remembered facing the court alone had been on her wedding night. That was also the last time she'd felt they might love her.

And did they love her now? Would they accept her fully, now that she was their best and only choice? Would they remember her as the queen who had saved the kingdom from being torn apart by civil war? Or would they always think that it should have been Lynet standing here, instead?

She held her head high, accepting their gesture, but part of her wondered if she had only traded the ghost of one queen for an-other.

22

LYNET

The merchant's cart was cramped, but Lynet was glad for it; the more people there were, the less attention she would attract. Tucked into the corner of the cart, Lynet tried not to fall asleep, but she was exhausted, and she pinched herself whenever her head started to droop.

The snow had become an unexpected resource. She now had a new dagger hidden under her cloak, and though she wasn't sure she would know how to use it, she felt safer knowing it was there. She hadn't eaten since leaving Whitespring, so she'd created some bread out of the snow and wolfed it down. She had a new purse with money now too, which she had used to buy her way south.

The cart belonged to a fruit merchant who was returning south to replenish his stock. When Lynet had seen others paying to ride part of the way in the empty cart, she had done the same. She had briefly considered trying to create a horse and cart of her own, but she still wasn't sure how her powers would work away from the snow. For all she knew, everything she had made could melt as soon as she crossed the Frost Line that separated the North and the South. The idea of creating a living creature intimidated her as well. She wasn't very familiar with horses—what if she forgot some crucial detail in its formation?

The others weren't going as far as she was. Lynet overheard a younger girl explaining that she had found a position working as a scullery maid at one of the northern estates. She'd only be able to take the cart to the nearest town, and then she'd have to walk through the snow the rest of the way. Lynet didn't know how she'd be able to make it that far; the girl's knuckles were already red and chapped from the icy wind. The gray-haired woman beside Lynet unwrapped a knitted shawl from around her shoulders and gave it to the girl, assuring her that she was returning from visiting family, and so she could make another shawl once she returned home.

Lynet shrank into her cloak. She was glad she had the heavy cloak to hide her finely made and embroidered dress, but she felt guilty knowing that she didn't truly need it when the others in the cart shivered under their thin clothing.

In Whitespring, it was a matter of pride not to show any sign of feeling the cold. But Lynet understood now that this was a game that only the wealthy could play, enduring the cold in public only to return to the warm fires and furs of their private chambers. She had been silently grumbling every time a splinter from the wood snagged on her clothes or hands, or whenever the rocking cart sent waves of nausea through her stomach, but now she only thought of what a blessing it was not to ever feel the biting cold.

The merchant stopped several times along the way, either to

feed the horses or to wait while the roads were cleared of snow or to sleep for the night. At each stop, Lynet took the opportunity to explore the northern villages, always hoping it would be different from the last.

Lynet had felt a thrill of excitement when she had first stepped into North Peak. Her father had never allowed her to go into town on market days, insisting that if she wanted anything, he would send someone to buy it for her. Still, Mina had told her stories of her home in the South, and some part of Lynet had imagined that all towns were the same—bright and bustling, full of color and movement. North Peak had been nothing like that. Lynet had walked past figures hunched over from the many layers of mismatched clothing they wore to protect them against the cold, their faces lined with fatigue.

No one looked at her. No one looked at anything. It was like . . . *like walking among ghosts,* she had thought with a shiver the first time. Of course she hadn't understood what it was like for northerners who couldn't buy their warmth at Whitespring—she never felt cold at all.

Wandering now through another bleak village, Lynet had the same feeling she'd had in North Peak, that she was walking among ghosts. She walked through the market, hoping to find a fruit stall, but most of the fruit had already begun to spoil. And there were no signs of the luxuries the North was so proud of—no gems or metalwork from the mines, no intricate wooden carvings—only necessities.

Nothing grows here, Nadia had said. With a pang of shame, she guessed that any food that stayed fresh during the journey north probably went to Whitespring.

Another girl near her age was also looking at the spoiled fruit, her nose wrinkling in disappointment. Still, she bought a single mealy apple and went on her way, while Lynet went the other direction, knowing that she could take a handful of snow and make her own fruit. She paused in her step, wondering if she *should* make an apple and chase after that girl, to offer her something better than what she could find here. And from there, her thoughts expanded—if she could make one, then why not a cartful? Why not feed an entire town if she had the capability to do so?

Because you're supposed to be dead, she reminded herself. She hadn't heard any news of either the king or the princess dying in her time traveling south, but she was sure Mina's soldiers had found the body by now. She couldn't afford to be heroic, either—she needed to be someone new and invisible, at least until she reached the South.

And perhaps it was selfish of her, but she *liked* being invisible. She had no name, no face, no connection to Emilia at all. She simply existed in her own right, and for the first time, the future was a vast unknown, a road cleared from snow.

She was walking back to the cart on the edge of town when a hand shot out and grabbed her by the arm. Lynet jumped, but it was only an old woman, wisps of white hair escaping from beneath her tattered shawl. "Is it you?" she muttered, peering past Lynet's hood to her face. "Are you the princess?"

Lynet went rigid in fear, looking around to make sure that no one was paying them any attention. The woman's grip on her arm was stronger than she would have expected from someone who looked so small and frail, but then, the woman would have to be strong to live so long in the North.

"No, ma'am. You're mistaken," Lynet managed to say in a broken whisper.

"I worked at Whitespring, in the kitchens," the woman said. "You wouldn't have noticed me, but I know your face—it was your mother's face too."

The woman was speaking more loudly now, and Lynet didn't

know how to make her stop, to release her arm. Bribe her? But that would only confirm her suspicions, and then she might tell someone else, and the news would spread through the North that the princess had been seen in one of the villages on the way to the South.

If Lynet wanted to get away, she would have to convince the woman that she was no delicate princess, no fragile butterfly. Lynet wrenched her arm from the old woman's grip, and the woman almost lost her balance from the violent movement. Lynet opened her cloak just a little, placing her hand lightly on the hilt of the dagger at her waist. "You're mistaken," she said again, more firmly this time. "Now leave me be."

The woman stared at the weapon as she retreated. "Of course," she said. "Of course. Sorry to bother you." And then she turned and hurried away.

Lynet let out a long breath as she continued back to the cart. She felt more shame than relief. She wasn't used to this kind of guardedness; it felt unnatural on her, like a dress that didn't quite fit. There was a kind of ache in her chest, a gaping feeling. *Is this how it feels to be strong?*

Back in the cart, she kept thinking of the old woman, of the girl and her spoiled apple, of how easy it would be for Lynet to step outside of the cart and clear these roads herself just by telling the snow what she wanted. She'd caught sight of a few workers along the way, shoveling snow off the road, and she was tempted to help them, to simply ask the snow to move aside and watch as it obeyed. Clean roads, fresh food—she could see the ways to counteract the hardships of Sybil's curse, yet she was running away.

But wasn't that what she had to do to survive? Hadn't Mina kept her own secrets rather than use them for anyone's good but her own? If Lynet wanted to match her stepmother's fierceness, to be stronger than she used to be, then she would have to learn to keep her own secrets as well.

The cart emptied a little more at each stop until Lynet was alone with the merchant, who thankfully paid no attention to her. She was fortunate she was alone when they crossed the Frost Line, because the moment it happened, she visibly jolted.

Even if she couldn't see for herself that the snow was gone, she would have known it at once. She simply couldn't *feel* the snow anymore. She had never thought she could feel snow in the first place, but now that it was gone, she could sense its absence, like a low buzzing in her ear that had suddenly been silenced.

And then there was the warmth that was slowly spreading through her body, making her feel heavy and listless. When she lifted her arm, it seemed to move more slowly than usual, like the air itself was trying to push it back down. Looking at her hand, she remembered her experiments with Nadia, and she wondered if her skin was still cold to the touch. She'd have to be careful not to let anyone brush against her here; her cold skin wasn't too strange in the North among the snow, but people would probably think she was ill if she was icy to the touch even under the sun.

I don't fit here, she thought suddenly, and she wondered if Mina had felt the same way when she had first crossed the Frost Line from the other direction. Mina always felt cold, no matter how many years she had spent in the North, and Lynet knew, without being able to explain why, that she would never get used to the heat under her skin now.

Lynet looked around and found an entire world she had never seen before. Green hills rose up near the horizon, and above them the sun was almost painfully bright now that it wasn't hidden by dense clouds. She had seen trees before, of course, but she only knew them to come in two varieties: green or bare. As the cart jostled along the path, she watched their surroundings change. She saw trees with red and gold leaves, trees with pink flowers, trees full of fruit or berries. She marveled at them all, thinking of Mina's rooms, her attempt to bring these colors to Whitespring. How faded those colors seemed now, compared to the sights in front of her.

They passed through miles of farmland, rows of wheat and other crops that Lynet didn't even recognize, but they never needed to stop—the road was smooth and unobstructed. Lynet closed her eyes and conjured the maps of the kingdom she had studied in her lessons, picturing the narrow strip of land, both protected and isolated by its heavy mountain ranges along the northern and western borders and the wide expanse of sea to the south and east. A little less than half-way down from the northern border was the Frost Line. Mina had once said that her journey north had taken nearly a week, but Mina's village had been closer to the kingdom's southern border. Lynet's destination, the largest city in the South, was farther north, not too far south of the Frost Line, and so the hardest part of the journey was already behind her.

They reached the city as the sun was beginning to set that night, almost three days after she'd begun the journey. Lynet stared, mesmerized, at the pinks and golds spread across the sky. Now she knew that she had never truly seen a sunset before.

The merchant would spend the night here before continuing on his way, so the cart moved on, slowly now, through the winding city streets, constantly stopping as people walked by with no regard for the horses. The air was warm and enticing with the smell of burning meat, and when they crossed a bridge over a river, the remaining sunlight reflected off the water so brightly that Lynet had to look away.

Mina had told her once that this was where Gregory went during his visits south, to the university that Mina had reopened not long after becoming queen. Thinking of the university made her think of Nadia, of course, but Lynet pushed her out of her head, trying not to imagine how different this journey might have been if Nadia had run away with her when she'd asked. It was risky, perhaps, to go to Mina's father for help, when Mina was supposed to think she was dead, but Lynet remembered the way Mina always bristled when she spoke of Gregory, and she remembered the way Gregory had been so pleased to see her the one time she'd run into him. She wasn't sure where his allegiance would lie, but he was the only one who could answer her questions, and so she had to take the risk.

When the cart stopped in front of an inn, the merchant helped Lynet step down, and she thanked him for taking her all this way. At first, all she could do was stand still on the street while everyone moved around her, the whole city spinning as she fought to keep her balance. When she'd recovered, she asked the merchant where she could find the university, and he simply pointed at a spot ahead. When Lynet looked, she saw a large dome rising up above the other buildings not far away. She thanked him and started walking in the direction of the dome.

But the streets here were not simple lines pointing straight ahead. They wound and curved, leading Lynet away from the dome, and then toward it again, and then slightly to the left. All the while, she was sweltering under her cloak and trying not to notice the strange stares people were giving her as they passed by in light, airy clothes, their arms bare. Lynet thought she must have looked like a storm cloud passing through.

And everywhere she went, she kept hearing Mina's name.

"Stop fidgeting," a mother told her child. "What would Queen Mina think if she saw how impatient you are?"

"To Queen Mina's health!" two men exclaimed as they passed a mug between them.

As she neared the university, she heard a rabble of drunken young students laughing and cheering. "To the queen!" one of them called out, and the others answered in turn, "To Queen Mina! To the southern queen!" *The southern queen*—how different those words sounded now, compared to when the Pigeons sneered them.

They love her here, Lynet remembered, pulling her hood farther down over her face. She had heard Mina tell her father about grateful letters she'd received, but she had never fully considered how important her stepmother must be to the South. To these people, Mina was their champion, and Lynet wondered, then, how they would have felt about her father's plan to give the South to his northern daughter.

The sun was a little bit lower by the time Lynet wound her way through the heart of the city and reached the university. She looked at the massive main building in awe. Glass tiles decorated the walls of the university in various patterns, shining brilliantly in the sunlight.

Lynet followed a group of students through the university gates, into an elegant courtyard with blooming pink roses climbing up the sandstone walls. In the center was a low, round fountain covered in colored tiles. Lynet would have liked to look more closely at a real garden, and a fountain that wasn't frozen over, but she didn't allow herself to become distracted. She went through the round arched doorway and marveled at the parade of color and light everywhere she looked, the setting sun throwing dramatic shadows of the arches and balustrades on the tiled floors. There were no straight lines here, none of Whitespring's sharp edges—from the tiles on the ground to the window frames to the roof above her head, the designs were all round or curved.

A grand marble staircase dominated the entry hall, and Lynet started her ascent, hoping to find someone who could lead her to Gregory. She had to pause when she reached a large stained-glass window on the landing. The remaining sunlight came pouring in through the window in a tapestry of color, and she wondered if the windows in the chapel at Whitespring had ever looked this way, in the days before the curse. Lynet looked down at her hands, the light painting her skin in different hues of orange and red and gold.

And then she looked up at the window as a whole, and she gasped at the image: a queen with red-tinged hair and golden skin, the sun rising behind her. The window was a tribute to Mina, in return for her reopening the university.

Lynet could only stand there a short while—the heat was becoming nearly unbearable to her—but she could still see the window's design behind her eyelids when she blinked. She kept thinking of Mina, who had grown up in the sun but now had to resign herself to lighting fires in an attempt to re-create its warmth. She felt strangely ashamed to be here now, like this was Mina's territory and she was trespassing, and she pulled her hood closer around her face.

Down one of the halls, Lynet found an older woman with a confident stride and stopped her to ask if she knew where she could find the magician Gregory.

The woman's eyes narrowed as she swept her gaze over Lynet's inappropriately heavy attire. "The queen's father? You won't find him here now."

The woman's stern tone made Lynet shrink back a little. "Doesn't . . . doesn't he live here, though?" she asked.

"He comes here often to visit the library," the woman said. "But no, he doesn't live on the grounds."

"If it isn't too much trouble, could you maybe tell me where he does live?"

She made a vague gesture in the air. "Somewhere nearby. From what I've heard, he keeps his home private because he doesn't like to be bothered, but if you're really so desperate to find him, you can try going to the apothecary. He may know more."

The woman continued on her way, leaving Lynet standing bewildered in the hall. She wished she hadn't backed off so easily or been so intimidated by the woman's forbidding attitude, but at least she had an idea of where to look next. Now she just had to find the apothecary's shop.

But not tonight. As she went back down the stairs, grateful that the darkening sky now obscured Mina's image in the window, she decided she would retrace her steps to the inn where the merchant had stopped and stay there for the night. And in the morning—well, in the morning, she would want to see the city in the light of day. The apothecary's shop could wait. After all, before that night in the chapel, even before her father's accident, she had wanted to come south to see who she could be when she wasn't just her mother's daughter. The discovery of Mina's powers—and her own—had made her forget her original reason for wanting to come south, but now that she was here, in a bustling city full of strangers, she knew what she really wanted to forget—the sound of Mina's voice in the chapel, the sight of her father on his deathbed . . . and herself.

Most of all, she wanted to forget herself.

LYNET

The South was much noisier than Lynet had anticipated. She'd felt a little nervous, but quite fierce, as she'd locked the door to her small room at the inn, lying down on the bed with her dagger beside her in easy reach. She had told herself that despite her exhaustion, she would have to sleep lightly, to be aware of every step outside her door. A girl alone in a city had to be vigilant.

But she needn't have worried about sleeping too heavily. At home, the snow had seemed to muffle all sound, creating a world of whispers and hushed movements. But here, that barrier was gone, the curtain lifted, and so Lynet did hear every step outside her door and on the floor above her. She heard the sounds of shouting and laughter on the streets outside her window. She heard the rattling of wheels and the clopping of horses. She heard every sound the city

had to offer, and when she rose early in the morning, the sun streaming in from her one window, she had barely slept at all.

The heaviness that had come over her when she'd first crossed
the Frost Line had never left. She still felt a little like she was trying to tread through choppy water, her movements a fraction slower
than she expected them to be. *You're not whole without the snow,* a
stubborn voice in her head insisted, but she ignored it.

Lynet emptied her purse onto the floor, counting the snow coins
that still remained. She was grateful they hadn't melted, and now
she wondered if she could dissolve them back into snow and make
more. Concentrating, she watched the coins become snow with the
same wonder as before. Then, before the snow could melt, she pictured double the amount of coins as before. But as soon as the snow
transformed, her body seemed to rebel against her—an ache in her
chest like something was wringing out her heart, a sudden fatigue
like the energy was draining out of her.

She shut her eyes, taking deep, labored breaths until the pain
faded, but the lethargy clung to her like a thick, muggy fog. Using
her power up north hadn't felt like this, but she had been surrounded
by snow there, so aware of her connection to it that it had felt like
part of her. And now, that connection was missing. She couldn't
afford to use her power again unless she had to, not if she wanted to
stay upright.

Gathering the coins back in the purse, Lynet eyed her heavy
cloak with disgust. Wearing it in the evening had been unpleasant
enough, but the idea of throwing it over her already heavy dress as
the sun beat down on her through the window was unbearable.
Even her thick hair seemed a burden, and she lifted it up off her
neck, wondering if she should just chop it all off.

And why shouldn't I? Her father would never have let her cut her
mother's hair, but her father was . . . her father wasn't here to stop
her. Before she could lose her nerve, she retrieved her dagger and

cut off her hair in an uneven line that stopped at her shoulders. She immediately felt cooler, and she let out a sigh of relief, some of her energy restored. But more than that, when she saw the mess she'd made of her mother's curls, she felt a curious kind of stillness come over her. Or no, not stillness—because her heart was pounding, and she thought she could even feel the blood flowing through her veins—but harmony. Every piece of her was finally moving together, no longer pulled in different directions to create that restless feeling under her skin.

She laughed, knowing that no one would hear her—or that it wouldn't matter if anyone did. Being alone in a city full of people was a frightening prospect at times, but now it made her feel bold. She ventured down into the city, following the road to the busy marketplace. She bought herself a new dress, the red silk sliding over her fingers like liquid. She would be happy to be rid of her wool dress, now torn and dirty from her travels, but she decided to keep wearing her cloak when she was out, despite the heat. Always in the back of her mind was the fear that someone might recognize her. She hadn't heard her own name since she'd run away, and she wanted to keep her identity a secret—at least until she found Gregory.

Tomorrow, she promised. She would try to find him tomorrow. She needed time to study her surroundings first.

For the rest of the day, she did just that. She wandered through the marketplace, letting the wave of the crowd pull her past baskets full of pomegranates, a stall twittering with the songs of caged birds, and carts of rolled-up woven rugs. She took note of a doll maker's shop, reminding herself to come back with the hair she'd cut this morning and see if he would buy it from her. She went down to the river that she had crossed last night and walked along its bank. She saw a group of children wading up to their ankles in a shallower part of the river, and she did the same, ignoring the echo of her father's voice telling her to be careful.

She did go to the doll shop the next day with a long braid of her hair, and before she left, her purse a little heavier, she asked the doll maker where she could find the apothecary. Following his directions, she went along the main road that snaked through the city in a large spiral until she turned down a shadowy road with a few scattered storefronts. She could tell which was the apothecary's just by the smell that surrounded it, a heady mixture of lavender and rosemary.

The smell was even stronger inside the shop. Bundles of dried herbs hung from the ceiling, and behind a long counter were shelves full of bottles and vials. There were a few other people inside the small shop, and Lynet waited her turn until she could speak to the apothecary. He was an old man, but he had a youthful air, a glimmer of amusement in his eyes as he handled his products with loving care. Lynet approached him with a smile and asked him if he knew where she could find the magician Gregory.

The glimmer in the apothecary's eye instantly went out as he peered at her over his desk. "Why would a young girl like you want to speak to the queen's father?"

But Lynet had been scared off once before; she had promised herself she wouldn't let that happen again. "That doesn't matter," she said, not breaking the old man's gaze. "I just need to know where to find him."

The apothecary shook his head. "I don't know."

"You don't know, or you don't want to tell me?"

He almost smiled. "He comes here often enough, but I don't know where he goes after he leaves my shop. He keeps to himself."

Lynet thanked him for his time and left the shop, wondering what she should do now. Before she'd gone more than a few steps, she felt a hand start to clamp around her arm.

At once, Lynet pulled her arm away and brought out her dagger, whirling around to face whoever was accosting her. The memory of being robbed in the woods was still fresh in her mind, and she was determined to put up a fight this time.

A young man with messy dark hair was facing her, his hands up to show Lynet that he meant no harm. She recognized him as one of the other customers in the apothecary's shop, and she lowered her dagger. "What do you want?" she demanded.

"I heard you asking about the queen's father," he said with a roguish smile. "I know where you can find him."

"Then tell me where," she said, and for a moment she didn't recognize her own voice. It sounded deeper to her, stronger, without any hint of uncertainty, and she wondered if it was because there was no one else to speak for her anymore. She couldn't afford to be anything but certain now. Perhaps she was slowly shifting, just like the snow, transforming into someone else.

The young man looked her up and down with an appreciative lift of his eyebrows. "I thought we could go together."

Lynet studied him more closely, noticing that despite his confidence and his height, he looked only thirteen or fourteen. "Thank you for the offer," she said, her voice softening, "but I'm not looking for a guide. Do you really know where he lives?"

The boy shrugged, his posture easing a little now that his attempt at flirtation had failed. "Sometimes he asks me to deliver things for him. When I do, I always leave them on the steps of the abandoned church behind the university."

"Thank you," Lynet said. "You've been very helpful." She pulled out a couple of coins from her purse and held them out to the boy, but he shook his head and backed away.

"No need," he said. "Just seeing your pretty face was payment enough."

Lynet hid a smile as he strolled past her and she set off to continue her search alone, but she soon began to wish she hadn't dismissed the boy's help so easily. Lynet traced the university walls around to the back of the grounds, and as promised, she found an old, abandoned churchyard down a short, dusty path, hidden behind some oak trees. But when Lynet marched up to the door, she found it locked.

Hands on her hips, she looked up at the church, thinking of a way to make it give up its secrets. The stone facade was water stained and overgrown with moss, and some of the higher windows were broken. A bird's nest peeked over the edge of the shabby tiled roof. Lynet had seen people come and go from a newer church with a high bell tower on the other side of the university, and she supposed Mina had funded it, considering the disrepair of the old church. But why, then, would Gregory ask that boy to deliver anything to him here?

Lynet gave the door another angry tug, but by now, the sky was growing dark, and the church was taking on a sinister appearance in the shadows, the water stains making the stones look like they were weeping. She was the only one on this hidden stretch of road, and she grew aware of how alone she was, not just in the churchyard, but in the whole city. There was no one here to help her, nowhere to go except for her room at the inn. Her heart lurched, and she felt like she was hanging out the tower window again, suddenly aware of how far she might fall. There was no one to pull her back inside this time.

I wish Nadia were here, she thought. She'd tried not to let herself think about Nadia before, but now the longing for her friend was fully formed and relentless, forcing her to acknowledge the shadows at the edges of her thoughts, the doubts she tried to drown out with the bustle of the city. Somewhere inside her mind was a dark void that had started to form the night she left Whitespring, and she worried that if she wandered too near it, she would fall in and never escape.

She headed back to the inn, looking for comfort in the light and movement of the city, but not even the city lights seemed as bright as Nadia's smile.

Her head was resting on something hard. She opened her eyes, and she saw only stone above her. *I'm in the crypt.* As soon as the thought struck her, she knew it was true. *I must be dead if I'm in the crypt.*

She sat upright on her stone bier, and all around her, the spirits of the dead sat up in their coffins. To Lynet's right was her mother, sad-eyed and insubstantial, like she was made of smoke. The dead queen waved shyly to Lynet.

"I don't remember how I died," Lynet said, but the words came out of Emilia's mouth instead. "I don't remember who I was."

She tried to speak again: "Where's Mina?"

"Mina is asleep. You forgot to wake her."

Lynet knew that voice. She turned to see Nadia on her left, sitting beside her on the bier. Her hair was loose, falling all around her shoulders. Mesmerized, Lynet reached out to touch it, but Nadia shook her head with a sad smile. "The dead can't touch the living. You left me behind."

"I didn't mean to leave you," Lynet said. Her own hair was growing, getting longer and longer until it was coiling around her feet like a tangle of snakes. She stared down at the snakes. They were hissing. "How did I die?"

Lynet was lying on her back again, though she couldn't remember doing so, and Nadia was kneeling over her, strands of her dark hair tickling Lynet's neck. "You weren't supposed to die," Nadia said. She bent even closer, her lips brushing the base of Lynet's throat. "You never told me what you wanted," she whispered against Lynet's skin.

Lynet's eyes fluttered closed. Just then she wanted *so much.* Even her heart was beating out the words. She started to say them out loud. "I want—"

"It's too late," Nadia said sharply, her head snapping up. Her face contorted, and Lynet couldn't tell if she was angry or sad. "Don't you see? Everything died with you."

"That doesn't make sense," Lynet tried to say, but she was dead, and the dead couldn't speak. She tried to get up, but the dead couldn't move.

"I'm going to cut off your hands now," Nadia murmured into Lynet's writhing hair. "But I'll keep them in case you want them again."

The pointed edges of Nadia's saw pressed against her wrist—

Lynet woke, her hair damp with sweat, and she immediately made sure her hands were still attached to her wrists. The dream came back to her in pieces—a mixture of pleasure and fear, but most of all a heavy feeling of regret—and she shoved it to the back of her mind.

It was that church, she decided later when she was walking through the city square. The old church was putting eerie thoughts into her head, but she couldn't let it scare her away.

But there were musicians playing in the square today, a few children dancing along, and the sky was bluer than she'd ever seen. Before she even knew she'd made any decision, she was sitting on the edge of the fountain that was built into a wall and watching people as they passed through the square.

She watched freely, openly, reassured by the fact that not a single person here knew who she was. And Lynet was thrilled not to know them, either, so accustomed was she to seeing the same faces at Whitespring. She only fully realized how small her world had been when she saw two young women strolling hand in hand, fingers entwined. One of them stopped to buy a flower from a vendor, and she placed the flower in the other girl's hair with such tenderness that Lynet knew they had to be sweethearts. Lynet tried not to stare too visibly, but her eyes couldn't help darting back to them repeatedly as they made their unhurried way through the square. Here was something she had never seen in Whitespring before. Her limited experience had only ever told her that men and women married each other and had children—she had never known there was any other option.

And why are you so interested in this knowledge? a voice whispered in her head. What did it have to do with her?

A loud burst of laughter from the children tore her away from her confusing tangle of thoughts, and she allowed the distraction, watching the children dance and play.

Her feet tapped the ground in rhythm to the music. She'd never danced like that when she was a child, eyes closed, spinning until dizzy. Her father always worried that she'd fall or tire herself, so he would scoop her up and tell her that she could dance all she wanted when she was a little older. But the measured dances of adulthood could never make up for the whirling abandon of childhood that she had missed. And finally she allowed herself to admit that part of her was glad the church had been locked yesterday. She did truly want to help Mina, but the sooner she found Gregory, the sooner she'd have to lose her anonymity and slip back into her old skin. Her mother's skin.

One of the little girls had spun too violently and nearly collided with the fountain before Lynet lunged to catch her. "Be careful," she said, but the child's laughter drowned out her warning.

"My friend thinks you're pretty," the little girl said, pushing her tawny hair off her forehead with her wrist. She pointed to a boy her age, six or seven likely, who was staring firmly at his feet, his face a little red. "You should dance with him."

"Oh, I can't—" Lynet started to say, but then she wondered—why not? When else would she have the excuse at her age to dance like a child again? "Actually, yes, I will," Lynet said, and she let the girl pull her by the hand over to the other children.

The boy was even redder now, so Lynet took his hands and said,

"Will you show me how to dance? I was never allowed to when I was a child."

He nodded, and soon they were spinning together in a circle, hands linked. The other children all wanted a turn, and Lynet danced with them all, one by one. She quickly grew breathless, and the heat of the sun weighed her down, but for a while, at least, she forgot that she had ever been anyone else.

And then, as she was mid-twirl, she received a vivid reminder.

Walking across the square at just that moment was Nadia.

That dark braid down her back, the sharp lines of her face— Lynet nearly stumbled over her feet as she fell out of the dance, so sure that she'd seen Nadia. But then she looked more closely, and she didn't recognize anyone in the crowd. Was her mind playing a trick on her by showing her what she wanted to see? That dream last night—

But if she *had* seen Nadia, then what was she doing here? The only way Lynet could imagine her leaving the king's sickbed was if . . . if the king didn't need a surgeon anymore, one way or the other. Suddenly all her old fears were upon her again, winding around her like invisible coils.

Lynet left the children behind to follow the apparition in the direction of the marketplace, hunting for one dark head among a patchwork of colors, but Nadia—if it really had been her—was gone.

She was still walking through the marketplace, glancing from face to face, when a large bell rang out. Lynet jumped at first, but then she remembered the bell tower that was part of the newer church. People were starting to head in that direction, and Lynet joined them, curious. By the time she reached the churchyard, she heard the sound of cheering, and she saw the same children dancing outside the gates.

Lynet approached the little boy she'd first danced with, kneeling down to summon him over to her. "What's happened?" Lynet asked him. "Why is everyone cheering? Why did the bell ring?"

He smiled brightly. "There was a message from Whitespring," he said. "The king and princess are both dead, but Queen Mina is still on the throne."

"To the southern queen!" a grown voice called out.

"To the southern queen!" the crowd answered.

The boy ran off then, leaving Lynet still on her knees.

The news rapidly spreading through the city was that the king had been seriously wounded in a hunting accident, and the princess, in her grief over his impending death, had flung herself off a tower. When the king heard his daughter was dead, he died on the spot.

There were three parts to the story—one Lynet knew was true, and one she knew was a lie, but the third . . . she had no way of knowing about the third.

It's my fault, Lynet thought as she wandered without direction through the city. She was barely aware that she was moving at all. *He died because of me—because of all the things I told him, because I ran away.* She suddenly felt a nauseating rush of guilt for cutting her hair.

Lynet ducked into an alley and doubled over, her body retching even though she had eaten nothing today. When her stomach relented, she huddled against the wall, leaning her forehead against her knees as her whole body shook with tears. It was silly to cry now, she told herself. She had known he would die—that was why she had wanted to leave in the first place. But now she wondered . . . if she hadn't decided to run, if she hadn't gone to the chapel to find Mina, if she had sat by her father's sickbed like a good daughter, then would he have lived? Should she have had more faith that he would make it through the night? And if he had lived, would she and Mina still have become enemies?

Mina. The gossip was that she had kept the throne in order to prevent a war of succession. Lynet could never go back now, not unless she wanted to fight Mina for the crown. Not that she wanted to go back—she wanted to *forget*.

But as she rose on uncertain legs and left the alley, she wondered if that was even possible. There was no use pretending she was another person anymore, not when her father's death had so sharply reminded her of who she was. She was probably the only person in this city who had cried for the king, and that grief defined her more clearly than her short hair or her new dress. She couldn't forget that the king was her father, or that she had loved him.

Even now, as she continued walking through the city, she saw signs of Mina everywhere, more reminders of the life she'd tried to leave behind. The bridge that she had crossed in the cart that first night was one that Mina had rebuilt. She passed by a group of workers who were digging a new road, on the queen's orders, so that the main road north would be less crowded. And always in the distance, over the hills, Lynet could see the shine of gold from what could only be the Summer Castle. Mina had moved to Whitespring so long ago, and yet Lynet still kept finding all these pieces of her that she had left behind. *What did I leave behind?* she wondered now. What pieces of herself were still in Whitespring?

The sound of a child laughing interrupted her thoughts, and she looked up to see a little girl of five or six sitting on her mother's lap by the edge of the fountain in the square. The mother was braiding the girl's thick brown hair, and Lynet felt a sudden stab of pain in her chest, her hand reaching for curls that were no longer there below her shoulders. *That should have been us,* she thought. *Mina should be here with me.* If they had known each other in some other way, if Lynet's father hadn't been a king, or if Mina and Lynet had both been made of flesh alone, no glass or snow in their hearts, would they be together now?

She moved on from the fountain with new purpose. She had delayed this moment long enough, hiding away and trying to forget the ties that still pulled at her heart. She had been relieved to feel alone and untethered before, but now felt herself tumbling into that black and empty void that kept threatening to swallow her whole. And yet there was still one way out from the void—Mina. Mina was her only family now, and Lynet couldn't let her stepmother go until she knew there was no way to cure her.

No more distractions. No more chasing ghosts or dragging her feet. Tonight, under cover of darkness, she would break into that church. Tonight, she would become Lynet again.

24

MINA

The funerals were over. The bodies of both King Nicholas and Princess Lynet had been laid to rest in the royal crypt beside the late Queen Emilia, the three of them reunited at last. Mina had bowed her head with the rest of the court as they all offered prayers to Queen Sybil in the Shadow Garden and the caskets were carried down to the crypt.

If the people of Whitespring thought her cold or unfeeling, she didn't care. She knew that if she fell apart in front of them now, they would never be able to believe that she could rule as queen, never trust her to be stoic in the face of hardship. And she knew, too, that if she gave in to guilt and grief, if she let them twist her face into something as ugly as her heart, that image of her would last forever, far longer than her beauty.

And so, though she was solemn, she was always composed, and

she tried to distract herself from the sight of Lynet's casket—so small and confining for a girl who loved to be under the open sky— by designing the Summer Castle in her head. She had lost her husband and her stepdaughter, but she still had her plans for the South.

Her first act as queen was to resume the Summer Castle's construction. She knew now why Nicholas wanted her to give up her project—even then, he must have been planning to give the South to Lynet—and so she knew that their deaths were the only reason she could continue with it now. But those thoughts troubled her when she dwelled too deeply on them, and so whenever they came, she devoted herself even more to the castle's completion. When she wasn't attending council meetings, she was poring over construction plans brought for her approval, overseeing every step.

Mina had wanted to believe that the court's attitude toward her would change. They had *chosen* her now, after all—chosen her as their queen rather than having to accept her only because the king had married her. And Mina was prepared to make an effort as well. She held back at the council meetings and let Xenia lead, knowing that if she were too aggressive from the start, they would all resent her for it. And so as each day passed, she slowly became nothing more than an attractive figurehead. Mina still had complete control over the South, but the council made its decisions on how to run Whitespring or how to settle grievances between its residents, and Mina said nothing. The only time she tried to disagree on some minor matter, Xenia had gently reminded her that the council had put Mina on the throne.

There was only one way she could think to win the North to her side, one act that would distinguish her reign beyond all others. If she could break Sybil's curse, then surely they would love her for it.

"I want to take down the statue of Sybil," she announced the next day to her council. She had suggested to Nicholas once that the answer to breaking the curse might have something to do with that statue over the lake, and even now she thought there could be some truth to it. After all, no one even knew when the statue had been built—it seemed to have appeared on its own sometime after Sybil's death.

As soon as she'd spoken the words, the entire council started clucking. "That would be the same as tearing down Whitespring itself," Xenia said, looking at her with a mixture of outrage and incredulity.

Mina waited with her arms folded on the table until they had quieted down, and then she said, "I know I don't always understand your northern traditions, but in this case, that may be a virtue. Over the years I've lived at Whitespring, I've wondered if Sybil's curse was somehow connected to her statue. If we tear it down, and lessen her power over Whitespring, perhaps the curse will lose its power as well." She turned to Xenia with an innocent smile, the kind she used to wear for Nicholas. "But of course, I would want the approval of my chief adviser in this matter." *And so will the rest of the council,* she thought. She only had to convince Xenia, and the others would follow without protest. "It would be a triumph for this council if we found a way to end the curse."

Xenia silently deliberated while staring out the window in the direction of the statue. Mina was sure she would agree—if tearing down the statue *did* end the curse, then Xenia would share in the glory, and if the attempt failed, she could simply blame that failure on Mina.

"I think the idea has merit," Xenia said quietly. "That statue is a reminder of Sybil's grief, as is the curse. Perhaps one won't exist without the other."

One by one, the other Pigeons all agreed, and Mina thanked them for their cooperation. The statue would come down, and then at least one gloomy shadow would lift from Whitespring.

Mina ordered her guards to take down the statue a few days later. She looked out into the garden from her window as they chipped away at the statue's base and threw rope around Queen Sybil's neck. Word had spread that the statue's removal might lift the curse, and so a crowd of people were gathered in the garden, waiting even now for the first signs of spring.

When the last pieces of the statue had tumbled into the lake, nothing had changed, except that there was now a blank square of soil that would soon be covered in snow. *Or maybe not*, Mina told herself. Maybe the change would be gradual, the snow melting a little at a time.

But the snow came down heavily over the following week, and soon Mina had to admit that she had failed. When she tried to address the council again, Xenia had coldly told her that they didn't currently need a southerner's perspective on northern matters. Mina's face burned with shame, and she didn't speak for the rest of the meeting, retreating again to thoughts of the Summer Castle.

Let the Pigeons have Whitespring, she thought. She would have something better in the end.

Late that night she found herself in the throne room. She couldn't remember making the decision to come here, but here she was, like a sleepwalker who had only woken now, surprised to be looking around at the glass mosaic tiles on the walls. Felix had followed her, as her personal guard, but he had said nothing as he accompanied her, carrying a candelabra that lit up the vast, dark room.

She had come to this moment the same way, one step and then another, not knowing where she was going, where her path was taking her, until suddenly she was here, shivering and alone, her husband and stepdaughter dead, ruling over a court of people who barely tolerated her. She remembered her first night at the banquet, a girl dreaming of being a queen, because then she would be loved. If only she could marry the king, she had thought, if only she could remain queen, if only she could sit on that throne, then she would have everything she wanted. . . . And what was next? What lie would she tell herself now to make her believe she was still only one step away from the love she craved?

But no, if she gave in to regret now, then Lynet had come to hate her—Lynet had *died*—for absolutely nothing. She still had the South, didn't she? The people there were happy she was their queen.

And then, as she stared at the two thrones at the end of the room, the idea came to her—as soon as the Summer Castle was finished enough to be habitable, she could hold court there instead, among people who loved her and would protect her claim to the throne. She'd considered the idea of moving court south before, but not seriously, knowing that Nicholas would never have agreed to it. But now Nicholas was gone. . . .

Maybe that was why she had come here tonight—to remember what she was still fighting for.

In the wavering light of the candles, the glass mosaics of the four seasons shimmered. "Keep away from the walls," she said to Felix. Then Mina held out her hands, feeling each piece of glass as though they were embedded in her skin, concentrated, and *pulled*.

The glass tiles all fell to the floor, glittering in the light. Mina concentrated again, and there was enough glass around her that she felt only the slightest twinge in her chest as each piece of the mosaic transformed into a grown man or woman wearing the finely made clothing of a nobleperson. *A court of glass*, she thought.

The members of Mina's new court all sank to their knees, kneeling to Mina with their heads bowed. In the center of the throne room, surrounded and protected by her own creations, Mina felt something close to safe and loved, and she reached for Felix's hand, because he was the closest to human of all of them. He took her hand, and he, too, went down on one knee, holding her hand to his forehead.

I should have done this before, she thought, but she had been too afraid to use her power so freely before, too afraid of anyone finding out about her heart.

But it didn't matter anymore. Mina didn't even have to wait until the Summer Castle was finished. She could replace all of her enemies with friends now. She could even create a family for herself if she wanted, a loving father and loyal mother, a devoted husband, a child—

Mina let out a small gasp, her hand going to her mouth. If she chose, she could take one of those pieces of glass and transform it into a perfect copy of Lynet, accurate in every way except that she'd be alive—mostly—and she would never hate Mina. She could have a version of Lynet from before the day of the accident, before Mina had destroyed everything between them, a girl who would never grow up—

A doll, Mina thought. *Everything Lynet didn't want to be.*

What a terrible insult to Lynet's memory that would be, to turn her into the very thing she had always feared—a shell, a body with no life or will of its own, a replica of someone dead.

How many times had Lynet come to her with that fear, sometimes unspoken but always lurking behind every word, every innocent question she asked? And how many times had Mina urged her to leave her mother's memory behind? Mina had thought at the time that she was giving Lynet the right advice, encouraging her to choose her own identity, but now that Lynet was dead, Mina could be more honest with herself. It was easy to guide Lynet on the path away from her mother when that same path also led away from the throne, away from Mina's crown.

Looking now at her loyal new subjects, at her throne at the end of the room, Mina shuddered in revulsion—at herself, at the life she had stolen from Lynet because she had been afraid that if she were no longer a queen, she would be nothing at all.

As soon as she'd allowed the thought to take shape in her mind, the glass court froze and shattered, glass littering the marble floor all around her. She thought for a moment that she had shattered with them, but it was only her resolve that had broken. Perhaps it would have been easier to live in the fantasy she'd created, a world of glass that reflected only the parts of herself that she could admire.

But every piece of glass on the floor was another lie to distract her from Lynet's memory, and so she returned them all to the walls, putting back together the image of seasons that the North had lost long ago.

She returned to her rooms, wanting to be alone, and looked at herself in the mirror. The gray hairs around her temple had grown back, and instinctively, she tore them out, not flinching at the pain, because she had performed this ritual so many times already.

A frown line on her forehead. Dark circles underneath her eyes. The cracks in her surface were starting to show. *If they love you for anything, it will be for your beauty,* she mouthed silently, watching her lips form the words. She brought her fingertips up to the glass, the cool surface warming under her touch.

Mina looked at her hands. They were growing thin, her fingers bony, and she could trace with one finger the protruding veins that traveled down to her wrists. Again she moved like a sleepwalker, going to the table by her bed, taking up the silver bracelet that still lay there, clasping it around her wrist as a reminder, as a punishment. Ever since placing the bracelet by the bed, she had developed a morbid fear of it, flinching every time she saw it out of the corner of her eye. But she had stubbornly kept it there anyway, because she refused to feel guilty or afraid.

She wasn't afraid now, either. She felt a strange kind of calm, an inexplicable relief at finally saying the words to herself, over and over again: *You drove her away. You killed her. You stole her throne. You stole her life. It's your fault she's dead.* The more hideous her thoughts, the more relief she felt, until finally she was driven to her knees, giving voice to all the truths she most feared.

Felix found her that way in the morning, bent over and clutching her wrist to her chest, still muttering words too low for anyone but herself to hear.

25

LYNET

The short climb up to the church's second-story windows should have been easy for Lynet, but she was still navigating around the disorientation that had come over her since she'd left the North. Her arms grew tired quickly and she had to pause several times, clinging to the edge of the building, until her head stopped spinning.

But she managed to reach one of the broken windows and climbed inside, careful not to cut herself on the glass. The room she landed in was dark, with dusty sheets draped over furniture. She peeked under one of the sheets and found a half-finished stone altar, much like the ones in the chapel at Whitespring.

She left the room, finding herself at one end of a long, narrow landing illuminated by a beam of moonlight coming from a window set into the slanted roof. To her side was a curving stairwell that led below, and across the landing were more dark rooms. Lynet tried to be as quiet as possible as she crossed the landing, but the wood still creaked under her feet.

She was reaching for the handle of the first door when she felt a blade pressing into the small of her back. Lynet froze, her hand twitching for the dagger at her waist.

"You're trespassing," said the owner of the knife at her back, and Lynet let her hands drop to her sides in relief. It was Gregory's voice.

"Let me turn around, and you'll know why," she said.

But she didn't even have to turn before she heard Gregory inhale sharply. "Turn," he said, and the blade at her back was gone.

Lynet turned toward him, wondering if he could recognize her in so little light. She could only see his silhouetted outline and the shape of the blade in his hand.

"Lynet?" he breathed, stepping forward into the moonlight to peer at her face. His eyes gleamed under his white eyebrows as he looked at a girl who was supposed to be dead. He was thinner than she remembered, his hair grayer. If Mina was a flame, Lynet thought, then Gregory resembled the curling smoke after the flame had been blown out.

"You once told me that if I ever needed help, I should come to you," Lynet said.

He nodded. "I remember. And I meant it. But how—" He started to reach for her face, his fingers thin and skeletal. Lynet almost flinched from them, but she stopped herself. He shook his head and took hold of her wrist, his grip surprisingly firm, his long fingers encircling her wrist completely. "There's more light downstairs," he said. "But tell me how you came here."

He led her back across the landing to the winding stairs, never releasing her wrist. Lynet wanted to pull her hand away, but he seemed so frail that she was afraid she might hurt him by accident. They moved at his slow pace, and she told her story selectively as they descended, skipping over certain details—not all of Mina's secrets were hers to tell. When she mentioned faking her death by using the snow, he halted suddenly, and Lynet nearly tripped on the step.

Gregory was staring up at her with wide eyes. "You're even more miraculous than I thought," he said, his voice reverent. "I've wanted you to know the truth for so long, but your father and Mina wouldn't allow it. I always hoped that one day, you would find out on your own, and then you would come to me willingly. . . ." He smiled, skin stretched out over bone. "And now you have."

"Are there others like . . . like me? Made with blood?"

His smile turned sour, and he started down the stairs again. "No, there are no others like you," he said. He paused, his voice strained as he asked, "Have you ever seen Mina wield the same power you have? Power over glass?"

Lynet swallowed. If Mina had kept her power secret from Gregory for all these years, then what right did Lynet have to tell him about it now? The thought of Gregory knowing this secret about her stepmother, when Mina hadn't even told Lynet, brought a bitter taste to her mouth. "No," she said, her voice strong and clear. "I don't think so."

Gregory nodded. "It's the blood. It's something that we alone share." They reached the bottom of the stairs, but Gregory still didn't release her hand, clasping it between his own and looking her in the eye with an almost feverish intensity. "In some ways, Lynet," he said, "*you* are my true daughter."

Lynet swallowed dryly, and she wondered how Mina would have felt to hear him make this proclamation. She remained silent as he led her to the main floor of the church.

In the dim candlelight, Lynet saw the remains of the church reformed into a makeshift parlor. The line of altars that would normally be at the front of the room were now all joined together in the center to form a table, with the sawed halves of pews serving as chairs. Along all the walls, blocking the windows, were shelves of books. There were more piles of books on the table and all but one of the chairs.

"You live here?" Lynet said, leaving out the *why* as she stepped farther inside.

Gregory moved the books off the chairs, onto the floor. "All I want is a quiet place to do my work without disturbance, without people constantly begging for my help. Either they want me to grant them some favor as a magician, or else they want me to ask Mina for something, as the queen's father." He shook his head in disapproval. "I choose to live near the university so I can stay at the forefront of progress and learning," he said, gesturing to the books around him, "not to pass messages to my daughter." He lit more candles and then he turned to Lynet and said, "But that's why you've come, isn't it? You want to ask me about Mina. You want to know how to defeat her."

Lynet swallowed, gathering the courage to speak the question she'd wanted to ask from the beginning. "Actually . . . I want to know if she can be cured."

One eyebrow went up in surprise. "A cure?"

"She says she can't love or be loved, but maybe she only thinks that's true because her heart is glass. If there were some way to make her heart real, then maybe . . ." *Maybe she'd remember how much we loved each other.*

He set down a candle and came over to her, forehead furrowed in contemplation. She seemed to have surprised him with the question, or else he'd never considered the possibility before. "I don't know," he said. "But perhaps, if we work together, we could find an answer."

She smiled, relieved. "That's why I came to you. You know more about Mina—and about me—than anyone else does. I want to help her any way I can."

He formed a steeple with his fingers, pressing them to his thin lips. "I think . . . yes, I think if I could take a sample of your blood, Lynet, then I could find out more."

Without thinking, Lynet crossed her arms. "What could my blood tell you?"

The candlelight flickered over Gregory's still face. "Blood is the source of our magic, Lynet. If I want to learn more about our magic and its capabilities, then I first need to study our blood. I could use my own, of course, but I'm . . . not as strong as I used to be."

"No, of course not," she said quickly. "You can use my blood."

His lips curled into a smile. "Thank you, Lynet. Let's do it now, shall we?"

He set off toward the end of the room and seemed to disappear behind a bookshelf, but then Lynet heard a door closing. She followed and found a small door in the corner beyond the shelf. In a few moments, the door opened again and Gregory reappeared, shutting it deliberately behind him. "My laboratory," he offered in explanation. He had a thin knife in one hand and a glass vial in the other. "I must ask you not to go in there by yourself, Lynet, not under any circumstances. It isn't safe unless you're with me."

"Oh, but—"

"Now just sit right here," he said, ushering her to a chair and kneeling beside her.

There was nothing to fear, Lynet told herself as she held her arm out for Gregory. She had never looked away when watching Nadia, and she didn't look away now as Gregory made a thin cut on her arm and her blood rose to the surface. He focused intently on her blood, drawing it from her vein into the vial.

Her blood in exchange for helping Mina. All in all, it was a small price to pay.

She thought she saw Nadia again the next day.

She was crossing the university courtyard on the way to the old church and she saw a flash of a dark braid from the corner of her eye. But when she turned to look, she saw no one resembling Nadia in the courtyard.

Lynet was still shaken by her own disappointment when she entered the church. Her head was full of ghosts today. When she'd woken that morning, she had a moment when she forgot that her father was dead. And then the memories flooded in, and it was like hearing the news for the first time again, the ringing of a bell echoing in her head.

Gregory had told her she could look through his books while he worked in the laboratory, and though she had the feeling he was humoring her, she browsed through the shelves, looking for something that might show her how to help Mina. But even as Lynet started to pull books from the shelves, she wondered if she was only fooling herself into thinking she could find the secrets to her stepmother's heart here. Gregory was the one who had shaped that heart—if he didn't know how to cure it, then how could Lynet?

With a stack of books balanced on one arm, Lynet reached up for a thick red volume on a higher shelf, only to feel the entire stack slip through her elbow and land noisily around her feet. With a sigh, she bent down to collect the books, hoping none of them had been damaged in their fall. As Lynet retrieved one book that was splayed across the floor, a folded piece of paper slipped out from between the pages. The paper was yellow around the edges, but it was still stiff, meaning it probably had been tucked away and forgotten.

Sitting on her knees, Lynet unfolded the paper, her eyes immediately going to the two names written there, one at the top of the page—*Mina*—and the other at the bottom—*Dorothea*. It was a letter to Mina from her mother. Had Mina ever seen it, though? Had she placed it here herself?

My dear Mina, it began, *I can't leave without saying good-bye. . . .*

Lynet told herself she shouldn't keep reading, but she couldn't tear her eyes from the page, and by the time she reached the final words, she was glad she hadn't stopped. Long ago, Mina had told Lynet that her mother, Dorothea, was dead. When Lynet had first started reading the letter, she had thought it was a mother's final good-bye to her daughter before she died. The letter *was* a good-bye—but not from a dying mother. Lynet read through it again to make sure she wasn't mistaken, but there was no question that Dorothea wasn't dying, only leaving.

And according to this letter, she had left because she was frightened of Gregory.

Lynet's stomach lurched, remembering Gregory telling her that she was his true daughter. She felt a pang of sympathy for the girl who had become her stepmother, living alone with a man who saw her as a failed experiment, a blemish on his own abilities. She was worth nothing to him, and Lynet knew that Mina must have felt it every day of her life.

If I'd had a father like yours growing up maybe I wouldn't care about being queen either.

Mina had told Lynet that no one could ever love her, but Mina's mother *had* loved her—the proof of it was here, in three words written at the bottom of the page. Lynet wondered if Gregory knew about Dorothea's letter, if he had lied to Mina about her mother's death. Glancing warily in the direction of the laboratory door, Lynet tucked the letter into the front of her dress.

She started to rise from the floor when a burst of pain in her chest forced her back to her knees. Her heart was racing, a frantic bird trying to escape tightening constraints, and when she tried to move, her surroundings all bled together and her head started to pound. She tried to take deep breaths, but they sounded more like sobs instead. Was this because she had been away from the snow for too long? Had she let herself grow too weak?

Trying to think clearly, Lynet emptied some of her purse into her cupped hands and let the coins become snow again. She nearly sobbed into the pile of snow, such a relief was it against her fevered skin. For the few minutes before the snow melted through her fingers, the world stopped spinning and Lynet started to breathe more normally. The pain had lessened, but her heart was still speeding, and she felt utterly drained, bloodless—

Bloodless. Lynet thought of the blood she'd given to Gregory last night. Was that why she was so weak today? Had the loss of the blood exhausted her beyond her limits, or were Gregory's experiments affecting her, pulling on some invisible thread between her blood and her heart?

Lynet staggered to her feet, tucking away her purse. She had to stop Gregory before he conducted any more tests. He must not have known. . . . But then, that letter from Dorothea proved that Gregory knew more than he revealed.

There was no lock on the door, so Lynet burst into the laboratory without warning, not giving Gregory the chance to deny her entrance.

The laboratory was larger than she'd expected, a round room with a high window that let in the golden sunlight of the South. The room reminded Lynet of Nadia's workroom—the same assortment of jars on shelves, the same long table, though this one was covered in glass apparatuses that she had never seen before.

And yet, this room was as different from Nadia's as Nadia was from Gregory. It was the difference between the natural darkness of night and the stale darkness of the crypt.

Gregory had been hunched over the far end of the table, but he looked up in surprise when he heard the door. "If you wanted to come in, Lynet, you only had to knock," he said.

"What are you doing with my blood?" she demanded.

"Exactly what I told you. And I'm very pleased with the results. Come," he said with an eager wave of his hand, "let me show you what you can do."

Lynet made her way across the room, passing shelves full of jars with unknown contents, including a withered, brownish lump that made her shudder violently for some reason. At the far end of the table was the now empty vial that had held her blood. She peered down at the table, trying to understand the relationship between the items of the strange collection gathered there. Alongside the vial were small piles of sand, as well as two open glass jars. In one of the jars was another pile of sand, but in the other was a small field mouse, its tiny paws trying to climb the side of the jar.

"Do you see?" Gregory said, gripping her upper arm to bring her closer. "The mouse is yours—made from sand and blood—*your* blood. You can only work with snow, but with your blood, I can shape anything. And the mouse has a heartbeat, which means it's truly alive, Lynet."

Lynet put her fingertip against the jar and watched as the mouse tried to paw at her through the glass. She heard the excitement in Gregory's voice, but all she felt was empty. "When you used my blood to make this, it nearly killed me," she said, her voice strained. She looked up at Gregory. "Did you know that would happen?"

Gregory snorted. "Oh, you're exaggerating. It's disorienting at first, I know, but that initial weakness will pass. Creating *you* nearly killed me, of course, but humans are complex, and I had a number of failed experiments before I managed to get you just right. Not to mention I was much older than you at the time, whereas you, Lynet . . . you're still so young, your heart so strong. You have so much life to give. . . ."

There was a hunger in his eyes as he reached out to touch her cheek, and Lynet flinched away. She still had her dagger at her waist under her cloak. She needed to distract him so she could reach for it without his noticing. "I . . . I'm still not feeling well," she said. "Perhaps I should go."

His eyes darted toward the door, and Lynet knew he was thinking that if he let her out that door now, she would never come back. He edged closer to her and shook his head in confusion. "You can't leave now. You're the answer I've been searching for. All these years, I've been trying to reverse the effects of your creation—my aging, my weakness. I even came here hoping medicine would help me since magic only worsened my condition, but to no success. Think of all that potential wasted, Lynet! I had only begun to discover what I could do before I grew too weak to continue. But now that *you're* here, we can unlock all the secrets of our magic together. If you stay here with me, there's no limit to what we can accomplish together. This is what you were meant for."

Lynet took a small step backward. She had always thought she was meant to become her mother—and now, finally, here was confirmation that she wasn't her mother, that she had a purpose and an ability that was all her own. She had been torn between wanting answers about the nature of her existence and wanting to leave her old life behind—and now Gregory could offer her both. She could be reborn in his image instead of her mother's. Was that what she wanted?

"Mina and your father kept you away from me," Gregory continued. "They made you scared of me, but I knew—I always knew—that there was a chance that we were alike, that you would share my gifts." He smiled at her, and perhaps it was only the way the light from the window hit his face, but he seemed younger now, some color in his wasted cheeks, a hopeful glimmer in his eyes. How different he was from her own father, how willing to let her see the most fearsome and powerful parts of herself.

He nodded, sensing her waning resistance. "In all the world, you're the only one who can help me," he said. "I've been wasting away for so long, Lynet—would you leave me now? Who else can guide you like I can?"

Who else? His words echoed in her head, overlapping each other in an endless, muddled stream. And then the answer came to her with the sharpness and clarity of glass—

Mina.

Mina had power over glass, and Gregory didn't know that. He had spent the past sixteen years trying to reach Lynet, but he had never even bothered to consider his own daughter. *He could never help me cure her. He doesn't know Mina at all.* And if he didn't know his own daughter, didn't understand why Lynet would want to help her, then how could he ever understand Lynet?

He took a step closer to her, and Lynet slowly backed away, her hand slipping under her cloak. Her fingers rested on the dagger hilt. "And if I refuse to stay with you?" she said.

The smile froze on his face before fading away, his eyes flat and dull. "Well, then I'd have to admit that I've been less than honest with you about my reasons for wanting you to stay. You see, the truth is that I don't need *you.* I just need your heart."

Lynet drew out the dagger just as Gregory lunged for her hand, his fingers wrapping around her wrist. He pushed her back against the table, the edge digging into her back, the dagger hovering between them. He had her other wrist in his grip now too, but they were locked in a stalemate, neither of them strong enough to overpower the other.

"You're not being fair, Lynet," Gregory said through gritted teeth. "I made you, sacrificed my power and my vitality to give you life. Now it's time for you to return it all back to me."

"By giving you my *heart*?" She tried to pull away, but she only ended up digging the table edge farther into her back.

"You felt that pain in your chest earlier, didn't you?" Gregory said. His fingers tightened, twisting her wrist, and Lynet's grip on the dagger began to loosen. "Blood is the source of our power, just as I said, but the heart is the source of our blood. I grew weak because I drained my heart too quickly, but with yours—so young and healthy, so full of magic—I would be more careful. I would be strong again. Doesn't that seem just, Lynet, that you should restore the life that you stole from me?" He gave a final twist of her wrist, and Lynet cried out in pain, her grip loosening enough to let him take the dagger from her.

"I came here to cure Mina's heart, not yours," Lynet spat. He still had her other wrist in his grip, but she could feel his hold weakening now that he had the dagger. If she could just distract him—

His face stretched into a hideous smile. "Do you still think you can help her? Let me show you what Mina really is. Look there." He gestured to the shelves beside them, and Lynet glanced quickly from the corner of her eye, not letting Gregory out of her sight, to see what he was pointing at.

But even before she looked, part of her already knew what she would see—that . . . that *thing* in the jar that had made her shudder. "Yes," Gregory was saying, "you saw it already, didn't you? That's what remains of Mina's heart. Even if you found a way to give her a new one, she will always carry that rotten heart inside. Do you see now how pointless it is to try to cure something that's already dead? It's too late for her, but not for me."

She kept looking back and forth from Gregory to the heart, trying to understand what that hideous thing had in common with Mina's radiance, Mina's fury. But even with her divided attention, she noticed that Gregory's breathing had become heavier, his grip on her wrist continuing to slacken. All this exertion was exhausting him, and so Lynet put any thought of Mina's heart aside and gave a final sharp tug. She may have been weakened, but years of climbing had made her stronger than she looked, and her wrist slipped free from his grip. She managed to make it down the length of the table before Gregory caught up with her, slamming both fists down on either side of her to trap her against the table. But Lynet had just remembered something about the dagger that was still clutched in his hand—she had made it from snow, and as long as she had the snow, she was never truly weak.

Burn, she commanded.

Gregory let out a cry as the dagger burned his right hand, and as soon as he had released it, Lynet reached for the weapon. Ignoring the pain of the burning metal, she held on to the dagger and drove it into Gregory's left hand, pinning him to the table.

He screamed in pain, and before he could recover enough to pull the blade out, Lynet was running out the door.

How much time did she have before he recovered and started to follow her? She needed a crowd, somewhere to lose herself so that even if Gregory came after her, he would never find her. Lynet raced away from the church, heading toward the university gates. If she cut through there, she could get back to the main road, and then he'd never find her.

Students dodged out of her way as Lynet ran down the main walkway between the university buildings. She crashed into a few of them, but she didn't let herself stop or slow down. She could see the pink of the roses in the courtyard in the distance—she was so focused on reaching the courtyard that she only barely noticed the blurry form of someone in her way, someone who wasn't moving aside even as Lynet came crashing through—

The breath slammed out of her as she collided with someone, both of them falling to the ground. Lynet hissed in pain as the burn on her right palm met sand, but she had mostly fallen on top of the other person.

She immediately started to scramble away, but then she paused, her arms holding her up as she looked down at the girl she'd run into, the girl who hadn't moved aside even when Lynet had come hurtling toward her—

After all those uncertain sightings, she'd found Nadia at last.

26

LYNET

At first they just stared at each other, both of them wide-eyed with disbelief. And then Nadia reached up and gently brushed her fingers against Lynet's cheek, testing to see if she was real. Her eyes lit up when her fingertips met solid flesh.

"*Lynet?*" Nadia whispered.

The sound of her name broke Lynet out of her trance, and she remembered that she was supposed to be escaping—and that she was still awkwardly positioned over Nadia. She quickly rose from the ground, as did Nadia, who was still staring at her in awe. No wonder Nadia hadn't moved aside when Lynet was running toward her—she probably thought she was seeing a ghost.

Lynet's frantic run had caught up with her; her chest hurt, her legs wobbled, and her head spun from getting up so suddenly. She glanced over her shoulder, looking for any sign of Gregory. "I can explain everything later," she said to Nadia, "but right now I need somewhere to hide."

Nadia didn't answer. She was looking at Lynet in a daze, perhaps still not entirely convinced she was real.

Lynet took Nadia's hand and pressed it firmly. "Nadia, *please*. Gregory—Mina's father—is looking for me, and I'm too weak to run."

Nadia had been looking down at their joined hands, but at the sound of the magician's name, her head snapped up, her eyes focused and clear. "I won't let him find you," she said. Keeping hold of Lynet's unburned hand, Nadia led her farther down the walkway, taking her through the side door of the main building that Lynet had visited on her first night here.

They were approaching the foot of the giant staircase when Nadia suddenly froze and pushed Lynet back into a small alcove in the wall, shielding her from view with her own body.

"What are you—"

Nadia shushed her, and Lynet heard Gregory's voice echoing in the large hall. He must have gone around and come in through the front gate—if she had reached the courtyard, she might have collided with *him* instead of Nadia. She quickly huddled behind Nadia's tall frame as she heard Gregory describing her to someone, asking if she had been seen. And then she heard his faltering footsteps coming toward them. Nadia leaned back against the opening of the alcove, and Lynet tried to make herself as small as she could. Surely Gregory would walk past them without a second glance—

But his footsteps stopped right by their alcove, and Lynet's heartbeat was so loud, she could barely hear him when he spoke. "Oh, it's you," he said. Lynet couldn't see the damage she had done to his hand, but his voice was hoarse and ragged. "What are you doing here?"

Did he recognize Nadia from Whitespring? Lynet had thought

he had already been away before Nadia arrived, but maybe she was mistaken.

"The queen sent me," Nadia answered, her voice stiff.

Gregory scoffed. "She found out, didn't she? Ah, well, it hardly matters now." His voice lowered. "Listen, I don't have time for questions, but come to the old church behind the university tonight. I have a new task for you."

Nadia hesitated for only the space of a breath, and then she nodded.

Gregory continued on his way, and when he was out the door, Nadia let out a long exhale. She turned to Lynet, her face tense with dread, but she didn't move aside. "I can explain," she said.

Lynet hadn't understood the full meaning behind Gregory's words, but her skin prickled with suspicion as she took in Nadia's guilty expression, and she felt the same as when she'd overheard Mina and her huntsman in the chapel. She recognized the bitter taste in her mouth as betrayal. "Let me out," Lynet said, her voice low.

"He described you to people. If you run out of here now, someone will recognize you."

Lynet was having trouble breathing in the close confines of the alcove. Her muscles were itching for movement. "*Move*," she said, with a note of rising panic this time.

Nadia reached for her arm. "At least let me—"

Something about Nadia's hand coming toward her made Lynet lash out. She tried to knock Nadia's arm aside, but her right palm screamed with pain as soon as she made contact. For a moment, she only saw red, and she sank to her knees, the last of her strength leaving her, and cradled her hand against her chest.

She didn't notice at first that Nadia had stepped away from the alcove, no longer blocking the way. *Run*, part of her urged, but she was so tired, so dizzy, and the truth of Nadia's words was now apparent: if she tried to run, she wouldn't get very far.

"Please listen," Nadia whispered, crouching down at Lynet's side. "You're hurt, and you're exhausted, and I can take you somewhere safe to help you with that burn. I'll explain everything, and then . . . if you never want to see me again, I'll understand. But I won't hand you over to anyone. If I had wanted to do that, I could have done it a moment ago."

The red haze of pain started to fade, as did the mounting panic from earlier. And now Lynet just tried to *think*. Gregory had said this disoriented feeling would pass in time, and time was what she really needed—time to heal, to rest, to wait until darkness could hide her features from anyone who might recognize her by Gregory's description. But what was this understanding between Gregory and Nadia? Could she trust Nadia now? Then again, Nadia was right—if she had wanted to hand Lynet over to Gregory, she had already had the perfect opportunity to do so.

"Fine," Lynet said. "I'll go with you for now."

Nadia helped Lynet rise from the ground, and if she was pleased that Lynet had agreed to her offer, Lynet couldn't tell. Nadia's face was as stern and impassive as when she was working. They crossed the hall carefully, Nadia peering closely around corners to make sure they were alone, and went out another side door. They entered an older stone building beside the main one, and Nadia led Lynet up a flight of stairs and down a hall lined with doors until she stopped to unlock one of them.

Lynet followed Nadia inside a small stone room, bare except for a desk, a chair, and a narrow bed along the back wall beneath a low window. And when Nadia shut the door behind her, Lynet's heart finally started to slow.

Nadia let out a sigh, her back against the door. Her hair was coming out of its braid, and she impatiently shook it out, letting the dark waves fall loose and free around her face. "Sit, and I'll take care of your burn," she said, gesturing to the bed.

Lynet perched stiffly on the edge of the bed, never taking her eyes off Nadia. She watched as Nadia opened a small chest beside her desk, inside which were two neat rows of jars. She selected one, and then, for one brief moment before she turned, Lynet saw Nadia's shoulders sinking under some invisible weight, her face shadowed by some unknown sorrow.

But when she came to Lynet with the jar, she was the perfect surgeon again, methodical and untroubled. Nadia took the chair, moving it across from the bed, and reached for Lynet's wounded palm.

"I'm sorry about your father," she said softly.

Lynet didn't respond, her throat tight.

"Would you tell me what happened up north? Why do people think you're dead?" Nadia didn't look up as she asked, her eyes focused on the angry, blistered skin of Lynet's palm.

Lynet might have told her—Gregory already knew, after all—but she remained cautiously silent.

Nadia didn't react to Lynet's silence as she started to apply the green ointment to her palm. "Would you at least tell me what happened between you and Gregory? Why he's looking for you?"

Again, silence.

This time Nadia shook her head a little, her mouth stretched into a pained smile. "No, of course you wouldn't," she muttered. "I'm the one who owes you explanations." But she was quiet as she finished with the ointment, and Lynet tried not to notice the way Nadia's eyelashes cast long shadows against her cheeks, or the way she still had grains of sand in her hair from when they'd tumbled to the ground. She tried not to care that the ointment was such a relief from the burn that she could now begin to enjoy the sensation of Nadia's thumb rubbing small circles against her skin.

"Explain, then," Lynet said, her voice thick.

Nadia released Lynet's hand and looked her in the eye with the same fierce determination as when she'd amputated the servant's foot. But what was she going to sever this time? What invisible thread existed between them that now was in danger of being cut?

"I told you before," Nadia began, "that it was often difficult for me to find work after my parents died. Imagine how I felt when the queen's father came to me and offered me a position at Whitespring. He was on his way south, passing through the village I was in, and he sought me out when he heard of the work I had done. Whitespring needed a surgeon, and he . . . he needed a spy."

Lynet could tell she wanted to look away, her eyes continuously darting to the floor.

Nadia took a breath and forced herself to meet Lynet's gaze. "It was so simple. All I had to do was keep close to you, tell you how you were made, and share with him what I'd learned about you. And before the year was out, if he was satisfied, he would give me passage south and a place at the university."

Lynet's heart beat in her ears, a bitter taste on her tongue. Her legs felt restless, and she stood, going toward the door even though she and Nadia both knew that she had nowhere else to go. Nadia turned in her chair but didn't rise or try to stop her, not even when Lynet reached for the door handle, gripping the metal with her good hand until it hurt. Lynet turned, her back against the door giving her the illusion of escape, of freedom.

"And so every time we spoke," she said, "everything I told you, or that you told me—it was all so you could tell *him*?" She thought of the night in the tower, of the strange connection that they had woven between them, as fragile and hidden as a cobweb, visible only at certain angles, in certain patches of light. Had those moments been dissected, recorded in letters to Gregory?

"No," Nadia said firmly, and Lynet was sure she was answering the second question, the one Lynet hadn't asked aloud. "I didn't tell him everything. I was only supposed to tell you enough to make you want to seek Gregory out. The journals I gave you, the experiments we tried in the tower . . . all of those were against my orders." She shook her head, her hands twisting her hair into a long rope as she looked away. "I wanted it so much—to go to the university where people would take me seriously so I could do my family's work. I told myself you weren't real, that you were just . . . a paper doll, an experiment, not even a real person. I told myself it didn't matter."

Lynet flinched at hearing Nadia voice all her worst fears. "And now?" The words came out as a croak. "Do you still see me that way?"

Nadia stood, looking at her in disbelief. "Lynet, I stopped seeing you like that the first time we met." She walked slowly to the door, giving Lynet enough time to move away or tell her to stop, but Lynet didn't move or say anything. When Nadia was standing in front of her, she reached tentatively for Lynet's hand—the left one, the one with the faded scar from when she'd fallen from the tree. Nadia brushed her fingers against the scar now. "You made me laugh for the first time since my parents died," she said quietly, keeping her eyes down.

Lynet let out a shaky breath. She wouldn't cry, not in front of her.

"I lied to myself to make the job easier, but then when I told you about your creation, I saw how deeply it shocked you. I wanted to help you learn more. I wanted . . . I wanted to be around you. I couldn't even write to Gregory anymore, not when you had become my friend." She looked up from their hands to meet Lynet's gaze, a fearful uncertainty in the depths of her eyes. "We *were* friends before, weren't we?"

In Lynet's mind, she had always seen Nadia as the fearless surgeon or the smiling girl, but this was something new, another part of her that Lynet had only seen in glimpses before. This was the girl whose parents had left her alone in the world, the one who had no letters or reminders of home in her bare room because she had no home.

Lynet looked away. She didn't trust her own feelings. Nadia was a friend. Nadia was a spy. She drew her hand back. "And now what?" she whispered, both to Nadia and to herself. "Am I supposed to forgive you because we were friends once?"

Nadia had no answer. She turned away and went to stand by the window, running a hand through her hair. But then her shoulders tensed, and when she faced Lynet again, the scared, lonely girl was gone, replaced by the surgeon who wanted to fix what was broken. "No," she said clearly. "Let me earn your trust again. Let me help you. I . . . I thought you were dead, and the whole world seemed to die with you." Her voice wavered, but her eyes were fierce, almost angry. "I'll hide you. I'll keep you safe."

Lynet shook her head, an idea forming. "I need you to do more than that. Gregory is already expecting you. If you go to him now and tell him that you saw me preparing to go back north, he'll believe you."

Nadia nodded slowly. "And he'd stop looking for you here." She thought for a moment, the deep orange of the setting sun passing over her face, making her seem alight with new conviction. "You'll keep hidden until it's safe?"

"I will," Lynet said.

Nadia walked over to her, her stare direct and unflinching. "Will you still be here when I return?"

Lynet held her gaze. "I promise."

"All right, then. I'll go now."

After Nadia left, Lynet waited a few minutes, watching the

shadows from the sunset grow long across the floor. And then she broke her promise and hurried out of the room.

And now where? she asked herself once she was on the main street. Her strength was returning, but all she had was a cloak, a half-empty purse, and the clothes she was wearing—

And the letter. She still had that, too, tucked away inside her dress.

Lynet froze on the street, and people jostled into her on either side until she started walking again, more slowly this time. She could find a way to send the letter north, to Mina. It seemed wrong that Mina shouldn't have it, that she would keep thinking her mother was dead. *I wanted to cure her,* Lynet thought, but she'd assumed Gregory would deliver that cure to Mina. Now she knew the only thing Gregory would deliver to Mina was more lies.

And what lies has my father told me?

Nicholas had already lied to Lynet and to everyone else about her mother's death. So few people knew the truth of Emilia's death— that she hadn't died in childbirth at all. It didn't seem fair, that a person's legacy could be twisted or forgotten so easily. Everything Lynet knew about her mother, she had learned from Nicholas. She was fragile, he said. She spoke in whispers and murmurs. She was sweet and gentle. *Like you, like you,* he said, but Lynet had never *felt* fragile, though she looked it. If her father had never truly recognized his daughter, then had he remembered his wife wrong as well? What if everything he'd ever told her about her mother was only how he'd seen her, not how she truly was?

What if she was more like me?

But there was no point wondering—even if she could remember a hundred different stories about her mother, told to her by different people, Lynet still would never really *know* her. She could ask and ask, but she'd never feel her mother's hands or hear her laugh or see her cry. Emilia was lost to her, and no story or portrait would ever truly recover her.

And for the first time in her life, Lynet missed the mother she had never known.

There was a crowd gathered ahead of her, forcing her to stop. She looked up and saw that she had reached the new church, the one with the bell tower that had rung for her and her father. Curious, she tried to peek through the crowd, and she managed to push herself through to the front.

There was a small fire burning in the churchyard, in a coal pit surrounded by stones. All around the stones were flowers and other offerings—straw dolls and ribbons and letters. Children seemed to be leaving most of the gifts, and Lynet watched a little girl take one of the ribbons out of her braided hair and leave it with the others. *A memorial for a child*, Lynet thought.

And then, with a shiver, she understood that it was *her* memorial.

She saw her name written on one of the letters in the circle, and then she tried to look at the rest—*Princess Lynet*, some of them said. *For the princess.* The celebration was over, then; now that they were secure in Mina's reign, they could afford to grieve for a dead king and his daughter.

They think I was just a child, Lynet thought. A girl who never had the chance to grow up or take one step out of the castle. And why shouldn't they? Lynet had led the life of a child in Whitespring—sheltered and carefree. She'd clung to her childhood as much as she could, running away as soon as she thought she'd have to step into the role of an adult—the role of a queen. No one would ever know that that princess had liked to climb impossible heights, or that she had survived an attack on her life, or that she had the power to control snow. This was all she was, all she would ever be—this girl who looked just like her mother, this child who died before she could grow up.

She thought of the shivering people she'd seen in the northern villages and of the work Mina had done for the South. And as she stared into the flame that burned for her short life, she knew this wasn't the legacy she wanted to leave behind.

I can do so much more. I can be *so much more.*

Lynet had wanted to become someone else in the South, someone other than her mother. She had spent years wanting to be strong, because she'd thought her mother was weak. She had wanted to be fierce and invulnerable like Mina, never seeing that Mina had become that way because she'd had to protect herself from the cruelty of her father. Weak or strong—she didn't know what they meant anymore. Maybe they didn't mean the same thing for everyone. All she knew as she turned away from the churchyard and headed back in the direction of the university was that it was time to discover what kind of strength lived in her.

She hid in the shadows by the dormitory building, waiting to see if Nadia would return alone or with Gregory—a final test to see if she could trust her. When Nadia did return alone, Lynet felt a weight lift from her, more relieved than she wanted to admit. She was still angry and hurt from Nadia's confession, but at least she wasn't as alone as she'd feared.

Nadia jumped when Lynet approached her. "You said you were going to hide," she whispered as she looked frantically around.

"I'm tired of hiding," Lynet answered.

"He's returning to Whitespring at once, but he wants me to go after you, to go north with you and hand you over to the queen," Nadia said. She frowned out the window, her arms wrapped around herself like she was cold. "And then . . . and then he wants to kill you."

"I know," Lynet said. She was sitting with her ankles crossed on Nadia's bed, her hands in her lap, her pulse curiously steady as she toyed with different ideas in her mind. She wished now that she had answered Nadia's questions about what had happened at Whitespring. She hated that Gregory had been the one to tell her about Mina's betrayal. "He wants to cut out my heart."

Nadia started to fiddle with her hair. "He wants me to do it," she said. "He said he would need my help transferring your heart to his body. He chose a poison from one of the shelves in his laboratory. It was called *Winter's Kiss*. When it's absorbed through the skin, it kills almost instantly, freezes you from the inside out. He said—" She twisted her hair more violently, lips pursed in disgust. "He said the poison will keep your heart from spoiling."

Lynet stood and turned away, nausea passing over her at the thought of herself carved up.

She felt the light pressure of a hand on her shoulder, heard the silence that meant Nadia was holding her breath as she waited for Lynet's reaction to this small gesture. And Lynet knew that if she turned and faced Nadia now, if she saw the play of moonlight softening the sharp angles of her face, she would also see the light glinting off that cobweb again, the threads spelling out something she couldn't yet read. If she turned now, she would be agreeing to forget Nadia's crimes against her.

Lynet jerked her shoulder away, and she heard Nadia's footsteps moving back to the window. When Nadia spoke again, her voice wavered at first, but then grew steady. "I don't intend to let Gregory come close enough to you again to give you that poison, but in case he does . . . I did something to make sure you'll still be safe. When he was out of the room, I found another poison similar to *Winter's Kiss*—the same color and method of delivery, but instead of death, it causes a deathlike trance that wears off in time."

"You switched the poisons?" Lynet asked. She turned to face her, now that the earlier moment had safely passed.

"I tried to persuade him to let me give you the poison myself, but he said it was too risky, and that you were too curious. But still, I had to do *something*," she said. "I know it's not much—"

"No," Lynet said, holding up a hand. "No, let me think." What did she have now? A cloak. A half-empty purse. A letter. A poison that wouldn't kill her. She could go to Mina, take the letter to her, and then even if the letter didn't work, even if there was no way to make Mina know the truth of her own heart, even if—*say it*— even if Mina or Gregory poisoned her, Lynet wouldn't die. There were so many risks, so many dangers she couldn't predict, so many questions—but the only question that mattered was whether she believed Mina was a hopeless cause, the love they had shared nothing but a lie.

That was one question she could answer, at least.

Nadia was watching her, eyes narrowed in confusion. "Lynet, what are you thinking about? What are you planning to do?"

"I'm going to walk into their trap."

Nadia studied her for a moment and then said incredulously, "You're serious."

"I need to see Mina again," Lynet said, and as soon as she said the words, she knew nothing could change her mind. "If you hand me over to her, then I can talk to her." *I can cure her.*

"Gregory said she tried to kill you!"

Lynet shook her head. "I'm not sure." She thought back to that night, trying to remember if the huntsman had ever said that *Mina* had been the one to want her dead. "She sent someone after me, but I still don't know if she ordered him to kill me. And even if she does try to kill me by giving me that poison, I won't die."

"You won't die, but you'll still be in Whitespring, surrounded by enemies. And what do you plan to do then?"

Lynet's heart thumped, but she knew what her answer had to be. "I'll take Mina by surprise. I'll . . . I'll kill her if I have to."

Nadia was shaking her head in disbelief. "It's too dangerous."

"That's what you told me when I wanted to run away on my birthday," Lynet said, her voice cold. She faced Nadia, staring her down until Nadia flinched and looked away. "You said I wouldn't even be able to make it out of the woods, that I wouldn't survive. But I *did* survive. I've already walked into Gregory's trap once and lived. At least this time I'll have a plan. You wanted me to trust you again, but first you have to trust me."

"I *do*," Nadia said, "but I don't understand why this is necessary. Maybe I can speak to the queen for you."

Lynet thought of the last time she had seen Mina, of the fear and rage in her eyes, the desperation in her voice as she had lashed out. That boy from the apothecary shop came to Lynet's mind—the way she had rounded on him with the dagger, only to find that she had been afraid of a child. But she hadn't been able to lower her defenses until she had known he wasn't a threat to her, until she felt safe. She wasn't sure if Mina had ever felt safe. "No, I need to speak to her myself," Lynet said. "I need her to think I'm defenseless. That's why you have to hand me over to her, the way Gregory planned it."

"Can't you just hide away for a little longer—"

"No," Lynet snapped. "I've already done that, too. I have to go back. Did Gregory tell you how I faked my death?"

Nadia shook her head. "What does that have to do with anything?"

Lynet knew she had to save her strength for the journey, so she selected a single coin from her purse. She held it out to Nadia, watching her face as the coin transformed into snow. Nadia stared at the melting snow in Lynet's palm with silent awe. "I have power over snow," Lynet said. "I can transform it and tell it what to do. I think . . . I think I could make the snow stop falling, if I wanted."

Nadia lifted her gaze to Lynet's face, eyes wide and shining with excitement. "You could break the curse," she said softly. "You could save the North."

Lynet stepped closer to her. "You'll go with me, then?" When Nadia didn't respond, her forehead creased with indecision, Lynet added, "I'm going back for my home, my family—don't you think any price is worth that? Wouldn't you do the same?" Her hand twitched, a sudden impulse to touch Nadia's arm, a promise to restore the connection between them—but Lynet stopped herself, not wanting to make a promise she didn't know she could keep.

But no promises were needed. Nadia nodded once, and all trace of doubt vanished from her face. "Yes," she said. "I would. I'll go north with you."

"We'll leave at dawn."

Nadia started to turn away with new purpose, but then she stopped. "You know that going back means becoming queen," she said.

"I know," Lynet answered. "But I'm ready now. I know what kind of queen I want to be."

"Queen Lynet," Nadia said, testing the words. She stared at Lynet, and then she tried to hide a laugh.

"What?"

Nadia approached Lynet and lightly touched one of her curls. "Your hair is a mess."

Lynet thought of how she must look, saying she would be queen with her unevenly shorn curls in a tangle, and before she could stop herself, she started to laugh too.

Still smiling, Nadia drew back her hand, and the backs of her knuckles brushed against Lynet's cheek, her touch as soft as cobwebs.

27

MINA

The knock at the door made Mina jump. That was silly of her—she knew it could only be Felix. No one was allowed to see her without going through him first.

Since that night in the throne room, Mina had lost the ability to pretend, even to herself. Her guilt was visible in every line on her face, and so she chose carefully who could see her and when, and she haunted her own rooms like a ghost.

"I wanted to be alone tonight," she told Felix when she opened the door.

He wore an apologetic look, but his arms were tense. "Your father is here," he said. "He claims to have urgent news that he wishes to share with you immediately."

Mina gaped at him. Gregory had been away for months, and he had sent no word of returning anytime soon. The news of

Nicholas's and Lynet's deaths must have reached the South by now, and so he had come to see his daughter, the queen. Would he be pleased with her for keeping the throne? Or would he blame her for the death of his creation? Either way, she knew if she refused to see him now, she would only regret it the next time she did see him. "Bring him here," she said, resigned.

Felix left, and when he returned, Gregory was with him. Mina stood aside to let them both in, Gregory striding into the center of the room while Felix remained by the door with his arms crossed.

Gregory looked older and frailer than when she had last seen him, and there was a bandage wrapped around his left hand. "Send this one away so we can speak alone," Gregory said, gesturing to Felix. Before Mina could say anything, he barked, "Leave us," at Felix.

But Felix didn't move, not even to wince at Gregory's rough voice. Mina hid a smile. "He'll only leave at my request."

"Then tell him to leave," Gregory said through gritted teeth.

She gave the appearance of considering this, so he wouldn't think she was following his order, and then asked Felix to wait outside, as she had always intended. She also didn't want her father to think she was afraid to be alone with him.

"Much has happened since you left . . ." Mina began, but Gregory waved his bandaged hand to interrupt her.

"I know all about your little power play," he said. "The king conveniently died and you saw your chance to take his place with the princess dead. Only you were wrong about something, Mina—the princess was never dead."

Mina shook her head. She must have misunderstood him. "But Lynet *is* dead. She broke her neck."

"No, Mina. That's what I came here to tell you. Lynet is alive."

Mina repeated the words to herself, but they didn't make sense. She felt faintly ill. "No, you're wrong. I *saw* her. She was dead."

"A ruse," Gregory said. "She has the same power that I have, only with snow. She created the body to stop you from searching for her."

Mina took a breath. She felt like she was moving underwater, all her movements slow and heavy. Lynet was alive. This revelation simultaneously burdened and unburdened her, relief and fear and shame all mixed together. She had been fooled, an embarrassing admission in front of her father, but did that matter when Lynet was still alive? The girl that Mina had watched grow into a young woman was still living and breathing . . . and she would return one day to take everything Mina had.

Mina had no doubt of that; despite her protests, Lynet would come back for her birthright, and on that day, one of them would have to lose. *It was easier when she was dead,* Mina thought. *Then I only had to hate myself, not her.*

She tried not to show any reaction at all, other than her trembling hands. "Lynet is alive," she repeated. "How do you know this?"

His expression darkened. "She wanted my help. I pretended for a while to have her interests at heart, but she ran from me before I could give her to you."

He was lying. Gregory had driven Lynet away somehow—and Mina wasn't surprised in the slightest. Mina had always tried to shield Lynet from him, but left alone, Gregory wouldn't always be able to hide his morbid fascination with the girl he had created.

"I know you remember her as a silly child, Mina," Gregory continued, "but she's . . . changed now." His eyes flickered down to his bandaged hand. "She is ruthless. I believe she'll do whatever is necessary to take back her crown."

Mina looked away from him. Why should Lynet have anything but hate for her? "She said that?" she asked.

"She thinks she can cure your heart, but what do you think she'll do once she knows that isn't possible? And more importantly, what will *you* do, Mina? Are you willing to kill her, when it becomes necessary?"

Kill Lynet again? But no, she hadn't killed Lynet the *first* time— Lynet hadn't even died. Mina eyed her father warily. "Why do you care? Why should you want me to kill her? You always wanted to be closer to her. Did Lynet not embrace you as her new father as much as you'd hoped?" Mina couldn't help smiling a little at the thought. "Is that why you suddenly want her dead?"

Gregory gave her a stony look, then quickly grabbed the back of her neck. Mina fought the urge to shake him off; she didn't want him to see her thrashing about like some caged bird.

"It shouldn't matter to you what my motivations are. As soon as the people of Whitespring know she's alive, they'll all be demanding your head. This is your last chance. If you indulge in any pity for that girl, you may as well hang yourself and save everyone the trouble. Now answer my question. Will you do whatever is necessary?"

"Yes," she hissed at him, her head bowing under the weight of his hand.

Gregory didn't seem entirely satisfied, but he nodded and released her at last. He took something out of the pocket of his coat and hid it in his fist. "I sent someone after Lynet to accompany her north."

"Another spy?" Mina spat out. She could still feel her father's hand on the back of her neck, and she was itching to rub at the skin there.

"The same spy, in fact. The surgeon you dismissed. She came straight back to me and told me Lynet was leaving for the North.

When they're near Whitespring, the surgeon will come to you and let you know where you can find Lynet. And then you'll give Lynet this."

He opened his fist now, holding out a small glass vial full of some clear liquid. From the handwriting on the label, Mina knew it had come from his own stores. "Poison?" she said.

"Instant and painless. It's absorbed through the skin, so you'll have to find some way to give it to her without making her suspicious. When she's dead, bring the body back to Whitespring, and I'll dispose of it."

Mina stared at the vial with growing nausea. "Take it, Mina," Gregory urged, and she obeyed, hoping he would leave once she had.

He did leave, satisfied that Mina would do what he wanted. As soon as he was gone, Mina rubbed at the back of her neck so viciously that it burned, but even that wasn't enough. Gregory was in her blood, in every part of herself that she hated.

Despite what Gregory had told her, Mina still didn't know if she should believe him. She had seen Lynet's corpse, and that horrible sight was still too strong and too insistent in her memory to yield to her father's words. That corpse lay in the crypt, and even if she went and looked at it again, she still wouldn't be able to tell—

But no, that wasn't true. If the body was made of snow, it would still be unspoiled, exactly as it had been the last time she had seen it. There would be no sign of decay at all. No sign that it had ever been alive in the first place.

Mina couldn't wait till morning. She lit a lamp and stormed out of the room and down to the royal crypt. Mina continued through the cavernous walls of the crypt until she reached Emilia's casket, undisturbed in its alcove. Beside it was Lynet's, in the place that had been marked out for her since her birth. As Mina slowly lifted the casket's lid, she didn't know what she hoped to find. Would she be relieved to know that Lynet was alive? Or would that only mean that she would have to find a way to get rid of her all over again?

Lynet's body looked the same. No discoloration, no shrinking of the skin around the fingernails. This body wasn't flesh at all. *Lynet was alive.* Mina had been fooled. All her sleepless nights and guilty thoughts had been for a trick of magic, a pile of snow in the shape of a girl.

Mina slammed the lid of the casket back down with a frustrated cry. She didn't understand why she was shaking with rage, why she felt so angry with Lynet for *not* being dead. *She let me believe she was dead rather than trust her life to me.*

She heard a sound in the darkness, and then Felix walked into the ring of light from her lamp. "My faithful shadow," she said. "I thought you would follow me."

How human he's become, she thought as he came to stand beside her, head down out of respect for the dead. Since bringing her Lynet's body, Felix seemed to have grown more distant from her—and yet he was with her more than ever before. Perhaps she only felt that way because he was becoming more himself, so many of his feelings now his own instead of hers.

He took her hand and stroked it softly. "The girl's death still disturbs you," he said.

Mina laughed, a shrill, weary sound. "No, Felix. My father brought me news tonight. He told me that Lynet is alive."

Felix looked up at her in surprise, and she looked into his eyes, wondering what would be reflected there. Relief, mostly, as well as confusion, but none of the creeping dread that Mina could feel in her stomach.

"But the body—"

"Lynet has powers of her own, it seems, and she's used them to fool me. There's nothing in that casket but snow. My father traveled all this way to tell me because he wants me to find Lynet and kill her."

"You won't," he said at once.

"The choice is to kill her or to let her kill me—which one is better, do you think?"

He shook his head. "No, you don't want to hurt her. I thought you did at first, but then I realized it wasn't true. That's why I—"

He stopped, and Mina frowned. "Finish what you were saying, Felix."

He hesitated. "That's why I let her run away instead of killing her."

"What are you talking about? You said you couldn't find her."

"I lied," he said, those two words falling heavily from his mouth. "I found her as she was climbing the castle walls. I had her throat in my hands, and I chose to let her go."

Mina slipped her hand out of his. "You kept this from me all this time." She lifted his head roughly by the chin, forcing him to look at her.

But his thoughts were locked away from her now, his eyes revealing nothing. "I'm sorry," he said. "I only wanted to protect you. I almost killed her because I thought you would be happier for it, that you even wanted me to do it. But she was so young, and I . . . I couldn't, not even when I thought you wanted it. And then I thought of the king, how I had let him be hurt because I thought you wanted that as well. But now I wonder . . . I wonder if it was only what *I* wanted. And I wish I hadn't done it at all."

Mina listened to his confession with growing fear. She wasn't afraid because Felix had spared Lynet, but because he had acted on his own impulses, and because he had been able to keep this secret from her. Even the simple fact that he had pitied Lynet frightened her. His knowledge of love was a lie that he'd learned from her, but where had he learned the semblance of pity? Of mercy? Not from Mina.

"I don't know who you are," she said softly. "You were mine, but now I've lost you."

He pulled her closer to him, resting his forehead against hers. "No," he said. "I'm here, as I have always been. I love you."

She pulled away from him. "You think you love me, because I told you that you do, but you don't know what love truly is."

He shook his head. "You're wrong. Maybe that was true once, but I remember . . . I remember one night soon after you married the king, after you started calling for me again . . . you brought peaches, and you told me that when you were a girl, you ate them all the time, but that you hadn't had one since the first day you'd come to the castle, and I heard such pleasure in your voice. You took the first bite with such relish, not caring what kind of mess you made, and some of the juice spilled down your chin, onto your throat. You were so content in that moment, so perfectly free. And even though I thought I had loved you before, I knew then that I hadn't understood love until that moment, when I would have given up my life just to keep you as content as you were eating that peach. I remember I reached out to wipe the juice from your throat, and when I touched you, it felt like the first time, the night you made me. I love you, Mina. And I know that you loved that girl."

His voice was low and gentle, and he reached his hand to brush a thumb against her throat, a faint smile on his face as he lived for a moment in his memories. But before he could touch her, Mina flinched and turned away from him. She couldn't bear to see the earnest look in his eye or hear the conviction in his voice. Nothing that he said was a reflection of her anymore. He had moved beyond her reach.

His fingers grazed her arm. "Mina—"

"Stop it," she said, turning to face him. "Do you think you're capable of love when I'm not? Do you imagine yourself more human than I am?"

He looked at her with concern and pity, and her chest ached. She'd made a man out of glass, had made him to worship her, and yet at this moment he was more flesh than she was. And she hated him for it.

"And what will happen when I grow old, while you remain as you are? Will you still love me then? Will you still want to hold me in your arms? Or will you find a new queen to serve? Maybe that's why you couldn't bring yourself to kill Lynet. Because you found a prettier face than mine, a new face to adore."

He put his arms around her, and even though she wanted to push him away, she clung to him instead. "You're wrong," he said, and she heard the rumble of his voice in his chest. "I don't think I'm more human than you. I think we are the same, and I think you give us both too little credit."

"I can't trust you anymore," she said, even as she held on to him. "You've lied to me. You've kept secrets. You've become . . . more than what I intended you to be."

"And yet I still love you."

"*Exactly,*" Mina said. She reached up and took his face in her hands. "And why do you think that is? You think you love me for my charms, for my sweet nature? That girl with the peach is dead, Felix. And one day you'll realize it, and I'll look into your eyes and see nothing there but contempt and pity." *It was painful enough when it happened with Lynet,* she thought but did not say. She could prevent it, though—with one thought, she could turn Felix back to glass, shatter him where he stood. She had almost done it once, and only his growing humanity had saved him. What would save him from her now? What would save Lynet?

Felix placed his hands gently over hers. "Mina—"

"No," she said, drawing away. She was horrified of her own

thoughts, of her urge to destroy anyone who came too close to her. She suddenly found the crypt suffocating. "Don't follow me," she said, and she moved around Felix to get away, half expecting him to reach out and stop her.

But he didn't, and when Mina stepped out of the crypt back into the open air, she thought of what she had almost done to him, and she hoped for his sake that he would never reach out to her again.

28

LYNET

As soon as the sun had risen, Lynet and Nadia set out on foot along the road north. Even after pooling their money together, they were reluctant to spend it until it was necessary, since Lynet didn't want to use her powers again until they crossed the Frost Line, where she hoped the snow would revive her.

Lynet didn't know if she should be sad to leave the South or excited to go home. *Home.* She had never had the chance to miss Whitespring before, to think of it as anything but the only place in the world. But now it was home—it was *hers*—and she already felt the pull of the snow calling her back.

Several times she noticed the wonder on Nadia's face as she took in the color and light of the South. Lynet remembered that Nadia's father had been southern, and she thought of what it must mean to Nadia to walk under these trees, knowing that her father might have once done the same. She had waited so long to come so far, and now she was leaving it all behind for Lynet's sake. Did Nadia resent her for it at all, or did she feel she owed this to Lynet, after giving her secrets to Gregory?

Lynet kept reminding herself of that betrayal, reopening a wound that was threatening to close. But when Nadia took her hand to help her climb over a fallen tree, or made excuses to stop and rest when she noticed Lynet's labored breathing, it was too easy for Lynet to let her guard down again, to remember only the sweetness of the friendship they had shared without the bitter taste underneath it. And yet, she knew Nadia never forgot the deal she had made with Gregory—Lynet could always see it in the shadows around her eyes, in the corners of her hesitant smile.

When night fell, they stopped to rest under the drooping leaves of a willow. Lynet laid her cloak out beneath her and looked up through the leaves at the visible patches of sky—a deep blue rather than a cloudy gray like at home—marveling at all the stars. Nadia settled beside her, both of them leaning against the wide trunk.

They'd only exchanged a few impersonal words between them since leaving the city. It hadn't been too noticeable when they were walking, but now, with the two of them sitting side by side, their shoulders barely touching, the silence surrounded them as completely as the willow leaves.

"Can I ask you something?"

The timidity in Nadia's voice was a sharp point pressing at Lynet's heart. This rift between them gave her no satisfaction, not when all she had ever wanted was to know Nadia better, to talk to her freely. She felt a fresh surge of resentment toward Gregory for having ruined their friendship before it had even begun.

"Ask me."

"Are you scared to go back?"

Scared? She had never wanted to admit when she was scared.

Mina was never scared, or so she had believed. "I'm only scared it won't work," Lynet said, her throat dry from having been silent for so long. She stared straight ahead at the outlines of the dangling willow leaves. *I'm scared I won't be enough.* "I'm scared that some wounds can't be healed."

"Some wounds never heal," Nadia said. She shyly reached for Lynet's right hand, turning it over so her palm was facing up. "But many do." Nadia's fingers ran over the scars that striped Lynet's palm where the dagger's handle had burned her. Her hands were soft, her touch soothing, so Lynet didn't move her hand away.

"How can you tell which can be healed and which can't?" Lynet asked in a whisper. And she knew they both heard the other question that hung unasked between them: *Which one are we?*

"Practice," Nadia said. "Experience." She hesitated and began to draw her hand away, but then she said, "Hold up your hand."

"What?"

"Hold up your hand, like this." Nadia held her hand up, palm facing outward. Lynet did the same, and Nadia pressed their fingertips together. "Now wait."

Lynet fidgeted, her earlier confession making her feel exposed, restless. But she waited until the only sensation was their twin heartbeats, Lynet's quick and jumping, Nadia's solid and even. Soon, Lynet's heart began to slow, and she couldn't tell whose pulse was whose anymore.

"My mother used to do this with me when I was a child, whenever I was afraid," Nadia said. Her voice layered over the beating of their hearts sounded like a song. "She said that if my heart was racing too quickly, I could borrow hers for a while, until my own was calm again."

Lulled by the rhythm, Lynet's thoughts turned to Mina. She could still remember the moment in the chapel when Mina had made Lynet feel her lack of a pulse, and Lynet wished she could return to that night and respond differently—to reach out to her instead of silently shrinking away.

Her own words echoed back to her like an accusation: *I'm going back for my home, my family—don't you think any price is worth that?* Of course Nadia had agreed—she had decided that spying on some girl she didn't even know was worth the chance to keep her father's memory alive. Wouldn't Lynet have done the same if she thought it would bring her closer to Mina?

Lynet let her hand fall, guilt stirring in her chest. "Nadia . . ." she started, searching for the right words, a safe ground between thanks and apology. "I want you to know that I understand what the South means to you, and that I appreciate your leaving it for my sake."

There was a pause, and then Nadia said, "Part of me did think I would find traces of my father here—in the people of the South, in the hands of other surgeons. In myself, maybe. But I think the truth is that I was trying to escape my parents, too. I wanted to stop seeing their faces, still marked from illness, right before we buried them in the snow. I thought if I went south, I could imagine them alive again. I could find something full of movement and life and energy to distract me from those memories." Lynet heard the rustle of Nadia's hair as Nadia turned to look at her. "But I didn't need to go south—I had already found what I wanted."

Lynet was keenly aware of her thudding heartbeat. "Where did you find it?" she asked.

"She fell out of a tree one morning."

Lynet hid her face, certain that even in the darkness, Nadia would be able to see the confused emotions written there. Anger and betrayal fighting for victory against forgiveness and something *else* that she didn't understand, the words hidden underneath her skin somewhere she couldn't reach. *I've missed this. I've missed her.*

But when Lynet turned back, Nadia wasn't looking at her, either. She was twisting her sleeves in her hands, her head bowed low, hair blocking her face. When she spoke, Lynet could hear the cracks in her voice. "Whenever I think of what Gregory wanted from you, whenever I think of the role I played . . ." Nadia lifted her head, turning to face Lynet with all of her sorrow and regret on display, and Lynet knew this was an offering. Lynet had told Nadia her secrets, and now Nadia was giving her the most difficult secret she possessed—that behind her air of competence and control, she was as lost and uncertain and lonely as Lynet had been. "Lynet, I'm so *sorry*," she breathed.

Lynet didn't look away this time. She could absolve Nadia with a word, if she wanted, and part of her did want to—her resentment was no raging fire that gave her strength, but a painful weight on her chest that made it hard to breathe. But she waited so long to answer, the silence stretching between them, that the moment for forgiveness passed.

She leaned her head back against the tree and shut her eyes. When Nadia spoke again—just Lynet's name, soft and questioning—Lynet pretended she was asleep.

At dawn, Lynet and Nadia continued following the main road until they came upon a group of merchants going north with bolts of colorful fabric. The merchants agreed to take them past the Frost Line in one of their carts in exchange for the contents of Lynet's purse, and so Lynet and Nadia left the South nestled between silks and linens.

Lynet kept her eyes shut for most of the journey—the rocking of the cart on the uneven road and the moving landscape around them made her feel nauseated. But then, on their second day traveling in the cart, Lynet felt a jolt all through her body, like she was suddenly waking up after dreaming about falling from a great height. Her eyes snapped open, and there, all around them, was snow.

They had crossed the Frost Line.

She nearly cried from the relief of seeing the snow. She felt like she'd been holding her breath for a long time and had suddenly released it, the world around her clear and vivid again.

But it wasn't enough just to see the snow. She needed to feel it on her skin, to sink into it and hear her heartbeat resounding all around her. *Soon,* she promised herself.

She had forgotten, though, how much slower the carts moved through the North, how often they needed to stop to clear the roads, and more than once Lynet wanted to test her power and sweep all the snow off the road with a wave of her hand. But she waited until the cart stopped at a crossroads. From here, the merchants would go west toward the estate of a nobleman whose name Lynet vaguely recognized. They didn't bother trying to sell their expensive fabric in the villages, taking them straight to the wealthy estates instead.

Lynet practically leaped out of the cart while Nadia thanked the merchants, and she headed north into the woods. Nadia hurried to catch up with her, but Lynet only went deep enough into the woods for the trees to shield her from passing view before sinking to her knees in the snow. She hadn't fully grasped how *warm* the South was until now, when the heat was finally seeping out of her.

She heard Nadia calling her name, asking her something, but nothing was louder than the blood rushing under her skin, nothing brighter than the white snow, like a beacon calling her home. She sank deeper into it, lying on her back with her eyes shut, and simply lay there for a while, breathing in and out to the rhythm of her heart until it grew steady—not too fast, not too slow.

She opened one eye and saw Nadia watching her from nearby, a fond smile on her face. Lynet remembered what she'd said about finding what she had been looking for in the North, soft words spoken in the dark, and she liked the version of herself that she saw in Nadia's eyes.

But when Nadia noticed that Lynet had seen her, she turned away, as if she had no right to watch her anymore.

It was almost evening, so they decided to walk to the nearest village and stay the night there before continuing on to Whitespring the next day. When they reached the small, crowded streets of the next village, Lynet remembered the last time she had passed through a village like this, how she had seen all the ways she could help and yet had shrunk away and even threatened a stranger. The memory shamed her. Perhaps returning to Whitespring was a mistake, but it was a mistake she needed to make.

Her cloak wasn't strange or out of place here, but she didn't want or need it anymore—it was one more layer between her and the snow—and so before she could talk herself out of it, she tore the cloak off and gave it to a young woman who was walking by, her own cloak thin and torn. She pressed the heavy cloak into the girl's hands, moving on quickly before the girl could refuse or ask questions.

She thought Nadia might worry about her being too visible in her bright red southern clothes, but she only said, "That was kind of you," before following Lynet onward to the village's dingy inn.

Lynet had a full purse, her magic effortless again, but for the rest of the journey, neither she nor Nadia mentioned the idea of riding in a cart, or even suggested that Lynet try making a cart out of the snow. With each step closer to Whitespring, Lynet's fears became harder to ignore, and so she was relieved to walk the rest of the way, to prolong these last stolen moments with Nadia before they returned to their roles of the princess and the magician's spy.

After four days of traveling, Lynet and Nadia finally reached the woods outside Whitespring just before dusk.

Nadia drew a long breath. "Are you sure about this?"

Lynet nodded, staring straight ahead. "I'll stay near the edge here, to the left, so it'll be easy to find me."

Nadia looked at her, and though she said nothing, her eyes spoke of fear, of remorse, of some forbidden hope. There was a question poised on her lips, but instead of asking it, she turned away, her hair hiding her face.

Lynet might have offered some reassurance that they would see each other again, that she understood why Nadia had acted as a spy, that she was finding it harder and harder to blame Nadia for what she had done. She might have reached out and brushed the snow out of Nadia's hair. She might have asked her own question, one that had been swimming in her mind since she'd seen those two young women in the city square. But now, so close to Whitespring, Lynet was becoming more fully aware of the danger ahead—not just for herself, but for Nadia as well. And so she knew what she had to say instead.

"You can still turn back if you want," Lynet said. "You don't owe me anything."

Nadia shook her head, facing Lynet again. "That's not why I'm doing this. If *you* want to turn back now, I'll go with you, but I'm not going alone."

"Then promise me that you'll leave Whitespring if Mina or Gregory poisons me."

"Lynet—"

Lynet held up a hand to stop her. "Here," she said. She pressed the full purse into Nadia's hands. "If anything goes wrong after I wake, or if Gregory figures out that you switched the poisons, I . . . I don't want anything to happen to you. Go south again if you wish, but promise me that you'll leave Whitespring as soon as you can."

Nadia didn't answer at first. She studied the purse in her hands, silently deliberating. "Is that your first order as queen?" she said at last.

Lynet tried to smile. "Yes."

"Then I promise."

She didn't say more, but Lynet saw the question forming on her lips again. And she knew, as strongly as she felt her connection to the snow, that if Nadia spoke now, this good-bye would become impossible. "You should go before it gets too dark," Lynet said, the words falling heavily to the snow at her feet.

Nadia gave a short nod, eyes glistening. She turned and started down the path to Whitespring without another word.

Lynet watched her go until the wind sent the snow flurrying up along the road, forming a white veil that hid her from view.

29

MINA

The snow had fallen over the patch of earth where Sybil's statue had once stood, as though nothing had ever been there at all. From her window, Mina frowned. The continuing presence of winter seemed to be mocking her, reminding her of her failure.

A series of quick raps on the door interrupted her thoughts. Mina knew it must be Felix. When she called him in, he fixed his eyes on a spot over her shoulder and said something about an urgent request to see her.

She kept looking at him, startled by the way his eyes were no longer blank and endless, but rich and full. He was an empty outline who had been filled in at last.

"Who is it?" she asked him. "Did you recognize the person?"

Felix nodded. "The surgeon you dismissed."

Mina turned away, thinking of the vial of poison that still sat by her bed. "I'll see her in the throne room," she told Felix. "Bring her to me there."

Two of her guards showed the surgeon in, with Felix behind them. Mina had gazed around in awe the first time she'd entered the throne room all those years ago, but the surgeon showed no reaction to the room's grandeur, her eyes fixed straight ahead as she approached the throne with single-minded focus. Mina wondered if the girl had to convince herself to turn Lynet over, or if this betrayal came easily to her.

She dismissed them all, except for Felix, who stood off to the side of her throne as Mina gestured for the young woman to come closer. "I know why you're here," Mina said, voice laced with disdain, "but I want to hear you say it anyway."

Nadia took a breath and then said clearly, "I've come here to give you Lynet."

Mina rose from the throne and stepped down so that she was standing level with the young woman. "And why does Lynet think you're here?"

Mina wanted to shame her, to make her cringe or look away, but Nadia did neither, never once breaking Mina's gaze. Her eyes gleamed, not with the coldness of betrayal, but with the fierceness of conviction. Whatever Gregory had promised her must have been something important to her, something that eclipsed even the shame of betraying a friend.

"She thinks I've gone into North Peak for food," she answered.

"And instead you've come here, to hand her over to me. What a wonderful friend you are to her."

Nadia's head lowered for a moment, a flash of guilt in her eyes, but she recovered quickly and met Mina's gaze again. "Your father promised to make me his apprentice. Not even Lynet can offer me what he can."

Mina wanted to have her killed on the spot. All she had to do was call for her guards, and they would do it, and nobody would even know that this young woman had ever existed. She thought of all the time this girl had spent with Lynet, all the trust Lynet had put in her, and it made her burn hot with rage. *You don't deserve her,* she wanted to say. But instead, she only said, "Yes, I can see why you and my father get along."

Nadia winced at that, which was one thing in her favor, at least—she recognized Mina's words as an insult. "Shall I tell you where she is?" she said, her voice slightly tense. "I can draw you a map."

Mina slowly circled her, not wanting the girl to notice her uncertainty over seeing Lynet again. But what Gregory had said was true—Mina didn't stand a chance against Lynet. As soon as the people of Whitespring knew Lynet was alive, they would unite against Mina immediately. *I have my powers,* she thought for a moment. But Lynet had powers too, and there was more snow than glass in Whitespring.

She had to find Lynet first, before she came out of hiding—and then? *And then I'm to poison her.*

Again, the thought sent waves of nausea through her. Poison was her father's plan, but that didn't mean it had to be Mina's plan. For now, all she needed to do was retrieve Lynet and contain her somewhere in the castle without anyone knowing. Gregory would be angry with her when he found out, but she'd faced her father's anger before, and even that wasn't as painful as the grief she had felt when she'd thought Lynet was dead.

"All right," she said, her voice a dull croak as she came to stand in front of Nadia again. "Draw me your map."

After she'd sent Lynet's unworthy friend away, back to her old workroom for the time being, Felix approached her, pointing to the newly drawn map in her hand. Lynet was in a spot in the woods surrounding North Peak, not far from the main road. "Shall I take that?" he asked her.

"Yes," she said, rolling the map up in her hands after blowing on the ink to make sure it was dry. "Wait a little longer, until it's fully dark, and then send four guards—it shouldn't take more than that. They'll have to take her quickly, by surprise, before she can use the snow to help her. Have them cover her head with a sack, but also tell them to make sure she can still breathe. Tell them . . . tell them that under no circumstances are they to do her any serious harm."

Felix took one end of the rolled-up map, but Mina didn't release the other end. "You won't be going with them," she said quietly, waiting for him to look up at her in surprise or confusion.

But he kept his eyes on the map. "No, I didn't think so," he said. "Not after last time."

"I have another task for you," she continued. While the surgeon had drawn the map, Mina had been thinking of where to put Lynet, where she would be contained and isolated, but safe. She couldn't imagine putting Lynet in a dungeon, but she thought of another place that would be similarly effective. "I want you to board up the window in the North Tower," she said.

She let him take the map from her now, waiting for him to go, but instead he lifted his head to look her directly in the eye. "You won't do it," he said.

Mina had wondered if he would say something to her about her plans, but even so, his words were a surprise. "I won't do *what*, Felix?" she said coldly.

He twisted the map in his hands. "You won't harm her."

It was strange speaking to him now and not seeing her own feelings reflected on his face. Strange to know that he had become something apart from her. "And how can you be so sure of that?" *How*, she continued silently, *when even I'm not sure?*

"Because I know you," he said. His voice was different too, richer, deeper—the difference between an echo and a human voice.

"But things have changed, Felix," she said, brushing her thumb against his cheek. "You've changed. Lynet has changed. Would you rather I die instead? Do you want a younger queen to serve?"

He flinched away from her, eyes narrowing with an anger that she had never seen in him before. "You believe the worst in everyone, even yourself." He turned and stormed out of the throne room, and this time it was Mina who watched him go without stopping him.

30

LYNET

Lynet ran her thumb over the folded piece of parchment in her hand. This was all she had now, this letter to Mina, but the paper seemed so thin. If she dropped it in the snow, it would likely dissolve, and then she'd have nothing but herself.

She was several feet away from the road, but with Nadia's guidance and her own red clothes announcing her presence here among the trees and the snow, she knew she'd be found easily. And she kept reminding herself that she *wanted* to be seen, to be found, despite the fear that seemed to be a living thing nestled inside her body.

They came after nightfall. Lynet heard the horses first, the pounding of hooves that echoed her pulse, and she held on to the letter like it would keep her safe from all harm, the paper creasing under her grip. Her legs started to buckle as she fought the instinct to run, but she kept still and tucked the letter into the sash at her waist.

When the horses appeared, she immediately looked for Mina among the riders, but saw only four soldiers, no queen in sight.

The soldiers surrounded her, two of them dismounting. They didn't draw their weapons, but she kept her distance, focusing on the snow in her mind, thinking of what she could shape to help her.

She backed up against a tree, the soldiers closing in on her. She noticed that the huntsman wasn't among them, and she didn't know if she should be relieved or disappointed. She didn't recognize any of the blank faces around her, but she knew by their glassy eyes that they belonged to Mina.

It was so tempting to run, to have the snow fight for her, but she needed to speak to Mina. If she wanted her stepmother back, she had to have faith that the years they had shared together hadn't been a lie. She had to trust that she knew Mina better than Gregory did. The shriveled heart she'd seen in Gregory's laboratory was no more Mina than the body she'd made out of snow had been Lynet. And if Lynet wanted to prove that, then she had to stand still for once and make a choice—just as she had to trust Mina to make *her* choice. Only their choices would determine who they were in the end.

"I'll come with you freely," she said, stepping forward. One of the soldiers approached her and bound her wrists with a cord, which she had expected, but then another soldier snatched the letter from her dress. "No!" she protested, but now her wrists were bound, her balance unsteady as she tried to move toward them. "I need to keep that."

"You're to have nothing with you," the soldier said, his voice flat and impersonal.

"But please, it's just a letter, you can't—"

He was already turning away from her, and she knew there was no use arguing with a man who wasn't really a man. Even the huntsman had seemed more human, more alive. These soldiers had their orders, and they would obey them no matter what Lynet said.

The soldier who had bound her wrists started to push her toward the horses, but she kept her attention on the one who'd taken the letter, trying to find some source of connection. "Please keep it safe," she said to him. "Don't destroy it."

He blinked at her, and whether he was responding to her plea or not, he tucked the letter into his belt. Lynet eyed it nervously as she was lifted up onto the horse, and then a cloak came around her body, a loose cloth sack over her head, and she lost sight of everything.

She went over different possibilities: The soldier would keep the letter. Mina would find it. He would lose it. He would toss it away. Maybe the letter didn't matter at all. Maybe it wouldn't have done any good anyway. Maybe it was all too late. Maybe Lynet was enough without it. Lynet spent her blind ride back to Whitespring trying to reason herself out of her worry, but none of her grasping thoughts could replace the feel of the letter in her hands.

When the sack was removed again, she was in the North Tower, the window boarded up to keep her from climbing out. There were still patches in the roof, though, and she could feel under her skin the snow on the roof, waiting for her command. She hoped she wouldn't have to use it, but she was glad she wasn't entirely helpless.

The soldiers started to leave, but one of them paused at the door, talking to someone outside of Lynet's view. And then he opened the door wider to let the huntsman step through, shutting Lynet inside the room with him.

All that had happened to her since she'd run from Whitespring was gone in an instant, and she was once again lying in the snow, looking up at a man with empty eyes who wanted to kill her. The huntsman stepped toward her, and she started backing away until she hit the boarded-up window. Cornered again, just like last time. *Just like last time . . .*

Had Mina sent him?

The huntsman was shaking his head, holding out his hands, but his hands were weapons themselves, so Lynet wasn't reassured. She swept her eyes around the room, looking for something *she* could use as a weapon, wondering if she should call to the snow. . . .

"I won't hurt you. I'll go outside, if you'd prefer. We can talk through the door, but I must speak with you," the huntsman was saying. "I must ask your forgiveness."

His words finally caught Lynet's attention, and she tried to push her panic aside as she took in the huntsman's appearance. After her first terror had passed, she noticed a change in him, subtle but undeniable. He seemed . . . *substantial* in a way he hadn't before, not the looming specter she had always feared. There were worry lines on his forehead that made him look older than she had ever seen him. And his eyes—she saw nothing of herself in them as he pleaded with her now.

It seemed wrong to be alone with him here, where she had once stood with Nadia—wrong to see his face softened by the moonlight instead of Nadia's face. She wanted to turn away from him and refuse to speak until he gave up and left her alone, but instead, she drew herself up as tall as she could and said, "What do you want with me?" He had only ever seen her as a scared little girl. Now, she decided, he would see her as a queen.

He bowed his head, breathing deeply, and then he said, "I did nothing to stop your father's accident. I didn't care if he died. I chased after you, nearly killed you. I let you run away, hoping you would die on your own." When he finished his string of confessions, he looked up at her, his eyes red and brimming with tears. "I feel such remorse," he exhaled, "and I don't know what to do."

Lynet watched him, trying to make sense of his changed demeanor. "What happened to you?" she said softly, taking a careful step forward.

"Do you know what I am?" he said, pushing back his sleeve to reveal his scarred forearm.

The night Lynet had run away, she had guessed, but now she was certain. "Mina made you out of glass."

He nodded. "She made me to be hers, but that night, when I let you go . . . I thought I was betraying her. I assumed she would want you dead, and yet I couldn't bring myself to kill you." He looked down at his hands, as though he didn't recognize them. "I acted from my own will instead of hers, and that changed me somehow. The only power she has over me now is what power I choose to give her."

Lynet tried to understand what he was saying, but one part kept repeating in her mind. "You said you *assumed* she wanted me dead. Tell me—*did* Mina ask you to kill me that night?"

He shook his head. "She wanted me to bring you back. I would have made a terrible mistake if I had killed you. I thought it would be easier for her if you were dead, but I didn't understand . . ." He clutched his heart. "There was so much I didn't understand."

Lynet almost wanted to throw her arms around him. Mina hadn't wanted her dead. Mina hadn't ordered him to kill her. "I'm so glad you came here," she said to the huntsman without thinking.

His pained expression softened, and his eyes turned hopeful. "Then you do forgive me?"

Lynet frowned. For a moment, she had been somewhere else—Mina's room, sitting in front of the mirror as Mina combed through her hair. At the huntsman's words, however, she was pulled back into the tower, standing in front of the man who had nearly killed her and who had let her father die.

Was he the same man, really? The man in the chapel who had confessed to Mina had showed none of the remorse he showed now. He'd had no conscience of his own—he only wanted Mina's forgiveness, Mina's blessing. And even then, he had still let Lynet run away rather than kill her.

Lynet shook her head. "I don't know," she said. "Even if I forgive you for what you've done to me, how can I forgive you for what you did to my father? I think . . . I think if I forgave you now, it would be a betrayal to him." She turned to the window, thinking of the crypt below them.

"I'll wait," the huntsman said from behind her. "I'll wait until you can forgive me."

Lynet turned. "That might be never," she said softly.

He shook his head. "That doesn't matter. I'll do whatever I can for you. Even if it isn't enough to make up for what I've taken from you, I'll try. I . . . I don't know how to live otherwise."

She walked over to him, thinking. "You'll do anything for me?"

He hesitated. "I can't let you escape again. Mina doesn't trust me as she used to. The guards are still waiting outside."

"I had something simpler in mind," Lynet said. "When the soldiers brought me here, one of them took a sheet of paper from me. A letter. I need you to find that letter and make sure that Mina reads it."

His face fell before he looked away from her. "I have no influence over Mina. She hears nothing that she doesn't want to hear."

"You have to try anyway," Lynet said. "That's all we can do for her. Just find the letter and give it to her."

"It won't . . . it won't harm her in any way to read it?"

Lynet shook her head. "I don't think so. I think it would only do her good."

He nodded. "I'll do what I can," he said. "I promise you." He left then, and she heard the sound of the door locking.

Lynet went to the window and clutched the stone of the windowsill, fiddled with her hair, twisted her skirt in her hands—anything to make her forget that she was empty-handed. That she had nothing to offer Mina now except her own heart.

31

MINA

As soon as the soldiers had left for the woods to find Lynet, Mina had gone to the empty council room with a candle to wait and look over the latest report about the Summer Castle. But not even her work could distract her from the thoughts running through her head. Had they found Lynet yet? Were they bringing her back even now? Would Lynet try to fight them, to use her newfound power over the snow, or would she be too defeated, knowing that the only ally she thought she had betrayed her?

"I've been looking for you."

Mina jumped at the sound of her father's voice. He was leaning against the doorframe, hidden in shadow. When he stepped forward into the light of the candle, she could tell from the way his veins stood out at his temple that he knew what she had done—what she had failed to do.

She had been leaning over the table, but she straightened now. "I know what I'm doing," she said softly.

"The surgeon arrived hours ago. That girl should be dead by now. You should have gone to her—"

"And why didn't you just go and kill her yourself?" Mina snapped. She came around the table to stand in front of him. "Why did you give me the poison? We both know why—because Lynet won't trust you enough to let you near her again. You *need* me. You've always needed me to get what you want." She paused, savoring the way he was trembling with rage. "I know Lynet better than you do. So I think it's best if you let me decide how to approach her."

"And the poison?" he said, his voice low with barely restrained anger. "Do you have it ready?"

"Yes," she lied. The vial was still sitting unopened on the table by her bed. She had considered emptying it out onto the snow, but something in her mind kept whispering that she might still need it. "I'll do whatever is necessary."

A slow, mocking smile spread across his face. "I know you will."

Gregory knew she would. Felix knew she wouldn't. She wondered which of them knew her better—the man who had made her, or the man that she had made. And again, she wondered how either of them could be so sure when, despite her assurances to her father, she still wasn't sure *what* she would do when she saw Lynet again.

A few hours before dawn, there was a knock at the door, and Mina jumped again, hoping her father wouldn't notice how tense she was. He had decided to stay with her for the rest of the night, and with Felix elsewhere, Mina was almost grateful for any company other than her own.

Mina went to the guard at the door. "You have her?" she asked in a low whisper.

The guard nodded. "She's unharmed. We locked her in the tower, as you ordered."

"Good," Mina said. "Give me the key."

He handed it to her just as Gregory appeared beside them. "It's done?" he said once Mina ordered the soldier away.

"She's in the North Tower," Mina said. "I'll go see her now."

But before she could step out the door, she felt Gregory's hand clamp around her arm. With the candlelight behind him, he seemed to glow red. "Don't disappoint me, Mina."

Mina pulled her arm away from him, but she didn't trust herself to respond. Even as she was climbing the stairs of the North Tower, she still didn't know what would happen when she and Lynet were reunited. She took a breath to steady herself, and then she unlocked the tower door and stepped inside.

Lynet was standing at the boarded-up window, peering through the gaps out at Whitespring's grounds below her. When Mina entered, Lynet turned to face her.

Lynet's hair was shorter now, and she was wearing southern clothes, the bright red silk standing out against the faded blue furniture and the pale moonlight coming from the patches in the tower roof. Anyone else would have been shivering from the cold dressed like that, but not Lynet. Mina had the urge to touch the red fabric, such a vivid reminder of her home, but she stopped herself. *I should have been the one to show her the South,* she thought. *That was mine to give her.*

The Lynet who faced her now had none of the restless energy— that sense of always moving, even just to tap her foot or play with her hair, like she'd jump out of her skin at any moment—that she'd had before. Instead, Lynet was completely still, especially compared to Mina's trembling hands.

Most startling of all, though, was that Lynet was alive. Mina could still see the corpse in her mind when she closed her eyes—it had been her last image of Lynet, an image that was so much like her and yet nothing like her at all, because there was no life in it. For those few moments after walking into the room, all Mina could do was stare at Lynet and marvel that she was standing there, alive.

She was suddenly back in the chapel, the night of Lynet's birthday, reliving the moment when she discovered that Lynet had heard all her secrets. *How can we ever move forward from this?* she had wondered then, and she thought it again now. They could never walk in step together again—one of them would always have to lose ground, until there was nothing left to do but fall.

Mina took a step toward her. "Don't be afraid," she said.

She'd expected Lynet to respond to that simple phrase as she always had—*I'm not afraid*, spoken quickly, defensively, trying to convince herself as well as anyone else—but Lynet simply returned Mina's stare. Her lips formed a word, almost too low to hear: *Mina*. And then she said, more loudly, "There's something I have to ask you, something that's troubled me. Were you with my father when he died?"

Mina was surprised by the question, but she said, "Yes. He asked for you."

"Did he . . . did he die because of me? Because he thought I was dead?"

She started to fidget with her dress, some of her old restlessness creeping in, and Mina knew that she would have lied to her if she had to, rather than allow Lynet to carry any of the guilt of her father's death. "No," Mina said. "I tried to tell him, but he didn't believe me. He was a little delirious toward the end, and he thought you were coming to see him."

Lynet's face scrunched up for a moment as she struggled not to burst into tears, and Mina wanted to reach out and smooth the lines on her forehead. *You don't want to spoil your beauty.*

Why didn't she go to Lynet at that moment and hold her, or let her cry onto her shoulder as she'd done so many times before? But she knew why this time was different—before, she'd always known how long to hold Lynet before gently pushing her away, so that she wouldn't notice the silence where Mina's heartbeat should have been. But now Lynet already knew, and so it was already too late—too late to push her away, too late to hold her at all.

Lynet composed herself, smoothing her hands over her dress. Now that she had asked about her father's death, she seemed lighter, like she had shed her last remaining doubts. But how could she seem so sure, so confident? Mina almost felt like *she* was the one who had been captured instead of Lynet.

"You're the only family I have left," Lynet said. "I was hoping . . ."

"Hoping for what? That we could be as we once were?" Mina hadn't known how harsh her words would sound until she saw Lynet start to shrink away.

"No," Lynet said. She took a breath, held it for a few moments, and then she straightened up again, looking Mina in the eye. Her voice was rich and clear as she continued: "I don't want things to be as they were. You kept so much from me, and I . . . I wanted to be you without really knowing who you were."

Mina tensed. "But I suppose you know now, don't you? You know exactly what I am. Of course you don't want to be just like me anymore."

"That isn't what I meant. We can't go back to the way things were before, but maybe . . ." She took a step toward Mina, walking right into a patch of moonlight that illuminated every scrap of hope and determination in her eyes. "Maybe we can make something new. I know more about you now than I ever did before, and I still want you to be my mother."

"Your stepmother."

"No," Lynet said. "It was always you I wanted, from the first time you found me hiding in that tree. My mother is the woman who watched me grow, who combed my hair every night with her own hands. You're the mother I chose, the one I love."

Lynet stepped toward her again, offering so much, *asking* so much, and all Mina could do was take a step back and look away from her. "You can't love me," she muttered. "You *can't*."

But Lynet was in front of her now, taking her hands, holding them tightly. "How can you believe that? During all these years, didn't you see how much I loved you?"

Mina pulled herself out of Lynet's reach, her back against the door. She had allowed herself to be cornered, and she resented Lynet for doing this to her, for making her words sound so true, so real, when Mina knew they never could be.

"You don't understand," Mina said. "You don't know me as well as you think you do." She swept Lynet aside so she could pass around her, almost tripping over the dusty armchair to reach the center of the room.

Her back was to Lynet, but Mina could still hear her say, "That's why I went south. I wanted to know more about you. I wanted to know myself, too. I thought Gregory could give me those answers. I thought he could help me find a cure for you, for your heart."

A laugh escaped Mina, scraping her throat. She turned to Lynet slowly. "And were you successful in finding a cure for my heart?"

Lynet shook her head, still standing tall, but her eyes betrayed her fear, her doubt. "If I failed, it's because I looked for answers in the wrong place. Gregory doesn't know you at all. He's never understood either one of us, or the bond we've shared. My father didn't understand either."

"So is there a cure for me, do you think?" Mina said, trying to sound cynical, but unable to prevent that one note of hope on the last word.

The silence that followed seemed endless, and Mina wanted to say something else, to stop her from saying anything at all, when Lynet answered, "I'm not sure that you need one, but—" Her voice wavered, and she took a breath before continuing. "But I brought something for you—a letter. Your guards took it from me when they found me in the woods, but it's for you. I wanted you to read it. And . . . there's something else I thought of." Lynet was fiddling with her dress, smiling shyly. "It's . . . it's childish, maybe, but . . ."

Lynet dropped the piece of fabric she was playing with and looked up at her. She walked over to Mina in the middle of the room and held one hand up in front of her, her palm facing Mina. "Hold your hand up, like this."

Mina didn't understand, but she held her hand up to mirror Lynet's, palms facing each other.

Lynet brought her hand closer until her fingertips were pressing against Mina's. "Now push," she said.

They pressed their fingertips together, forming a web of flesh with their fingers. "What is this for?" Mina said.

"Just wait," Lynet said. "Close your eyes."

She waited until Lynet had closed her own eyes before doing the same. More time passed, and she was beginning to wonder if Lynet was setting some kind of trap for her.

And then she felt it.

There, in the tips of her fingers, she felt the steady beat of Lynet's pulse. But the longer she held her fingers there, the harder she pressed back, the more it seemed like the pulse was coming from inside her own body. Or rather, it became impossible to tell whose body it came from. It was Lynet's pulse, she knew, but it was also, miraculously, her own. It reverberated through her hand, down her arm, into her chest, and she wondered how she'd lived all these years without that gentle rhythm.

The pulse that was and yet wasn't hers seemed to dislodge something in her, her blood flowing more freely now, and she felt everything at once—the grief of Lynet's death combined with the shock of hearing she was alive, the shame Mina had felt in seeing her again, together with the hope she'd heard in Lynet's voice as she insisted that she loved her as a mother.

Mina's eyes stung—she was crying.

Startled by Mina's tears, Lynet moved her hand away, and Mina was overwhelmed with the sudden emptiness of their broken connection. Lynet was staring at her with worry, and Mina could have embraced her then, this girl whose heart was so strong and so full that it could beat for the both of them.

Mina ran for the door, needing to get away from Lynet before she gave in to fear and her father's voice, always whispering in her head.

"Promise me you'll find that letter," Lynet called after her, her own voice ragged with the start of tears.

Mina fumbled for the door, ignoring her.

"Mina, please promise me you'll read it!"

But Mina was shutting the door behind her, muffling Lynet's voice. She started to lock the door out of habit, but then she stopped, leaving the key in the lock. What Lynet did now was up to her.

Lynet's last words still rang through her head as she went down the tower stairs. *Promise me you'll read it.* There was a letter, something she supposed Lynet had written for her. But when Mina came down from the tower, she went straight to the chapel, some invisible line pulling her there whenever she needed refuge. She fell to her knees in front of the altar, and she put her hand over her chest, half believing that she would feel the gentle pressure of her own heartbeat, transferred from Lynet to her.

But there was nothing, of course. Nothing had truly changed. The truth still hung like a vicious blade between them: Only one of them could be queen. Only one of them could win.

32

LYNET

She'll read it, Lynet told herself as she paced around the circular room, biting her thumb. *She'll read it, and she'll come back to me and everything will be all right.*

Lynet hadn't wanted to tell Mina the letter's contents or even that it was from Dorothea, unsure that Mina would believe her unless she read the letter herself. But there were still so many dangers. Did the guard who had taken the letter from her still have it? Would Mina track him down and read it? And even if she read it, would it make any difference at all?

Lynet had tried to reach out to Mina as best she could, with her words and with her heart. Ever since the night under the tree when she and Nadia had pressed their hands together, Lynet had wanted to see if she could use the same trick to give Mina the sensation of a real heartbeat, even if only temporarily. But Mina had hurried away, and now, as Lynet stood alone in the empty tower, she knew the letter was her last chance. She stopped pacing, standing in the same spot where she had first noticed that Mina was crying. She had never seen Mina cry before—surely that meant she had stirred Mina's heart in some way.

Each time Lynet went around the room, it seemed to grow smaller and smaller, the boarded-up window making her feel like she couldn't take a full breath. She wondered if there was anyone guarding the door, if they could bring her some water, something to make her feel like she wasn't inhaling the same stale air. She tried knocking on the door, but instead of hearing an answering voice, she heard something clatter to the ground. Lynet frowned, listening with her ear against the door for sounds of movement. If she didn't know better, she would have thought it was a key that had fallen from the lock.

Mina had left so quickly . . . was it possible she had forgotten to take the key with her? Had she forgotten to lock the door at all? Or had she *chosen* to leave the door unlocked? Hardly daring to believe that she would be successful, Lynet slowly turned the door handle, amazed when it gave way, the door starting to inch open. She didn't let it open fully, though, in case there were guards waiting outside. She still wasn't sure this wasn't some kind of test or trap.

But now she had a choice—she could stay here, waiting and wondering what would happen next, and where the letter was, if the huntsman had found it, or if Mina would read it, without any control at all. If the unlocked door wasn't a trap, though—if Mina had really forgotten or chosen not to lock the door—then Lynet could sneak through the castle and look for the huntsman. She could try to retrieve the letter and hand it over to Mina herself.

Lynet stared intently at the door, going back and forth in her mind several times before deciding that she couldn't lose this chance to regain control of her plan. She didn't think Mina would design a test for Lynet to fail, especially not after the moment they had shared. Lynet reached for the door again—

But before her fingers had touched the handle, the door creaked open to reveal Mina standing at the threshold, half in shadow. She stood calm and composed, her face smooth and impassive, her hair no longer loose but braided neatly in tight coils around her head.

"Mina!" Lynet said, startled. She hadn't heard footsteps approaching the door at all.

Mina stepped forward, edging Lynet farther back into the room. Lynet tried to see if her eyes were red or still full of tears, but they were hidden in shadow. She saw that Mina was holding something in her hand, but it wasn't the letter.

"Did you find the letter?" Lynet said at once.

Mina frowned slightly. "Yes," she said, her voice perfectly even, "but that's not why I'm here. I have something for you, something I forgot to give you before."

Lynet watched Mina in confusion and almost wondered if their last meeting had been just a dream. Mina was acting like none of it had happened, like they'd never shared a heartbeat. But Mina was holding out her hand, unfolding a black cloth to present to Lynet her silver bracelet.

All of Lynet's worries faded away in a moment. If Mina seemed stiff or formal, it was only because she was nervous to make this gesture—a gift to remind Lynet of the first time they had met under the juniper tree. Mina must have kept it after finding it on the body Lynet had made—she had kept it all this time, waiting to give it back to her.

"Mina, thank you," Lynet said. "I was worried that . . . but it's all right between us now, isn't it?"

Mina's lips curled into a smile, and she ducked her head to avoid Lynet's eyes. "I hope so, Lynet. You'll take it back, won't you?"

"Of course." Lynet took the bracelet and clasped it around her wrist. Its weight was familiar and welcome. "And now we can—"

Her words froze in her throat. An unfamiliar feeling, almost like pain, was spreading down to her hand, her fingers becoming stiff. *Cold,* she thought. *This is what cold feels like.* Mina was watching her, folding up the cloth. *Why did she use a cloth? Why not give me the bracelet directly?* Lynet had thought it was simply for embellishment, to surprise her, but now she couldn't stop thinking that Mina had never touched the bracelet herself.

Poison.

She had hoped—had wanted to believe so badly—that Mina wouldn't hurt her. She'd thought that letter would be the cure she'd been looking for—a reminder to Mina that she was more than what her father had made her. She had hoped, and she had been wrong—naive, even. Weak. *This* was Mina, standing in front of her, choosing to give her a bracelet coated in poison. Choosing to kill her.

The cold was spreading through all her limbs now, and she had to remind herself that Nadia had switched the poisons, that she wasn't really about to die. But as her arms and legs grew stiff, she kept thinking of how easily Gregory might have discovered Nadia's trick. What if he had dropped the original vial and had to choose a new one? What if he had changed his mind about which poison to use? *What if I'm really dying?* All the risks she had been willing to take seemed foolish to her now, the result of her misplaced trust.

She didn't want Mina to see how frightened she was. "You won't go until you see it happen, is that it?" she said, her voice as icy as the poison in her blood. "You want to see me die?"

Mina didn't respond. She only tilted her head, waiting. In the dim light, she seemed ten years younger, her face almost unnaturally smooth, even the cluster of gray hair around her temples hidden away.

Lynet sank to her knees. She wondered if the poison would stop if she took the bracelet off now, or if it was already too late. It didn't matter; she couldn't move her arms anymore. She was turning to ice, freezing from the inside out. *It's not real. I'm not dying.* But then why did the cold going through her feel so much like death?

Her vision was blurring, but something caught her attention—a heavy step, a flash of gray near the door. A familiar voice said, "Isn't it finished, yet?" And then her vision sharpened as Gregory stepped into the room.

But no—Lynet had thought of this—he would need Nadia before removing her heart. Nadia would stall him until she had a chance to wake again—

But I made Nadia promise to leave if I was poisoned. Why had she done that? What had she thought would happen after she was poisoned, if no one was there to protect her from Gregory while she slept? *I thought Mina would never poison me in the first place.* And so she had let her emotions weaken her judgment yet again. For all she knew, Nadia had been mistaken, and Gregory could perform the surgery without her if necessary. Or maybe he didn't need Nadia to remove the heart, just to transfer it to him, and Gregory was about to cut out her heart while she was still alive.

"No—" Lynet choked out. She tried to rise to her feet, but she merely inched forward on her knees a little, fighting to keep upright. She tried to cover her heart with her hand, a futile but instinctive attempt to protect herself, but her hand wouldn't obey. And despite everything, she looked to Mina to help her, as she always had. "Don't let him—"

But Mina did nothing, said nothing, as Gregory came to stand at his daughter's side. "It shouldn't be long now," he muttered. "Stay here until she's dead. I'll return shortly."

He left, and Lynet was alone with Mina again, her face as blank as snow.

Snow, Lynet thought, her mind growing foggy. *I still have the snow.* She could use it to protect herself, to keep Gregory away—but when she called to the snow on the roof, a spasm of pain went through her chest, and she cried out. The poison was shutting down her heart, freezing her blood, and freezing her magic with it.

And yet the most painful detail of all was that Mina could just stand there and *watch.*

"It wasn't supposed to happen this way," she muttered through gritted teeth, her head bowed from its own weight. "I had too much faith in you—or too much faith in myself, to think I knew you so well." Her tongue grew heavy. "I know you now. I see you." With a final effort, she lifted her head to look Mina in the eye. Now, finally, she saw those eyes clearly—they were black, shining, and empty, two glassy stones placed in a human face.

Lynet looked away before she saw herself die in them.

33

MINA

Mina huddled in the chapel, shivering at the cold wind that came in through the broken windows. Her thoughts were as chaotic and confused as they'd been when she'd first run from the North Tower, Lynet's heartbeat still echoing in her chest.

What a queen I am, she thought bitterly. *Hiding away from a girl half my age*. And what would a true queen do? Strike down any threat, of course, even if it meant killing her own stepdaughter. That was what her father would have her do.

Mina was wrenched out of her daze by the sound of hurried footsteps. When she heard them at the chapel door, she didn't even turn around.

When Mina did look up, Felix stood over her, his voice cold and impersonal as he said, "This is for you." She looked up, and he was holding something out to her—a folded sheet of paper, yellowing at the edges.

Lynet's letter. She looked up at Felix in surprise. "You went to see her?"

He nodded. "I did her a terrible wrong, and I had to atone."

How easy he makes it sound, she thought. Just like Lynet—Felix was too inexperienced to understand that sometimes it was too late to atone, too late to stop moving forward on the chosen path. She snatched the letter from him. "Do you really think this letter can change anything?"

He shook his head slowly. "I don't know. I just promised her I would find it and take it to you. I warned her that I couldn't make you read it if you didn't want to."

Mina sighed and unfolded the paper, glancing quickly at the first lines as she leaned back against the altar.

My dear Mina, I can't leave without saying good-bye. . . .

She frowned, wrinkling her nose at the musty smell of the old paper. She had thought it was only the paper that was old, and that Lynet had written a letter to her, but this wasn't Lynet's handwriting. She didn't recognize this hand at all. Her eyes swept down to the bottom of the page, and the name *Dorothea* made her suck in a sharp breath.

Felix tilted his head. "Should I leave you?"

"No," she said quickly. "Don't . . . don't go." She had no desire to be alone with her mother's ghost. Felix sighed and settled beside her, careful not to let even their shoulders brush against each other.

At first Mina imagined that this letter was her mother's last good-bye before taking her own life, but as she read—going over some of the sentences several times—she started to frown in confusion. Her mother's words didn't match what Mina knew, what she expected. Mina couldn't understand the words until she put aside the story she knew and focused on the one she held in her hands now.

The letter wasn't just a good-bye. It was an apology—and not for killing herself, but for running away.

I wish I could take you with me, but I don't know where I'll go, if I can take care of myself, let alone a child your age with your poor health. Your father says your heart is stable thanks to what he's done, but I can never tell if he's lying, if he's only trying to trick me. I've never been alone before. No one ever told me how hard it was to be a mother, how much of a child I would feel even when holding my own child in my arms.

The paper was stained in places—smudges of ink during hesitant moments, stains that might have been tears.

I know I should stay, and that it's wrong for me to leave you here with him, but I can't stop myself from hating him and I know that he sees it in me, and that he hates me for it too. And I'm sure that if I stay, he would do me some harm. But he wouldn't hurt his only child, not after he worked so hard to save your life. I've failed you too many times, and I don't deserve your forgiveness, though I hope that one day you might still try to think kindly of me. I won't look for you, in case you don't want me, but I'll always be waiting, in case you ever find your way to me again.

And then, miraculously, the words that made the least sense of all—

I love you, Mina. I love you so much. I wish I could be stronger for you.

Mina's hands trembled, both from anger—*She left me*—and from joy—*She loved me*. She ran her fingertips over those last words again and again, wanting to hold them, to transform them into something with weight and shape, something she could carry with her. All these years, this letter had been hiding the secret of her mother's love. Where had it been? How had Lynet found it?

She had gone to Gregory, Mina remembered. Lynet was always so curious, always snooping where she shouldn't be. Gregory had kept this letter, or perhaps he had forgotten about it, but he still *knew* that Dorothea hadn't killed herself. He had lied to Mina— about her mother's death, about her mother's love, about the way her heart worked. *You cannot love, and you will never be loved,* he had said, and he had been wrong.

Didn't you see how much I loved you? Lynet had asked.

No, no, she'd only ever seen the world through her mirrors, sur- rounding herself with distorted images and believing that they were real. *Lynet is younger and more beautiful than you, and she will replace you,* one of them had told her, and she had believed it while ignoring the joyful smile on Lynet's face as she talked with her stepmother, the love that poured out of her with every word. Mina had let reflections fool her, too afraid to look beneath them for a heart she didn't think she had. She wondered when she had started to imagine that Lynet was as cold and heartless as she saw herself.

Felix now put a tentative hand on her shoulder. "Mina?"

Mina dropped the letter carefully on the ground and turned to take Felix's face in her hands, studying him intently. All those times he had said he loved her—had he truly meant them all? Even now, when he was angry with her, he had stayed with her simply because she had asked him to. She shyly ran her thumb along the line of his mouth, and she remembered what he had said to her in the crypt. *And when I touched you, it felt like the first time, the night you made me.* She felt that way now, because it *was* the first time—

the first time they were both alive together, separate and yet the same. The first time she felt an unfamiliar warmth spread through her chest and knew that she loved him, as he loved her.

"Oh, Felix, I'm sorry," she breathed, thinking of how she had almost wanted to kill him that night.

She started to draw away, but he caught her hand in his and brought his head down to press his lips to the veins on her wrist, where her pulse should have been, embracing the parts of her that she thought were broken, just as he always had. And then they were both in each other's arms—him holding her fiercely, one hand buried in her hair, her murmuring "You love me" over and over again against his cheek.

"Lynet was right," he said, pulling away from her. "She said that letter might do you some good."

Mina couldn't answer. Her mother had still abandoned her, leaving her to her father, and Mina felt a wave of resentment, a dizzying sort of despair as she wondered how her life might have been different if Dorothea had been brave enough to stay or to take Mina with her. *I wish I could be stronger for you.* And yet when Mina said those words to herself, she didn't hear her mother's voice, but her own—*I wish I could be stronger for Lynet.* Dorothea had run away from being a mother. Mina had not run away, but she had still failed Lynet. It was only the dead mothers who were perfect—the living ones were messy and unpredictable.

Is there a cure for me, do you think?

I'm not sure that you need one.

Lynet had known. She had understood that Mina's heart wasn't as damaged as either Mina or Gregory had claimed. She had read the letter, but more than that, Lynet had *loved* her. Even now, Lynet loved her. And Mina . . . Mina made her decision at last. She would do what her mother hadn't been able to do—she would protect her daughter.

Mina rose from the chapel floor, picking up the letter, and walked toward the door. Felix followed close behind. "Is she still in the tower, do you think?" she asked him. "I left the door unlocked."

"I would think she is," he answered. "The guards said she came freely, without trying to run or fight."

Mina would go to her, then, and Lynet would see that she had the letter, and she would know at once—that Lynet had understood her better than Mina understood herself. *And the crown? The Summer Castle?* a treacherous voice whispered in her ear. *Only one of you can be queen.* It was true. She faltered in her step as she hurried down the long hall that led to the east wing, and Felix held her arm to keep her from stumbling. But what was the false and fickle devotion of Whitespring compared to the love that Lynet had shown her? What was the heavy feeling of a crown on her head compared to the pressure of Lynet's fingertips against hers, as she had lent Mina her heart? It was only the South that she still wanted, the South that gave her reign any meaning at all, but would Lynet even want to take that from her, as Nicholas had?

I have to trust her, she thought. *I have to earn her trust in me.* She continued toward the stairs that would take her up to the North Tower—

—where she nearly collided with her father, headed in the opposite direction. He looked worse than she had ever seen him before, his skin stretched taut over his bony frame, and he jumped when he saw her, reaching for the wall to support him.

Mina ran her thumb along the paper in her hand, remembering the words written there. Her mother had run away from Gregory because she didn't know how to protect her child from him. Mina wouldn't allow herself to do the same.

"I won't do it," she said as she approached him near the stairs. "I won't poison her."

Gregory laughed weakly. "I'm not surprised," he said, waving his hand dismissively in her direction. "You've always allowed that girl to manipulate you."

For a moment, Mina's vision went red, and then she thrust the letter at him. "Is that why she gave me *this*?"

He took the letter from her, but there was no sign of recognition as he frowned down at it. He unfolded the page and only then did his face fall, his hands tightening on the paper. "Where did you get this?" he hissed.

"Ask Lynet. She's the one who found it, probably when she was with you. You told me my mother was *dead*. You told me she killed herself because she *hated* me—" She cut herself off, her voice wavering dangerously as she spoke aloud words that she'd only ever thought to herself in shame.

He looked ready to tear the paper in two, he was clutching it so tightly, and so Mina snatched it back from him, tearing a corner of it in the process. "I didn't hide that letter from you," Gregory said, his voice a low growl. "I must have tucked it away somewhere and forgotten about it; otherwise I would have burned it. Does it matter whether your mother is dead or not? She abandoned us both."

Mina shook her head. "No, it doesn't matter. What matters is that she loved me, as much as she could, and you told me that I can't love or be loved. Was that a lie too?"

He hesitated, eyes darting still to the letter in her hand. At last he said, "I don't know."

She choked back a whimper. "Of course you don't know. You've never known anything about love."

But that wasn't entirely true. He knew that if he raised his daughter without love, and that if he told her often enough that she wasn't capable of it, she would soon start to prove him right, if only because it was all she'd ever known. He had reshaped her in his own image, not by taking out her heart, but by convincing her that she was as unable to love as he was.

Gregory's face contorted, and he started to reach for her when his eyes went to Felix, standing aside in the hall. His hand dropped, and he said in a fierce whisper, "You're nothing like me. If you were, that girl would have been dead hours ago."

"I'll protect her from you," Mina said. "I won't let you near Lynet ever again. Nicholas was right to keep you away from her. Do you understand? I will not hurt her, and I won't let you do it either."

Gregory pouted at her in a semblance of pity, but his eyes were glittering with some secret amusement. "Oh, Mina, you're the one who doesn't understand. It's already been done."

She took a startled step back. "What did you say?"

"Don't you hear the footsteps?" he said, standing aside.

Mina *did* hear them now, echoing down the curved stairwell with each even step, a mockery of the heartbeat she didn't have. She watched in growing horror as she recognized the figure now descending the stairs with perfect grace—first her dainty foot, taking small, careful steps, and then the hem of her familiar green dress, until a woman as composed and elegant as Mina could ever hope to be emerged from the shadows of the staircase. She wore Mina's face, except there were no wrinkles to disturb her beauty, no signs of age or distress. She wore Mina's hair in braids, not a single hair in disarray, no gray hair peeking out around the temples. She was Mina's reflection come to life, identical in every way—except for the eyes. The eyes were chilling in their emptiness.

For a moment, she simply stood there, looking at herself—a version of herself without any feeling, any heart at all. *This is what he wanted me to be,* she thought. And just the sight of her made her realize how wrong she had been all this time, how deeply she could love—because Lynet was possibly dead at this moment, and while Mina could feel the blood draining from her face, this other Mina didn't care at all.

Gregory snapped his fingers, and the other Mina collapsed in a pile of glass shards that scattered along the stairs. "I had to use what little strength I had left to make that thing because I knew you wouldn't do it," he said, his voice weary but dripping with contempt. His face was a mask of loathing as he turned to Mina. "Do you see, Mina? I don't need you after all."

Mina shoved him aside and nearly tripped over the pieces of glass as she raced up the stairs, cursing herself for leaving the poison in her room, for leaving the door unlocked, for marrying Nicholas and getting involved in Lynet's life at all. When she reached the top of the stairs, the door gaped wide open, and she ran inside, letting out a strangled cry when she saw Lynet's body sprawled on her back on the floor, her hair spread out around her head. One of her arms was stretched out at her side, and Mina saw the glint of a silver bracelet on her wrist—the bracelet that had been on her bedside table, next to the vial of poison. Her father had taken this first gesture of trust between them and used it to kill her.

She's not dead, she can't be dead. Mina fell to her knees beside her daughter's limp body, cradling Lynet's head in her lap. *She died thinking it was me—that I killed her.*

Mina felt rather than heard another presence and looked up to see Felix standing in the doorway. "Your father is gone," he said. "I don't know where he was going."

"That doesn't matter now," Mina rasped. She leaned down to kiss Lynet's cold forehead. "I'm sorry," she whispered. "I'm so sorry. I didn't want this to happen, I—" *I love you,* she wanted to say, but the words caught in her throat. She'd never been able to say them to Lynet when she was alive, and so it seemed wrong only to say them now that she was dead. Using the fabric of her skirt to protect her skin, she managed to unclasp the bracelet and slide it away, hoping its removal might revive her. She put her fingers to Lynet's wrist to check her pulse, and for one breathless moment, she was sure she would feel Lynet's heartbeat echoing through her again, but instead she felt only her own emptiness, Lynet's heart now as silent as Mina's.

She was still sitting on the floor, crouched over Lynet, her body in her arms, when the surgeon appeared in the doorway, breathing heavily. "Your father told me to come at once. He said—" She broke off as she took in the sight of Lynet's lifeless body.

Mina almost ordered the surgeon away. *She* had been the one to lead Lynet into this trap in the first place, setting this whole disaster in motion. But then a sliver of hope—so small, but still so dangerous—made her reconsider. Was it possible that Lynet wasn't dead yet? The court surgeon would know better than she did.

Mina gently let Lynet's body lie on the floor, still and unmoving, and rose in an attempt to recover some sense of dignity in front of this young woman. Nadia wasn't looking at her, though; her eyes remained on Lynet, her mouth hanging open as she reached for the doorway to steady herself. There wasn't time for her regret, though. "Has this poison definitely killed her? She put on the bracelet just a few minutes ago. Is there any chance she's still alive?" Mina said.

Nadia shook her head, still staring at Lynet.

"Just *come here*," Mina ordered, raising her voice. "I'm sure you've seen plenty of corpses before."

Nadia swallowed and nodded, coming to kneel beside Lynet and check for some faint pulse that Mina had missed. Mina waited, hardly breathing, until the surgeon lifted her head and gave Mina her answer without even speaking.

Tears filled Mina's eyes, and she turned aside, not wanting the surgeon to see her cry. "I don't understand why you're so upset," Mina said. "You got what you wanted, didn't you? You didn't care if Lynet had to die for it."

"You're right," the girl said, her voice laced with disdain. "We both have exactly what we wanted, my lady."

Mina ignored her, turning now to Felix, who was waiting at the door. "Take her down to the crypt," she told him for the second time. "Don't let anyone see you." To the surgeon, she said, "You're dismissed."

After one last hesitant look at Lynet, the surgeon left, but Felix remained. He started toward Mina, but she held up a hand to stop him. She didn't deserve to be comforted when Lynet was dead. She looked up at the patches in the roof, now letting in the cool light of dawn. How could Mina have forgotten such a careless detail? Lynet could have used that snow to her advantage. But she hadn't fought. She had trusted Mina, and she had died for her trust. And now there would be no more chance for escape, not from the crypt.

"Take care with her," she said to him. She couldn't stay in this room any longer. She swept past Felix without letting him touch her. She was covered in fractures, and she was sure that if he placed just a finger on her, she would shatter into a million pieces at once.

34

MINA

She pressed her fingertips to the glass of her mirror, but of course, she felt nothing. Mina had often considered forcing her heart to beat; glass obeyed her, after all. But even if it worked—and she wasn't sure it would, or if her heart would crack with the effort—it would still be a lie.

The steady pulse in Lynet's fingertips hadn't been a lie.

Lynet had died thinking that Mina had killed her, that her efforts to reach out to her stepmother one last time had failed. *You're the only family I have left.* That was what troubled Mina the most— that Lynet may have died believing that she was unloved.

Maybe we can make something new.

Not now, Mina thought. *Not anymore.* Nothing new ever happened in Whitespring.

What happened now that it was all over? Mina had won, and here was her victory, here in the mirror: a miserable queen, a hollow reflection. Mina wished she could finish her father's work and replace each piece of her with a shard from her mirror. First her bones and then her flesh, until she became a living mirror, always reflecting out, but never in, so no one would see that she was once again carved out and empty, her heart dying with Lynet.

She couldn't stand to look at herself anymore—her disheveled hair, her red eyes, her skin no longer smooth but lined with grief. She took up the little stool that sat beside the mirror and with one swing smashed it into the glass. The mirror cracked, and Mina swung again, until pieces of glass were falling like snow.

"What are you doing?"

His body was warped in the broken mirror, but she knew her father's voice.

"Why is there broken glass everywhere? Did you do this?" She felt his heavy step reverberate underneath her, and without thinking, she pried one of the loose shards from the mirror frame, not caring when it cut her hand.

He grabbed her by the shoulders and turned her to face him. "What's the matter with you? I've never seen you so careless before."

"Because I have nothing to care about anymore," Mina said, wrenching herself out of his grasp. "Isn't that what you always wanted? For me not to care about anything or anyone? I thought you'd be proud."

He waved at her with a dismissive gesture. "I don't have time for this. Where is the surgeon? She's not in her workroom and she was supposed to—I can't find her anywhere."

"How should I know?" Mina said. "I hope she's gone."

He frowned at that, shaking his head in confusion. "And you put the corpse in the crypt?"

Mina narrowed her eyes in suspicion. "Why would you ask me that?"

Did he hesitate before answering, or did Mina imagine it? If he did hesitate, it was only for a moment. "You were so distressed before. I have to make sure you were thinking clearly enough to get rid of the corpse."

"Stop *calling* her that," Mina snapped. Her grip tightened around the glass in her hand, and she felt a trickle of blood spill from between her fingers.

"I don't have time for your hysterics," he said. "Clean yourself up. If you show any sign of weakness now, you'll be deposed before that girl's corpse is cold." He chuckled as he turned away. "But then, I suppose it was cold from the start."

Mina started to fling the piece of glass at his head, but then he let out a sharp cry, clutching his chest with one hand while reaching for the doorway with the other. Mina watched him but made no move to help. "What's the matter?" she said, her voice flat. "A weak heart?"

He chuckled feebly. "Yes, Mina, exactly that." He muttered something under his breath—Mina thought it sounded like "But not for much longer"—and then he was gone.

Her father was right about one thing. If she faltered now, or even showed up at the Great Hall in disarray—her eyes red from weeping, her hand red with blood—not even her glass soldiers would be strong enough to keep her on the throne. And she had to stay on the throne—what else did she have now, except her dreams for the South? If she lost her crown, there was nothing left. She would have to follow Lynet to the crypt.

Why did he ask if Lynet was in the crypt? Mina wondered, still questioning that moment of hesitation before he answered. If he had been lying, then why? What could he possibly want from Lynet now? She remembered he had spoken of Lynet this way, like

she was just a dead body, when he had first given her the poison—
*When she's dead, bring the body back to Whitespring, and I'll dispose
of it.*

Why the insistence that she bring the body back to Whitespring?
What did he want from Lynet that he could only take from her
now that she was dead?

He had been looking for the surgeon—

What's the matter? A weak heart?

Exactly that . . . but not for much longer.

Mina let out a low groan. She should have known. She should
have sensed it at once—when her heart had weakened as a child,
Gregory had replaced it. He'd told her once that creating Lynet
had drained his heart, and so now he planned to take Lynet's—to
reclaim the life and the magic that he had given to her. He would
open Lynet up and leave her heartless, just as he had done to Mina.

I won't allow it, Mina promised herself, her hand tightening
around the glass. All the thwarted love that had collected in her
heart, stagnating there for years without any release, came to life
now, transforming into something as sharp and dangerous as the
piece of glass in her hand.

Her hair was still a tangled mess. There was blood on her hands
and skirt. Her face was bare and stained with tears.

It didn't matter. She had been too late before, but not this time.
She clutched her weapon and ran from the room to find her father.

Felix was beside her in an instant, and she wondered if he had
been waiting outside her rooms since returning from the crypt in case
she called for him. "Mina, what's the matter?" he asked as he caught
up with her quickly. His eyes went straight to the blood on her hand.

She stopped and reached for him with her free hand, pulling
him toward her by the fabric of his shirt. "I need you to take the
guards—*all* of them—and stand watch outside the crypt. Don't let
anyone pass through the door, not even me."

"But why—"

"Go the back way, from the servants' door, not through the courtyard. I don't want my father to see you. *Please*, Felix."

He heard the note of panic in her voice, and he nodded, reassuring her that he would do exactly as she asked.

When he was gone, Mina continued down the hall, turning a corner and going to a window that looked out on the courtyard. Yes, there he was—Gregory was just stepping out into the courtyard, taking slow, labored steps. From the window, in the light of the early morning, he looked so small, and she was struck again by how feeble he appeared when he wasn't looming over her, one hand gripping her by the wrist. She always felt like a child again in those moments, and so she had never believed that she could break that grip—never thought she could escape him, even if she tried. But she wasn't a child anymore, and now, for Lynet's sake, she had to believe that she was capable of stopping him.

With a fresh surge of determination, she raced down to the courtyard.

"Father!" she called, hurrying across the snow to block his path. She didn't care that he wasn't alone, that there were people watching.

He looked at her disheveled appearance in horror, and she heard a nearby gasp, probably at the trail of blood she was leaving behind. "Go back inside," Gregory said in a frantic whisper. "What are you *doing*?"

She didn't bother to lower her voice. "I won't let you have her. I won't let you have her *heart*."

His eye twitched in response, but he simply put his hands on her shoulders and said, "You've had a trying day. Now go back inside before anyone else sees you like this."

He tried to shove her aside so he could reach the arch that would lead him around through the Shadow Garden, to the crypt door at the base of the tower. But Mina shook off his grip and blocked him again. He was still looking nervously at the passersby who had stopped to see this spectacle of the queen fighting her magician father, and Mina suddenly remembered the night of her wedding, when he had tried to use the public eye to pressure Nicholas into giving Lynet over to him. He had lost, though, because that same crowd had made it impossible for him to argue when Nicholas had stood his ground. If Mina wanted to win, she had to keep him here, where everyone could see them. Her father was always at his most cruel when he had her cornered and alone.

But Gregory must have known that if he turned back now, he would never have another chance to step foot in the crypt. Mina would have him guarded day and night. "Mina, stop this at once," he said. "You think you can turn me away by causing a scene, but you'll do more damage to yourself than to me."

"Only if I stay silent. I may have driven Lynet away and made her a prisoner, and I may have been too late to save her, but *you*— you're the only one who *killed* her."

The whole courtyard came alive with excited murmuring. More people were starting to gather now, including some who were watching from windows and balconies above. Once, Mina would have cared that they watched with something like glee at seeing their hated queen come undone at last.

Gregory was noticing the crowd too, and he shot Mina a look of absolute loathing, his lips curling to show sharp teeth. "You'll regret that, Mina. Never put a man in a position where he has nothing more to lose."

"You should have remembered that before you killed Lynet," Mina shot back.

She thought that would have made him angrier, maybe even scared if she was lucky, but instead he was smiling, and she was the one who was suddenly afraid. "I'll give you one more chance, Mina. Let me through."

"I won't let you near her."

"Then you won't have a choice."

He lifted his hand, palm facing toward her the way Lynet had done not long ago in the tower, but then he closed his hand into a fist, and Mina felt a blinding jolt of pain in her chest.

"You've told my secret," Gregory said. "Perhaps it's time to reveal yours. Have you forgotten, Mina, that when I create something, I also have the power to destroy it? I made your heart out of glass—that means I can shatter it with just a thought."

The pain forced Mina to her hands and knees in the snow, and she heard Gregory's words echoing in her head. The truth was that she *had* forgotten—she had always thought of glass as hers. But her heart had always been her father's creation, just like the mouse he had made from sand all those years ago.

Felix and the glass soldiers still guarded the crypt, but even weakened, Gregory could use his powers to strike them down, knowing that Lynet's heart would restore him. If Mina wanted to keep her father away from Lynet, she had to stop him here, now. She tasted blood in her mouth, and she tried to stand again, but she sank back to her knees as her court continued to watch.

She was so tired of being strong, so tired of fighting enemies both real and imagined. And now she would die because in the end, she was as easily broken as a piece of glass. She wondered if Lynet would have appreciated knowing that her stepmother was the delicate one after all.

"Give up, Mina," Gregory said from directly above her. "You have no other weapon to use against me. It's all over now."

Mina kept her head down, not wanting him to be the last thing she saw before her death. And instead, she saw—herself. A fragment of herself in a piece of glass. The pain had become so consuming that she had forgotten about the broken mirror shard that she had brought with her, which lay in the snow now beside her hand, still stained with her blood. That was the one secret she had managed to keep from Gregory over the years—and Lynet must not have told him either. Even when they were enemies, Lynet had kept Mina's secret.

I have to keep fighting for her, she thought, *for Lynet*.

She kept her eyes on the piece of glass in the snow, and then with the strength she still had left, she concentrated.

"You're wrong," she said, choking on her own blood. She lifted her head to see her father staring down at her, a satisfied grin on his face. "I do have one more weapon."

A flash of light passed across Gregory's throat in the space of a single blink, and then the glass shard fell to the snow at Gregory's feet as a red line formed across his throat.

The blood started to spurt out an instant later, and Gregory clutched at the wound, his eyes wide with horror. He was gasping, keeling over, and landed beside her. He grabbed at her wrist, but she pulled her hand away.

She had made the cut deep, so that he would bleed out before he could do more damage to her heart, and she watched him as his limbs stopped jerking and his face went still, the blood still pouring from the gaping wound at his throat.

It's done, she thought, and even through the pain in her chest, she felt safer than she had ever felt before.

She heard a dull roar in her ears that came from the crowd, horrified at the violence they had just witnessed, but not so horrified that they had done anything to stop it. They were probably pleased that she and her father had finished each other off.

Mina coughed, spraying more blood across the snow. It couldn't be much longer now until she either died or the pain made her lose consciousness.

Another collective gasp filled the courtyard, and Mina wondered if it had happened at last, if she was dead, but she noticed that they were all pointing at something behind her, above her. *Princess,* she thought she heard. *Lynet.*

But that was impossible—Lynet was dead. Or maybe Lynet's vengeful spirit had returned to see Mina die. Somehow, impossibly, Mina pushed herself up to her feet and turned to face the girl she had failed.

With her black hair and red dress cutting through the white haze of snow, Lynet was as vivid as a bolt of lightning against a dull gray sky. She stood outlined by the stone arch, and behind her were at least a dozen men, their faces blurred, carrying sharp and solid swords. Her beautiful face burned with rage, and she was vengeance itself, her own hand carrying a dagger as well.

Mina stumbled toward her as the pain continued to tear through her chest, and then she fell to her knees again at Lynet's feet. Her fingers found the hem of Lynet's dress, and it was so solid, so *real*—how could a ghost feel so real? "You're alive," she murmured, hardly believing the words even as they fell from her mouth. "This is real. You're alive." Death meant nothing to her anymore—Mina could endure a thousand deaths knowing that Lynet was alive and safe. A painful laugh tore out of her as she lifted her head.

"I'm ready now," she managed to say through the blood. "I'm ready to die."

35

LYNET

Lynet had woken with a scream trapped in her throat. Her heart—Gregory was going to cut out her heart while she was still alive—

But then she'd felt a painful thud in her chest as her blood began to thaw inside her veins, and she might have laughed from relief, except she couldn't move at all. The relief didn't last—she was still alive, but her eyes wouldn't open, no matter how she tried, and so she didn't know where she was, if she'd soon feel the pain of a knife splitting her open.

That interminable space between waking and being able to move again was even worse than the moment she knew Mina had poisoned her. The scream was building up inside her whole body, growing louder, and she almost thought that it might tear her open in order to get out.

A scream of helplessness, yes, like the itch she always felt under her skin when she came out of the crypt every year, but a scream of rage, too, because the reason she was lying here, half dead, was because she had put her trust in Mina. Perhaps Gregory had been right, in his own way—there was no cure for Mina, no way to heal the rift between them. Now Lynet understood what Mina must have known all along: one of them had to die.

And as she finally began to feel a tingling in her fingertips, Lynet was determined to live.

Her heartbeat grew louder, stronger, and soon she was able to open her eyes. There was no knife hovering over her, no sound to indicate that Gregory was near. She was in the crypt, lying in one of the bare alcoves, and she had never thought she'd be so glad to find herself here.

"Lynet?"

The whisper was so soft, so uncertain, that Lynet thought she'd imagined it at first, but then she heard it again:

"Lynet? Are you waking?"

Lynet had told Nadia to leave, had convinced herself that she *wanted* Nadia to leave for her own safety. But Nadia's voice had never sounded sweeter, nor had she ever looked so beautiful to Lynet's eyes as she did now, peering down at Lynet from beside her, a candle in her hand.

"I'm awake," Lynet breathed, her voice weak, her tongue heavy. "I'm alive."

At once, Nadia set the candle down and leaned over her, feeling for her pulse at her throat. Lynet's memory stirred. The crypt— Nadia's hair brushing against her skin as she lay on a bier. *We've done this before*, Lynet thought. But no, that had just been a dream. This was real.

"You promised you would leave," Lynet said.

Nadia smiled down at her, but her shimmering eyes betrayed how worried she had been, how relieved she was that Lynet had woken. "I'm tired of following orders," she said. Lynet couldn't help a faint laugh at the response, an echo of her own words when Nadia had found her wandering outside the university.

Nadia helped Lynet down from the alcove, an arm around Lynet's waist to hold her up, and Lynet shuddered to imagine how much worse it would have been to wake up in the crypt alone, knowing that no one alive loved her anymore. She was grateful to have someone to trust, someone to hold her. She curled her fingers against Nadia's shoulder, clutching at the fabric of her shirt. "I'm glad you didn't listen," she murmured, her lips almost brushing Nadia's neck. "Thank you for keeping me safe."

Nadia's hand fell from Lynet's waist, and she gently tipped Lynet's face up to look at her. Her face was serious, her eyes intense. "I wanted you to know," she said, her voice low and heavy, "that I chose to be here with you—that I chose *you*."

Again Lynet saw the unspoken question on her lips. But this time—this time, she could feel the answer burning under her skin, finally rising to the surface. *What do you want?* Nadia had asked her once. *You never told me what you wanted,* she had said to Lynet in a dream.

With a heady mixture of joy and relief, Lynet answered.

She closed the space between them, touching her lips hesitantly to Nadia's, waiting to see if this was right, if this was the meaning buried beneath words and glances and stray touches, the desire she had felt but not fully recognized till now.

Yes, Nadia answered, pulling Lynet closer, and Lynet melted into the softness of her, her hands winding around Nadia's neck. When her nails grazed the skin there, Lynet felt Nadia shudder, felt their two hearts fluttering between them in a frantic but still perfect rhythm. Even though they were in the crypt, even though Lynet was pushing back the despair of Mina's betrayal, she still knew that this moment had been waiting for them ever since Lynet had fallen out of the juniper tree—or maybe even from the morning she had seen Nadia for the first time, mesmerized by the promise of a life different from her own.

They broke away but still held each other close, their foreheads touching. This was what it meant to feel truly alive, Lynet knew. It wasn't the magic in Gregory's blood, and it wasn't the slow thaw of waking from the poison—it was the way she felt at peace in her own skin, the person she was and the person she wanted to be in alignment at last. And it *was* her own skin, because when Nadia looked at her, when Nadia touched her, Lynet was herself and no one else, her future hers to shape as she chose.

But soon the stale air of the crypt forced Lynet to remember why she was here. She reluctantly pulled away from Nadia, her arms going around her own waist defensively.

Nadia sensed her change of mood, and she said, "I'm sorry about your stepmother."

"Did Mina tell you she killed me?"

Nadia's jaw tensed. "No, but she wanted me to make sure you were dead."

Of course, Lynet thought. *She didn't want to make the same mistake as last time. That's why she had to watch me die herself.*

The memory of Mina's impassive face watching her as she fell into unconsciousness made the scream start to build up inside her again. But she wasn't frozen now, and so this time the scream did rip out of her body, echoing against the vaulted ceiling of the crypt as she pounded her fist against the nearest wall.

When her rage was spent, she sagged against the stone. She could smell blood on her knuckles. Nadia's hands rested gently on her shoulders. "Don't lose your strength now," she said. "You'll need it for what's to come."

And she was right. Lynet knew that any chance of reconciliation with her stepmother was lost—and that the only way to ensure her safety was to kill Mina. She had acres of snow at her command, and the advantage of surprise. But she would need more than that—she would need the will to go through with it.

Lynet backed away from the wall that she had suddenly assaulted, and she saw that it was the partition between the alcoves that held her parents' caskets. She had seen her mother's casket plenty of times, but the space beside it had always been empty except for a bronze plaque above with her father's name. Lynet couldn't look away from the plain wooden casket. She'd hardly had time to mourn her father, and she couldn't stop thinking that if she opened the casket now, she could see his face again and say goodbye one last time.

But she knew it wouldn't be him, just as she knew that no matter how many times her father had brought her here, Lynet had come no closer to knowing the woman he thought of as her mother, Emilia. She'd been frightened of the crypt for so long, but now it seemed so harmless, so completely empty. Even as her ancestors surrounded her, she knew she and Nadia were alone here.

"How can I kill the only family I have left?" she asked softly, to no one in particular.

Nadia answered from behind her. "When my parents died, I thought I had no family, no loyalties, anymore. But I was wrong— you just have to choose your own family from now on."

"I loved her so much." A tear was spilling down her cheek, though she didn't know which loss she was crying for now—perhaps all of them at once. "But she'll never believe it, will she? If she could just stand there and watch me die without any feeling at all, then why shouldn't I be able to do the same?"

Lynet shut her eyes and drew a long breath, forcing herself to say good-bye now to the Mina she once knew, so that when she went to find her—to kill her—she would have no hesitation, no doubt.

"I'm ready," Lynet said finally, turning to Nadia.

They passed through the crypt, Lynet walking the same path she walked once a year with her father, but this time with her head held high, without any fear. She had been one of the dead lying here; how could she fear what she had once been? Even the Cavern of Bones seemed more somber to her now than frightening, and Lynet didn't bother to offer the customary prayer to Queen Sybil to end the curse of winter. She knew now that she would have to break the curse herself.

As Lynet followed Nadia, climbing the winding stairs that led them to the crypt door, she thought she heard sounds of movement coming from the other side. She stopped and took a moment to concentrate, to feel the snow that lay beyond the door. As long as she had the snow, she knew she would be kept safe.

The moment Nadia opened the door for her, she focused her thoughts into shapes. She summoned soldiers of her own now, the snow rising up into human forms, blank and faceless, but all carrying swords. Their task was to defeat Mina's soldiers and clear her path until they reached Mina herself.

She stood back in the darkness of the doorway as the sound of clashing swords broke the stillness of the air. Nadia took a tentative step outside, only to be slammed against the wall and pinned there by a familiar scarred arm.

"Felix!" Lynet shouted, emerging from the crypt at last, stunned by the light outside.

The huntsman had acted on instinct, and now he seemed startled to see Nadia, his grip loosening. And then he saw Lynet and his arm fell away from Nadia completely. Lynet sent the snow swirling up all around him, transforming it into coils of rope that wrapped around his wrists, his ankles, as he fell to the ground. He barely seemed to care; he was too busy gaping at Lynet.

"Mina . . . she didn't kill you," he said finally.

"No. But she tried." Lynet wanted no more apologies, no more excuses, so she used the snow to form a gag and cover his mouth as well.

"Stay here and keep watch over him," Lynet said to Nadia. She nodded, pulling a small knife from a sheath at her side. Lynet stepped around the huntsman and continued through the fray with one goal—to find Mina and end this.

The soldiers were still locked in combat with each other—none of them could die, and so they would keep fighting like this forever, until Mina or Lynet ordered them to stop.

She summoned more soldiers as she passed through the dead trees of the Shadow Garden. She didn't know how to wield a sword, so she created a long dagger to carry. In the distance, she noticed that the statue of Sybil was gone, leaving only a blank patch of snow in its place. There was no time to wonder at that, however, so she headed on to the arch that led to the courtyard, a dozen or so soldiers behind her.

Lynet had thought she was prepared for anything now. She would storm the castle, looking for Mina, to finally end this war between them. But she still wasn't prepared for the sight that greeted her in the courtyard, the collective gasp from so many of the faces she'd known all her life, the people of Whitespring, who surrounded a gruesome, bloody scene.

Red stained the snow, and Lynet saw that most of it had spilled from Gregory, who was lying dead, his throat split open. And beside him, clutching her chest, blood on her face and hands and seeping from her mouth, was Mina, not far from the juniper tree where they had first met. This Mina was nothing like the cold and composed woman who had given Lynet the poisoned bracelet—her face was ashen and twisted in agony, and her hair, flecked with blood and snow, streamed down over her shoulders. She was no longer a single burning flame but a wildfire, her pain spilling out around her.

The world seemed perfectly still for a moment. Lynet couldn't hear the crowd anymore, not even as they murmured her name. She wasn't aware of anything except for Mina, and the dagger clutched in her own hand. She seemed to hear every one of Mina's ragged breaths. She saw the tears that were still stuck in her eyelashes before they could fall down her cheeks. And when Mina looked up to find Lynet standing there, Lynet saw with perfect clarity the stunned joy on her stepmother's face and heard the startled laugh that escaped her bloodstained lips.

Mina pushed herself up from the ground with enormous effort and staggered toward her before landing on her knees again at Lynet's feet. "You're alive," she was muttering, her hands clutching at the hem of Lynet's dress. "This is real. You're alive." She turned her face up in some kind of pained rapture. Her eyes were red and glistening, not black and empty as they had been in the tower—and Lynet was beginning to doubt that the woman in the tower had really been Mina at all. "I'm ready now," Mina said. "I'm ready to die."

Even in her shock, Lynet had managed to keep hold of the dagger, and she looked up now to see nearly the entire court watching. They were leaning forward eagerly, waiting for their newly resurrected princess to slay her usurper and take her rightful place on her mother's throne. This was an era they would all willingly forget, and perhaps one day, years and years from now, Lynet would start to forget some of the details too. She would forget that she had loved her stepmother, forget the nights they had spent in front of the mirror, sharing secrets. She would forget that her father had tried to push Mina away from her, forget the part that Gregory had played and that it was probably his blood on Mina's hands. She would forget the way Mina looked now. All she would remember was the story that would be passed down by those watching: the cruel stepmother, and the wronged princess who had returned from the dead to strike her down and take back what was hers.

She didn't want their story to end this way. And more than that, she knew she had the power to change it. They both had the power to change it. She remembered what Mina had told her once, and those words now resounded in her mind, in her bones, in every heartbeat: *You'll find something that's yours alone. And when you do, don't let anyone take it from you.*

She thought she heard someone calling her name behind her, but she ignored it, ignored everyone who wanted to take Mina away from her. Lynet let out a breath, and in that same moment, all the snow soldiers behind her fell apart, dissolving back into snow that whirled around her and Mina both, shielding them from the court's hungry view. The dagger fell from her hands and she dropped to her knees beside Mina, taking her stepmother in her arms.

They clutched at each other, Lynet allowing herself a moment to cry into her stepmother's shoulder, but she could feel Mina's body shaking with pain, and she knew she didn't have time to lose. She gently drew Mina away but kept her hands on Mina's shoulders to help her stay upright. "Mina, what happened to you? Did Gregory wound you?"

Mina wrapped her arms around her own waist and let out a pained laugh as she struggled not to double over. "He cracked open my heart. I can feel it splitting open. I'm dying. There's nothing you can do now. . . . And Lynet . . . please don't remember me too harshly, if you can help it."

Lynet thought frantically. Gregory's powers were her own, after all, and she wondered if she could fix what he had broken—but she had power only over snow, not glass.

Mina had power over glass.

"Mina, listen to me," Lynet said, worried at the deathly hue Mina's skin was taking. "You can command your own heart to heal itself. It's just glass, isn't it? You can fix it yourself."

Mina was shaking her head. "Too tired to fight anymore, too

weak . . ." She started to wobble, so Lynet gathered Mina in her arms, resting Mina's head against her shoulder.

"Your father is dead now," Lynet said. "He has no more power here. Lean on me if you feel weak, but please, please, just *try*."

"Lynet . . ." Mina rasped. Her tears soaked through Lynet's dress, hot against her shoulder. "Lynet, I love you. All this time . . . all this time, I loved you, and I couldn't see it. Thank you for help- ing me see it."

Lynet let out a sob as she held Mina tighter. Her stepmother— her fierce, unbreakable stepmother—now felt so small and frail in her arms. "I love you too," she said. "You've always given me strength—let me do the same for you now. We still have so much to do together. Please don't give up."

With great effort, Mina pushed herself out of Lynet's arms and tried to sit up. She wavered a bit, and so Lynet gave Mina her arm to help hold herself up. Mina took a breath and closed her eyes.

Lynet wished she could do more, but she knew that only Mina could heal herself. All Lynet could do was lend her arm when Mina started to falter, and continue to shield them both from view with the curtain of snow falling around them. She wouldn't let anyone take Mina from her now.

Mina concentrated, and every time she started to double over, Lynet helped to keep her upright. When Mina let out a low moan of pain, Lynet stroked her hair and murmured comforting words, telling her she would be all right, that she just had to keep fighting a little while longer.

Mina's breathing grew heavier, and fresh beads of sweat formed on her skin. "I think it's happening," she managed to gasp. "I can feel it happening." Her hand tightened on Lynet's arm, and then she cried out, clutching her chest as her hair hid her face.

"Mina!" Lynet cried, her skin clammy with fear. She thought of her father on his deathbed, how scared she had been to see him there—but now she was too scared to look away or even blink, in case Mina would be dead before she could open her eyes again. "Mina, please, are you—"

But when Mina looked up, her skin was quickly regaining its normal color. "I did it," she breathed. "I can feel it. It's still . . . it won't beat, but it's . . . it's whole, at least."

"I knew it," Lynet said, breathless with relief. "I knew you could do it."

Mina took Lynet's face in her hands. "But you," she said, her voice still ragged, "how are you here at all? How are you alive?"

Lynet didn't answer. She didn't want explanations, yet. She only wanted to throw her arms around her stepmother's neck, to bury her face in her stepmother's shoulder, and to stay here behind the snow shield for a little while longer, in a separate world where nothing could tear them apart again.

36

Normally a coronation at Whitespring would have been a grand, public affair, but Mina had insisted that Lynet be crowned as soon as possible, and so it was only a small crowd that gathered in the castle's throne room.

Mina was not part of the crowd. She stood at the front of the room, before the two empty thrones, with a golden crown in her hands. That was the tradition at Whitespring—the person who performed the coronation was always a noblewoman who had been designated as the spirit of Queen Sybil, passing the crown to the next rightful ruler. Lynet had cautiously asked Mina if she would play the role of Sybil today, and Mina had agreed at once—she wouldn't have allowed anyone else to crown Lynet as queen. It was her crown to give, after all.

An uneasy peace had settled over the castle in the days that had passed since Lynet's miraculous return. Numerous stories spread from the start about what had happened to Lynet. Mina heard a few of them—some said the princess had never been dead in the first place, and that the queen had lied in an attempt to chase her rival away; others said that Lynet *had* died, but that she had returned through some kind of magic, the same force that kept Sybil's curse in place. Mina didn't care what they said; only she and Lynet needed to know what had happened.

At first it had seemed like nothing had really changed. When Mina placed her hand over her heart, she still felt nothing. She was still a queen on the brink of losing her crown. And yet—

And yet nothing was the same. For the first time, Mina felt like she could take a full breath. She sometimes wondered if she should feel horrified or guilty that she had killed her own father, but mostly she just felt a profound sense of relief. The ever-present sense of dread that twisted her stomach was suddenly gone, and Mina hadn't even been aware of it, not until the moment she knew her father was dead.

But who was she now? Without the bitterness that seeped out of her heart, the certainty that no one could ever love her, who would she become? She didn't understand who she was now that she wasn't unlovable.

She wasn't a queen anymore; she knew that much. And rather than cling to a crown she wasn't even sure she still wanted, she had decided to pass it on to Lynet as soon as she could. Mina had kept the crown from her long enough.

When Lynet appeared in the doorway of the throne room, her hair pinned up, wearing a light blue dress trimmed in white fur— the colors of Whitespring—Mina knew she had made the right decision. Lynet was already a queen. She would save Whitespring just as she had saved her stepmother, never questioning the worthiness of those she helped.

To the people of Whitespring, Lynet must have seemed as self-assured as any queen. She walked down the length of the throne room, the crowd forming an aisle between them, without a single faltering step. She kept her head high, her gaze only on Mina as she moved toward her. But Mina knew her stepdaughter, and she could see from the way she was taking shallow, uneven breaths that Lynet was nervous. Both of them had dreaded this day for so long, both fearing what they would become—what they would lose—when the crown passed from one to the other. Mina gave Lynet the slightest nod, and she saw Lynet slowly exhale the breath she'd been holding.

And at that moment, Mina made a decision. She couldn't ever allow herself to hurt Lynet again, and Lynet should have more important things to worry about than the emotional state of her traitorous stepmother. It would be easier for them both if Mina followed her mother's example and simply disappeared.

I can go south, she thought as Lynet came to kneel in front of her. Mina still had her mother's letter, the paper already smudged with her dirty fingerprints and worn even thinner from Mina's constant folding and unfolding. At first she had been so stunned by those last lines, that profession of love, but lately Mina's eyes had kept falling to a different line: *I won't look for you, in case you don't want me, but I'll always be waiting, in case you ever find your way to me again.*

Dorothea had kept her promise, if she was still alive. She would have known that her daughter had become queen, surely, and yet she had never tried to find her, to take advantage of Mina's position. She didn't even know that Mina had never seen the letter until now. Perhaps she still thought that Mina hated her. And part of Mina *did* still resent Dorothea for abandoning her, but that resentment offered Mina less comfort than the idea of knowing the mother who had loved her, even if her love had been imperfect. *I could try to retrace her steps. I could find her.*

Mina said the words that would make Lynet queen, thinking it amusing that she was upholding the spirit of Sybil when she was the one who had taken down Sybil's statue. She remembered the words from her own coronation—*I charge you with the care and keeping of this kingdom, to rule in the memory of those who came before you*—and she wondered for one terrible moment how different her life might have been if she had never become queen or never left the South. Who might she have become if her mother had never left, or if her father had been a loving man? The thought made her newly healed heart want to break, but then she remembered that she would never have known Lynet. And she had done some good for the South, at least, during her reign. It hadn't all been for nothing.

She placed the crown on Lynet's head, and when Lynet stood, Mina was no longer a queen.

While the nobles went forth one by one to promise their service to their new queen, Mina slipped out the back door behind the thrones and found Felix waiting outside in the empty hall. He opened his arms to her at once, and Mina threw herself into them, grateful she didn't have to explain her feelings to him now—her pride at seeing Lynet become queen or the gaping sense of loss she couldn't ignore. "I'm going to return south," she said into his shoulder. "I'm going to try to find my mother."

He stroked her hair and said, "We'll go whenever you say the word."

He would come with her, of course—neither one of them had assumed any differently. That was one small change, at least—she used to believe that she would be completely alone if she lost her crown. Now she knew she never would be.

When she returned to the throne room, the procession was nearly over, and finally the crowd started to filter out of the room. Lynet was to remain on her throne, as was customary, until the last person was gone.

But Mina was the last person in the room, and so Lynet let out a long sigh as soon as they were alone. She was happy, though—Mina could tell from the way her eyes shone.

"Queen Lynet," Mina said softly as she approached the throne. "Your father would be proud."

"I hope he is," Lynet said, taking the crown from her head and turning it over in her hands. "Even though I'm not quite what he asked for."

Nicholas was a fool, and you're more than anyone could ask for, Mina thought, but instead she said, "I have something to tell you."

Lynet looked up in concern. "What is it?"

"I've decided to leave Whitespring. It'll be better this way."

Lynet stood from the throne, her forehead furrowed. "Where will you go?"

"Home," Mina said, "to the village where I grew up. I thought . . . I thought I might be able to find out where my mother went when she ran away." She didn't say, *I don't have anywhere else to go.*

"I've decided something too," Lynet said. She placed the crown carefully on the seat of her throne and stepped down from the dais so she was level with Mina. "I was going to wait to announce it at the banquet tonight, but perhaps I should tell you now."

Mina's eyes kept shifting to the crown, but she forced herself to turn away from it and look only at Lynet. "Tell me what?"

Lynet almost seemed a little girl again, biting her lip as she prepared herself to speak. "I never wanted to be queen until I saw how much good you had done for the South and knew that with my powers, I could do the same for the North," she said in a rush. "But that doesn't mean I want to neglect the South again. This kingdom is broken, and I can't fix it alone." She was gaining confidence in herself, her words becoming firmer, a spark of fire in her eyes. "Do you understand what I mean now? The North needs me, but the South needs *you*. This kingdom needs us both."

No, Mina didn't understand. She was too busy watching her stepdaughter, the girl who had peered at her from a tree so long ago, transform herself into a queen, assured and clear in her purpose. "What are you saying, Lynet? We can't both be queens."

Lynet shook her head, her excitement growing. "I know that, but we can't keep doing things the same way as before—it hasn't helped anyone. We have to tear the old way down, so we can build something new. I'm creating a new position—a governor to rule the South in my stead, someone who understands what the South needs and who will work with me to unite the kingdom. And I'm naming you as the first governor of the South."

Mina was finally beginning to understand, to believe. She had always thought that one of them would have to lose, but Lynet was offering her a different kind of victory. For years, she had depended on the crown to define herself and give her the love she so craved, but now . . . now she could rebuild herself even as she rebuilt the South. "I could still finish the Summer Castle. . . ." she murmured. The fondest dream of her childhood, to live in the Summer Castle with its magnificent gold domes, would come true.

Mina's eyes stung and she turned away. She still wasn't used to these pangs of the heart that brought tears to her eyes. Once, she'd thought she couldn't cry at all, and now it seemed she couldn't stop. She took in the mosaics on the wall, the changing seasons that she had missed so much since coming north. *Home. I'm going home.*

She turned back to Lynet, who was waiting patiently for Mina to recompose herself. "Do you accept the position, then?" she asked with a growing smile.

We still have so much to do together, Lynet had said to her when she'd been bleeding to death in the snow. And she was right—there was more to be done. Mina could never earn back the devoted worship that Lynet had felt for her as a child, but Lynet wasn't a child anymore, and for the first time since she'd realized how quickly Lynet was growing, Mina believed that they could build something new, something even stronger than before. It would take time, but she had time now. She had more time than she'd ever had in her life.

Mina nodded, her voice only slightly trembling as she said, "Yes, I gladly accept."

Early the next morning, greeted by freshly falling snow, Lynet walked down to the lake where Sybil's statue had once been. She had to admit that the grounds already seemed cheerier without the weeping statue overlooking them.

She had moved to a new set of rooms now that she was queen. Not Mina's, of course—those would remain for her whenever she chose to visit Whitespring. But the new rooms were larger than her old ones, and she couldn't help feeling small when she stood in the middle of them, surrounded by so much space, so many expectations.

But she had become queen without dying, without transforming into her mother, without losing her sense of self. She had felt the crown's weight on her head without fearing that it would break her neck. There was so much to be done, and she was relieved Mina had accepted the position of governor. Lynet was sure they could work wonders together—they already had.

"It's strange not to see Sybil there anymore," Nadia said from behind her.

Lynet had left Nadia a note last night to meet her here in the morning. She had left a note for Mina, too, but she had wanted to talk to Nadia first. Lynet felt the familiar pull as she turned to Nadia, the link between them strong and clear now. But she couldn't forget the reason she had called Nadia here, or ignore the worry that came with it.

"Come walk with me," Lynet said.

They walked together along the edge of the lake, their hands finding each other, fingers entangling. These casual touches weren't heavy with meaning, as they had been before, but Lynet found an entirely different kind of pleasure in the lightness of them, the ease with which she could lean in and brush her lips against Nadia's cheek.

At the coronation banquet last night, Lynet had placed Mina to her right, Nadia to her left, and no one had said a word to oppose her. Lynet knew the court was still too amazed that she was alive to find fault with her now, but she was sure she would hear the Pigeons cluck in disapproval eventually—because Nadia was a commoner, or because they still didn't like Mina, or for whatever reason they chose. Lynet didn't care; she knew now that she was strong enough to fight for the people who were important to her, and so she was ready for that day, should it ever come.

But fighting for the people she cared about didn't always mean keeping them. Her hand tightened around Nadia's.

"Are you going to tell me what's bothering you?" Nadia said quietly.

Lynet halted, her hand slipping away. "I want to ask you something, and I want you to answer me honestly," she said. "Do you promise?"

Nadia smiled. "Do you still trust my promises?"

"I'm serious," Lynet said firmly.

Her smile faded away, and she said, "Yes, I promise," giving the words a special weight.

"I've been thinking of ways to bring more progress to the North, not just short-term relief from the snow, but something lasting," Lynet said. She had been so scared of being a queen, but right now being a queen was easier than being Lynet. Her voice was firm, her stance solid, and she wondered if she looked like Mina. "One of my plans is to build a school here, something small at first, but that could eventually mirror the university in the South—"

"Lynet, that's a wonderful idea!" Nadia said, her face blooming with excitement. Snow was falling on her loosely braided hair and on her collarbone, and Lynet's fingers itched to brush it away, looking for any excuse to touch her. It would be so easy to pretend she didn't have anything more to say.

"Well, actually," Lynet continued, tearing her eyes away from Nadia to the small lapping waves of the lake behind her, "I thought maybe you'd like to be a part of that, to use what you've learned to help others. But . . . but I also know how much you wanted to leave the North, and I wouldn't want you to stay just for my sake. So if you wanted to go south again, instead, if you wanted to stay there . . . I would understand." She swallowed, and finally she glanced back at Nadia for some hint of her preference, but her face revealed nothing. "*Do* you want to go?"

Nadia blinked, and then she looked away, a sad smile on her face. "Lynet . . ." she said. And then she shook her head and pulled a familiar purse from the pocket of her trousers. "I brought this to give back to you," she said, holding it up, the coins jangling faintly inside. "I wanted to tell you that I wouldn't need it, because I don't intend to go anywhere."

"But I thought—are you *sure*?" Lynet said, hardly trusting her own relief.

Nadia laughed, her face open and bright, with no shadow to mar her joy. "I *would* like to go back south someday to visit. But when I said I wanted to go before . . . I thought going south would make me feel less alone, but I was still so lonely there. The only time I didn't feel lonely was . . . when I was with you." Her eyes fluttered down, a shy smile on her face. "If I had left Whitespring after you were poisoned, I would have made the same mistake as when I agreed to spy on you. I would have been chasing ghosts and memories instead of fighting for something real."

She pressed the purse into Lynet's hands and bent her head to lay a gentle kiss on Lynet's mouth. "That's why I still choose you," she said, her lips brushing against Lynet's. "I want to stay with you and help you heal the North."

Lynet leaned in, and for a while, neither of them spoke.

"Keep this," Lynet said, giving the purse back to Nadia. "In case you ever change your mind. It's only snow, after all."

Nadia hesitated, but then she took it. "I'll save it for the new school," she said with a grin. "I can't think of a better way to honor my parents than to teach others what they taught me."

They walked back toward the garden, discussing plans for their school, Lynet's step lighter than before.

A few minutes later, Mina came striding across the grounds, still every bit a queen. She offered a civil nod to Nadia and then she turned to Lynet with a smile as warm as summer.

"Now that you're both here," Lynet said, "I wanted to show you something."

Nadia and Mina both spoke at the same time. "What are you—"

"Hush," Lynet said. "Just watch."

She hadn't tried this before, but she knew it would work, because she knew *this* was her true purpose—not to become her mother, but to end this curse at last. The snow was still steadily falling on them, but Lynet turned her face up to the gray clouds and told the snow, simply, to *stop*.

And it did.

Nadia's forehead wrinkled as she looked at Lynet's face, watching as she'd been ordered. It took her several seconds to look up and notice that the snow had stopped falling. But Mina—Mina had noticed at once, her eyes widening in awe.

"The snow stopped," Mina whispered.

"Did you—?" Nadia started saying at the same time.

Lynet laughed. "I think the snow deserves a rest." She turned her attention to the place where the statue had once stood, and she concentrated again until the snow there melted, leaving a square of damp brown soil. "A little at a time," she said. "People will need to adjust gradually, and I'll have to keep some of the snow, or else I'll grow too weak. But I want to make the North bloom again, to make life easier here. I have to try, anyway."

"If anyone can do it, I know you can," Nadia said, gazing at her fondly. "I think—" Nadia stopped and frowned as something over Lynet's shoulder caught her eye. The frown softened into that expression Lynet had seen on her before when she was studying her books—an expression of curiosity and amazement that there was still so much in the world to discover. "Lynet, look," she said.

The first thing Lynet noticed when she turned was a flash of green. She thought it was just a trick of the light at first, but then she saw it clearly: a long, thin stem with a perfectly formed leaf. When Lynet examined it more closely, she saw that the budding plant was real, a single sign of life in place of Sybil's statue.

"*Lynet.*" From behind her, Mina spoke with such breathless wonder that Lynet wasn't sure what she would see when she turned around.

Mina was pointing to the trees in the Shadow Garden. Lynet stepped closer, coming to stand beside her stepmother, and saw the scattering of leaves and the closed pink buds that were beginning to grow on the dead branches.

The two of them walked through the garden without speaking, and Nadia seemed to know not to follow for now—this was something Mina and Lynet needed to share alone. Mina was looking around in amazement at what was probably the first new life she had seen since leaving the South, and Lynet went up on her toes to examine the delicate leaves, brushing her fingers carefully against their edges. They were so small, like little pink and green stars against the dark wood, but they held the promise of spring.

"We broke the curse, Mina," Lynet said softly.

"*You* broke the curse," Mina said, tearing her gaze away from the trees.

Lynet shook her head. "You're the one who tore down the statue. It took both of us to break the curse."

Even as she said the words, she was sure they were true. Sybil's garden. Sybil's statue. Perhaps the dead queen had only been waiting for someone to put an end to her grief at last, to offer her some kind of hope that life would return to the North.

A small smile crept over Mina's face. "Maybe you're right," she said, her hand slipping into Lynet's.

And as they walked back from the garden together hand in hand, Lynet knew that *this* would be their legacy, the story they had chosen—two girls made of snow and glass who were more than their origins, two queens who had come together to reshape their world.

ACKNOWLEDGMENTS

First and foremost, thanks to my family. This book wouldn't exist without you.

To my mom, Gilda: Thank you for listening to my late-night panic sessions when I was convinced I was doing everything wrong, for believing in me more than I believed in myself, and for your wisdom, advice, and unwavering support. To my dad, Barry: Thank you for suggesting that I take a book with me out to recess in second grade when I complained about being bored, for encouraging me to be the best I can be, and for always being there for me. And to my sister, Roxanne: Thank you for being proud of me, for your irrepressible enthusiasm and encouragement, and for always looking out for me like a true big sister.

To friends both online and offline who have generously given me their time, their support, and their encouragement as I decided to follow this dream. To name just a few, thanks to Meaghan Hardy, Emily Drash, Laura Rutkowski, Elizabeth Ayral, Chelsea Gillenwater, Emily A. Duncan, Jamie Taker-Walsh, and Jessica Lynn Jacobs. Thank you for reading, for listening to me fret and worry, for believing in me, and for inspiring me with your passion and your immense and varied talents. And thank you to Rhiannon Thomas for taking me under her wing and making this whole debut experience feel a little less intimidating.

A huge thanks goes to my agent, Meredith Kaffel Simonoff. You *get* me. From the very beginning, you understood the heart of this book, and I owe so much to your insight and your advocacy. You've been my compass during this journey—whenever I was unsure of the direction I was going, I only had to check with you and know which way was true north. Special thanks, too, to Ashley Collom for her valuable early feedback.

To my incredible editor, Sarah Dotts Barley, thank you for taking a chance on me and helping me turn this book into something so much more than what it once was. It's magic, what you do. Thanks as well to Caroline Bleeke, who stepped in with her sharp eye and keen insight while Sarah was on maternity leave.

Thank you so much to Amy Einhorn and everyone at Flatiron and Macmillan—to Patricia Cave, Molly Fonseca, Nancy Trypuc, Jenn Gonzalez, Lena Shekhter, and Liz Catalano. Thank you to Anna Gorovoy, Keith Hayes, Erin Fitzsimmons, and Kelly Gatesman for making this book look so beautiful and elegant inside and out. I'm so proud to be part of Flatiron's list. Thank you all for turning my pages and pages of a Word document into a real live book.

And lastly, to the women who taught me the power of fairy tales: Shelley Duvall taught me as a child the value in different versions of the same story. Donna Jo Napoli taught me as a teen to look at those stories from all angles. And Angela Carter taught me as an adult how to dig beneath the surface of fairy tales and find the vulnerable, beating heart underneath. I can trace my path to this book through the three of them.